BURN DOWN THIS WORLD

Burn Down This World

A novel

by

TINA EGNOSKI

Adelaide Books
New York / Lisbon
2020

BURN DOWN THIS WORLD
A novel
By Tina Egnoski

Copyright © by Tina Egnoski
Cover design © 2020 Adelaide Books
Cover Image by Lynne Taetzsch, artbylt.com

Published by Adelaide Books, New York / Lisbon
adelaidebooks.org

Editor-in-Chief
Stevan V. Nikolic

All rights reserved. No part of this book may be reproduced in any manner whatsoever without written permission from the author except in the case of brief quotations embodied in critical articles and reviews.

For any information, please address Adelaide Books
at info@adelaidebooks.org
or write to:
Adelaide Books
244 Fifth Ave. Suite D27
New York, NY, 10001

ISBN: 978-1-951214-82-1

Printed in the United States of America

Author's Note

Burn Down This World is based on events that took place at the University of Florida in May of 1972. The book is a reimagining of those events and is not intended to be an historical representation. The characters were created wholly from my imagination. Any resemblance to real-life figures is coincidental. The 1971-72 academic year on campus was rife with change and controversy. The first African American student body president was elected and *The Florida Alligator* was kicked off campus for publishing a list of abortion clinics. While I had all this rich material to work with, I reluctantly had to narrow my focus to the upheavals surrounding the Vietnam War. To the best my ability, I adhered to the chronology of events, taking liberties only when the narrative structure or character development required. One exception: Leonardo's Pizza, a student mainstay at 1245 West University Avenue for over forty years, didn't open until 1973. Including it in the novel was a personal indulgence.

The wildfires that ravished Florida in 1998 took a toll on nearly every county in the state. By the time they were under control, 474,000 acres had burned. Over 300 homes were damaged or destroyed, along with at least 33 businesses. Hundreds of thousands of residents on the East Coast were forced to evacuate. In my research, I learned that no lives were lost, by either firefighters or residents. I tried to remain factual in my treatment of the wildfires. I strayed from the timeline and specifics for continuity of plot.

*For my brother Kenneth –
once lost, now found*

Contents

Author's Note   *5*

Contents   *9*

Prologue   *11*

PART ONE   The Present and the Past   *15*

    The Goddesses of Fire   *17*

    The Highwayman Poet   *34*

    Strange Days   *49*

    The Smallest Seed on Earth   *73*

    Cherry Bomb   *109*

    Chase Your Pleasure   *133*

    Centripetal Force   *158*

PART TWO   The Past   *191*

    The Blind World   *193*

    Ocean of Storms   *220*

    Year of Vulnerability   *247*

PART THREE   The Present   **275**
    Fireproof   **277**
    Pleasure and Pain   **308**
About the Author   **327**
Acknowledgements   **329**

Prologue

We're moving again. This time from Texas to California. Our father, another shiny bar on the shoulder of his uniform, has taken a new post. The date circled on the wall calendar is May 21, 1959. I'm five. My brother, Reid, is eight.

The van comes and eats all our belongings. That's how I think of it, as a Brothers Grimm ogre who swallows my bed and dresser, my stuffed animals and Raggedy Ann doll, my dresses and Mary Janes.

To stop my crying, Reid says he'll teach me to say goodbye in all the languages he knows.

"It's like magic," he says.

We stand in my room. I'm a red-eyed, red-faced mess. Clear-eyed Reid, Mr. Expert, holds my hand.

"These words are like abracadabra," he says.

Oh, I like that.

His shaggy black hair hides his forehead, his eyebrows. He's always shaking the curls out of his eyes. He's taller and I look up to him, in so many ways.

"Okay, you ready?"

"Yes," I sniffle.

"Ten-hut!" he says. I adjust my posture, soldier on a parade ground.

"Say *au revoir*," he says. "*Au revoir* to your dollhouse."

I do.

"That's French. Now, say *adios* to your dresser. That's Spanish."

I do.

"*Ciao* to your hairbrush. Italian," Reid says.

I like that word, *ciao*. I like this game.

In Hawaiian, I say *aloha* to my coloring books. In German, I say *auf wiedersehen* to my puzzles. Reid knows saying goodbye to my dolls will be the biggest, saddest one of all, so he saves the best for last. I'm allowed to bring one doll in the car with me, my favorite Betsy Wetsy, but all the others have to be packed.

"I'm going to tell you the most beautiful word," he says. "It's Japanese."

I hold my breath. I hold my tears. I hold the pee that's about to trickle out.

"*Sayonara*," he says.

I breathe and pee a little in my pants. These are big foreign words and Reid, strong and confident, knows them all. I don't pronounce them correctly, but my brother has distracted me long enough for my tantrum to pass.

The van lumbers away, gut-heavy, sated.

Yes, I'm grim. I sulk in the back seat all the way across the southwest, the desert highway long and bleak. I shake my head when my mom urges me to stand with Reid in front of a huge saguaro cactus outside of Phoenix. I refuse to get out of the car when we stop at the Grand Canyon. We take more detours. The lights of Las Vegas hurt my eyes. Panning for gold in Carson City is a bust. I grow nauseous on the switchbacks of the Sierra Nevadas. When Reid describes in gruesome detail the ill-fated Donner party's journey over these same mountains a hundred years before—the nibbling of fingers, the chomping of femurs—my father has to pull over so I can be sick on the side of the road.

To cheer me, my mother says we're going to live in Hollywood.

"Not even close," my father says. "Hollywood is four hundred miles south."

"Same state," my mother says. "It's like we're living in Hollywood."

"What's Hollywood?" I ask.

"Movies, stupid," Reid says. "You know, like westerns. John Wayne and Audie Murphy."

"Don't say stupid," I say.

He pinches me.

"And don't pinch me," I whine.

"Don't pinch your sister," my father says.

Grim turns to grin when we arrive in Fairfield. The yards are green grass, full of bougainvillea, palm, citrus, banana, avocado. All smiles, I hug every tree. This is a great new place. Flowers. Fruit. Movies. Better than Texas. The moving van comes and spews out all our stuff. Reid teaches me to say hello in all the beautiful words.

We dance around our new quarters, singing to the furniture: *hola, bonjour, guten tag*. We sing *ciao* and *aloha*. These are truly magical words because they mean both goodbye and hello. To all my toys and clothes, I sing *konnichiwa, konnichiwa, konnichiwa*—now my favorite, more beautiful than *sayonara*. We jump onto the couch, bouncing and singing. Reid takes my hands.

Bonjour, couch. *Aloha*, table. We bounce higher, sing louder. He's my big brother, so smart. He knows everything in the whole wide world.

PART ONE

The Present and the Past

The Goddesses of Fire

It was the summer of fire, 1998. The east coast of Florida burned. Seven counties, from Duval to Martin. I had a house smack dab in the middle, on the St. Johns River. My neighbors and I lived at the edge of miles of water, 310 miles of it to be exact, the length of the river from source to mouth, and all around us hardwood blazed and pine scrub smoldered—the irony didn't escape me.

Most mornings, as on this first Wednesday in June, I made coffee and the dog and I walked the well-worn path from the back door to the river, fifty or so long strides that Penny turned into a shin-bashing frolic. My copper-colored mutt, for her this was the best part of the day and she wanted me to hurry. Once we reached our pier, she was off, leaping into the water, splashing through squishy marsh. A flock of black skimmers, interrupted in their hunt for breakfast, circled and scolded her, their calls plaintive.

Coffee mug in one hand, postcard from my brother in the other, I stood and scanned the horizon for fresh plumes of smoke. These warning signs, so commonplace, let me know if or where another blaze had flared. In the distant northwest, I spotted a billowy spire. It might be Union Park or maybe Bithlo, towns like ours that, so far, had been spared.

It hadn't rained in months. Afternoon thunderstorms—those much-loved, much-hated storms that came up just after lunch, dumped what seemed like a foot of rain in a matter of minutes, and vanished before you unsnapped the umbrella—had failed us. As spring turned to summer, the temperature soared and the humidity dropped. Fires seemed to ignite spontaneously, kindled in a pressure cooker of heat and dry underbrush. It made us brittle, a little mean. I felt it myself. In my bones. In my interactions. Just the other day someone cut me off in traffic. I gave him the finger and he gave it right back.

Penny bounded out of the shoal grass and right for me, rubbing against my leg, jostling the postcard from my hand. I set down my mug and picked it up. On the front was a picture of quaint downtown Manitou Springs. On the back, in tight cursive, it said:

Mountain to ocean
I walk the earth west to east
Hibiscus split open.

A haiku, cryptic, but I got the gist: my brother was coming to visit, hitchhiking—his favorite mode of transportation—from Colorado to Florida. Typical. Every few years he sent one of these missives, and in three days, or three weeks, he'd hurricane into town—the famous poet returned. He whipped up the equilibrium, toppled our hearts, mine and my mother's, flimsy as saplings, then he left. I counted back. It had been nearly four years since we'd seen him.

His timing, too, was predictable. He had a knack for arriving between the lows and the highs. When our father died, Reid was still in Canada. On the day of my wedding, he was on the isle of Ithaca, communing with the spirit of Homer and Odysseus. He didn't meet my son until after the terrible twos. A year ago, when I called to let him know I was selling our mother's house and moving her to assisted living, he was otherwise engaged: mourning the death of Allen Ginsberg in a sweat lodge in Taos.

Writing as Reid Layman and known as the Highwayman Poet, my brother was a member of the second wave of beat poets, famous for his sparse, sometimes humorous, sometimes poignant, poetry. He spent his life hitchhiking around the country, from small town to small town, towns with colorful names like Bucksnort, Knob Noster, and Bird-in-Hand. He set up temporary shelter, usually in a tent or maybe at a fleapit motel, and found odd jobs, staying long enough to take in the local color. After he made pocket money, he was back on the road. But not before he immortalized the town with language described by critics as "illuminating," "elegiac," and "in praise of bottom-of-the-barrel humanity."

We were, if such a relationship existed, sporadically estranged.

My plan was to rip up this postcard, toss the pieces in the air for the pelicans and herons to pad their nests. Instead, I folded it into a crude airplane and let fly. It arced, sputtered, and nose-dived into the water. Out loud, the meter all wrong, I said:

Save your soles
Fly the friendly skies
You ass.

Taking my words to mean our morning ritual was over, Penny trotted up to the house. A creature of habit, she wanted a drink and a quick shower. Because of the odd-day, even-day water restriction, quick was all any of us got. Mud poured off her fur. She found a place to sun herself.

I had my own habit. After the walk to the pier, I stood outside Evan's bedroom door and took bets. My son, at fourteen—would he be smug and sullen? A downright grouch? Today, maybe he'd wake up and be his old self, a cheerful and joking boy. The stakes were high and the spread a mile wide. I couldn't even make an educated guess. When he was in first grade, he caught the flu and it turned into pneumonia. From a fevered stupor, he said to me, "I feel like I'm the cousin of a volcano." These days, he ran both hot and cold. One minute he erupted and spewed—like his cousin—and the next he froze me out. His long-lost second cousin, the iceberg, had come to visit.

I knocked. No answer. I knocked again and cracked the door.

Instead of my son, I found another boy curled peacefully in his bed, dreadlocked and pierced, studs through both eyebrows. I assumed he was one of the stray boys from the community center Evan had begun to bring home this summer.

I knocked again, harder. The boy sat up, rubbed his eyes. No shirt, his torso pale and stark against navy sheets.

"Who are you?" I asked, trying to keep levity in my voice.

"Zink," he said, matter of fact.

"Zink who?"

"Just Zink."

He was a few years older than Evan, his face more mature, any traces of baby-fatted jowls replaced by angular cheekbones. He hadn't washed his hair since, I estimated, the beginning of the decade. Run-of-the-mill juvenile delinquent, the kind of boy every mother hopes her son won't become or befriend.

"Well, Zink, nice to meet you."

I meant it sarcastically, but he, politely, said, "Likewise."

From the floor on the other side of the bed, Evan jumped up. "Don't go ballistic, Mom." He was wrapped in a quilt. "You were already asleep when Zink came by."

"You guys should get up," I said and closed the door.

I needed more coffee. It was then I noticed, from the kitchen window, a Mustang parked diagonally in the driveway, front tires on the grass, crushing my already struggling snapdragons and impatiens. Nice car, a shimmering red convertible, obviously brand-new, obviously belonging to Zink. He could easily have spent the night in the back seat of that beauty.

Just then, Evan made his way slowly down the hall, hang-dog, tail between his legs. Zink bounded after him, a heedless puppy, fully dressed in baggy jeans, T-shirt, and tire-tread sandals. His T-shirt read "Don't Worry Be Happy," but the H in Happy had been X'd out with permanent marker and replaced with the handwritten letters SN.

"Good morning, Mrs. Banks," he said.

"Do you have a real name, Zink?" I asked.

"Stephen," he said, pinching free a cluster of grapes from the fruit bowl and firing them one at a time into his mouth.

"Stephen what?"

"Byers."

He was a boy of few words.

"Where are your parents? Won't they be worried about you?"

"They're not what you would call traditional parents."

"Well, maybe you should go home. Just to check in," I said.

"Aye, aye, Mrs. Banks," he said.

"Actually, it's Leahy," Evan said. "Ms. Leahy."

Zink double-eyed me. "Ah, a devotee of Gloria Steinem. Cool."

Maybe I had misjudged. One didn't hear that name from your typical teenager.

"Way cool," I said. "You can find your way out, I assume."

"Yeees, ma'am," he said, supercilious. Giving Evan a half-salute, he pocketed more grapes and headed out the garage door. I stared at Evan, at the peach fuzz on his upper lip and the scattering of pimples on his cheeks. He had his father's olive complexion, dark eyes, and brown hair. Recently, he'd had the barber give him a close crop, and, although I couldn't see it right this minute, I knew there was a peace sign shaved into the back of his head.

We heard the Mustang engine start up and rev. I expected Zink to give us a splashy spin-out, but he eased onto the road. No burning rubber or bridges. He'd be back.

"So, Dad knows Zink?" I put a frozen waffle in the toaster oven and poured Evan a glass of OJ.

Keith, my ex-husband and Evan's father, was director of the Yost Community Center. It was an after-school and summer program for low-income boys. This summer Evan was spending weekdays there, volunteering, helping to entertain the 10-and-under set, a group he kept busy with basketball, soccer, and swimming.

He nodded. "I wasn't trying to get away with anything. It was late and he needed a place to stay. I didn't want to wake you."

The toaster oven chimed and Keith honked from the driveway. I smeared peanut butter on the waffle and folded it into a taco for him to eat in the car.

"Next time, ask first," I said. "SOP from here on out." He was used to my military speak, knew that meant Standard Operating Procedure.

I stepped closer to him, commanding his attention. I was about four inches taller and wanted to remind him, *I'm still bigger and stronger than you.* I knew this difference wouldn't last much longer. Keith is six-two. Once Evan had his growth spurt, I'd be dwarfed.

He grabbed his backpack and skateboard and headed out. I waved to my ex from the door.

Before I left for work, I went into Evan's room. A recent convert to snooping—he was a teenager, of course he was hiding something, many things—I looked under the bed. Nothing. I slid a hand between mattress and box spring. Did kids these days hide things there? Evan sure didn't. I refused to be a parent who looked the other way. I picked up the quilt and folded it. I smelled a hint of nicotine-laced smoke. Oh, great, Evan, under the influence of his new friend, was probably smoking now.

My drive to work, from neighborhood to downtown office, was a guilty pleasure. Time alone in the car when I didn't have to fight Evan for the radio. He was a station surfer, hunting for his favorites: Busta Rhymes, Spice Girls, Usher, Barenaked Ladies. Not my taste. I was loyal to WRBZ. They played what Evan called moldy-oldies and I called goldies. I turned up the volume and sang along. The Rolling Stones want you off their cloud. Buffalo Springfield want you to see what's going down.

A news brief let me know what was happening in the world. Clinton knee-deep in the Lewinsky scandal, GM factory workers on strike, and an earthquake in Afghanistan. An ad for Sun Power, Inc. came on, the solar panel installation company I worked for. My boss, Russell Morris, his tone perfectly serious-causal, touted the cost benefits of using the sun's rays to power your home. Not only had I heard this spot a million times, I had written the copy. The tagline: *We specialized in solar before it was hot!*

While I could talk convincingly about silicon layers, electric fields, and metal conductor strips, I wasn't particularly gung-ho about saving the world one solar panel at a time. It was a job with a flexible schedule that paid well. Russ let me take off whenever I needed to shuttle Evan to soccer practice or my mom to a doctor's appointment. My title, communications liaison, though fancy, meant that I did the administrative scut: answering the phone, word processing, database management.

Our digs were in a storefront in the heart of the pedestrian mall. Around us was a collection of Spanish Revival buildings that housed mom-and-pop shops and restaurants. When I arrived, Russell greeted me with a glum "Good morning." Our bottom-line had plummeted in the past few months. Right now, solar was a reminder of how inflamed we all felt.

With no appointments scheduled, we tackled long overdue spring-cleaning projects. Russell sorted the store room; I answered email and worked on a new inventory system. We kept on the radio, one ear tuned to the news. For lunch I picked up sandwiches and ate at my desk. Russell ate standing in front of the patchwork of east coast county maps he had taped to one wall. To keep track of the fires, he used a multi-colored push-pin system: red for hot-hot-spots, yellow for smoldering patches, black for scorched earth. Our corner of the county was free of all color, a quadrant of land defined by a perimeter of yellow.

"Blasted sun," he said. Since he left banking to become an entrepreneur, Russ always wore a pair of Bermuda shorts and a Hawaiian shirt. He claimed he never again wanted to be restrained by a suit and tie.

"Those are fighting words," I said.

"I feel like I'm being tested. Like I'm Job of the South. Boils, pestilence, drought."

I rose and did a little dance, a cross between a cha cha and a high-speed shuffleboard game shuffle. "That's my best rain dance," I said.

"I appreciate the effort. I really do," he said. "Why don't you go home? No—better yet, go see your mother."

"You're the boss," I said, not about to raise an objection.

"Give that lovely woman a kiss for me," he said, as I walked out the back door.

Poor Russell. I left him standing in front of the maps, contemplating his profit/loss ratio.

My mother had lived at Garden House for eleven months, four days and—I looked at my watch—five hours. I knew this because she never let me forget. At some point during my visits she asked, "Do you know how long I've been here?" It wasn't a rhetorical question. I tried at first to answer with humor. "Who's counting?" That didn't work. She was. Then I tried not answering at all. So she answered for me, throwing in, for good measure, for a turn of the knife, seconds and nano-seconds. I wasn't sure how accurate the tally was. Her memory, which a year ago I might have described as sieve-like, letting names, dates, and the location of keys slip through mere fissures, was now sink-holed: years had plunged into the chasm. Still, this bit of timekeeping remained fresh.

Here's another thing she liked to say: "I knew what I was doing. I knew that pot was on the stove."

Naturally, I saw it differently. Was it fluke or fortune that on the day she burned down her kitchen, a social worker from Garden House called to let me know we had reached the top of the waiting list and they would be happy to offer a residence to my mother? And she lived here as if a queen *in residence*. The staff were her minions. "I think I'll take my lunch in my room today," she was fond of saying when summoned at noon to the dining hall. They humored her. We all did. I was, no doubt, the biggest court jester. Come to entertain, come for an almost daily ration of rebuke.

Garden House was built to look and feel like a twenty-room manor. *Cozy* and *homey* were the most repeated words in the brochure. The décor was oriental rugs, antique tables, and upholstered sofas. It smelled of lilac air freshener and Gold Bond.

If I timed it right, my visit felt more like a chat than a chore. That time was 1600 hours—or four o'clock for civilians—when staff brought tea to the residents and a glass of wine to guests. It was another way Garden House distinguished itself from a nursing home.

Her room was first on the right. She sat in her favorite chair, one we had brought from home, the radio turned to a big band station.

"Hi, Mom," I said and bent so she could see my face.

She put a hand to her head and pulled down the glasses perched on top. "Estelle, there you are."

Celeste? Estelle? It was close. Estelle was the name of her long-dead sister, the sister who died of polio in 1944 at the age of twelve. She started calling me that the day I moved her here. I tried not to take it personally. I tried. I tired. Disorientation was part of the deal, and it could be especially acute after a move like the one she experienced, leaving her home of thirty-two years.

Except for her mental decline, my mother remained in large part ageless. She was slim and nimble. Her skin was smooth, with wrinkles only around the eyes and mouth. She made sure her salt-and-pepper hair was kept short. Every six weeks she said, "Don't you think my hair's getting a little fluffity?" That was the kind of word—the endearing *fluffity*—my mother could get away with.

She held up the newspaper folded on her lap. "Have you heard about this fire?" On Sunday she had asked the same question.

"I have." I sat on the bed.

"It's just terrible. Right here it says that thirty-six thousand acres have burned in Volusia County alone." On Sunday she had quoted the same figure. In the last seventy-two hours, 10,000 more acres had been destroyed.

Sophie, the young attendant my mother often called Celeste, came in carrying a tray. She wore pink scrubs with white bunnies all over them. She was new, still timid.

"Here you go, Margaret, your favorite, raspberry tea." She set the tray down on the bureau.

"Lovely," my mother said. "Thank you, Celeste."

In a moment of confusion, I said, "You're welcome," and Sophie said, "You're welcome," and then we both said, "Oh, sorry." She backed out of the room, stopping at the doorway. I thought she was going to say something solicitous, something absurd, like, "Will that be all?" Instead, she did a little bend-and-dip. Was that a curtsy?

My mother sipped her tea. I gulped my wine, cheap and tart. Above her bureau hung two collage frames filled with family photos. I had painstakingly selected and ordered the pictures, believing if I got the right pictures in the right order, I could create a narrative thread through the labyrinth of her memories. Two pictures stood out now. The first was of my father as a young man in his Air Force uniform. He was twenty, maybe, with a cocky grin and a cocky slant to his cap. The other was of Reid and me at college. We're standing in front of the library, a brick Gothic building with arched windows. We have our arms around each other and our smiles are big, toothy—we look like we're in mid-laugh. We had overlapped just that year. I was a freshman, he was a senior. This was one of the last pictures taken of us together.

A Garden House resident, Mrs. Kline, stopped in the doorway. She leaned on her walker, looking left and right, as if she'd lost her way.

"Mrs. Kline, can I help?" I asked.

"What are you doing here?" she asked. Sprightly and slightly deaf, her attitude was: Everybody's business is my business.

"Oh, Agnes, turn around," my mother said. "Your room is back that way."

"I'm on to you," Mrs. Kline said, shaking her finger at me.

For her, we visitors were a suspicious bunch, showing up and disappearing all the time.

After Mrs. Kline hobbled away, my mother held up a postcard. The same one I had drowned in the river that morning. Had my origami been plucked from the water, smoothed flat and dried out? Of course not. Reid had sent her one too, probably not written in haiku.

"Isn't it the best news ever?" She snapped it, like a playing card, picture-side up, on her bedside table.

"It is," I said.

She didn't mention Reid by name or say what *the best news ever* was. This was the first postcard he had sent to her new address. At least the first I knew about. What had he said to her? I wanted to know and I didn't.

"Let's have a party," my mother said. Her eyes widened. She looked a bit mischievous, as if she were proposing something strictly against the rules.

"We can have any kind of party you want."

I lifted a corner of the postcard, but could read only the first five words. *I've read about the fires.* I lifted further—*and devastation.* Oh, why pretend? I flipped it. *We inflict damage on Mother Earth. We inflict damage on those we love. Time to heal the past. Mother, I'm coming home.*

She pointed to a roll of purple crêpe paper, which I hadn't noticed earlier, but was right there on her bed. "We'll decorate the house with it," she said. "This is his favorite color."

Inflict damage? Heal the past? What kind of New Age woo-woo was that?

"Sure, we can decorate," I said.

I'm coming home? That sounded like more than a visit. The bitter smell of my empty wineglass caught in my nostrils. I stood, needing to get away from the words, needing to leave before I quashed my mother's joy. I kissed her check and told her I'd see her tomorrow.

"Don't forget," she said.

She frequently said this when I left. It was jarring. Did she mean not to forget her or not to forget to visit? Maybe it was anxiety about her own forgetfulness. Today, though, there were more things to not forget. Reid was coming. We'd have a party. His favorite color was purple. In truth, I didn't know his favorite color.

I carried the tray out to the reception desk. Sophie took it and said, "You don't have to do that." The queen's daughter was immune to menial labor.

"It's no problem," I said.

"She's so excited about your brother's visit. Do you know when he's coming?" She looked fresh out of high school. Her blonde hair was cut short with wispy bangs over her large forehead.

"Your guess is as good as mine." My tone was more abrasive than I intended.

Heal the past?

"He's so cute," she said. "For an old guy. No, I mean, for someone his age." She reddened. "Oh, I'm sorry. I just meant—".

"Don't worry about it. I know what you meant."

"My mom has all his books."

When *Buried Portraits*, his fifth and most well-known book, was published in 1991, women all over America—well, women who read poetry anyway—fell in love with him, his photograph on the back cover highlighting his spiraling black curls and earthy, gem-stone green eyes.

"Have you read any?" I asked.

"Uh, poetry, I just don't get it," she said.

"Me neither," I said.

This wasn't true. I owned and often re-read collections by Adrienne Rich, Carolyn Forché, and Marge Piercy. They were there on my shelf next to Reid's books. I said it to make her feel better—she was so young, so nervous.

"I should go, Sophie. I'll see you in a few days."

"By then your brother might be here."

"Maybe," I said.

I stopped at the grocery to pick up an oven-roasted chicken. Let Publix do the cooking tonight. I experienced a moment of squeamishness at the deli—my arms goose-fleshed—watching poultry turn in the rotisserie oven. Still, we needed dinner and for all I knew we would have a third. My brother. And maybe a fourth. Zink might join us.

Who was Zink, a.k.a. Stephen Byers? He was well-off—the Mustang a clear giveaway—and he was well-educated, what with that nod to Steinem. He looked reasonably well-fed and well-dressed in a slumming-it kind of way. His hair? I couldn't get a handle on that mess.

I had grown used to Evan befriending and bringing home boys from the community center. They were typically being raised by a single parent, usually a mother, who worked long hours. Scrawny and trash-talking, they were sweet-natured underneath all the bravado. Hygiene wasn't their strong suit. When they appeared at my house, I gave each one the benefit of the doubt and then later called Keith for a background check.

I pulled into the driveway. No Mustang. Just before I turned off the engine, the local news broke in with a report. Another blaze had flickered to life in a woodland scrub near Deland. Flames were jumping from tree to tree, coming as close as a mile from some homes. A dozen firefighters had been taken to the hospital for exhaustion and dehydration. Another prayer circle was scheduled that evening at city hall.

All over town people had gone stupid with fear. Some gathered for vigils in Monroe Park. Some held sunset rain dances at the beach, complete with rain sticks. One group had created a shrine in front of the public library. Anyone could add a good-luck charm to the pile: rabbit's foot, horseshoe, four-leaf clover, the socks you wore when your team won the big game.

That was what I needed: an altar of my own, right in my backyard.

I put away the groceries and let Penny out. We stood in the garage, so full of stuff, boxes of my mother's belongings and furniture that didn't fit in her room at Garden House—it was more storage unit than car park. I had been meaning to sort it and sell it.

There in the corner was exactly what I needed. An old tiki totem, a relic from patio parties my parents used to throw. I dragged it out and, with a rusty axe, guillotined the thing into three separate heads. The wood split easily—it was old, rotting.

Penny thought this was great fun. She sniffed around the wood, wagging her tail. It felt good to wrap my hands around the handle of that axe. What began as a tentative act turned into a clobber-fest. All the messy parts of my life on the chopping block. Bash the frustration of a mother with dementia. Thrash the eye-rolling disdain of a fourteen-year-old son. Smash the when-will-he-show or will-he-even-show games of my brother.

I wheelbarrowed those ghoulish heads, along with a toolbox, down to the pier. One by one, I nailed them to the railing. It wasn't as straightforward as I expected. The top rail wood was new and dense, the nails bent. I was sweating and the muscles of my upper arms ached.

I christened them the goddesses of fire. They were obviously male—what tiki in the 1960s wasn't?—but I had decided that gender bending was in order. Their colors were faded, the reds more ochre, the blues gone bland. Their grimacing faces were rather sweet. One gal had a wide, open mouth, turned up at the ends, giving her more sneer than scowl. I named her Pyra, the head honcho. The other two were her gal-pals, Myra and Tyra. Myra sported a jagged set of bottom teeth, like a jack-o-lantern.

Watching the wood crack and then reassembling it, reusing it—being both destroyer and architect—felt like I was doing *something*. Just like the chanting, the rain sticks, and the vigils, they meant nothing and they meant everything. One final *thrawk* secured Myra, but—ping, crack—two nails came loose from Pyra and she sagged, head bowed, sorrowful. I put my hands on either side of her splintery cheeks and straightened her.

I had lost sight of Penny. She couldn't be far, probably in the reeds under the dock. I whistled for her. Then, tossing the hammer in the tool box, I pushed the wheelbarrow back to the house.

In the hazy dusk, I saw a figure walking toward me from the end of the driveway. At first, I thought it was our neighbor. Derek walked his dog at this time of night, just home from his job as a pharmacist at Walgreens. The dog, Buddy, was a one-hundred-pound black lab. He and Penny would sniff each other while Derek and I exchanged pleasantries: how was your day, how about this weather.

But I didn't see Buddy, and besides, this man was too young, too tall. He stopped in the yard and dropped a duffel bag. His hair was long and coiled around his neck. He wore a T-shirt and jeans. No shoes. I recognized Reid's familiar stance: stiff shoulders, head cocked to the left.

He stepped forward.

"I'm home, Celeste," he said. "For real this time."

My throat constricted.

I knew, from all I had read, that heat radiating from a forest fire can blister human skin after a mere one-second exposure. In that same time eyelashes disintegrate, hair sizzles to brittle wire. After four seconds of exposure, your clothing combusts, your skin chars. All this before the flame has even reached you.

The Highwayman Poet

Reid wasn't barefoot after all. I stepped close enough to see he wore sandals, a complicated contrivance of wisps of leather woven around his feet, attached to nearly imperceptible soles. The straps had taken on the color and elasticity of skin. My brother had hitchhiked across the country on tissue paper. He wiggled his toes.

Like a petulant child—how quickly I devolved into a little sister around him—I stomped on his foot. Not hard, I had on flip-flops, but enough to elicit a wail.

"I think you broke my toes," he said.

"I doubt that," I said.

He pulled me to him, a forced hug. His height surprised me, as did his broad shoulders and muscular back. Had he grown taller? Most of us shrink with age. He drew me tighter, squeezed the breath right out of me. My body went limp, leaned into him, his bony torso against my own fleshy trunk, our knees knocking. I pressed my forehead against his sternum in a way that was both nuzzle and head-butt.

Penny bounded around the side of the house and skidded to a stop. She barked. Protective by nature, she knew an interloper when she smelled one.

"Who's this?"

"This is Penny." I rubbed her ears.

The last time he visited, I was dogless. I was still married and living downtown. Keith and I were slaves to commerce. He was an assistant manager at May's department store and I worked at an office supply warehouse. Evan had just turned ten, sweet, sweet ten—no natural disasters—when everything was backyard forts and soccer and comic books.

Reid held out a fist and Penny slinked over for a sniff. She barked again and came to stand beside me. Good girl.

"It's good manners to invite your guest inside," he said.

"You're not my guest," I said. "You're my stupid brother."

"Spoken like a true hostess," he said.

He picked up his duffle and followed me through the garage. All he owned, I was sure, was in that bag.

"Do you have a tent in there?" I asked.

In the past, he had refused to stay with either me or my mother. A house? Too pedestrian. He insisted on remaining true to his lifestyle and pitched a tent at the Whitmore campground.

"Not this time, I'm hoping to stay with you."

"Do you mean inside? Like a mere mortal?"

"God, I missed you."

I had half a six-pack of Heineken in the fridge. Alcohol probably wasn't recommended in this situation, but who cared. I handed him one and we each took a long swallow. The beer—a slice of ice down my throat—felt so good, so cool. Another swig steadied my hands and my wildly pumping heart.

We leaned against the counter, facing each other. Reid's jeans fit loosely. His T-shirt was a tie-dyed swirl of blues, greens, and yellows. He was the epitome of an aging hippie. His face, tanned and leathery, was branded with deep furrows—frown lines similar to the ones my father had developed in his fifties.

A primitive smell hung off his clothes. I couldn't pinpoint the scent. Motor oil? Pine tar?

There was a picture of Evan on the fridge, taken on a camping trip with Keith last summer. They had gone tubing down the Ichnetucknee, a spring-fed river in Central Florida. Evan is standing waist-high in blue-green water, holding the inner tube high over his head.

"This is Evan?" he asked. "He's all grown up."

"He's fourteen. Rather unbearable right now. You'll see. Holly calls him hormone-infused. As if he's been injected like a Butterball."

"Good ol' Holly," he said. "How the hell is she?"

Holly Matteson was my oldest, my dearest friend, the first friend I made when we moved to Florida. She was married to Grant Matteson, the owner of a Chevrolet dealership. They had recently built a new house on the beach, a Tudor-style, five bedrooms, with stainless steel appliances in the kitchen and a stunning view of the Atlantic. She had two daughters, smart and lovely girls, both in college, one at Vanderbilt and the other at Sweet Briar.

"The same," I said. "You know her, she's been the same since eighth grade. She and her husband built a house on the beach. A big, big house."

Reid whistled, implying *impressive*.

The back door slammed. Evan. I hadn't even heard Keith's car. Penny had missed it, too. Usually she was right on top of Evan the minute he arrived. As he rounded the corner, he stopped and gave Reid the stink-eye.

To me, he said, "Got a date?"

Reid chuckled, amused by this smartass comment. That would be all the encouragement Evan needed—he'd keep it up. As with my mother, there was a charm to his acerbic wit.

"Don't be a dope," I said. "You remember your Uncle Reid."

"I know, I know. Just kidding." He hugged his uncle. "Hey, wait, did something happen to grandma?"

"No, no. Hold on," I said. "Nothing bad has happened. Reid's just come—"

"Okay, good," he said. Turning to more immediate matters, he asked, "What's for dinner?" These days he pounced—beast of prey—on every meal.

"Chicken. Why don't you go wash up?" I said.

"Huh?" Evan said.

Never, not once in my life, had I uttered that phrase. It was a line from a 1960s family sitcom, where everyone sat down for a meal at the end of the day, the disaster, whatever it may have been—a white lie, a misunderstanding, an innocent prank taken too far—was resolved. Mom spooned out peas, Dad reinforced the moral. Yes, The Beaver was always washing up for dinner.

I backtracked. "Go scrub every trace of Yost out of every pore. That place is a germy breeding ground." My need to be motherly, or rather to be perceived so by my brother, gave my voice a false note.

"Mind if I wash up, too," Reid said. "The car that picked me up broke down on the highway."

Ah, that was the smell on his clothes: grease. With all his time on the road, he must be a decent mechanic. The bathroom, I told him, was down the hall, first door on the right.

I made a salad. I skinned the chicken and pulled meat off the bone, happy for something to occupy my hands and my mind. Penny stayed by my side, waiting to see if I dropped any morsels. For background noise, I turned on the radio. I didn't want to hear the news, any news, good or bad. Classical seemed pretentious. Pop was too pop-y, too young. Jazz? Also pretentious. Why was I so self-conscious? I settled for my regular station. Three Dog Night was singing the bullfrog song. Yes, we could throw away the cars, the bars, the war.

When Reid came out of the bathroom, he stood at the sliding glass door, looking out at the river. Penny checked out the hem of his jeans and wagged her tail. He might be okay. Let's wait and see.

"This is a nice place," he said.

"Way out here in the boonies," I said.

"That's why I like it."

Me too. I had purchased the property after the divorce. Its selling point was the river and the fact that it was as far away from downtown as I could get and still have Evan in the same school district. The house itself was modest, a cedar shingle ranch, three bedrooms, squat, compact, built in the 1950s. The shingles were old. Several in the front were missing or crooked, hanging on by a lone nail, like teeth—or the lack thereof—in a six-year-old's mouth.

Dinner was ready. Evan and I rarely sat at the dining room table, but I set it now, making sure the dishes matched, getting out the cloth napkins. I took two more beers out of the fridge, this time pouring them into glasses. We sat.

"Put your napkin in your lap," I said to Evan. He pulled the same amused face as earlier, the pinched forehead and gaping mouth. Had I really not civilized my son? In truth, we were sloppy about dinnertime, sloppy about table manners and at times general cleanliness. All too often Evan carried his plate into his bedroom. I ate while doing a crossword, pleased to have a quiet moment. On the weekends, Evan was with Keith. I was so slothful I had dinner in front of the television and then sometimes left my dishes right there on the coffee table until morning.

Now that I was sitting, all energy left my body. I felt gangly—loose-armed and nerve-charged. Clumsy. Just handing Evan the bowl of salad made me tired. Reid was here, staying in my house. For real this time, he had said. *Heal the past.* In silence, we passed the serving dishes. Silence except for the clink of silverware against china.

Evan broke in with, "So, Uncle Reid, where have you been all these years?"

I took a pull of beer.

Reid wiped his mouth. He had better manners than either of us.

"Up until about five days ago I was living in Colorado, up in the mountains. Manitou Springs to be exact. Been there off and on for a year."

It seemed an appropriate place for him. Those tight-lipped westerners keep to themselves. They don't ask too many questions.

"Are you married?" Evan asked.

"Nope," Reid said.

"Have you ever been married?"

"Nope."

"Do I have any mystery cousins?" Evan asked.

"None that I know of."

Should I interrupt this cross-examination? Reid's curt responses implied he was uncomfortable. But I was curious. I had a few questions myself, like why he hadn't told me he was living in Colorado. We Southerners, transplanted and native, didn't hold back.

"What do you do there?" Evan picked up a chicken leg and ripped the meat off in one large bite.

To me, the chicken tasted rubbery, the salad dressing too oily. Fork tines against my teeth echoed through my skull.

"I'm a poet," he said.

He wasn't just a poet. He was the voice of his generation. Our generation. His first book came out in 1974. He was in Nova Scotia, but the book was issued by a small, well-respected American publisher. Nightingale Press. A mimeographed, stapled flimsy of a pamphlet, all of twenty-five pages, it was entitled *Bled in Hand*. On the cardstock cover was a drawing of a fist smashing an American flag. Done in pen-and-ink, the fist appeared to both embrace and tear the flag. Like this image, the poems were full of rage and tenderness, as well as a whole lot of Nixon bashing. His last book, *Silver Alley*, took aim at middle-class complacency and included a whole lot of Clinton bashing. While it won the National Book Award in 1996, it was both praised and mocked as a mix between *Howl* and *The Bridges of Madison County*. That must have been bittersweet. Reid idolized Ginsberg and hated pop culture. To be compared to Robert James Waller—ouch.

"Sure, I know that," Evan said. "I've seen your books. I mean, how do you make money?"

"I write. That's it," Reid said.

He didn't just write. He experienced, then he wrote. Before there were laws about such things, he hunted buffalo with the Lakota Sioux and harpooned bowhead whales with the Inuit. In a snake handling ritual in Harlan County, Kentucky, he was bitten 14 times. The bites were like venom track marks on his forearm, an arm displayed and photographed for the *Paris Review* interview.

"Must run in the family. Mom writes copy for a solar panel company." He was poking fun at me, good-naturedly. Still, I heard the edge in his voice. My profession lacked prestige. I wasn't a community leader like his father. I didn't have the hip life of a poet.

"Solar panel company?" he said. "Very progressive. Energy of the future."

My belly did a belly-flip. I had pleased him. Approval from my brother—I had always craved it. To receive it now was like hitting a dive straight as an arrow, no splash.

I knew how it felt to receive the opposite—disdain—in a very public way. In his third book, *Foraminifera*, Reid wrote about a married couple living on a street of identical houses with quilt-patch lawns and sidewalks like *pent-up fences*. The husband drove a minivan and barbequed in the backyard dressed in Izod and boat shoes. He was a *sub-hub*, a derisive term Reid coined for a suburban husband. The sub-hub's wife—me—was a *glom-mom*—again a made-up word; it meant a mother who held on to her son so tightly—glommed on—that she didn't allow him the rough-and-tumble experiences necessary to grow into a man.

That book came out in 1988—Evan was four and I was a full-time mom, focused on my only child. Reid, skewer of convention, had visited us a year earlier. We were living downtown, after just purchasing our first home, a house very much like the one described in his book.

I had to look up the term foraminifera. My old Webster's said, in short, that foraminifera were amoeba with shells covered in minute holes. The holes allowed them to stick out their tiny, tiny feet—pseudopodia—to move around, to find food. That was the scientific definition. Poetically, it meant a living being defined by and confined within a sheltered life. It was a veiled reference to my life, or maybe it wasn't so veiled. It stung.

I put down the fork, unable to eat another bite. My fingertips tingled. So did my armpits.

"What's with the peace sign?" Reid asked Evan, meaning his haircut.

Evan put his hand to the back of his head. He was tracing the outline, just as I had when he came home with the new cut. The stubble, I remembered, was bristly to the touch.

"It's hair art," he said. "Better than a tattoo or a piercing. And way less painful."

"You know, that's not something to be taken lightly." His voice suddenly coarse. "Do you even know what a peace sign means?"

Evan looked at me, uncertain. Peace meant peace, right?

"It's nothing," Evan said. "Just something I did on a bet."

"That's no joke, little man. People lost their lives in Vietnam. You should understand the politics before you adopt the symbol."

"Reid, cut it out," I said.

"It's no biggie, Mom," Evan said. "I get it, your generation was all peace and love and bare asses."

He was talking about streaking. For some reason, this antic had come up in his history class when they were talking about the 60s. I had told him streaking came into vogue in the 70s, but I was no match for a teacher who would show them pictures of men running across a football field with no clothes on.

"I'd like to stay and catch up with you folks" he said, standing, ready to make an escape. "But I've got some stuff to do."

"Take your plate to the kitchen, please," I said.

"Don't I every night?" He was into the groove of our make believe.

After Evan stalked off to his room, Reid said, "Cute kid."

"None cuter," I said.

"They grow up so fast," he said.

"There's never enough time."

"Out of the mouths of babes," he said.

Our banter was cliché, spoofy. It was the Leahy family way—we covered awkward with shtick—and we quickly fell back into it.

Reid helped with the dishes. The narrow kitchen felt claustrophobic as we worked side by side. I washed, he dried. We didn't talk. I noticed when he put the glasses in the cupboard, he placed them rim down, something our mother always did. I stored the glasses rim up. It seemed more hygienic.

"You haven't told Evan anything about your past?" he asked.

A plate slipped out of my hands and back into the soapy water. He had circled back to the peace sign. But, really, he was circling the real issue, circling our past and the reason—reasons—he never came home for more than these short visits. *Heal the past.* I didn't want to have this conversation now. A part of me thought I could live the rest of my life without having it.

I did what I did best: made a joke. "It wasn't exactly pep rallies and sock hops."

"No, but he should have a sense of history. Your history especially," he said.

I did what I did second-best: went on the offensive.

"Don't lecture me on political correctness or parenting, or, well, anything," I said, putting my hands, still wet, on my hips. A defensive stance.

"I know it's strange, me showing up and inviting myself in like this."

"It's not about that," I said. "You had no business making that comment about his hair. You're not his uncle. I mean, you are, but you don't even know him. You don't know *us*."

"Duly noted," he said.

That was all he was going to give me on the subject.

Dishes done, we made up the bed in the guest room. This seemed like such an intimate gesture, parachuting the sheet, tucking the corners in, military-tight, the way we were taught, finishing up with the tent-flap—that's what our father called the bottom corner on morning inspection. It had to be snug, pointed, with a knife-edged pleat.

We fluffed the pillows. My fingers began to prickle again. His duffle bag was in the corner, as were his shoes, the straps coiled like snakes. I looked for and found the scars from the real snake bites on the inside of his left arm, pocked skin, parallel nips all the way to his elbow.

"I'm in a bit of a—I don't know what to call it—a slump or a transition. I'm not writing and it feels like everything has gone to shit," he said, taking coins from his pocket and putting them on top of the dresser. "If you'll have me, I'd like to stay for a while."

Hesitation, timidity, a trace of fear—I had never heard any of these from my brother. I was so surprised I didn't ask how long *a while* was or what he meant by *slump*. I softened. The air in the room—the tension between us—softened as well.

It was time again for my jokey self. "You're welcome to stay until one of us brandishes a weapon."

He laughed and again that zig in my belly. I had amused my brother.

"How's Mom?" he asked.

This was his first mention of our mother. I felt protective. Finally, she was settled at Garden House. This stasis, though, seemed precarious. Would Reid disrupt it? Or the opposite—would his presence make her new home feel more like *home*?

I gave him the brief version of our mother's decline, the spotty recall of names, dates, and essential numbers—social security, telephone—the losing of keys and the losing of her way home from the store because all the streets of her neighborhood looked the same. I suggested she see her doctor. *Oh, what's a doctor going to do? Tell me I'm old?* That was her flippant answer.

I made an appointment with a neurologist. He checked her reflexes, her muscle tone and strength, her coordination. He gave her blood and urine tests. He asked her a series of basic questions. What day is it? What year? Who's the president?

Her answer to the last question was, "William Jefferson Clinton, the man who can't keep it in his pants."

Both the doctor and I laughed. This pleased my mother, the ham.

"See, I still got it," she said. Her sense of humor and her sanity.

The final test, a CT scan, revealed no tumors or fluid buildup in the brain, no sign of stroke damage. All these tests were more a process of elimination than firm diagnosis.

Holly recommended I call Garden House. It was where her mother had lived for the last year of her life. Helen Turner kindly turned me away. Too much demand, not enough rooms. There was a waiting list. It was like enrolling a toddler in a coveted preschool. To be in the running you had to be on a list.

Not even two weeks later, I received a call from the fire department. She had set her kitchen on fire. It wasn't a complete inferno, but she needed a new stove and repairs to the charred wall and ceiling. Later that day another call: Helen Turner. She had a room available.

Now, I sat on the bed and said to Reid, "I wish you'd been here for the move. For the sale of the house. The whole thing was kind of—lonely." I had wanted to say *brutal*. It better described the experience and would have upped the guilt factor. But Reid wasn't easy to guilt.

All he said was, "I know. Me, too. But you know why I couldn't."

I knew. Everyone knew. When Reid emerged from his sweat lodge mourning of Allen Ginsberg—six days with minimal nutrition—he published an article about the vision he had of the poet dancing in hell with William Burroughs. Four months later, Burroughs died. Reid was hailed as a literary mystic and was very much in demand: readings, radio shows, conference panels.

He sat next to me, his weight forcing me to tilt toward him. This was what I had wanted, right? Yes, but I wanted it a year ago. It should have been Reid at the wheel, driving my mother to Garden House—the coronation of the queen. He would have called my Toyota her chariot and hummed "God Save the Queen" all the way there. He would have made her laugh and kept me from breaking down. As it was, I, all nerves and edge-of-tears, spent the whole drive afraid that once we arrived, my mother would refuse to get out of the car. Then I'd cave and drive her back home. In the end, that didn't happen. My mother was cooperative. She charmed her way into the hearts of the staff members as they helped her get settled.

It should have been Reid and I cleaning her house, him Ajax-ing the bathrooms and me Pledge-ing the surfaces. We should have fought over the furniture and cried over old photographs. Just once it would have been nice to have a normal sibling interaction.

"This will be a whole lotta closeness," I said. "You ready for that?"

"I'm ready for anything." He bounced up and down, grinning like a kid.

I took his hand and felt a row of calloused skin. Abrasive, rigid—it reminded me of when we lived in Cheyenne and my father gave him a BB gun. Reid spent hours teaching himself rifle drills, like the ones we saw at military parades. *Present, arms. Trail, arms. High port, arms.* His hands became coarse from repetition. Sometimes a blister burst and bled. I didn't care about drills or guns, but I stayed and watched him, fascinated by the brisk chain of moves, the way he spun the gun like a baton.

I rose from the bed and kissed my brother's cheek, whisker-y rough.

"I'm glad you're here," I said.

"Night-night, sis-sis," he said, still bouncing, still with the playful smile on his face.

Penny was waiting for me in bed. She hadn't stayed with us at dinner. Instead, she retreated to this comfort spot. Typically, I didn't let her sleep with me, but she looked at me with sad eyes—her routine had been disrupted—and I relented. The bed was warm and soft. I wanted it to envelop me, to carry me away to sleep. For a time, it did.

Then I woke thinking about BB guns and Cheyenne. About our days as military nomads—six states in fourteen years—and our arrival in Florida, the longest we lived anywhere. I thought about peace signs, the one Reid wore on a beaded necklace in high school, and how he and my father fought over it. For us, at the time, the peace sign wasn't ironic or funny. It wasn't commodity or slogan. Even now, it wasn't abstract or throwback or nostalgia. And it certainly wasn't an emblem used to define our *look*.

Evan had never asked about my pre-mom days and I hadn't been forthcoming. I had never told him about the year Reid and I spent in college, the early 1970s, at the University of Florida, in Gainesville. While I had lived in a dorm, I spent most of my time at the house Reid shared with three other guys. I still remembered the address: 621 N.W. Fourteenth Terrace. We called it, simply, The Terrace. It was in that house, fueled by a sense of indignation at the leaders of our country—Nixon, Secretary of Defense Laird, General Abrams, Congress—and at the president of the university, Stephen O'Connell, that we planned our rallies, hand-printed our posters, tore bed sheets to make banners. We wrote op-eds for the school newspaper and shouted our demands from a makeshift podium on the quad.

We, along with hundreds of other students on campus, had raised our fists against the war and lowered our butts to the floor of the administration building. We wore peace sign armbands and made Molotov cocktails out of rags covered with hand-drawn peace signs. We dodged police and guardsmen, got caught in the crossfire of tear gas and the cannon spray of fire hoses.

It was those events, one event in particular—a sit-in that turned from peaceful protest to street brawl—which led to the use of the Molotov cocktails, to my arrest and return home, and which sent Reid out into the world, without a home.

Strange Days

My brother and I were Air Force brats, schooled in the art of acronyms, crisp bed corners, and yes-sir, no-sir. We recited the phonetic alphabet and told time by the twenty-four clock. We had firm handshakes. We had backbones of steel and, when necessary, expressions as impassive as granite. Underneath it all, our hearts, especially when it was time to move, were as gooey as the inside of a campfire marshmallow.

Reid was born in 1951 in Illinois, at the base hospital in Rantoul. Three years later, I took my first breath of the genteel air of Charleston. I've been told I once swallowed a mouthful of sludge from the Guadalupe River during our time in San Antonio. I started kindergarten at Travis Air Force Base in Fairfield, California. In the chalky air of a Department of Defense classroom, I practiced duck-and-cover drills. In the stucco bungalow of base housing, I watched Kennedy's brain blown to bits and Oswald take one in the gut.

Our friends were fellow brats, who, like us, had dirt from one end of the country to the other under their nails. Some even had crescents of Germany or England or Japan. In fourth grade, just as I settled into my assigned seat, we moved to Wyoming. I started my period and had my first kiss in Cheyenne. I saw snow for the first time, the landscape disappearing in what

I thought of as a torrent of white rain. Trees turned to skeletons, as if bark, like skin, had been peeled away to reveal only bone. The cold went right to my bones and I knew it wasn't for me. When the PSC carbon copy appeared on the dining room table—Permanent Change of Station orders—I pitched both my winter boots and pink cowgirl boots. Our destination: the east coast of Florida.

On the long and boring drive south, I held an atlas on my lap and traced the highways, the ones behind us and all the miles we had yet to go. We bisected the country. As we left each state, I tore out the page and shredded it. Good riddance to the Equality State. Too-da-loo Cornhuskers. See ya later Show Me State. Arkansas, Mississippi, Alabama. They were all confetti by the time we reached Florida.

My father drove right to the beach. We walked to the shore of the Atlantic. It was August. Hot, hot. Waves curled around our ankles. My toes were sucked down among periwinkles and cockles. We had traded dust for silty soft sand. This landscape: palm trees, humid air, ocean—these were in my marrow. From now on, my go-to shoes would be a pair of sandals.

There was no base housing at Dad's new post. For the first time, we lived in what I thought of as a real house, a post-war ranch with three bedrooms and—a luxury—two bathrooms. There was no base school, so for the first time we attended what I thought of as real school. Public school. I found the social scene disorienting. My clothes, hair, and accent were all wrong. Most of the kids had been friends since birth, going to the same schools all these years. They spoke in shorthand: best hangouts, beaches, movie theaters. How would I fit in? Where would I fit in?

My mother used to say, on the first day of school, no matter where we lived, no matter if we were starting in the middle of the year or on the first day with everyone else, "Bring home one new friend today. I'll make cookies." Both Reid and I did, and all four of us sat at the kitchen table nibbling around the chocolate chips. The next day she told us to bring home two new friends. There were six of us and ginger snaps. The week progressed, many friends, many sweets.

I was too old for the cookie trick, but I used it in a new way. I bought a bagful of drugstore makeup and each morning laid it out in the girls' bathroom. Soon I had a crowd, shoulder-to-shoulder in front of the mirror, experimenting, sharing advice. I was a fair and freckly girl, with auburn hair inherited from my Irish paternal grandmother. I had braces and wore glasses. Makeup tips were more than welcome. My first friend, Holly Carter, taught me how to apply rouge so I didn't end up looking like a clown. She was also new that year, having just moved from Little Rock. We bonded over the misguided belief that life so close to Cocoa Beach would be full of the hijinks seen on *I Dream of Jeannie*.

My brother never worried about fitting in. He made friends easily, had no trouble finding his place. He didn't even need to find it, he simply started his own group. In high school, that was the Peace Coalition. Mr. Jessup, the history teacher, let Reid use his room for meetings. We moved aside all the desks and sat on the floor making plans for sit-ins in the cafeteria in support of civil rights and early morning vigils on the front steps to demonstrate against the war in Vietnam.

I was almost fourteen, in the ninth grade. I had a December birthday, so was always the youngest in my class. I hung on every word Mr. Jessup and my brother said. Reid, at seventeen, was almost six-two, spindly and ruddy-faced, with hair down to his shoulders and jeans down on his hips. He wore moccasins. He wore a handmade peace sign necklace. Fashioned out of wire and beads, an alternating pattern of red, white, and blue, it had been made by his girlfriend Beverly. He never took it off, not to shower or to swim. It was a sign of both love and defiance.

Florida, in those years, the mid-1960s, was gripped by the same tensions as the country: racial strife at lunch counters in Jacksonville, Miami, and Tampa; antiwar demonstrations at state colleges and at the capitol building in Tallahassee; the space race at Cape Canaveral, just 60 miles north of where we lived. Television brought it all into our home.

We watched the nightly news in the living room, our Swanson frozen dinners on tray tables. As we forked Salisbury steak into our mouths, Walter Cronkite announced the day's body count. As we twirled gravy into mashed potatoes, soldiers crawled commando-style through jungle brush. Lift foil off a square of chocolate brownie and a protester put lighter to draft card. Between these images were commercials for cereal and antacid and paper towels. For half an hour, it felt that life, as presented by network news, was too real—wounded soldiers carried to choppers on stretchers—and at the same time surreal—Buddhist monks setting themselves on fire. We were fed words and images that made our stomachs hurt and then sold products to ease the pain. Maybe Bounty could clean up this mess.

It was usually during the first commercial break that my mother announced she'd lost her appetite and went to the kitchen. I often joined her, my own stomach turned sour. My father and Reid watched Cronkite until the bitter end.

I heard Dad say, "We can't leave now. Our boys are invested." He believed the war was not only necessary but righteous. It was our responsibility to protect the people of South Vietnam and stop communism from spreading around the world.

"You sound just like Westy," Reid said. He meant General Westmoreland, the Czar of Death. To Reid, the war was unjust. Our government was a killing machine, lining its pockets on the backs—and with the lives—of young men and innocent South Vietnamese.

"Those two," my mother said. "They're too stubborn for their own good." She lit a cigarette, the window above the sink sucking out the smoke.

"Or for our own good," I said. "We're the ones who have to put up with them."

She laughed. "We're perfect, of course. We don't argue. We don't complain."

"These are bad for you," I said, taking the half-smoked cigarette from her and running it under the tap. She had grown thin. She seemed to smoke her breakfast, lunch, and dinner. She was the wife of a recruiting officer and the mother of a boy who would soon go down to the post office to sign up with the Selective Service System.

One evening in late October, 1967, we watched the coverage of fifty thousand protesters in Washington, D.C., marching from a rally at the Lincoln Memorial across the Potomac River to the Pentagon. They chanted and sang, taunted the police, linked arms and walked in unbroken chains. Abbie Hoffman, all bushy-headed and tied-dyed, claimed they were going to levitate the building. By meditation.

At this, my father guffawed. "What a kook," he said. He was late coming home from work that night. He still had on his uniform, hadn't even sat down for dinner.

While I thought that was silly—it wasn't possible to lift a building simply by willpower—I believed all those people in that one place, with their loud, angry, and, yes, kooky voices, could change minds. The President would see them, hear them.

"I agree with him, so what do you say to that?" Reid said. "You have a son as crazy as Hoffman."

My mouth was dry and the smell of rubbery meat permeating the room was stifling.

"Don't start, you two," my mother said.

One of the protesters, a blonde boy in a white turtleneck sweater, broke rank and walked right up to the line of military police.

I got up and moved closer to the television, drawn to the scene, to that boy. He carried a handful of flowers—carnations? daisies?—and began to slide them into the barrels of the rifles, a peace offering.

My mother shouted, "Get out of the way."

I thought she meant me, that I was blocking her view, but she meant the boy. My skin prickled hot and sticky. I was frightened for and in awe of the boy. He seemed brave to me.

"Who do these damn kids think they are?" my father said. He loosened his tie and unbuttoned the top shirt button. I had watched Dad do this dozens of times. Tonight, he struggled, fumble-fingered, the collar so tight his neck bulged.

"He's going to get himself killed," my mother said.

The MP's were ramrod straight, stoic. Except for one, one on the far end, he reached forward and brushed the flower out of his barrel.

"Damn pigs," Reid said.

"Watch your mouth," my father said. He still hadn't sat down.

"What do you care?" Reid said, standing up. "Every day you send boys over there to get killed."

My father grabbed Reid's necklace and yanked. The string gave easily, beads skittered across the floor. Reid lunged. He got my father around the neck, in a headlock. I thought he would take him to the ground, but Dad matched his strength. They wrestled, standing up.

"Stop it!" my mother yelled.

Reid let go, backed away. He said nothing. None of us did. The television droned on. Cronkite had moved on to other news, the Dow Jones and a raft of Cubans landing in Miami. Several of the beads pinged against my sandals. I bent and picked some up. Tears, a salty sting, rose in my eyes, wavered but didn't drop. I held out my hand, ready to give the beads to Reid.

"It's a just necklace," I said. "You can restring them."

He stomped down the hall to his room, ending the argument the way so many ended: Reid slamming the door, my father yelling, "Don't you ever slam that door again."

My mother left the living room and returned with a broom and dustpan. "Now look what you've done," she said to neither one of us or to both of us.

From that day until Reid left for college in fall of 1968, I woke every morning to an argument between him and my father. Maybe it wasn't every morning, but it felt like a daily refrain that buzzed in my ears, irate and loud as an alarm clock. I buried my head under the pillow, but the feathers were an ineffective buffer. They fought about hair. Reid's was too long and too greasy. They fought about jeans. Reid's were too long and full of holes. They fought about chores—*take out the trash, mow the lawn*—about the car—*No, you can't use it tonight*—and the state of Reid's room—*deplorable*. Underneath all this, they were, of course, fighting about the war.

I gave up all hope of getting an extra ten minutes of sleep and threw off the covers. Reid and Dad were in the hallway, at opposite ends, a stand-off.

"Hey, can you hold your fire long enough for me to get to the bathroom?"

I brushed my hair and my teeth. I washed my face. For several minutes, the faucet drowned out the voices on the other side of the door. When I turned it off, all was quiet. I opened the door and stuck out my head. All clear. Time to make a break for the kitchen. My mother, still in her robe, her hair tied in a loose bun, leaned against the counter, smoking.

"So far this morning I've counted sixteen *disrespectful*s and five *establishment*s. Now we've reached a whole new level of *pigs* and *hippies*."

"Can't you talk to him?" I said, meaning Dad.

"Can't you talk to *him*?" she said, meaning Reid.

For a second, we stared at each other. We had no control and we knew it.

She set a plate of toast on the table. I put jam on a slice and ate it.

"What's going on with your brother?"

"How should I know?"

"Who are the kids he's hanging out with?"

"They're not derelicts, if that's what you're asking," I said.

Derelicts was the word my father used to describe boys who didn't wear a belt. That day at the Pentagon, the streets had been full of derelicts.

"Your father doesn't like them."

"No matter what Reid does, Dad won't like it."

Dad came into the kitchen. He was in his uniform, ready to leave for work.

"Morning, Pumpkin," he said to me, kissing the top of my head.

I knew he considered me his easy child, but I felt like that boy in the turtleneck sweater. While I wasn't passing out flowers, I was being good, being all the things Reid wasn't, trying to bring peace to our home.

Reid came in, wearing his own uniform, those frayed jeans dragging on the floor.

"Put some wax on those hems and you can clean the floor for Mom," I said, unable to resist making a joke at his expense.

"Don't start." He had his hair pulled back in a ponytail.

"I wasn't. I'm not." I dropped my toast on the plate and put up my hands. "I'm just trying to eat my breakfast."

"Can't we have one morning of quiet?" my mother said.

I gathered up my books. "Come on, it's time to go. We'll be late for school."

I hated the war, but I loved my father. He was the man who had nicknamed me Pumpkin, for the color of my hair. He was the man who told awful knock, knock jokes.

Knock, knock.
Who's there?
Rufus.
Rufus who?
Rufus the most important part of your house.

At the time, I thought this was hilarious. He was the man who surprised us one Sunday with a new television set, a color television, so we could watch *Walt Disney's Wonderful World of Color* that night. Strict but kind, the only time he raised his voice at home was during the epic battles over Vietnam between him and Reid. He was a thinker who acted only after he had thoroughly analyzed a problem or an issue. He believed in hard work and a job well done. Loyalty to country and family was his motto.

I hated the war, but I loved my mother. She was the woman who had tea parties with me and my stuffed animals, the woman who made all those cookies for our new friends.

When we lived in Cheyenne, she and I loved to watch the shooting stars together in the summer sky. She taught me the names of the constellations, and not just the easy ones, like Orion and both dippers. Cassiopeia—five stars in the northeast, a W or M, depending on the time of night, a queen banished to the skies as punishment for bragging about her beauty. Lyra—an asymmetrical square with a handle star; Vega, the fifth brightest star in the sky; and sad, sad Orpheus' cast-off harp. She told me about the Pleiades, the seven sisters who Zeus transformed first into doves and then into stars so they could comfort their father Atlas, who held up the sky. She stroked my hair and told me I was named for the sky. For the heavens. Celeste. I was *heavenly*.

I hated the war, but I loved my brother. He had a gift for imitations. His Jimmy Stewart got a laugh from boys at the lunch table and four-star generals at the officer's club. When we were younger, he shared his issues of *Galaxy Science Fiction*. He once let me paint his toenails pink and kept it on for a whole week. In return, I held the plastic pieces of his model airplanes between my shaky little fingers as he applied the faintest, straightest line of glue. He could shoot a BB gun, unhook a barb from a fish gill, and skim a flat pebble seven, eight, nine times. If dinner was MRE (Meal Ready-to-Eat), which it often was, we slurped and burped our way through. And, of course, he had taught me all those beautiful words for hello and goodbye.

All this love, all this war. In our new house.

Reid drove us to school in our father's Oldsmobile. It was now rusty from the salt air and the bumpers were dented, but Reid didn't care. Possessions weren't his thing. Well, certain kinds of possessions, like cars or clothes or money or status.

He worshipped at the threshold of three things: sex (Beverly, it was rumored, put out); drugs (weed, speed); and rock-and-roll (The Rolling Stones, The Grateful Dead, The Doors). Albums spun all hours on the stereo, a soulful, moan-ful, sorrow-bitten, angst-ridden sound reverberating through the bedroom wall we shared.

As we pulled out of the driveway, I lit two cigarettes and handed him one. No, I didn't want my mother to smoke, she was old, she was susceptible to lung cancer, but I was young. I was invincible.

"I didn't appreciate that crack about my pants," Reid said.

I patted his shoulder, poor baby. "You're a big boy, you can handle it."

At the next stoplight, I perched my cigarette in the ashtray, removed my glasses and applied mascara.

"What exciting things will we talk about at Peace Coalition today?" I asked.

"I'm open to suggestions," he said.

I snorted, smoke rushed from my nostrils.

I pulled a copy of *Life* magazine from one of my folders. "This," I said. "This is what we need to talk about." The cover story was about American prisoners in North Vietnam.

He liked that idea, liked it so much he began a soliloquy about the bourgeois leanings of lazy Americans. They cared more about having a bright shiny new car in the driveway or lush green, even-heighted grass in their front yard. The war, he pointed out, was being fought by the working class, the poor.

Bourgeois—this word, all of the sudden on his lips. Reid had a faint inch-long scar on his chin. I looked at it with triumph and shame, a remnant of our younger selves. I had pushed him off the top of our bunk bed. When he spoke like this, I couldn't take my eyes off it.

Did Reid think we were bourgeois? Yes, our family had certain privileges. My dad, given his position, could keep Reid out of the war. He could afford to send Reid to college, expected him to go, even if there hadn't been a war. In fact, there was no question of us both going to college. From a young age, we had been taught the path of education was elementary school to middle school to high school to college. There was even graduate school, where you went to earn a Ph.D. When I asked, my father told me a Ph.D. was a doctor of philosophy. When I asked, Reid told me philosophy was the meaning of life. To me, the mystery was why everyone didn't become a Ph.D. We should all—not just clergy—know the secret of life.

Reid's friends, the ones my parents were so concerned about, the *derelicts*, were members of the Peace Coalition, guys and gals from all grades, freshman to senior. Beverly, his best friend Parker Smythe, and a boy named Greg Davis. Greg was a crew-cut science grind longing to be hip. Anyone could join. I had talked Holly into coming to meetings. New students showed up, checked us out. Some stayed for a while, others drifted away. It was fine. We weren't about rules or definitions. Come as you are—pothead, brainiac, or jock. We were about making the world a better place, free of prejudice and war.

Mr. Jessup's room was a safe haven. I especially liked having a place to talk about the war that wasn't as confrontational as it was at home. Mr. Jessup was our father's age and he seemed, in his horn-rimmed glasses and white buttoned-down shirts, to be trying too hard to be cool. But he was a valuable source on military history and he subscribed to the *New York Times*. We spread out the paper and read stories aloud.

When we got to school, just before we pulled into the parking lot, Reid said, "Ready, set, go," and we threw our cigarette butts out the window at the same time. There was no smoking on school grounds, so we liked to leave our daily butts, an ever-growing pile, at the entrance. A personal mutiny.

I often wondered how our move to Florida played a part in the changes in Reid. If we had lived on a base, where conformity was compulsory, would he have grown his hair long? Would he have started the Peace Coalition? I couldn't imagine my father or the teachers would have allowed either. We were no longer cloistered or constrained by protocol. Our entertainment was no longer the base movie theater or the base bowling alley. The chances of us running into our father's commanding officer—a man who would have much to say about Reid's hair and clothes—was limited by the numbers of times we were now on base. A lot of boys from Air Force families still kept their hair short, still dressed conservatively. They stood out at school. Most of them were in ROTC. Maybe none of this mattered. Maybe the changes in Reid were a convergence of adolescence and the times—the 60s. Everything—everyone—was changing.

While I wasn't defiant or outspoken about the war—I was my father's Pumpkin and my mother's confidante—I did have a secret. A rebellion all my own. One that was, in my opinion, harmless, but directly impacted Reid. When everyone was away from the house—Reid out with friends or his girlfriend, my parents out to dinner—I snuck into my brother's room and played his albums.

I was forbidden to touch them or his stereo. This was one possession he was possessive about, which made it all the more enticing. Before I played anything, I memorized the set-up: which record he had on the turntable, the position of the empty sleeve on the shelf. I didn't want him to notice anything out of place.

I lay down on the floor, my head right between the speakers. The Beatles, Bob Dylan, The Byrds. I was gone. And that was only the B's.

When we moved here, our parents allowed us to paint our bedrooms any color we wanted. Because we had just left behind dreary, dusty Wyoming and because the house had wall-to-wall green shag carpeting, I painted the walls sky blue. My room matched the landscape, with lush earth underfoot and a wide-open horizon.

Reid had painted his room deep gray, installed a black light, and hung up posters of rock groups: Moby Grape; The Kinks; Blood, Sweat and Tears. Some of them glowed, appeared to quiver. With long, thick nails he'd hammered a stop sign deep into the plaster. A real stop sign, one he claimed to have found, discarded on the side of the road. I was pretty sure he had stolen it. His bookshelves were full of the model airplanes he had made when he was young.

My two favorite albums were by The Doors. We had seen them on *The Ed Sullivan Show*, the soulful voice I had heard through Reid's wall belonged to Jim Morrison. He sang "Light My Fire" and lit me right up.

I always started with the first album, *The Doors*, and moved on to *Strange Days*. I knew exactly how long it took to play each one from Side A to Side B, and I knew there was a scratch on the 4th song on Side A.

Most of my friends liked the cover on the first album best. They loved Jim's pouty lips and devilish eyes. *Strange Days* was my favorite. The group wasn't even pictured on the cover. As I listened to "Soul Kitchen," I studied it, a circus act scene in a New York alley: acrobats, a dwarf, trumpet player, juggler, and strong man. On the wall was a poster advertising a Doors concert. This, I thought, was a brilliant photographic representation of Jim's chaotic but genius mind.

As I changed albums, lifting the needle and putting it down, I whispered to myself, gently, gently, don't scratch it, gently. I turned the volume low and put my ear close to the speakers. Jim was talking only to me. The music pulsed through bone and sinew. I felt as if Jim had cranked open my chest, slipped in a hand, not the gloved hand of a surgeon, but his bare, bare hand, and was caressing my heart. By now I knew every word of the lyrics and the songs followed me through daily life—while I walked through the halls at school, grocery shopped with my mother, rode my bike home from Holly's house—a soundtrack, the Morrisontrack of my life.

Sometimes on our drive to school, Jim Morrison came on the radio and Reid and I sang together. He beat his thumbs against the steering wheel. While Holly was crazy for the Beatles, while she covered her folders with lyrics from "Penny Lane" and "Strawberry Fields Forever"—I covered mine with "No one remembers your name when you're strange" and "When the music's over turn out the lights."

I could have bought my own records, but I liked being in Reid's room. I felt close to him there. Our love of music, particularly The Doors, was something to be shared, not split. A duplicate set of albums under the same roof, in two separate rooms, that went against the natural laws of rock and roll.

Here, for the briefest time, I didn't have to be anyone other than who I was. I didn't have to be my parents' good girl or Reid's little sister. I didn't have to be defined by my place in the family or defend my brother unconditionally. I could just *be*.

Besides, Reid had introduced me to Jim. Yes, we were on a first name basis. I learned from Reid—this was one subject he loved to talk about—all about Jim's bad behavior, his arrests in New Haven and Las Vegas. I knew that Jim and I were born on the same date, December 8, eleven years apart. I also learned that he had been born right here in Melbourne. The Morrisons were also military. Jim's father was a Naval Officer. They lived in Melbourne until Jim was nine months old. Aside from Florida, we shared, geographically, Texas and California. I liked to think of our journeys as orbiting the same circuit and occasionally touching, coming within miles of each other, intersecting on a bizarre space and time continuum of my own making.

I wanted, at all times in my life, to be in his music.

1968 was a year of sorrow: the Tet Offensive was launched; Martin Luther King, Jr. was assassinated, followed by Robert Kennedy; there were race riots in Washington, D.C., Detroit, Baltimore, Pittsburgh, Louisville, and riots at the Democratic National Convention in Chicago; Richard Nixon was elected. In the middle of all this, on his eighteenth birthday in March, Reid went down to the post office and signed up with Selective Service. At home he stuffed the paperwork into the trash. My mother fished it out and slipped it into a drawer. When the fat manila envelope arrived from the University of Florida, his acceptance, he studied it with intent. These papers were like gold to young men. Their ticket out of the war. He declared his major: political science.

On the weekend Hubert Humphrey was nominated for president, Reid stripped his room of everything that made it his: the posters, the black light, trophies for the debate team, the model airplanes, the stop sign. Those boxes he crammed in his closet. He packed his clothes in three suitcases. That was all he was taking to college.

On Monday morning, he handed me a slim stack of albums.

"They're all yours, sis," he said.

Only The Doors albums. Not the Stones, the Fugs. Not Creedence Clearwater Revival. This was a sly nod to the fact that he knew, had known all along, that I was sneaking into his room, listening to his music.

Instead of hugging my brother, I punched him in the forearm.

In my bedroom, I intermingled Reid's records with my Rolling Stones, Aretha Franklin, Laura Nyro, and Donovan. When I missed my brother, all I had to do was close the door and put Jim on the turntable.

I started tenth grade and emerged from my ugly duckling phase, orthodontia removed and contact lenses in place. I wasn't exactly a swan, but I wasn't a pelican either. Maybe a flamingo. With their longs legs, comical knees, and large angled beaks, flamingos might not be beautiful, but they're interesting to look at. I was a so-so student. New teachers asked if I was Reid Leahy's sister. This question meant either was I as smart or was I as difficult. I was neither, so in some cases I was a disappointment and in some a relief.

In late December, NASA launched Apollo 8. Its mission was to orbit the moon and return safely, the first mission to do this. For the launch, my dad, mom, and I stood with dozens of others on a beach as close to Cape Kennedy as we could get. We listened to the countdown on the transistor.

It was seven in the morning, the sun low on the horizon, but strong, warming our arms. Reid hadn't joined us. He was home for break, just having finished two terms. He had announced he was switching majors, from political science to English. He wanted to be a poet. My father said, "Oh no, you're not. That isn't even a profession." Reid said, "Sure it is. Look at Shakespeare. Look at Whitman." Who could argue with Shakespeare? My father. He threatened to not pay the tuition bill. "I'll quit," Reid threatened, which meant he'd lose his student deferment. My father would never let that happen. They were not, at the moment, speaking at all.

From just a few miles away, on the launch pad, we heard the bellow of the lift-off and, moments later, the blast of first stage ignition. Eyes to the sky, we craned our necks. At ten minutes to eight in the morning, our hearts soared, along with the missile, at first an arc of light against temperate blue, then a trail of vapor. Days later, on Christmas Eve, the astronauts, out in the great beyond, read from the Book of Genesis as we sat in front of the television, staring at a live-feed from the window of the Apollo, a trapezoid of the moon.

For the next three years, our house was suffused with silence. I was no sparring partner. I wasn't going to argue with Dad about the war; I wasn't going to argue with my mother about the too-short skirts most girls wore to school—I had never cared all that much about clothes anyway. I was comfortable in cords, long denim skirts, Poor Boy shirts and thong sandals—all of these my mother could live with.

My father put on his uniform and went out to bring more boys into the fold. He was, if nothing else, consistent. My mother began a part-time job at a gift shop downtown. She became involved in community events. She seemed to want to be out the house as much as possible. I was never sure she forgave my father for the hostile wedge he forged with Reid.

At school, the Peace Coalition fell apart. Reid had been the glue. Parker Smythe enlisted in the Army and was waiting to go to basic training. Beverly graduated. Greg Davis, now a senior, moved on to the Science Club. Holly stopped come to meetings.

The nightly news still brought us the horrors of war aboard and the turbulence on the streets at home: troops in Cambodia, the My Lai massacre, the killings at Kent State and Jackson State. When Reid visited, he punctuated the silence with stories of protests on campus. He had joined SMC, the Student Mobilization Committee. Students and faculty wore black armbands stenciled with peace signs and sang "Give Peace a Chance" at rallies. Those lyrics, crystallizing our desire for the war to end, rang in my mind. Reid had befriended a vet who shared his experience in Vietnam. In turn, Reid shared those stories with us, the indiscriminate burning of villages and the trophies vets brought home, dismembered ears or fingers of Viet Cong captives. My mother begged him to stop. I didn't know if those stories were true or not, but by the end of each visit I was ready for him to go back to school. He disrupted an equilibrium I worked hard to maintain.

On the night of December 1, 1969, silence was broken by a historical moment: the live broadcast of the first draft lottery in twenty-nine years. CBS journalist Roger Mudd interrupted *Mayberry RFD* so we could learn the fate of thousands of young men.

My father explained that the lottery system hadn't been used since the beginning of World War II and now the government was playing catch-up. This lottery was for draft-age men—anyone under twenty-six-years-old—born between 1944 and 1950. Reid missed it by a year.

Catch-up, a new and dangerous game brought to you by President Nixon. It was all a big show, with Mudd, his voice calm and stately, as the MC. The first blue plastic capsule was pulled from a glass container. A gray-haired man split it open and unrolled the piece of paper. The first birth date was chosen:

September 14. Men born on that date would be the first to go to Vietnam.

"This is barbaric," my mother said.

"Margaret," he said, curt, as if these three words questioned everything he stood for. For him, there was no distinction between his professional and personal lives. Love of country, love of family.

"Well, it is," she said. "You can dress it up, put it on TV, and make it all look official, but come on, William, they're sending these young men to war by their birth date, for chrissake."

Usually he called her Maggie and she called him Bill. That night, I heard angry words exchanged from behind their bedroom door. My parents never fought in front of us, but that didn't mean they didn't fight.

While the station broke for commercials—the most memorable was from Norelco, Santa sledding downhill on an electric shaver, *ho ho, ho*—the drawing continued. Each birth date was stuck onto a large board next to numbers 1 through 366. After one of those breaks, the camera panned the board. There was Reid's date: March 3. His number would have been 267. A good number, high enough to be considered out of draft range. I couldn't help listening for my birth date, even though this had nothing to do with me, a girl. December 8, it was 105. Not good. I would definitely be drafted.

Six months later, there was a second lottery, the real lottery as far as we were considered. Reid's lottery, for men born in 1951. His number: 207. On the cusp. Anyone with a number below 250 was at risk.

"Don't worry. He has his deferment," Dad reminded us.

"What about next year and the next?" my mother asked. "What about all the years this war might drag on?"

"Maggie, Maggie," my father said and put his arms around her.

After that, my parents didn't exchange anymore harsh words. They didn't exchange any words that I heard. Silence returned. Three months later Jimi Hendrix died. The following month Janis Joplin overdosed. Parker Smythe left for basic training in Alabama. By the end of 1970, 6,000 more Americans were reported dead.

I, too, had a new my lottery number—323, Reid and I had reversed places—and couldn't stop thinking about it. I made a mantra out of both numbers. Two oh seven three two three. Two oh seven three two three. Mine didn't count. I was never going to war. But I repeated it just the same, at night, trying to fall asleep. I said them forward and backward, believing that if I didn't make a mistake, Reid would be safe. My father's military status, Reid's student deferment, the rising voices of those trying to stop the war, my ability to keep a series of numbers straight—all these things would keep my brother safe.

I felt compelled to fill the silence in our house. So, along with Holly, I tried out for cheerleading. I would bring home cheer, with pompoms, saddle shoes, and a gold and blue uniform that barely covered my ass. It was also a way to keep me out of the house. After school I was at practice. Every Friday night in the fall I was on the sidelines of a football field. During basketball season, I was in one stinky, sweat-oozing gymnasium after another.

I decided I was tired of frozen dinners, so I taught myself to cook. I roasted chicken, I braised lamb shank, I layered lasagna. Soup, salad, fish, blanched vegetables. My mother was happy to let me take charge.

All the cheerleaders were dating football players. The boys acted like they were owed sex. If we didn't submit, they would get blue balls. I didn't know what that meant and was too afraid of looking stupid to ask. But it seemed to be an ailment that for some reason was a girl's job to relieve. Holly dated the quarterback. For a few weeks I went out with a boy named Shane, more bench-warmer than player. He was crass and boisterous and talked only about football. Around him I felt cold, none of the warm and fuzzy feeling all the girls said they experienced when making out.

At the suggestion of the guidance counselor, I applied for three state colleges. My grades were decent. Nothing exceptional, unlike Holly, who was the salutatorian. When I received three fat envelopes of acceptance, there was, for me, no question: I'd join Reid at the University of Florida.

Holly decided to attend Florida State, the historically female campus that was now known as the place to catch a husband. That was exactly why she was going there.

My last summer at home was free and easy. I spent most of my days at the beach with friends. We read *The Catcher in the Rye* and *On the Road*. Oh, Kerouac, I've been on the road all my life. We watched the surfers and waited for them to notice us. We turned up the transistor and listened to the Rolling Stones. We imagined Janis and Jimi making music together in heaven. At night we built bonfires. We passed whatever bottle anyone of us brought: cheap wine, vodka, gin, Kahlua. Joints and cigarettes—they were interchangeable. If it had a filter, you just didn't inhale as deeply.

When I grew tired of sitting on the sidelines, I decided to try surfing. One boy, Adam, caught my attention. He walked out of the surf with water glistening on his chest, dripping from the ends of his shoulder-length hair. I asked him to give me lessons. I splashed and crashed the first few times I tried to stand, my body tumbling, colliding with the ocean floor, salt water stinging my open scraps. The first time I stood up and rode a wave all the way to shore, struggling to keep my balance, I felt better than any time I had been on the sidelines cheering for the accomplishments of boys. I had agency—I was on top of the curl—and I would ride it into the next phase of my life.

Adam and I had a two-month romance. We surfed, then lay on the blanket and kissed for hours. The sun burned our necks and backs—our whole bodies, really. The kissing burned our lips. We did it all, except for it. *It* being, back then, the thing we could hardly bring ourselves to say. Not that I was saving myself for marriage, like Holly, but I wanted my first time to be with someone I loved. Not just a boy who was convenient, who happened to be a great kisser.

By the end of the summer I was a decent surfer. I was tanned and my legs were muscular. Adam and I separated, a civilized break-up. He was going to North Carolina, to attend Duke. I still had my virginity.

In July, Jim Morrison died in Paris. He was twenty-seven. I spent the day in bed just listening to his music. I now had all the albums. *The Soft Parade, Morrison Hotel, Absolutely Live, L.A. Woman.* I put them on the turntable, beginning with the first and going through chronologically. By 1800 hours—six at night—I had a horrible headache. No food and all that bass. My mother knocked on my door and told me to turn it off. I shot her a bird through the door.

"I saw that," she said. She didn't really. She probably thought I had rolled my eyes.

For weeks, I spun the albums over and over. Lifting the needle and placing it down at the beginning again and again.

Strange days, indeed. I had moved right into the Morrison Hotel. The roof was percussion, the foundation a melodious bedrock. I was waiting. Listening and waiting, waiting. At the same time, I couldn't wait to be away from home, to be with Reid. I played those albums until they were needle-nicked, gutted, until it was time for me to join my brother.

The Smallest Seed on Earth

The next morning, Reid's first full day back, I broke with tradition. Yes, I brewed the coffee and listened to the radio for fire updates—no homes had been destroyed in Deland and they had the blaze 80 percent under control—but instead of walking to the pier I decided to make a proper breakfast. Eggs, bacon, pancakes.

In the living room, Penny was waiting for her morning swim. I let her out. By herself. She didn't like it one bit. She stood wagging her tail, waiting. She whined.

"Go on," I said. "You're a big girl."

I stepped out with her and saw Reid in lotus position on the pier. My back went up, along with the hairs on my neck. And I wasn't the only one. Penny growled. This stranger from last night was in her spot. Our spot. In less than twenty-four hours Reid had made himself quite comfortable.

Penny trotted off, did her business, and came back inside. She sat down at the door, staring at Reid, her world off-kilter. I scrambled the eggs. I mixed the batter. The image of my brother on the pier, calm, not a care in the world, propelled the whisk deep into the batter. I dropped in a handful of blueberries—no, I rat-tatted them in, one at a time, little peeved explosions. Why hadn't I just gone out there? I could have staked my claim. Or joined him. But meditation wasn't my thing. I didn't want to interrupt him and I didn't want to be his audience.

Evan came into the kitchen, saw Penny sitting at the door. Not even the smell of bacon was keeping her from her vigil. Following her gaze, he noticed Reid out on the pier.

"What's he doing out there?"

"My guess, meditating."

"Huh," Evan said. "Penny's not a fan."

"That's an understatement."

"And what is that I smell?" he asked. "You're making breakfast?"

"Don't sound so surprised." I whipped him with the dishtowel. He grabbed the end and pulled it out of my hands.

"New world order," he said and turned to the dog. She was now dancing around him, thinking she'd get in on this tug-of-war. "You better get used to it, Penn."

Reid slipped in the door. The air behind him smelled dewy, refreshing.

Click, click—Penny's claws across the kitchen floor, cautiously greeting him.

"Morning. What can I do to help?" he asked. He had on the same jeans as the day before, but with a new T-shirt, gray and wrinkled.

"Flip those pancakes while I get orange juice," I said.

"I can do it," Evan said. Spatula in hand, he lifted the edge of a pancake to see if it was brown enough.

The kid knew his way around the kitchen. Determined not to send a helpless man-boy into the world, I had, beginning when he was six and old enough to respect the burner, taught him the basics. With him beside me on a step stool, we boiled, poached, fried. Over the years, we advanced to baked chicken, roasted vegetables, lasagna. All that stopped when he turned thirteen. Suddenly he was too cool for the colander.

"You've got a regular little life going here, sis," Reid said.

Regular? Little?

"I think I should take offense at that." The bacon puckered, sizzling in a way that made me think of burning kudzu.

"No, no. I'm serious. Nice homestead, a nice kid."

"Nice kid? That's debatable."

"Here I am helping you and you dis' me like that, Mom," Evan retorted.

Reid attempted to wrestle with Penny. "And look at this girl. She's the sweetest thing."

Penny backed away, ears down.

"Sweet, but protective," I said.

"Coffee?" I held up the pot.

"No, thanks. Don't touch the stuff. Juice is fine."

"Pancakes are ready," Evan said. He slid them onto plates.

We sat down, the table getting more use than it had in months.

"I have to ask, what's with the tiki heads you've got up out there?"

I had forgotten all about the goddesses. That trivial exercise eclipsed by Reid's arrival.

"What are you talking about?" Evan got up and went to the window. "Geez, Mom, what have you done?"

"I put them up, you know—." I didn't want to say the words out loud: altar, prayer. "They're like good luck charms."

"Oh, this I've got to hear," Reid said, chuckling.

My face warmed with embarrassment.

"To scare off the wildfires."

Now he really laughed, a hearty full-belly chortle. This time I got no swell of pride at having amused him. It felt too much like being his poetic subject.

"Oh, well, it all becomes clear to me now," Evan said. "My mom's a witch."

I rose to clear the dishes. Sitting still made me a sitting duck. Evan would keep at me.

"What can I say? It seemed like a good idea at the time."

"I've got an idea," Evan said, addressing Reid more than me. "Let me skip Yost today, in honor of the return of the prodigal son?"

Prodigal son? Where did this reference come from? Keith and I had given him, at most, a marginal religious education.

"No way," I said. "Your dad depends on you to be there."

Reid guffawed. "Let the kid stay home. You weren't always the law-abiding citizen I see in front of me."

Evan leaned in, cupped his ear. "Tell me more."

I gave Reid a look I hoped would implore him to zip it. But we were long out of practice with this kind of sibling communication.

"Let's just say, she didn't not skip school," he said.

Evan had a slice of bacon poised between his lips, trying to suss out the double negative. Not that it mattered, the magic words being "skip school." He bit into the bacon, ripping it in half. To him, Reid was the fun uncle. He showed up every once in a while, brought exotic gifts—ancient Greek coins, bone dice, a dream catcher—and slept in a tent at the campground. This time was different. Reid's treasure was hidden knowledge about my past. Evan was shrewd enough to know how to use this to his advantage.

"Guilty," I said. Then in an attempt at vagueness, wanting to dismiss my behavior as simply bad influence, I added, "Yeah, for about a year I ran with a tough crowd."

"Oh, yeah. Like Holly," Reid pitched in.

"Aunt Holly?" Evan drew a bead on me. Reid had just handed him a box of ammo he could pocket and, at a later date, pull out and take aim.

I wasn't talking about Holly at all and Reid knew it.

We heard Keith honk. "See," I said. "That's your father."

"Bye, Uncle Reid," he said, pointedly not including me, and disappeared out the back door.

I looked at my brother.

"Seriously," I said. "I'm trying to raise a halfway respectable human being. A human being—do you know how hard that is?" Once again, I was attempting to win him over with humor. I needed Reid on my side, not working against me.

"What? What did I say?" He held his hands up. *I'm innocent.*

"Last night I said I was glad you were here. I wasn't even sure I meant it, but now I'm pretty sure I didn't."

"You always were contrary." He flashed his audience-pleasing smile.

"Anyway, I don't want to get into it. We need to go see Mom."

It would take only a few key stories from Reid to erode the last shreds of my authority. Reid thought he needed to know my history—he was owed the right to know it. How would I control what was said or not said? Should I preemptively sit Evan down and tell him everything? That was parental suicide. The midst of adolescent mutiny was the worse time to confide in him.

Maybe this was what the goddesses were all about. They were strong and silent. In the coming weeks, to keep Reid from spilling my secrets, I'd have to be like them: guarded and on guard.

I called Russell to ask for the next few days off. It was Thursday. If I didn't have to return to work until Monday, that would give Reid and I four days to reconnect, to settle in. If he was really planning to stay for a while—weeks? months?—he needed to learn the routine, get into our groove.

The first thing Russell asked was if my mother was sick.

"No, nothing like that," I said. "My brother's in town. Visiting."

I cradled the phone against my shoulder and tossed off my robe.

"I didn't know you had a brother," he said.

"Doesn't everybody have a long-lost brother they keep in the closet?"

I slipped on a sundress, awkwardly multi-tasking.

"No." He obviously wasn't from a family of secret keepers.

"Well, I do and now he's here."

I didn't tell him who my brother was.

"Intriguing," he said. "Take all the time you need."

Russell was hurt I had never shared the fact that I had a brother, but he wasn't alone. I had plenty of friends and acquaintances who didn't know I was Reid Layman's sister. The more his fame grew, the less I mentioned him. It was just easier. When our connection was discovered, I heard the most intimate details from fans. I once met a woman who had, way back in the early 1980s, picked up Reid on a highway outside of Amarillo. Being a poet herself, she gave me a vivid description of the afternoon: the air sizzling with humidity and the peaks of Duro Canyon turning orange in the setting sun. They slept that night in the back of her car. Sleep being a euphemism for *sex*.

I was shown tattoos of his words in places on bodies I wished I could erase from my memory. I was shown Polaroids of him in comprising positions. During Reid's last visit, he gave a reading at the bookstore—he read from *Buried Portraits* and the store was packed, the crowd winding between shelves, all the way back to the cash register. Afterward, a man with the adopted name Bear Moon cornered me. He told me about sharing peyote with Reid in the Arizona desert. "That was the best trip of my life," he said. "And I've been to Morocco, if you know what I mean." I didn't. Was *Morocco* a sex or a drug euphemism?

Just this past spring, Evan's English teacher read a part of Reid's poem, "Between Carnage," in class. Evan was so excited he told the teacher Reid was his uncle. The teacher called and invited me to class. He thought I could offer the students insight into Reid's work. I demurred. I had no insight. "I'm a college dropout," I said, because I knew it would shut him up and it did.

Unconventional lifestyle aside, Reid was a public figure. I enjoyed anonymity. In this town where I had lived for over thirty years, I did lead what Reid had already labeled "a regular little life."

They did have a garden at Garden House. Two gardens actually. One in front that greeted visitors with crotons and spider ferns, with hibiscus blooms like fat, rouged cheeks and bromeliad spikes as shiny as lip-glossed lips. Just as we reached the door, Reid bent and pinched off a single red hibiscus petal.

He had changed into olive khakis and a button-down shirt, a shirt I didn't even think he would own. He wore moccasins, and pulled his hair into a ponytail. He was nervous. I could tell because he was fidgety, rubbing his thumbs and middle fingers together. Between his pads, the petal curled and uncurled. He hummed, a low *om*.

Today, the halls bustled with families, many with young children. Senses on high alert, I smelled Vicks and ammonia. I smelled snot and piss just under the surface, the bodily emissions they couldn't hide under cleaning chemicals. The walls were scuffed from wheelchairs that didn't cooperate. The upholstered chairs were lovely but fraying at the seams. The antique tabletops were stained with glass rings. Yesterday I had noticed none of this. With Reid beside me, I saw only imperfection. Did he see it? Would he question my decision to move my mother here?

Several nurses and aids greeted me by name. They were gathered around the reception desk, whispering behind hands, smiling at Reid, the dopey smiles of the enchanted, which meant some of them recognized him. Sophie waved to me.

We passed Mrs. Kline as she shuffled her way down the hall with her walker. We passed her on the left, in the fast lane. The able-bodied lane.

"Hello, Mrs. Kline," I said.

"Hello, dearie," she said.

At the door to my mother's room, I asked Reid if he wanted to go in alone.

"God, no," he said. He had worried the petal into a tube of crinkled flesh. "All of a sudden I don't want to go in."

"Don't be silly. Go on. It's why you're here, right?" I took the petal from him and stuffed it into his front pocket.

My mother was standing in front of the bureau, brushing her hair. When she saw Reid, she put down the hairbrush, laid it calmly on the bureau, and went to him.

"My boy. My sweet boy." She put her hands on either side of his face. "I knew you'd come today."

She didn't look confused or uncertain. She didn't need to search for a name or an identity. Of course. Of course. I should have known. Her memory, when it came to Reid, was the proverbial steel trap. He was locked inside, with all the minutes and seconds she'd been counting. We—Celeste and Estelle—were on the outside. Easily mistaken, easily dismissed.

I left the room.

A paved path—good for wheelchairs and walkers—wove through the back garden, which was shaded by windmill palm, wild plantain, and bamboo. There was a bench by a koi pond. I sat. The koi, mostly orange and white, two black, brought their mouths to the surface. Open, close. Their tails fanned the water.

In the ripples, I saw my mother's face the moment she recognized Reid: her bright eyes, her gleeful smile. When I had returned home after I was expelled from college, there were no parties. No fanfare at all. Only silence. I took responsibility for Reid's actions and came home to accept my punishment. I took on the blame and the shame. For nearly two years I never saw my mother even crack a smile. She carried her own shame, believing she had failed as a parent. Both she and my father carried it. Their son was gone and their daughter was here, having wasted a year in college.

Real joy didn't return to my mother's life until Reid came home in 1977, when President Carter pardoned the so-called draft dodgers. I didn't think of Reid as a dodger. He was a war resister. But circumstance and choice took him to Canada. It was true he had lost his student deferment and had never checked in with his draft board. It was true he had spent the last five years there in exile—what I thought of as self-imposed exile; he was where he wanted to be—but his draft number had never been called. Just by being in Canada, though, he was conferred comrade status—he was a hero to other writers north of the border.

The first place he landed back in the States was Buffalo, where he joined the Outriders Poetry Project. That was when his second book was published. *Rust Devil*. From there, he traveled west across the upper half of the United States, all the way to Alaska. Then he made a sweeping L down the coast of California, through the Southwest. There were postcards from Cannon Beach, Oregon; Winslow, Arizona, with a reference to the Eagles song; and Blessing, Texas. By the time he made it to Florida, he had transformed himself whole-heartedly into Reid Layman. He spoke not only for the men affected by the war, but also for those hit by the recession—the working man.

I was living in an A-frame on the land of the nursery where I worked. It was in a small town called Fellsmere. There was no reason for Reid to have ever heard of it, although its depressed economy fit with the places he wrote about. Dry Branch, West Virginia, which he described as *rasp-rapping an existence out of coal phlegm crusted lungs*. Mars Hill, North Carolina, which he christened the *Blue Ridge buck-back belt-notch of the South*.

Fellsmere was no more than trailer parks and convenience stores, but the nursery itself, called Paperbark, was for me a haven. It was the perfect job for a flunky. We sold all manner of exotic tropicals and woody ornamentals. We cultivated orchids. There were, I learned, over 25,000 species of orchids. I couldn't pronounce most of them. *Dendrophylax lindenii, haraella retrocalla*, and *cypripedium*. Their seeds are so tiny, a billion per gram. I planted them. I watered them. I tended and transplanted the seedlings. When they bloomed, I took pride in the variations: ruffled petals, triangular sepals, freckled throats. With my hands in soil all day and my mind blank, I didn't have to think about the past or the future, focusing only on the living things right in front of me. It was a job I loved, but a bare-bones life. I subsisted below the poverty level. I was the working woman.

I didn't know what Reid thought about the way I lived. He never came to see me at Paperbark. At the end of his first visit, he shoved his books into my hands, as if they were proof that his decision to leave was justified. *See, see, it all worked out,* he seemed to say. He was a published poet, and if sacrifice—mine—had been necessary, so be it. The books were tangible, permanent in a way flowers could never be. Flowers withered; they died.

Reid even signed his books. My mother clutched her copies to her chest and cried. I hate tears. Mine and others. In this way I'm my father's daughter: stoic, disciplined about emotion. But as I held Reid's books, I cried, too. He hadn't brought himself to us—his flesh and blood, his love and attention—he offered the same thing he gave everyone else: his persona.

I wasn't an adoring fan. I was his sister. I didn't need his autograph.

Just this morning Evan had called him the prodigal son. While no livestock had been slaughtered in celebration, my mother had recognized him. In the modern world, in my world, that was the prize for returning.

I wondered if Evan even knew the full Bible story. When Keith and I decided it would be a good idea to give him a moral, if not a spiritual, foundation, we church-hopped, trying out the religions that didn't speak in tongues or froth at the mouth: Methodist, Congregationalism, Lutheran. We went to an Episcopal church. It was Lent and Evan liked the ashes they put on everyone's forehead. He called it the fire church.

Both Keith and I had been raised Protestant, but at the end of our search we joined a Unitarian church, which, from what we could tell, simply followed the Golden Rule. That was fine with us. Did Unitarians even teach stories from the Bible? I didn't remember Evan talking about his Sunday school classes, except to say they had the *mostest wonderfulest* animal crackers at snack time.

Reid and I had learned biblical parables in Air Force base chapels, primarily in Texas and California. Our Sunday school teachers illustrated them on a felt board. The figures were like paper dolls and had interchangeable clothing: red robes and blues sashes and white headscarves. The teacher moved the floppy men around as she told of Jesus healing the sick or Jesus working in the vineyard. Everything on that board was static, one-dimensional, except when the bond between felt and figure came loose and a peasant lost his grip. His arm drooped, hanging by a fabric shoulder joint. Or a disciple slumped forward, as if bowing. Only then did the stories come alive for me.

In the prodigal son story, when it came to the slaughter of the animals, my teacher used sleight of hand. One minute the cows, goats, and lambs were grazing in a pasture and the next they were pinched off the board and replaced by the roasted versions of their parts.

This reminded me of another story. The Parable of the Mustard Seed. A mustard seed was so small you could barely see it—no bigger than a mote of dust—but when planted, grew into a tree a hundred times larger, no, a billion times larger, than itself. Its branches spread strong and wide. They provided shelter for birds, shade for people. And so it was with the kingdom of God. It was expansive, all-encompassing.

The teacher poured some seeds from an envelope into her hand. They were tiny and smelled spicy. On the felt board, Jesus had a seed in his palm, the mere hint of a dot, maybe made with the nib of the teacher's pen. Next to him was a tall tree with a sturdy brown trunk, topped with what looked like a green cloud.

When the teacher mentioned how important trees were to us, a boy raised his hand and said, "Oxygen."

"Pardon?" the teacher said.

"Trees give us oxygen."

"Of course," she said, taking a deep breath and exhaling, exasperated—this was religion not ecology. The seeds in her hand flew up into the air and we all sneezed. They were not seeds at all, but pepper.

Back inside, director Helen Turner intercepted me in the hall. My mother always remembered Helen's name, but she called her Helené. It added to the air of sophistication she had created around her life at Garden House.

"I'm so happy your brother's here. I was just in her room. She's beside herself."

Helen, tall, with a page-boy haircut, was no-nonsense. Her voice was soft but direct. "This is a lot of excitement. She does look tired."

"She remembered my brother right away," I said.

"That happens. She'll have these lucid moments. They'll come and go. Listen, I wouldn't let him stay too long today. Short visits each day."

"Sure, I understand," I said.

She squeezed my arm and went to her office.

I trusted Helen. When I first moved my mother here, I had been alarmed by what I thought of as her quick decline. She was crankier, more forgetful. I mentioned my concern to Helen. She was reassuring. She said, "She's still Margaret. Just love her. The old Margaret and the new." It took a while, several months, for me to do what Helen suggested, to stop noting every lapse, to stop pushing my mother to be her old self. I had, finally, accepted the new Margaret. She barely recognized me and called by her sister's name. I did love her. Now I had to accept this: no matter how long it had been since she'd last seen her son, she would never forget him.

In my mother's room, she and Reid sat on the bed, laughing. His hair was down and she had her hands in it, running her fingers to the ends, ruffling, tousling.

"I always loved your hair," she said.

I had a sense she was in a different time, back in our teenage years, when Reid first grew out his hair.

"I loved that you defied your father," she said. "I shouldn't say this, but it gave me a perverse satisfaction."

"I didn't know that," I said.

She turned to me. Her eyes were red-rimmed and the skin underneath was thin and pale. "Oh, Estelle, we need eggs," she said. "It's your turn to go out."

The spell was broken.

"I think there are eggs in the fridge," I said. I had been counseled by Helen to not contradict her. It was best to just answer and move on.

"Nonsense. You always make me go out." She was back in time, back on her parents' farm, talking to her sister. "And I don't want to. It's too cold. When Mother comes home, she'll want eggs and I'll have to tell her you wouldn't go out."

Helen was right. It was time to go. I nudged Reid.

He started to object, but Sophie came in. It was time for lunch and she was here to escort my mother.

"I don't need an escort," my mother said, huffy.

"No, Margaret, but I do."

That made my mother snicker. She stuck out her arm and Sophie took it. I didn't know if Helen had sent her to help pave the way for us to leave, but Sophie impressed me. The guile and gift of youth allowed her to pull off this transition beautifully.

On our way out, Helen offered to call later and let us know how Mom was. After the sun went down—it was called sundowning—many Alzheimer's patients became anxious, restless. Pacing was the symptom my mother exhibited. There were times, on a day I had just been there, that Helen called and asked me to return, to sit with her, to calm her.

In the car, Reid said, "She looks good. The way you acted, I thought she was going to be a total vegetable or something."

"Did you not hear that she called me Estelle? Did you not hear all that about the eggs?"

"Well, sure, that was weird." His profile reminded me of our father: the long, thin nose, the equally thin jawline. A bird-like silhouette. An eagle. A regal eagle. He was handsome. Both he and my father had those searing green eyes.

"Don't I know it," I said. "You, my dear brother, have no idea what it's been like."

When Reid and I got home, three cars were parked in the driveway: Holly's BMW, Keith's Jeep, and Parker Smythe's pick-up truck.

"Ah, you have a welcoming committee," I said.

This confluence of people could only have been brought together by Evan. Evan told Keith, Keith told Holly, Holly told our old friend Parker. Those last two genuinely liked seeing Reid when he came to town. I had planned to call them. We usually got together. Did it matter if it was right here, right now?

And Keith, why was he here? It wasn't unusual for him to stop in and stay a while when he dropped Evan off. We discussed our schedules, checked-in about Evan. We had remained friends and took co-parenting seriously. Today, though, I was sure Keith was curious, a rubbernecker at the site of a collision. Or a collision-to-be, since Reid and I knew how to be civil, especially in public. We had been trained by our father. In fact, our talents allowed us to keep up the charade even when it was just the two of us.

Reid pulled his hair back and rubber banded it. "Not sure I'm up for this. It's been a long day already."

I was drained from the visit to Garden House, but I hadn't thought how Reid might feel. He and my mother had hugged and talked and laughed. I figured his earlier show of nerves was a rare emotional blip.

"No, it'll be fun," I said. "These are your friends. Used to be. They're my friends. Well, not Keith. No, yes, Keith. I love him. I do. I just can't live with him." I was tangled in this web of interconnections.

"Yet another example of your contrary nature."

"You bet," I said. How did he do that, utter a sentence that on the surface was simple and spoken in a light-hearted tone, but came off with a hint of a putdown?

Penny ran out to meet me. She twirled, she barked. *We have company. Come and see.* They were sitting on the back patio, three six-packs on the picnic table, two beer, one root beer.

"There he is," Parker said.

Both he and Holly got up to hug Reid.

"Good to see you, man," Reid said.

"Dad's here," Evan said, pointedly to me.

"I see," I said.

Keith offered me a beer.

"Thanks," I said.

"How ya doing?" he asked with a sheepish-wolfish grin, fully aware that I was aware his curiosity had gotten the better of him. I clinked my bottle against his, acknowledging his cunning.

Holly put her hand on my arm, as if to say, "Isn't this nice?" Her long brown hair was tied back with a paisley headband. She had on a top with the same pattern. She favored coordinated outfits like this.

Under the river birch and carrotwood that surrounded the patio, we caught up. I only half listened. These *were* my friends. I didn't need updates about their lives. Parker lived in Viera, not too far from me. A mechanic and collector of classic cars, he operated his own shop. We saw each other on occasion. I took my car to him for repairs. If I needed to leave it for a day or two, he gave me a lift home and stayed for dinner. He had offered to help Evan find his first car when he turned sixteen. If I needed something fixed around the house, a small job like a ceiling fan installed, Parker was my go-to guy.

"So, where are you staying?" Keith asked Reid. Ah, he was being protective. He was the only person who knew the full story of what happened in college. On Reid's previous visits, he acted as a buffer. It was nice to know he still had my back in the most basic way.

"With us," Evan said. "He's in the guest room."

Keith side-eyed me.

I shrugged.

Inevitably, talk turned to the fires. They were strongest in Flagler County, a hundred and twenty miles north of us. Fifty-four homes were now in ashes and the poor air quality was jamming up emergency rooms. Anyone with lung or heart conditions had been told to leave or avoid being outside in the vicinity of the fires.

For us, today, the air held a hint of ash-haze coming on the eastern wind from Deland. It smelled, Reid said, acrid. Such a show-offy word.

"You mean like acid?" Evan asked.

"What high school do you go to again?" Reid asked, implying that I sent him to a special school with a curriculum decidedly against teaching words like acrid.

"The same one we went to," I said.

"That school sucked," Parker said. His gray hair was short. He wore carpenter pants, a slight paunch hanging over the top.

"Here, here," Holly said, raising her beer bottle.

Evan drained his root beer and burped.

"Excuse yourself," Keith and I said together.

"S'cuse me," Evan said.

Parker, like a teenager himself, said, "There's no excuse for you."

I stood and offered to make dinner. Inside, I clicked on the air conditioner. The house was stifling, the air unhealthy, acrid. I knew what it meant. I wondered if air-conditioning was too bourgeois for Reid. He might think of it as a conspiracy of the military industrial complex, meant to lull the masses into a comfort that kept them from rebellion. He hadn't yet complained.

I rooted around the cupboards and fridge. Isn't there a Bible story about Jesus feeding the multitudes with a loaf of bread and a couple of scrawny fish? On the Sunday school felt board, our teacher had made the most rudimentary of loaves. They were just beige circles. The blue fish had triangle tails, like something I might have drawn at that age.

I pulled together a plate of cheese and crackers. *Here's Jesus breaking a loaf of bread into thousands of pieces.* I opened some cans of tuna and whipped up tuna salad sandwiches. *Here's Jesus plucking the flesh of a fish into thousands of bite-size morsels.* I plopped a bunch of grapes in a bowl. *Here's Jesus working in the vineyard, turning grapes into jugs of wine.* There was always enough to fill the bellies of his followers.

When I returned to the table, I heard Reid say, "It's somewhat over-packaged for me. Strip mall after strip mall. A drugstore on every corner."

"We were just talking about how the town has changed over the years. You know, since the good old days," Keith said.

He was a pro in these kinds of social situations. Years in retail before he took the job at Yost had taught him the art of small talk. Keith—in an Izod shirt and boat shoes, just as Reid had written years earlier. I was happy to have him here. Reid might think it strange, but to us, it was natural.

Our divorce was primarily caused by the fact that we didn't speak the same parental language. Intuition was my guide. Keith was a strict disciplinarian. He expected me to toe the line, his line. We were out of sync and it fed discontent. These days we were amiable, could share a beer together among friends.

"Hey, Holly," Reid said. "I hear you live in a McMansion."

"Guilty," she said. "And by the way I feel no guilt at all about that. We work hard for our money." That was Holly, unashamed of her wealth. She not only lived in a million-dollar house, she sold them. When her daughters were in junior high, she took night classes to get her real estate license. A suitable career for a full-time mom.

"We used to have just that one movie theater," Parker said. "What was it called?"

"The Van Croix," Reid said.

"I think I saw *The Sound of Music* there," Holly said.

"And we didn't have any fast food joints like Burger King or Hardy's or Taco Bell," Parker said. He and Reid were of the same mind: all the tacky parts of capitalism had turned our town into Everytown, which made it a non-town. "All we had back then was Burt's Burgers and The White Bridge Café."

"You people," Evan said and rolled his eyes. The words *back then* were death to a teenager.

"Whatever happened to your boyfriend? Adam Something?" Reid asked.

"I haven't thought about him in years. I have no idea where he is," I said.

"Was he one of your delinquent friends?" Evan asked.

"Oh boy, what have you been telling him?" Holly asked Reid.

"Way too much," I said.

"Not enough," Evan said.

We ate. We drank. Penny circled the table, hoping for dropped nibbles. It was cool in the shade, even though the leaves were brown and limp. The Spanish moss was waiflike, the strands grayer, more shriveled than usual. The sky, beginning to dim, was cloudless, as it had been all summer. In the distance, the river ambled along.

"Did you see the witchy statues my mom put up?" Evan asked. "They're some kind of altar or something. She prays to them."

That wasn't true. When it came to God, I was a user, an abuser. I didn't pray. I begged. I bargained. Always to my advantage and without qualification: no situation too small or too big. *Please bring me a pony for Christmas. Please don't let my father die.* There was no pony, ever. My father died. I cursed. It was an appalling relationship.

Everyone turned toward the pier. Keith stood and craned his neck for a better look. From this distance, in this light, the goddesses were mere outlines with smudged faces.

"Oh, it's silly. I had some crazy idea that I could, I don't know—" I stopped, finding it difficult once again to explain the impetus for my actions. "I call them my goddesses. I've convinced myself they're going to keep the fires away." I was a big girl, I could take some ribbing.

"I thought you were an atheist," Keith said.

"These days I'm more of a seeker," I said.

"They're great," Holly said. She took my hand. "I believe in your girls."

"I believe in them, too. Right now, we need help from anywhere and everywhere," Parker said.

"I think she's insane," Evan said. He tossed a grape up in the air and caught it in his mouth. When he bit down, I heard the snap of skin breaking between his teeth. I was reminded of Zink. I should take Keith aside and ask about him.

Before I got a chance, Keith stood to leave. He was meeting his girlfriend for a movie. This was a new relationship, only a few months old. I didn't know much about her, had chatted with her a few times when dropping off Evan.

He told Evan to be ready at eight the next morning, no excuses. I had a feeling Evan had tried to talk his way out of going to work so he could spend the day with his uncle.

Parker was next. He hugged everyone goodbye, even my son. He was a hugger and it didn't matter if you were or not. You succumbed to the embrace. He and Reid agreed to meet later in the week. I walked Holly to her car.

"This is weird, right?" I asked.

"It's weird and wonderful," she said.

"Did I tell you he's staying here? I mean here, in my house." I thought of his sandals in the corner of the guest room, his duffel bag spilling rumpled clothes onto the floor.

"I never understood what happened between you two," she said.

When I returned home from college, abruptly and with no explanation, Holly accepted me, even after the way I had treated her—unkindly, with judgement. She didn't ask questions. At the time, it felt good to not be judged.

"We're just different people," I said.

"He's here. It's a kind of miracle," she said. "Like your goddesses. Maybe they conjured up all this. Maybe it was just meant to be."

"Now look who's getting all spiritual," I said.

Maybe she's right, I thought. Maybe not. Like all my other pleas, both large and small—ponies, death, fire—maybe neither God nor the goddesses would hear or heed.

Later that night, I went to Evan's bedroom to say goodnight. He sat at his desk, all of Reid's books piled on top, a spiral notebook open in front of him. He hadn't cracked any type of book, not even the one required for summer reading, since school ended. I knew enough not to ask what he was writing.

"Uncle Reid is so cool," he said. His hair was still wet from a shower and the room smelled of steamy soap.

"He is." Why fight it, I thought.

Then came a rapid-fire string of questions: How long was he staying? Could he come to Yost, see where he worked? Why hadn't I ever invited him to stay with us? He was in awe and barely heard my answers: I don't know. Yes. I've invited him many times.

"Wake me up in time to meditate with him tomorrow morning," he said.

"That's at, like, six," I said.

"I know. Get me up. No, forget it. I'll set my alarm." He picked up the clock and fiddled with the knobs.

"Let me ask you something," I said. "You know that thing you mentioned this morning, about the prodigal son? I'm just curious, what do you know about that story?"

His answer was what I expected. Sure, he said, he knew what prodigal meant. Like gifted, on the violin or the piano. He was talking about prodigy.

"No wait," he said. "That's progeny."

He had dropped into a language pit. The words—prodigal, prodigy, progeny—so similar but with very different meanings. At this point, he couldn't tell them apart.

"You say potato, I say *potahto*," I joked.

"Look, I know what it means." His ears stuck out in a cute way, kind of baby-ish, though I would never tell him that. "The dude went out and made his fortune and when he returned his father slaughtered a bunch of pigs or something. The son who stayed around was all jealous and suicidal."

"I wouldn't say suicidal." This conversation was suddenly too real for my comfort. I was the dude who stayed home. I didn't have the heart to tell him he was wrong, on so many accounts. The son didn't go out and make his fortune. He squandered the one he had been given. Prodigal by definition meant extravagant, wasteful. And sure, the other son was envious at first, but the lesson, the moral of the parable, was simple: all for one and one for all. Everyone rejoices and feasts on the bounty.

Now, I thought, the smallest seed wasn't mustard or pepper. It wasn't poppy or strawflower, a nib of orchid or a pip of celery. It wasn't an organic thing. Not vegetable or floral. It wasn't even visible. The smallest seed on earth lived right here in my hard-hearted heart. It was resentment.

After Reid's visit in 1977, his nomadic lifestyle began in earnest. At any given time, I knew and didn't know his whereabouts. His primary form of communication was postcards. He sent them to both my mother and me. She never let a postcard pass without informing me of its arrival. She wanted me to know she knew where he was. Of course, by the time we received the postcards, he was already gone.

Even though postcards are, in essence, public—even the postal carrier knew what Reid had written—I made a point of finding a quiet moment alone to sit and read them. I was looking for clues, for hidden messages. For an apology, a real acknowledgement that he understood what I had given up for him. Instead, I received snippets of travel updates and personal musings.

When I wanted to get in touch with him, I called his publisher. The message was delivered and Reid called back. Sometimes. When he did call it was collect. Our conversations were as exasperating as his postcards, his answers to my questions veiled and self-important. I'd ask how he was, and he'd say something like, "How are any of us, sis? The world's a mess." I'd ask where he was, and he'd say something like, "I'm standing in front of the Yellow Jacket Bowling Alley. Believe it or not, it's painted black-and-yellow. Stripes. Like the name implies." I was paying for the call and I got nothing.

All his visits home mirrored the first one. Adulation and attention. Distance and disregard. He pitched his tent at the campground, he hitchhiked around town. I received sighting reports. *Hey, I saw your brother get in a Chevy on New Haven Avenue this morning.* If the visit coincided with the publication of a new book, which they often did, he gave a reading at the bookstore. We sat in the audience, all of us: Holly, Parker, Keith, my mother, me. Others: my mother's friend Shirley and our former history teacher Mr. Jessup. My mother beamed. I had always thought the idea of someone beaming with happiness was a cliché. An invention of the movies or the greeting card industry; the domain of sappy poetry. But that was the effect Reid had on my mother.

He never stayed long. He was too restless. In between visits, between postcards and collect calls, we read about his life in his books, in interviews and articles. When he sunk a nail into his palm at a reading in Washington, D.C.—his bloody protest against Jessie Helms' threat to defund the National Endowment for the Arts in 1989—the *New York Times* wrote about it.

When he won the Conway Award for *Foraminifera* in 1988, I heard on NPR that he gave the prize money, $25,000, to a shelter for homeless veterans in Pittsfield, Massachusetts. That was the Reid I knew—generous, unconcerned with monetary gain. I wished at that moment to be near him.

Through all this, my life inched forward. I lived and worked at Paperbark. After a day in the company of mostly plants, I walked across the property to my tiny house. The bathroom had only a tub and I filled it and soaked, the water clouding with grit. Crickets serenaded me; geckos skittered around on the floor. For a long time, I thought this was no better than I deserved. Then, as time passed, I thought of it as the life I wanted.

I met Keith about two years after I first started at Paperbark. We worked side by side for months, exchanging little more than pleasantries. He had moved from Madison, Wisconsin, to live with and take care of his grandmother. When she died and his parents sold her house, he had no job and no place to live. He decided to stay in Florida. He found the job easily—the nursery always needed an extra set of hands willing to get dirty—and found it an easy job with rich rewards.

Keith Banks was a man with soft dark eyes and beautiful, smooth, pale Midwestern skin. He hadn't been in Florida for long and he didn't seem to have his bearings. Like me, he was going through a change. We were in the middle of molting. Except it was the opposite of molting. It was a form of quilting, overlaying new patches or ripping out the stitching of old patches, turning them, re-sewing, skewing the pattern to create something unique and different on top of the original.

He was no-frills, no-games. What you see is what you get. I liked that. I didn't want to have to think too hard. Our dreams, in the middle of this major shift, were similar and meager: make a little money, live simply but close to the earth.

In early 1981, we married. I let my mother plan the wedding. At the time, I thought it was the least I could do, after all the trouble I had caused. I wore the Cinderella dress in the church of her choice and sat down to a chicken dinner complete with champagne fountain. The one thing I didn't concede was my name. I remained a Leahy. My first act of feminism as an adult.

Two months later, I received a collect call from Reid. He wanted to congratulate me on my marriage.

Evan and I quickly absorbed Reid into our lives. Our daily ritual went something like this: At dawn, he and Reid rose and went down to the pier. They remained in lotus position for a good twenty minutes, the stillest I had seen Evan in years. I watched from the comfort of my couch, unable to take my eyes off them. Coffee and contemplation, my own moment of Zen. Penny had abandoned me. After she took her swim, she settled next to them. Buddha dog. I took solace in the fact that she chose to sit next to Evan.

Breakfast was self-serve. Cereal, oatmeal, toast, a banana, a peanut butter waffle taco. Afterward, we went our separate ways: Evan to Yost with Keith. Me to work. Reid to Garden House. I never asked how he got there, since he refused a ride from either of us. I supposed he walked to the main road, then hitchhiked.

On my drive to and from work I found no respite in Fleetwood Mac or Three Dog Night or The Who. Janis, either one—Joplin or Ian—did nothing for me. Neither did Jim or Jimi or Mick. The news was bleak. I couldn't stand to hear about Lewinsky's little blue dress or how the new Nigerian president was just as corrupt as the old Nigerian president. I listened to fire updates, each day an assessment of damage and risk. Voluntary evacuations had been announced for residents in Ormond Beach. A hundred firefighters from throughout the state had arrived to help local firefighters. It was the slow slog of containment. I turned off the radio.

I was thankful for my no-count job. I didn't have to concentrate. Russell was awe-struck when I told him my brother was Reid Layman. Of course he knew Reid's work. *Rust Devil* had meant so much to him when he was in college, an aspiring poet himself. I promised to bring Reid in soon, so they could meet.

I stayed away from Garden House, but I called every day to talk with Helen. She said everything was going well. Reid was a dear. No, a *dearie*, as Mrs. Kline would say. He had started a poetry group, featuring Ogden Nash and E.E. Cummings and William Carlos Williams. The red wheelbarrow, the plums in the icebox. Short, easy poems. They must love that. They must love the word *icebox*. Reid was trying to get them to write. Even staff members were participating.

At the end of the day, we came together for dinner. Reid began to cook, the prodigal son providing the feast, his way to earn his keep. I didn't argue. Items and ingredients I didn't own showed up in the cupboards and on our plates: quinoa, tempeh, wheat germ, green tea. He kept a bottle of Fuenteseca tequila on the counter. When he cooked, he had a glass by his side. As soon as I walked in the door, he poured me one. Maybe I could drink my way through these days.

Fuenteseca, he told us, balancing the bottle in his palm, as if showing off the biggest diamond in the world, was the *only* brand he drank. He first tasted it in Mexico in 1979, when living with the Aztecs in Guadalajara. The red volcanic soil in the area produced the sweetest, most aromatic blue agave in the world. They harvested a million plants a year. It was aged for twenty-one years in oak barrels. Agave, he said, his voice low and smooth, was the nectar of the gods.

"Cool, red dirt makes blue plant," Evan said, trying to slide into the conversation. "I'll take a shot."

"Oh no, you won't," I said.

I still wondered why Reid was here. Why now? *Heal the past.* Hmm. Around him, I did feel vulnerable. I could succumb to his charm so easily. At the same time, just his presence reduced me to a snappish, huffy, hands-on-hips, stomp-my-foot child. I pecked and poked at him. I took out my resentment in snide remarks and insinuation. Like Evan's metaphor about volcanoes and icebergs, I was alternately molten and frozen. Either way, the core—my heart—was solid.

I kept watch, studied his actions. I dwelled on each word, each *inflection* of each word, listening for clues. Was there a big announcement on the horizon? Did he have a terminal illness? Was he moving back permanently? Or he just might up and leave. Advance, retreat. It was my brother's MO.

After dinner, while Evan and I did the dishes, Reid stayed at the table, opening a canvas satchel that held a knife, basswood, and a cache of carved figures. He was learning to whittle. It was, he said, a replacement for writing. He was working on a series of small animals and birds. Most of them were misshapen, blobs with a beak or short tail. I remembered the callouses I felt the night he arrived. His hands, his very skin, were acclimating to this new skill.

He had been like that with the model airplanes he built as a kid. At first, the parts didn't fit together correctly and the glue was a globby mess. But he remained diligent. Before long, the pieces lined up straight and the seams were invisible. He hung them with fishing line from the ceiling of his room, as if they were flying, proud of his accomplishment.

Later, at dusk, all three of us walked to the pier. All four of us, Penny included. She couldn't resist an evening swim. Evan ran ahead, urging his uncle to walk with him, eager to get him alone, away from my nagging. As they made their way down the slope of our backyard, they pretended to box. Reid faked a left hook and Evan gave him a few belly jabs.

Leaning over the railing, Evan pointed to a lone flat bottom boat in the middle of the river. The two men were fishing. Evan imitated their actions, casting and recasting an imaginary line. When he was excited like this, he couldn't stay still. He was a constant hiss of motion. He boxed with the goddesses. I heard him say, "I'll knock your block off."

The sun was low in the west, tipping the upper branches of the willows. The water took on an orangey-pink tinge. Soon mosquitoes would come out, followed by lightning bugs. We watched the final half-pie of sun drop behind the earth.

I loved it here on my riverfront property. I loved the river, so lazy, never in a hurry to get anywhere. Evan had written a fifth-grade paper on the natural geography of Florida. The St. Johns is the longest river in the state. Like a handful of other U.S. rivers, like the Nile, it flows south to north. The total drop from its source in the swamps south of town to its mouth near Jacksonville is less than 30 feet, and it flows about one inch per mile.

The tributary I lived on, me and a dozen other families, was called Jigsaw Lake. Beds of pepper grass created the marshy edge where Penny swam every morning. Twisted roots of mangrove clung to the earth bank, as did sweetbay, their leaves green and lush. They thrived on this dry weather. From here, I couldn't see any of the other houses. I couldn't even see the bank on the opposite shore. Sometimes it felt like I lived at the end of the earth.

After the divorce, I fled to this place, away from the hub-bub of downtown, which was where Keith and I had lived for years. Away from the *sub-hub*. I wanted to cultivate the land. I planned a vegetable garden. I planned a flower garden. Gladiola, bird of paradise, and laceleaf—inconsequential but beautiful. We all need beauty in our lives. I longed to once again stick my hands into the earth, the way I had so many years earlier at Paperbark.

But in the three years I had lived here, I never planted the flowers or the vegetables. Once I settled in, there was too much to do—my mother was beginning to decline, I had to find a better paying job, the house needed constant upkeep. Because we lived so far from town, I spent more time in the car. Everything took longer, even a trip to the grocery store. It seemed frivolous, a waste of time given all that. I was ashamed now, with Reid here, of my smallness, the small goal.

Evan ran up behind Reid and, acting more like a high-strung seven-year-old than a surly teenager, jumped on his back. Reid jogged a few paces, giving him a piggy-back ride.

Their ease with each other puzzled me. When was the last time Evan had touched me? Had let me touch him? When he got his last haircut, I reached out to run my hands through the close crop and he ducked. "Don't, you'll mess it up." I had made him stand still, so I could trace my fingers around the peace sign, feeling his scalp in the sheared circle. Still, the general sentiment was that my greedy hands—any involvement at all by me—would only make a mess of things. My son, full of shrugs and shrug-offs.

Could Reid be a good influence? Could he have changed? He seemed so at home. Maybe that was all this visit was about: reconciliation. Maybe he just wanted to be a part of our family.

The goddesses glowered at me. They certainly had an opinion.

My mother wanted a party, so we had a party. An afternoon dessert fête at Garden House. The star—aside from Reid—was a six-layer vanilla cake with the words *Welcome Home* stenciled in purple icing. Purple crêpe paper bows were taped to the backs of the dining room chairs. It was, after all, his favorite color.

My mother was glammed-up in coral lipstick and rouge, done, I imagined, by Sophie. Her hair was freshly washed and set. No *fluffity* today. Sophie herself was dressed in street clothes, jeans and a crop top. Evan, drawn to her ample chest, struck up a conversation. I stepped in, telling her how pretty my mom looked and thanking her for all her help.

"It's amazing what a little lipstick can do," she said.

I licked my bare lips, said, "You're allowed to wear your own clothes to work?"

"Oh, I'm not working today. I just came in for the party. My mom's here, too." She pointed to a woman with brown-gray hair down to the middle of her back. She was my age, dressed the way we all did in the early 70s, a flowing skirt and madras shirt—a true Reid Layman groupie. She had him cornered, talking fast, wigwagging her hands.

"She made the cake," Sophie said.

"Cool," Evan said.

Holly arrived in a sweep of real estate agent flair, in between showings: navy suit, panty hose, heels. Her hair was in a tight chignon. She hugged my mother.

"Do you see who's here?" my mother asked.

"I know, Margaret. Isn't it great?"

"It's wonderful, darling."

My mother's lipstick had migrated onto her front teeth. Holly took a Kleenex from her purse and, with social aplomb I admired, swiped it away. I felt—and I felt this with no animosity; it was simply a fact—that Holly was the daughter my mother wished she had. Her clothes were classic 50s to my 70s hippie chic. I was more like Sophie's mom than I cared to admit, with my sundresses, denim skirts, and espadrilles. Holly had followed the conventional path: from college to marriage to children to suitable career selling houses. Criminal activity had not derailed her.

I finally got my chance to introduce Russell to Reid. To my surprise, he was tongue-tied. He spoke in platitudes. *It's an honor to meet you. I'm your biggest fan. This is one of the top five highlights of my life.* Between him and Sophie's mother, Reid was monopolized much of the afternoon. He acted humble and humbled. Maybe it wasn't an act. I didn't know.

Overall, the party was a lovefest, and I was feeling the love. It was so nice for my mother to have Reid here, to have family and friends together. Sophie took pictures on a digital camera. We stood behind the dessert table, the cake beginning a Leaning-Tower-of-Pisa tilt, and said, "Cream cheese."

This was the first digital camera I had seen in action. We leaned over the small screen to see the results. Immediate results. Instant gratification. No waiting for one-hour processing. We were all smiles. In one, Evan snuck bunny ears behind my head. The last picture, though, gave me pause. I took the camera from Sophie. In it, everyone was looking at the camera except my mother and me. She gazed lovingly up at Reid, who stood next to her. I also stared at my brother, but the look on my face both surprised and saddened me. Instant gratification turned to instant humiliation. *Miffed* was not a strong enough word to describe that look. Scorn—that was a better word.

The other good thing about a digital camera, I discovered, was that with a tap of a finger pictures disappeared. Petty moments can be instantly erased.

We ate the cake—it was delicious—and helped the staff clean up. It was time to leave, but I didn't want to go home. I wasn't ready to spend the rest of the day ricocheting between Evan and Reid. One trying to bait me, the other switching loyalties so fast I couldn't keep up. To my relief and after a bit of organizational maneuvering, it was decided that Russell would drive Reid and Evan home. They would take Penny for a walk and have dinner without me.

I walked downtown, sat on a bench at Monroe Park, and stewed about the picture. My childish feelings were evident right there on my face: suspicion, downright jealousy. Was I that spiteful? I guess so. Reed had what I wanted: my mother's full attention.

There's a saying—not one my parents ever used or I myself had ever said to Evan when he was a grump—*Turn that frown upside down*. I don't even know the origin. Was there a way, with a simple gesture, to change the dynamic between Reid and me? The goddesses used their smirky smiles to good effect. They were perpetually amused, and whenever I saw them, I had to smile as well. Could a shit-eating grin really make a difference?

A slight breeze cooled my arms. I closed my eyes, wanting quiet. What I got was the noise of skateboarders who had overtaken half the park. They jumped curbs, slid down the handicapped ramp, banked off the lip of the fountain. Basically, they had commandeered public property, forcing pedestrians off the sidewalks. It irked me, and a lot of people. Evan was a skateboarder, but I only allowed him to practice at our house. He and Keith had built a set of ramps, rails, and benches that could be pulled from the garage to the driveway. There were probably liability issues I hadn't thought of, but I liked watching him and his friends out there doing tricks.

One of the skateboarders took a tumble. His cry—*shhiiiit, man*—pulled my attention. He was on the ground and the others, instead of helping him, laughed. When he got up, I recognized him. It was Zink.

I had seen these kids dozens of times and never took any notice except to curse them under my breath; they were inconsiderate and unconcerned about the destruction of property. I wondered why the police didn't hustle them away. Zink, like all the others, wore baggy shorts and untied tennis shoes. They were shirtless and so skinny. Their ribs, exposed and taut, were like strings over the fretboard of their torsos. With each trick, Zink's braids flew up, splaying, like the flying swings at a carnival. I searched the parking lot for his Mustang but didn't see it. Bringing it here would ruin his street cred.

An old man approached the boys. They spoke, but I couldn't hear the conversation. Zink bummed a cigarette from a friend, lit it, and gave it to the man. What a good Samaritan.

I was reminded of the first few weeks after we moved to Florida, the summer of 1966. While my father went off to work and my mother unpacked, Reid and I rode our bikes around town, trying to get our bearings. We went to the bakery for bear claws and the five-and-dime for gum. We'd hit the library and the public pool, always ending up at Monroe Park.

Back then, it was just a bunch of picnic tables under the live oak trees, old men occupying the tables. They sat in shorts and undershirts, canes across their knees. Reid smoked and, if asked, he took out the pack and offered one. He talked to anyone, to everyone. Polite and interested in the stories of others, ready to offer a hand, he was the good Samaritan of our time.

I drove home with the sun still strong, causing a glare on the windshield. It seemed to take forever, this drive. Not because of the sun or traffic lights that refused to turn green. It was time itself, a maze of fractured and flitting increments. How long had Reid been here? Two weeks and it seemed like days. As I sat at the intersection of Sixth and Newman Streets, waiting for my turn at the light, the seconds moved colossally slow. It felt like a lifetime. It was easy, too easy, to slip into the past.

This corner, for instance. It had once been an orange grove. It was owned by a man named Solomon Jones who sold citrus all winter at a roadside stand. The air, at harvest time, was overpowered by the smell of orange blossoms and the drone of bees. We had ridden our bikes past here hundreds of times. After Jones died, the land was razed and paved. Half of it went to build a much-needed elementary school and the other half for a drive-in movie theater. Later, when the population tripled and a new, bigger school had to be built west of town, when a six-cinema complex went up by the interstate, the land was turned into a 700,000 square-foot mall. I shopped there. I had bought my wedding dress in our once-beloved orange field. I had bought a bassinet for Evan where I had first watched *Love Story*, holding hands with my boyfriend Adam in the front seat of his Mustang. Keith had even worked there.

Every building, every street was a memory-bomb. I wondered if this is how my mother felt every day, living simultaneously in the past and the present. In her case, she dwelled primarily in the past, everyone forcing her back into the present with reminders. "Time to take your pills, Margaret," the nurses said. "My name is Celeste, Mom. Remember?" I said.

I wondered what Reid, now so enmeshed in my day-to-day, thought of my life. I was middle-age, middle-class, middle-of-the-road. I was a property owner. I drove a foreign car. My living room was overstuffed with furniture and its focal point was a twenty-five-inch Zenith television set. These were all things he held in contempt. My divorce was humdrum, as was the fact that I hung out occasionally with my ex. Evan, too, was a typical adolescent, his rebellion uninteresting: smoking, befriending neglected boys.

What the hell did it matter what Reid thought? That was the problem, it did matter. Of course, without my small, small life, without me, the one who stayed, or I should say, the one who returned and took care of all the small, small tasks of daily life, Reid wouldn't have his larger-than-life life.

Cherry Bomb

I arrived on the campus of the University of Florida in the fall of 1971, ready to join the fray. That was how I thought of the protests taking place all over the country, on college campuses and in cities like New York, Chicago, San Francisco—an unraveling of what my father called *the fabric of society*. When he used that phrase, he meant the mores and morals of America. Duty and discipline. I wanted to be a part of those at the ragged fringe.

Already I had missed so much. I missed Gentle Wednesday—October 15, 1969—when students and faculty gathered on the quad and chanted "Give peace a chance." I missed the candlelight march to President Stephen O'Connell's house after the Kent State shootings. I missed Jane Fonda at Graham Pond in January of 1971. I missed, only months later, Black Thursday, a sit-in by black students at the administration building, demanding the hiring of more black faculty and the establishment of a black culture center. I missed the strike on the first anniversary of Kent State when thousands of students refused to attend classes, forcing the university to shut down for two days.

I didn't want to lose another minute.

First, I had to check in at my dorm. I stood on the sidewalk in front of Mallory Hall, flanked by my parents. It was eleven in the morning and the sun was strong, the humidity high. Around us, students and parents unloaded suitcases and boxes, their shirts stained with perspiration. At the information table, the RA, a girl with a nametag that read Kim L., welcomed us and gave me my room assignment: fourth floor, at the end of the hall.

"Oh, it's right next to mine," she said. Her smile was as big as her hair, a teased bouffant. "If you need any help finding your way around, just let me know."

"Thanks," I said.

Behind the table, along with Kim, was a boy nametagged Matt R. He had a sweat moustache that was starting to develop into a goatee. He handed me an *F Book*, a pocket-size student handbook full of university history, policy, and advice for freshmen.

"Study it, memorize it, live it," he said, stern and serious.

"You bet she will," my father said, a connoisseur of rules and regs.

Matt winked and I got the joke—his line was a put-on for the benefit of my parents.

I slipped the book into the back pocket of my shorts.

We unloaded and began the trek upstairs. The hallways were overrun by girls, hugging and screeching. *How was your summer? Who's your roommate?* It was a stew of estrogen. Mallory was the last all-female dorm on campus. My parents no doubt thought of that four-story brick building as a fortress, a safe place to house their daughter, to keep her away from the grabby hands of boys. The curfew was a moat and the doors, locked at all times, were as secure as a drawbridge.

My room was basic and sparsely furnished: two identical metal frame beds pushed against opposite walls, two desks, a long bookshelf between them, two bureaus, and a mini-fridge in the corner. Since my roommate hadn't yet arrived, I took ownership of the bed and desk closest to the window. My mother dug the sheets from a box and we made the bed. In another box, she found my spread. She smoothed out the wrinkles and tucked in the bottom corners.

"Well, this is home," my mother said.

My father kneed open the door and dropped a box on the floor. He wiped his forehead with a handkerchief. "Do you really need all this stuff?" he asked.

"Yes, Bill, she does," my mother said.

I opened the box and found it was full of soap—shower bars and boxes of laundry detergent—from the base commissary. For some reason my mother had decided soap was the ultimate comfort. I had enough to last until I went home for holiday break. In my mother's mind, I'd be virginal and squeaky clean.

All around me were signs of the exact opposite. The mini-fridge could be filled with beer, the bureau could hold a ton of condoms. The window right next to my bed could be opened so my RA wouldn't smell the smoke. Sure, the outside doors were locked at all times, but doors could be shimmed. Sure, I had to sign in and out, but that's what roommates were for, to forge your name on the roster.

After my parents left, I walked across campus toward Reid's house. I knew my way around, had been here when we dropped off or picked up Reid for breaks and just this summer for freshmen orientation. The brick buildings around me were magisterial and gothic in style, with arched doorways, gabled roofs and ornamental buttresses. Stately, intimidating. Only a few, like the science labs, were modern, with concrete façades and no charm at all.

Past the Fine Arts Center and Little Hall, I arrived at Tigert Hall, the administration building, site of many sit-ins and protests. I cut west and continued over to the Plaza of the Americas. This was another gathering spot for students, and not just for rallies but for sunbathing, study groups, practicing tai chi, eating lunch, and playing Frisbee. That day, move-in day, it was nearly empty. A trio of boys tossed a football.

I took off a sandal and dug my toes into the soil. Trees—oaks necklaced with Spanish moss, magnolias bobby-pinned with yellowing blooms—shaded the green. Century Tower was at the southern end of the Plaza, a guidepost, fifteen stories high, you could see it from anywhere on campus. A glance at the *F Book* gave a brief history. The Tower was built in 1953 to commemorate the centennial of the university. Right next to it, a stand of American holly trees were planted in the shape of the letters U and F.

History, tradition. I was surprised by the sense of reverence I felt. This conflicted with my anti-establishment sentiments, with what I hoped to do here: join Reid and his friends to promote change and help stop the war. Of course, I was a product of the establishment. The military was in my blood. I was raised to respect custom and ritual, to honor hierarchy. But every institution had faults and reading further in the *F Book* let me know that in the name of tradition, women had been kept out until 1947 and black students much longer.

I put the book back in my pocket and crossed University Avenue.

Where Reid lived was known as the student ghetto—rented houses that students used and abused, one rundown ranch after another, weedy front lawns littered with couches and folding chairs. His house was painted barn red. The wood around the windows was rotting and the shutters were cock-eyed. It was on N.W. Fourteenth Terrace. "The Terrace," we called it. From the street, I heard strains of Black Sabbath.

Inside, four couches, all different sizes, were pushed together to form a lopsided rectangle. Students lounged on every surface. They had their feet in each other's lap or on the coffee table in the middle. The table was covered with ashtrays, bongs, plates with dried food, half-filled glasses, empty beer bottles, a teak box that looked like a treasure chest. Tuffs of stuffing poked out from several corners of each couch, as if a dog had used the cushions as a chew toy. The whole living room was thick with smoke, tobacco and weed.

I slammed the door, loud enough to get everyone's attention.

"Whoa, there she is." Reid jumped up and scrambled out of the pile of bodies. He hugged me, spun me around.

"Everyone, this is Celeste. Celeste, this is, well, all the guys."

"All the guys except for me," said a woman in jeans and a pink tank top. She was rolling a joint.

"Oh, Billie, you're one of the guys," said a boy with horn-rimmed glasses. He had an unlit cigar in his mouth.

I said hi, swung a leg over the back of the nearest couch, and slid into an open spot. The guy next to me bumped my shoulder.

"Hey, I know you." It was Matt, from the dorm registration table. He had given me the *F Book*. "How's the roommate, is she dreadful?" he asked. He had a red and black armband tied at his bicep, a symbol of solidarity for those who lost their lives in Vietnam.

"I don't know. Haven't met her yet. But I took the best bed."

Billie handed me the joint, said, "Welcome to the mad, mad, mad house."

I took a long drag. I hadn't smoked since Jim Morrison died. The buzz was instant.

Soon I would come to know and love everyone there that afternoon. In my memory, the light coming from the front window—a window with no curtains or blinds because who in that house cared about window coverings—was diffuse, a perfect soft focus. Our arms and legs were entwined. The room smelled of warm necks and sulfur. They were all seniors, all moving quickly toward life after college. I was just beginning.

Billie DeCampo was from Brooklyn. She had a round, lively face with dark hair, frizzy and long. My mother would have called her, respectfully, *bosomy*. She could roll a joint, fat and tight, with one hand.

The guy with the glasses was Paul Fielder, editor of *The Florida Alligator*, the student newspaper. His bushy hair and eyebrows—those glasses, that cigar—made him look like a modern-day Groucho Marx. For some reason he thought a cigar in his mouth made him look reporter-y. He was rarely without one, even if he never lit it.

Cal Jeffers ran Vietnam Veterans Against the War. VVAW. He was a loudmouth. He had to be. As a vet, he had firsthand knowledge about what was happening over there and felt he had to be loud—louder than everyone else—to get out the truth. Like Paul, he had bushy hair, and his beard was bushy, too. He dressed in camo vests and ragged jeans.

Matt Ryder had blonde hair, straight and shoulder-length, tucked behind his ears. He was head of SMC, the Student Mobilization Committee. He also had a work-study job on campus, which was why he was helping at registration.

Someone made popcorn, poured it into a large bowl and placed it on the table. It was slightly burned, but realizing I hadn't had lunch, I dove in with both hands.

Black Sabbath ended. Paul got up and put on the Moody Blues. All around me noise swirled: conversation, music. No one paid any attention to me and that was fine. I was, like Billie, just one of the guys. She opened the box on the table. It was stuffed with baggies of weed. She dug around for a packet of rolling papers.

Matt put his head on my shoulder and said, "You're in Mallory? They keep you girls locked up over there."

"I'm in Broward," Billie said. "But let's face it, most of the time I'm here."

I pulled out the *F Book*. Matt cackled.

"You still have that thing?"

Not for long. I snatched a lighter and touched it to the booklet. The corner caught quickly. In my dreamy pot haze, I let the flame grow bigger as it spread and gathered momentum, ate up the cheap pages. Heat rose to my chin. When it got too close to my fingers, I dropped it on a plate. Pages curled, all the rules and regs up in smoke.

By the time I got back to my dorm, my buzz had worn off and I was rife with sweat. All I wanted was to soak in a tub of cool water. Not possible. There were only showers in the bathrooms. My roommate was on her bed, crying. Her name was Doreen Carlisle, and she was from Cairo, Georgia, which she pronounced, with a sweet drawl, *K-Row*. She said, between sobs, that she didn't want to be here. Her boyfriend—no, her fiancé, they had been together since the eighth grade—was back at home. Before she could return and marry Dwight, she had to fulfill the deathbed promise made to her father that she would be the first in their family to graduate college.

Blue mascara raccooned her blue eyes. She had brown hair that she teased at the crown and flipped at the ends. She was petite. Her white clam diggers revealed thin, fine-boned ankles. An admirer of British royalty, she thought it romantic that Prince George left the throne to marry an American.

"I mean, the most powerful position in the British Empire. A love like that, stronger than the crown—" She didn't finish the sentence. She had elevated her and Dwight's love to the same lofty heights. In their case, four years and a liberal arts degree stood in their way.

I tried to bring her down to earth. "The prime minister actually runs the country, you know," I said.

She ignored that and reached for a stuffed dog. She cradled him. He was tan and fluffy, with a pink felt tongue and blue eyes made of glass.

"This is Rascal," she said. "At least I have Rascal."

I had been given the straightest girl in the world as a roommate. She reminded me of Holly. Their situations were different—Holly was going to college to *find* a husband—but their life goals were the same, to get married and have children.

The telephone rang in the hall and someone yelled, "Doreen? Is there a Doreen here? Phone's for you."

She jumped off the bed and ran out the door, saying, "That must be Dwight. His ears were burning. He knew I was talking about him. That's the way it is with us."

I finished unpacking. I put my books on a shelf. Steinbeck, Dickens, the Brontë sisters. I set my stereo on top and sorted my albums below, alphabetically. The Doors—I owned all eight albums—Pink Floyd, Joni Mitchell, Santana.

I hung up my knit and chambray shirts, my denim skirts. Doreen's half of the closet was filled with lace-collared dresses and chiffon blouses in pink and lavender. I put my flip-flops and tennis shoes next her wedge sandals. On her desk was a flowered blotter with matching letter opener, pencil holder, and stationery. Her eyelet bedspread was appliquéd with a similar rose and ivy pattern. She had all the paraphernalia, neat and tidy, but her heart wasn't in it. Her heart was back in Cairo.

I unfurled the one poster I had brought from home. With four thumbtacks I gave Jim Morrison the prime real estate above my bed. Doreen might squawk. The Doors didn't seem like her scene, but too bad. Staring into his soulful eyes, I heard Jim whisper these words: *Chase your pleasure*. A line siphoned from side A, song 1, of the debut album. That was exactly what I planned to do over the next four years.

I gathered my toiletries and went to the bathroom. It smelled of Noxzema. Someone was taking a shower and steam hung in the air. I brushed my teeth without even bothering to wipe clear the mirror. I was that tired.

Doreen was back, under the covers and sniffling. Rascal was tucked under her chin. I climbed into bed, the mattress squishy and lumpy. That's okay. This was my new bed. I said goodnight and Doreen gave me a pitiful *nite-nite*. She probably wished she was back in her girlhood bed. Not me. I was right where I wanted to be. Finally, I was away from home. I didn't have to be a military brat. No saluting here, no devotion to hierarchy. No dressing up or dressing down. I was Reid Leahy's sister, yes, but here that was a fact, not an identity. This campus, as opposed to our high school, was big enough for us both.

From the hall, I heard a shriek of laughter. Or maybe it was sob of despair. Music pounded through the wall we shared with Kim, the RA. I expected her to be a girl who listened to Bread, who knew all the words to "Make It With You." But she was a lover of Three Dog Night. It reminded me of home, of listening to Reid's music. I fell asleep that first night under the benevolent watch of Jim and the familiar sounds of rock.

The next morning the Plaza was jam-packed with students. Clubs and organizations had set up tables and were hawking their wares, enticing us to join, join, join. The Florida Players needed actors for *Hair*. Florida Glee needed tenors. Greeks needed pledges. Signs were everywhere. *Take pictures for the Seminole Yearbook. Save the planet with the Environmental Action Group.* At the intramural sports table there were sign-up sheets for archery, golf, tennis, volleyball, and square dancing. The Residence Halls were organizing get-to-know-you socials. The air was pungent with homemade brownies the girls from Chi Omega had baked.

Paul walked around encased in a sandwich sign that advertised *The Florida Alligator*. His bare legs were pale and hairy. He had a cigar in his mouth and one behind each ear. He looked like a cross between a Roman emperor in a toga and a Mafia boss.

This carnival display of possibilities was overwhelming. I couldn't sing. I couldn't act. I hated volleyball and tennis. How would I choose? I was drawn to the Environmental Action Group table. Here was a place I could make a difference. I could pick up trash and plant seedlings and educate others on the hazards of pollution. As I looked at the display pictures of club members doing all those things, I heard, above the din, one voice, the voice of a skilled and insistent barker: "Ladies, step right up to the Mortar Board table. If you want your voice to be heard on campus, this is the place."

It was Billie, standing on a chair, waving a clipboard. Her gauzy cotton blouse had mirrored sequins embroidered on the sleeves. When the sun caught them, they glittered, winked. Her frizzy dark hair was held in place by a floppy leather hat.

"Hi," I said.

"Celeste, there you are." She acted as if she had been waiting for me. "Here." She shoved the clipboard at me and gave her pitch. Mortar Board was the first all-female honor society, founded at Cornell a hundred years ago. It was our responsibility to show scholarship and leadership, to promote community service. As women, we had to make sure everyone on campus knew who we were and what we did.

I signed up.

"Good," she said. "Now we can be friends. Sit down, sit down."

I sat with her behind the table, watching students mill around. It was another steamy day. The spire of University Auditorium punctured the sapphire bright, almost too bright, sky.

"Look around," Billie said. "What do you see?"

I did look around, but I didn't need to respond. She answered her own question.

"Most of these tables, except ours and all those sorority lovelies, are manned by guys. It's the way of the world."

Cal, Matt, and others were at the VVAW table. Matt held a tattered American flag on a stick. He swung it over his head.

"End the war in Vietnam. Bring our soldiers home," he shouted.

"Now, *he's* a good guy," Billie said, meaning Matt. "I like him. He's the only one who really listens to us." *Us*, I figured, meant women.

"Not so for that guy over there. Stuart Burgess. He's president of Florida Blue Key."

Stuart was pudgy, with a slight overbite. He wore a homemade Uncle Sam hat, cut and taped together out of construction paper. As if he sensed we were talking about him, he headed our way.

"When are you going to let women join your little boys' club?" Billie asked.

Florida Blue Key was the all-male honor and service society, the most powerful organization on campus. That I knew. They planned Homecoming, the annual debate tournament, and the Miss University of Florida pageant.

"The only thing we need from you gals is to get us coffee," Stuart said.

"If you had any brains, you'd know we need to pool our resources," Billie said. "Conquer not divide."

I had the feeling this banter was something they engaged in regularly.

"Don't worry, Billie, some day," he said. Then, as he walked away, he began to sing "Someday Your Prince Will Come" from *Snow White*.

"You're an ass, Burgess. Pure and simple." She was determined to have the last word.

For the next half an hour she regaled me with her opinion of everything UF. She said the best place to eat was the Union Grill and the place to drink was the Rathskeller. The beer there was cheap and cold. She had a toe in every social door. She was a member of student government, president of Mortar Board, and secretary of Accent, an organization that brought speakers to campus. An English major, she was associate editor at the *Florida Quarterly*. Billie, I now understood, was full of more vital information than the *F Book*.

A girl named Stacy came to the table. She was Billie's roommate and here to take her turn at the Mortar Board table.

Gathering up her purse and a stack of flyers, Billie said, "Anyway, gotta jam," and just like that she was gone.

Classes began. I had no idea what I wanted to major in. Math and the sciences were too cut and dry for me, too fact-and-formula based. I had thought about journalism, or maybe English, like Reid. I liked to read big, messy, saga-driven novels.

Not that it mattered. For now, I sat in large lecture halls with all the other freshmen taking the requisite survey courses: composition, algebra, biology, humanities, history.

My first class—Western Civilization—was first thing in the morning. I dragged myself out of bed, dressed quickly and quietly, not wanting to wake Doreen. All her classes were scheduled for the afternoon. She picked them carefully, needing, she said, beauty sleep. Sleep was followed by two hours spent curling her hair and putting on makeup in front of a lighted, magnified mirror.

In the bathroom, I splashed water on my face, put my hair in a ponytail. I sleep-walked across campus. Sunlight bit my eyes, made me blink. Professors and other students rushed to class. The sub-arctic temperatures of the air-conditioned buildings kept us awake. But it was no small feat at that hour to care about the class system of Babylon or to memorize the dates of the Stone Age and the Bronze Age. When the wheel was invented, I thought, finally, some movement. When sticks and stones were fashioned into weapons and war broke out, I thought, against my pacifist tendencies, halleluiah—murder, pillage.

At the end of the first week, I had yet to purchase my texts. The chore seemed daunting. When I got to the bookstore, it was a chaotic scene. The lines at the registers weaved through the store in a pattern I couldn't understand. I gave up and went to the classics section. I wanted the familiar, books I had read a million times. I sat on the floor with Jane Austen. I didn't care that I was blocking the way or that students had to step over me to get to the Shakespeare and Zola.

I heard someone say, "Mr. Darcy, I presume."

I pulled my thoughts away from the 18th century, looked up, and saw Matt.

"Wrong book," I said. "Besides you're mixing your literary references."

"My sister loves Austen. I picked it up one time, read it and just couldn't figure it out. What's so great about Darcy? Yeah, he has the shiny buttons on the uniform and the fuzzy mutton chops. But, he's cold. He's unattainable."

"Until the very end," I said.

"There's always some big misunderstanding, like a mix-up with a letter. They don't talk to one another. I can't stand that."

A guy who has read Austen? Intriguing.

"It was another era. What do you expect?"

"I expect him to walk right up to her, take her face in his hands, and say, *Let's do it, babe*."

I decided to enlist his help. I needed my books and I figured he knew how to navigate the maze of aisles and lines.

I was right, it didn't take long: I had my textbooks.

While we walked across campus, I learned that he had grown up in Cleveland and had been at Case Western Reserve before transferring. Tuition was cheaper and it didn't snow. He was a sociology major.

Over the next few weeks, Matt courted me. He found out where my classes were and he waited for me outside the building. He brought me a sandwich on the days I had a tight schedule. At The Terrace, we sat on his bed and he played guitar. His repertoire was limited. He didn't know any Doors tunes. He was more of a balladeer. "Blowin' in the Wind," "Both Sides Now," and "If I Had a Hammer." When I watched him, his eyes closed, fingers on the frets moving gracefully, I felt like the only person in the world.

I quickly found a balance between going to class, attending meetings of the Environmental Action Group, studying at the library, hanging out with Doreen, and going to The Terrace to be with Matt and the others. Most mornings, after Western Civ, I went to the Union to get my mail and to have breakfast.

Both Kim and Stacy were in that class, so we ate together. Stacy—very pale, with long blonde hair and sunken eyes—was a theater major, which surprised me. I thought actors were supposed to be boisterous, but she was quiet and reserved. Kim surprised me in other ways. She wasn't at all what she appeared to be when I first met her. She had parties in her room that spilled out into the hall and into mine, if Doreen wasn't around.

My afternoon classes were a bore. I had imagined college to be students sitting around conference tables and debating ideas. Professors pushing us, asking probing questions, forcing us to think critically. But it was just one lecture after another in echo-y halls. Sometimes he—all my teachers were male—wasn't even a professor, but a graduate student. No one even cared if you showed up or not. I soon figured out that if I was going to survive, I had to show up and do the work, even if no one was keeping track.

It was never boring at The Terrace. Someone was always there. Cal might be at the dining room table counseling a local boy about how to avoid the draft. Billie might show up and fire up the bong. Guys, some students, some not, plopped down on the couches, drank a beer, smoked a joint, then left. Girls, some students, some not, drifted in and out of the bedrooms. Were they friends, girlfriends, just an afternoon fuck? I didn't ask. I didn't care.

I could study in the midst of all this activity. While I read about Hammurabi's laws—eye for an eye, unless you killed a commoner and then all you had to do was pay a fine—Cal railed against the apathy of Americans. They had no idea what was really going on in Vietnam. The real enemy was American imperialism. They accepted, blindly, the greed and capitalism of our country. While I did math—variables, coefficients, tangents—Paul talked about his investigation into the university's Foundation funds. He was trying to find out where all the money came from. Who were the donors? If O'Connell's taking money from the war machine in the form of defense contracts and Dow Chemical donations, where did his true loyalties lie?

I let all this sink in and often I thought about Parker. In the weeks before he left for boot camp, I'd see him at the beach. He parked his car at the boardwalk and just sat there, no shirt on, his feet on the dash, a cigarette hanging between his lips. Holly and I tried to get him to come down to the surf, but he refused. His eyes were vacant. He wore fatigues and combat boots from the army surplus store, as if by changing into this uniform, he was changing into the person the Army would soon make him into. A gold cross hung down the middle of his chest, buried in the dark fuzz. His hair was tied with a bandanna. He looked as if he hadn't shaved in days. A banner of whiskers dirtied his chin.

Anytime we stopped to talk to him, he said, "I just want to remember this place, just like this." I had been too selfish, too wrapped up in cheerleading and suntanning—activities I now saw as foolish—to really pay attention.

One afternoon in mid-October, Billie and I were having hamburgers in the Union Grill. She was enlightening me on the virtues of Matt Ryder. She thought he was a perfect match for me. He was fun and funny. Way more sensitive than all the other guys at The Terrace, several of whom she had slept with.

She stuffed a trio of French fries in her mouth and said, "You were a cheerleader. Am I right?"

"So," I said, defensive.

"I was always jealous of girls like you. Skinny, cheery."

"But I was also a surfer." I thought this might make me cooler. Being a girl surfer had made me stand out back home. She wasn't impressed.

"What's your major?"

"Don't know yet. All I know is that when I graduate, I don't want a job where I have to make coffee for guys like Stuart Burgess," I said, remembering the condescension in his voice when he spoke to Billie.

"Oh, he can go blow it out his arse," she quipped.

I had never met anyone like her. So open, so ready to take charge. To bite the world. To growl and be loud. Billie took up space. Something I had tried *not* to do at home. She knew exactly what she wanted to be: a writer for the *New York Times*.

I liked her for all those reasons, but also because she was a friend I had made independent of one of our moves. I hadn't been forced to make friends with her because we lived on the same base or because we were both the new girls. Up until now, that was how it had been. And all too quickly my friends left or I left. A girl named Karen became a girl named Marty became Sharon became Theresa became Holly. Now there was Billie. We were friends because we liked each other.

"Well, Cheery, let me ask you another question?"

I had a feeling she was going to ask me something about Reid, like if he was dating anyone. I had no idea. I didn't keep track of his love life.

"Have you been with a guy?"

I didn't answer. Didn't know how to answer. I liked her candidness, but now her curious gaze was on me. My cheeks burned. I slouched in my seat.

Of all the hours of kissing Adam that summer, what I loved most was that it was pure. An emotional and physical connection that was an end—*the* end—in itself. It wasn't going any further. He never pushed me; I never pushed. There were moments when we stopped and looked at each other. *Should we?* We asked with our eyes. We shook our heads, both knowing this was only for the summer.

"It's not like I'm saving myself or like I'm against it, you know, morally. I just haven't met the right guy." I thought of Holly. I thought of Doreen. Both saving themselves, both so eager, like Billie, to talk about it. Only Billie was talking about the sex *she* was having.

"Your brother," she offered, "is good in bed. No, he's great in bed."

"Ugh. I don't want to hear this."

"Sorry, you're right. A sister shouldn't know anything about her brother as lover."

Lover. Geez. So sophisticated. I said it silently, under my breath. Lover. It was foreign but fun to say. It forced my tongue into a curling shape that rolled in my mouth pleasingly. I regularly used the word fuck. Everyone did. No curling of the tongue there. Just the front teeth on the bottom lip in a way that hurt if you said it in anger.

"I think Matt might be the right guy for you," Billie said. "But before you find out, get these." She pulled a plastic disk from her purse. The Pill. I had never actually seen this small round miracle that revolutionized women's control over our bodies. The packet was bright aqua—the color of a headband I had in fifth grade. Why did they make it so dazzling, so eye-catching? My face flushed again. This whole topic was awkward, although Billie didn't think so.

"And you may need some of these."

She rummaged in her mammoth purse. What all did she have in there? Apparently, among other things, a variety of birth control—she tossed two condoms onto the table.

Again, the bright colors, one blue, one red. Embarrassed, I grabbed and stuffed them in my purse.

"Don't trust anything alone. You miss a pill, condoms break, and, uh oh."

Matt, I felt, even without Billie telling me, was different. I tried to hide this from Billie, even from Matt—I didn't want to be just another girl in the house. I was like one of the guys, but being a girlfriend, a lover, as Billie put, was serious. A commitment. I still thought of my time here at school as carefree, no strings attached.

"Listen Cherry, when you're ready, go to health services. They'll fix you up with whatever you need."

So now I was Cheery and a Cherry.

It was Homecoming weekend. On Friday, classes were canceled for the parade. In my former life as cheerleader, I would have been on a float shaking my pom-poms. Now, I would be part of the Vietnam Veterans Against the War march. We were bringing up the rear, unsanctioned but undeterred. It wasn't enough to just carry a banner. It wasn't enough to chant and shout. We needed to bring our cause front and center.

This was where Stacy shined. I saw that she wasn't a theater major because of acting, but because of her directing skills. She didn't teach us recitation or stagecraft, but Guerrilla Theater. It was loud and frenzied, intended to prove a point. Over the course of the week we coalesced into a well-prepared troupe. Our staging ground was The Terrace. Our costumes were basic: fatigues from Cal's closet. Our script was minimal: *Make love, not war. Stop the killing.* Our program was mimeographed leaflets with a list of statistics: men killed in action; men wounded; civilian casualties; prisoners of war. The stark realities of war in numbers. Our props were few: toy M-16's, blood packets, banners, signs, firecrackers, cherry bombs, a plywood coffin draped with an American flag.

In *The Alligator* that morning, Paul published an editorial questioning the relevance of Homecoming. "Why do we continue with the frivolities of dances, skits, and banquets, when our country is at war?" That was our question, why did people—our parents, our professors, the administration—O'Connell himself—go about their lives and the business of the university—as if 55,000 men had not died in Vietnam? Was the war, as it dragged on, just background noise?

Today, parade day, we would bring it to the foreground. It was a cool afternoon, finally some relief from the humidity. The street was lined with families and students. The air was sugary and salty, like a Payday candy bar. Billie and I were audience plants, along with a half dozen others. We stationed ourselves at the corner of University Avenue and 13th Street, the crossroads of city commerce and academia. Four corners: a hotel, a gas station, Leonardo's Pizza, and the official *Welcome to the University of Florida* sign.

We were next to a family: father, mother and their three kids, two boys and girl, between four and ten years old. The parade was standard fare: sorority and fraternity floats, county high school bands, high-stepping majorettes. The kids clapped and danced to the bands. They scrambled to get candy the sorority girls threw into the crowd. I stepped out and picked up a piece. No shame in wanting a Mary Jane. The homecoming queen waved from her perch. I was reminded of Holly. She won homecoming queen in our senior year. Just last year. A world away.

Shriners on mini-bikes spun around.

"Oh, look, aren't they cute?" Billie said. "I bet those scooters are crushing their balls, though."

The mother turned and looked at us with disgust.

I was antsy, fingering the cherry bombs in my pockets. Soon they would become the smoke of firearms, symbols of warfare. I worried I might fumble it. If I did, if I couldn't light them or if my timing was off, I'd reveal myself to be the novice I was. Just the little sister, a hanger-on.

Several of the floats depicted the team mascots: wire mesh and papier-mâché figures of our fighting Gators and the Maryland Terrapins, the team we would play on Saturday. Alligators tromping on turtles. Turtles on their back, looking distraught.

"The only mascot stupider than an alligator is a turtle," Billie said.

"They're terrapins," I said. This was the kind of banal thing I knew that drove Billie insane, that made her think I was silly and cheery.

"Oh, the mighty, mighty terrapins. Sorry, I didn't realize."

Up ahead I saw Cal and Matt carrying the banner we had made. It read THE (IM)POSSIBLE DREAM? NO MORE WAR.

The question mark was essential. The night before we had debated this squiggly punctuation for hours. Matt wanted the I and M in Impossible to be in parentheses. This would offset the letters and imply a double meaning. Is it a dream that was possible or impossible?

"This isn't English 101," Billie had said.

"Maybe we should put it after No More War," Reid said. To him, a writer, punctuation was important.

Cal said, "You guys don't even see the point. This is all so beautifully academic and by beautifully I mean ugly. No one in the war cares about your question mark."

That shut us up. Cal pulled up his shirt and drew a question mark on his chest. He circled his belly button three times to make the point.

"You're crazy, man," Reid said.

When he put down his shirt, wet marker bled into the white cotton.

"We love you, Cal," Billie said. She got up and kissed his forehead. Mama Billie. She always knew how to make us feel loved.

Now, here was Cal and Matt holding that banner. Behind them was a line of marching veterans, a solemn column. At the rear, Reid and three others were the pallbearers of the coffin we had made. When they reached the intersection, they dropped the coffin and pulled the toy guns from their camo jackets.

"Look, Mommy, those guys have guns," said one of the little boys.

Reid and Paul pretended to fire into the crowd, making the *ratatatat* of real machine guns. That was my cue. I lit and rolled a cherry bomb into the street. Smoke caught in my throat. I lit another, and another. The mother beside me stepped back onto the sidewalk, pulling her daughter close to her. The girl screamed and covered her ears.

Her screams made me laugh. It was theater. These were just my friends. But then Paul stepped closer, a black bandanna tight across his mouth and nose. He was firing—his machine gun imitation loud through the cotton. The smoke and the sound, it felt, for a moment, even to me, real.

Billie tossed blood packets that splattered on the asphalt, the scene before us turning into a simulated battlefield. VVAW members fell to the ground, wounded, moaning, groaning, writhing. Fake blood hidden beneath their clothing blossomed forth. Cal fell to the ground, so did Paul.

I lobbed three more cherry bombs, then three more. I had the hang of it—the ease of flipping the lighter, twisting together the fuses before I lit them. They fizzed and popped, a series of high-pitched explosions that made my ears ring.

The father beside me took off his shirt and put it over his daughter's nose and mouth. The mother did the same things for her youngest son. She was now in her bra.

More vets, friends of Cal's, brandished rubber knives. They wove through the crowd, thrusting. Screams came not only from the kids, but also the adults.

Stacy walked around calmly handing out the leaflets. "What you've witnessed, ladies and gentlemen, is a dramatization of what's going on in Vietnam right now. If you lived there, this could be happening to you."

I raised my fist and chanted, "Unjust war. Unholy war. Unlawful war."

The father hustled away the kids. The mother came over to me.

"You should be ashamed," she said. Her breasts, large and straining against her bra, trembled as she spoke.

Anger hardened my spine. She was the kind of person we were trying to reach. She just didn't get it.

I got close to her face. Spit flying, I shouted, "You're a sheep. All of you are sheep. Following one after the other down the chute of war." I lobbed insults and accusations. She had blindly bought into the American Dream. She woke up, went to work, came home and drank her boredom until it was time to go to bed, and the next morning she continued her sheep ways.

The cherry bombs gave me power. It made others fear us. Fear me. I embodied the rage I had listened to all month from Cal, Matt, Reid, and Paul. I gave voice to my feelings, thinking of Parker in his car, taking in the beauty of the beach before going to war. My words, like the cherry bombs, had power. She needed to open her eyes to the reality of what was happening in Vietnam. No more sitting on your comfy couch.

No more following along with all the other sheep, who let the government send innocent boys to die.

Billie grabbed my arm and pulled. Other families, those nearby, watching, panicked and hurried away.

"That's right, run away. Cowards," Billie called after them.

The parade was over. Our shirts were bloody and our hair was smoke-filled. My eyes watered. But we laughed. We were exhilarated by the fake deaths.

"That was brilliant," Billie said. "You were brilliant. You gave that woman what for."

We were the first ones back at The Terrace. We flopped on the couches, giddy with triumph. I thought of the look on that mother's face when the first bombs went off. I was proud to have been the one to wipe that complacent smile off her face. She was one of them, the mindless Americans who worshipped at the feet of the Nixon war machine. She had to see the truth. She couldn't be shielded from it and neither could her children. I had popped my cherry and let go of my cheery self. I was no longer a protest virgin.

Chase Your Pleasure

Betty Friedan was coming to campus. The founder of the National Organization for Women and author of *The Feminist Mystique* was to be the keynote speaker at the Mortar Board banquet. Billie called her The High Priestess of Women's Liberation. She had been in negotiations for months to bring her in for this speech. She raised funds from car washes. She sent every member of Mortar Board out onto campus to shake donation cans. I had done that myself.

Our banquet was held opposite the Florida Blue Key banquet, which was considered the "real" event that night. The men had secured the gym, while we had a ballroom in the Union. Their keynote speaker was Senator Edmund Muskie. Billie thought this unfair—they had the larger space and a prestigious political leader—but she was confident Friedan would ignite sparks on campus.

The day before the event she came to my dorm, ping-ponging around the room, saying, "I'm so excited I can't stand still."

Doreen was at her desk writing her weekly letter to Dwight. I lay on my bed, feet on my headboard, just staring up at Jim Morrison, burned out from studying.

Billie snatched Rascal off Doreen's bed and snuggled with him. She noticed the picture of Dwight on the shelf.

"Who's this?" Billie picked up the frame and turned it toward me but asked Doreen.

"My fiancé," Doreen said. "His name's Dwight and if you don't mind, I'm in the middle of writing him a letter."

"Cute," Billie said.

I didn't know if she was talking about Dwight or the fact that Doreen was writing to him. Dwight was cute, in a clean-cut, slightly buck-toothed kind of way.

"And he's all mine." She took the picture and held it to her chest.

I was amused by their interaction. From the first time they met, in the dining hall, they clashed. Doreen was, in Billie's eyes, too goody-goody, too sorority. For her part, Doreen thought Billie was brassy. At moments like this I felt caught in the middle. I liked them both and didn't know who to be loyal to.

With the picture in one hand and her notebook in the other, Doreen said, "I think I'm going to finish this in the common room, where it's quieter." She snatched up Rascal on her way out.

"You could be a little nicer," I said.

Billie flopped on her bed. "She'll never make it. My prediction, she'll be home by Halloween. Definitely Thanksgiving."

It was just over a week until Halloween. I didn't see any signs that Doreen was cracking.

"But she made a death-bed promise to her father," I said.

"You're kidding. Oh God, how Southern Gothic of her."

"She's sweet. I couldn't ask for an easier roommate."

"Don't worry, soon you'll have the room all to yourself."

She picked up my copy of *The Feminist Mystique*, a hardback with a red tattered cover, tattered from so many handlings. Long passages were underlined and exclamation-pointed.

I had seen Friedan give interviews on television. She had even been a topic of conversation in our house. My father definitely had opinions about her. She was as much of a kook as the hippies and the Yippies.

"What, do you want men and women to share bathrooms?" My father's question dripped with sarcasm.

"That's not what it's about, Dad," I said. "It's about equality. Equal pay."

"Can you hump a hundred-and-ninety pound man on your back while under machine gun fire?"

"No, Dad, you know I can't do that. You're exaggerating."

"No, I'm not, you're not thinking this through."

"William, we get it, men are stronger than women," my mother said. "So what? Celeste is right. There are other ways to be equal. Equal education, equal pay."

I had never heard my mother speak about equality or feminism. And Dad—he had never cooked a meal, washed a dish, folded his own laundry. At least not since he married my mother. For Reid the chores were traditional, mow the lawn, take out the trash. I was the one who helped my mother around the house. I cooked. I cleaned.

Billie tossed down the book. "Does your roommate know you're a radical?"

"She knows I've read that book. She suggested we use it as a door stop."

The following night, I was running late for Friedan's lecture. The dress I planned to wear needed ironing and even though I knew what Billie would think of me taking the time to iron—she would say *The iron is a chain around a woman's ankle* or *I wield an iron like a sword for equality* or *Every man, woman, and child should learn to iron for themselves*—I wasn't going to show up wrinkled.

By the time I got to the ballroom, Friedan was at the podium.

"Ladies! All you bright and beautiful young ladies! Women, young women! When I say beautiful, I mean smart and capable. I'm honored to be here, but talk is a cheap substitute for action. Our issues are national issues, issues that concern both women and men. You need to get involved. Whatever the organization, we need you."

Friedan's voice held a smoker's rasp, but she held us all rapt.

"When you graduate, run for office. Become a voice for women. Become, if need be, a thorn in the side of every senator and congressman. Men will try to shut us up. Don't let them. Let your voice be heard. We need your voices."

Applause rocked the room. The floor shook under my feet.

She wore a voluminous peasant dress. Every time she waved her arms, the flowing sleeves danced. Her hands never stopped moving as she spoke. She chopped the air, she pounded on the podium. She spoke of transcending the roles society forced on us. There was no inherent reason why men worked and women stayed at home. Men and women could join together to take care of the home, to raise children, and to work. She spoke of men who were strong enough to be gentle. Men who are the other half of our struggle, the struggle for women's liberation.

Every word she said was a trip-wire that set off a flare of yes, yes, yes in my brain. Mini-explosions of connection: Yes, of course, you're so right, yes—that's exactly how I feel, what I think. It was as if she had read my thoughts and now expressed them out in the open. I had never heard anyone articulate these thoughts with such precision. I felt the same way, but when I tried to explain it, to my father or to the guys at The Terrace, I tripped over my words, clumsy and emotional. When Billie tried, she sounded shrill. The discussion devolved into defensive retorts instead of facts and empirical evidence.

Here was Friedan, a woman in power with the ability to state her vision clearly, with passion, and bring that vision to thousands of people.

"But remember, men are not the enemy," she said. "It's not men I'm against. We are our own worst enemy. We don't have the self-confidence. We silence our own voices. Be the good girl, society says. Be quiet and helpful. I say *no* to quiet. *No* to being just good girls."

When she finished, she opened the floor to questions. Billie, of course, was first at the microphone. "Right now, on the other side of campus, there's a banquet being held by the all-male honor society. It's like they've hung a no-girls-allowed sign on their clubhouse door. It's an honor society that, in my opinion, has no honor."

"Here's what I have to say to that," Friedan said. "Let's go over there and have a chat. Let's show them who we are." She stepped down off the stage and went to Billie. "Lead the way."

Friedan slipped an arm through Billie's and they pushed through the tables and were out the door. For most of us, this turn of events hadn't yet sunk in. Stacy, quick on her feet, took the mic and said, "Anyone who wants to have her voice heard at Blue Key should come with us. Those who wish to stay, by all means, stay. Have dinner."

Most of the room got up and followed. We filed down the hall, down the stairs. Outside, the group coalesced into rows of three and four women, arms linked. In the front was Billie, leading the charge, and next to her was Friedan, with Stacy on the other side. I raced to catch up and slipped my arm through Stacy's. We chanted "Women's liberation now" all the way across campus. Being a part of this march was different from being a part of the Homecoming parade. This fight was domestic, in more ways than one.

As we climbed the steps of the gym, two security guards stepped in front of the entrance, blocking our way. Our chant changed to "Let us in. Let us in." Billie stepped around them and tried to pull open the door. The guards nudged her back. During this distraction, Stacy wedged her foot in the door and shouldered her way in. We—there were about a hundred of us—took the left corridor down the length of the gym, snaking between the tables, and took over the dais.

Stuart Burgess, head of Blue Key, had the microphone.

"Ladies, ladies," he said, his tone a dismissive bleat.

We booed him.

He tried a different tack, an appeal for cooperation. Co-operation in the form of *Get out, leave us to our important matters*. He said all the right things—*We respect you* and *We believe in your right to speak*—but really he was just trying to shut us up and get us out.

Friedan interrupted him and said, "Gentleman, we're here not as voices of dissent, but as voices of collaboration. We want to join forces with you. We want you to join us in a fight that involves all women and all men. This fight is your fight. I know you, too, want women to be equal. To not be tied only to children. Only to the house—"

In mid-sentence, Burgess pulled out the cord on the microphone. In a resonant voice that didn't need amplification, he said, "Senator Muskie has been more than patient with you gals." As if patience was something men had so little of.

Billie, her voice deep and loud—Burgess was no match for her—said, "We won't hold up these gentlemen and their fine speaker. We've had our say. We've made our point."

She and Betty led us on a march around the room to the door. We filled the air with our call, "Women's liberation now." We didn't need a mic. Together our voices were as loud as thunder.

Once outside, we straggled back to the Union. Some went up to the ballroom to finish dinner, others to their dorms. In the lobby, Billie called a taxi to take Friedan back to the hotel. Before she left, Friedan embraced us, Billie, Stacy, and me. We soaked up every ounce of her citrusy perfume and her powerful words.

"You're going to take over the world, girls," she said. "I'm counting on you."

We waved goodbye, true groupies who could never get enough. Billie sat down on the sidewalk, as if she were exhausted, and said, "My life is complete."

"Best fun I've had all week," I said.

That night I fell into bed with a congratulatory sigh, the smell of Friedan's perfume still in my hair.

Halloween was upon us. Campus was alive with creatures of the dead: mummies and vampires, skeletons and devils. Parties everywhere, the biggest one at The Terrace. Come one, come all. All who dared.

I got dressed in my room. I was a gunslinger, with chaps, cowboy hat and a toy six-shooter. Doreen helped me slick back my hair. She drew on a Snidely Whiplash moustache with an eyebrow pencil.

The dorm floor buzzed, everyone preparing for a party somewhere on campus. Girls ran up and down the hallway, from room to bathroom, in various stages of undress and dress-up: a ruffle-skirted gypsy with no blouse, a clown without her curly red wig and floppy shoes. Candy bars were tossed from hand to hand. *I hate Snickers, give me an Almond Joy. Licorice for me.* Doreen, dressed as a princess, tiara and pink gown, was going to a party at a fraternity house.

I met up with Billie at our usual spot, the gates of Hull pool, halfway between Mallory and Broward Halls. As a barmaid, like Miss Kitty from *Gunsmoke* but with a sharper wit, she wore a gunny sack dress and black fishnet stockings. Wrapped around her neck was a white feather boa. Her lipstick was bright red and she had glued on false eyelashes.

"And just who are you going to bat those big beautiful eyes at?" I asked.

"I have always relied on the kindness of strangers," she said.

"That line coming from those lips in that get-up, it just doesn't work."

"Blanche DuBois ain't got nothin' on Miss Kitty," she said.

The same energy in the dorm—excitement, anticipation—whipped up the air all over campus. Witches, pirates, and Frankensteins streaked passed us, cackling, calling to friends. It was just after nine, the moon high and the air cool. A slight breeze rattled the leaves as we walked through the Plaza. Spanish moss swayed from the branches, pallid flying ghosts. Just the right amount of spooky.

"I never want to graduate," Billie said. We were near the Murphree statue. Albert Murphree was college president during the 20s and 30s. He started the newspaper where Paul was now editor and the *F Book* I had burned on my first day. He established ROTC, which we were now trying to get off campus, and fraternities, which Billie called dens of sexism. In bronze, he was seated, hands raised as if in oration. These days, students climbed up there and placed beer cans in his open palms.

Billie jumped on the plinth and began a personal plea to the university. "Fair UF, home of the gator, of Albert E. Gator to be exact, keep me in your bosom always. Do not force me out into the cruel world of jobs and mortgages and responsible adulthood. You are my home and I shan't forsake you."

She waved the ends her boa like a maestro's baton, revealing her deep cleavage. Feathers fluttered around her face.

This was the first time I had seen Billie show a hint of vulnerability. Maybe this was the only way she could risk exposure, in a public demonstration.

"You can't write for the *New York Times* from here," I said, taking her hand and helping her down.

"I know, I know. But my mother doesn't care about the *New York Times*. She cares about marriage and babies. *Make me a grandmother*, that's all she says to me."

I didn't know Billie got the same pressure from her family. My mother didn't come right out and say she couldn't wait to become a grandmother, but the expectation—or implied belief—was that I'd marry, settle close to home, and have children.

"I could blow all my classes," she mused. "Or I could fake a nervous breakdown and live in the infirmary for an extra semester."

"That's crazy." I thought of all those boys who faked mental illness or cut off digits to stay out of the war.

We crossed University Avenue, car horns and the sound of catcalls greeting us. Blocks from The Terrace, we heard Jimi Hendrix and his singing guitar.

"We must be in the right place," I said.

The house glowed orange with jack-o-lanterns. Two stereo speakers were propped against the living room screens. The door was wide open. Students streamed in and out, dancing on the front yard and in the street. There were clowns, mobsters, ghosts, other cowboys. I hitched up my jeans, tightened my bolo and dove in. Instantly I lost Billie.

I danced under the oaks in a swarm of bodies. Someone knocked my hat off and I bent to recover it. A pirate pinched my ass.

"Hands off, Captain Hook," I shouted.

He grinned and I recognized him from my biology class. We danced until Jimi turned to Mick and Mick turned to Neil.

I needed a drink. I shoulder-slammed my way into the house. It smelled of candle wax and pizza. Dozens of Leonardo's boxes were stacked on the coffee table. The booze was set up on the dining room table. Billie was there, performing barmaid duties.

She put on her vamp and said, "What can I get you, pardner?"

"Whiskey for me, ma'am," I said.

She fixed me a screwdriver. "Drink up. No whiskey in this place."

"What kinda saloon you runnin', ma'am?" I scratched my crotch, faked a tobacco spit.

"Cut the ma'am shit," she said. "You're really getting into this. Maybe you were born in the wrong skin."

I took a sip and said, "Tastes like swill."

"Okay, Jesse James. Cool it." A stray boa feather was stuck to her cheek.

Matt came out of the kitchen carrying two buckets full of his famous cranberry lemonade punch. Only Matt knew the proportion of juice to rum. Sweet and tangy and refreshing, the first glass went down quickly. I didn't even taste the alcohol. Billie poured me another.

"Slow down," Matt said. He was yet another pirate, with an eye patch and a feather in a three-cornered hat. The hat was more Minuteman than Blackbeard.

"I'm thirsty," I said, kissing him.

"You're going to get sucker punched in a minute," Billie said.

"What do you mean, you're going to hit me?" I plucked off the feather and blew it into the air.

"No, but the rum will," she said.

Stacy showed up as Little Orphan Annie, her curly red wig blinding us.

I spotted Reid across the room. He was watching me, laughing. I sauntered over, tipped my hat. "Evening, sir."

"You've got to be kidding," he said.

"Billie thinks I was born the wrong gender."

An inmate, Reid wore a black-and-white striped outfit. He had a plastic ball-and-chain around each ankle.

"Those are so you don't have to dance, right?"

"You know me too well."

Dancing embarrassed him.

Cal walked by, an American flag pinned around his naked body, an off-the-shoulder mini-dress. It didn't quite cover his ass. His left cheek was the moon under a ragtag of stars. I gave him a quick pinch.

"Nice ass," I said.

"I've been waiting for that all night," he said. "Here's your treat." He dropped a handful of candy corn into my palm. Nestled among the orange cones was a Quaalude.

I swallowed it with cranberry punch.

Someone behind me stuck his tongue in my ear. "Oink, oink," he whispered. I turned to find Paul, dressed as a pig: fuzzy, pink, footed pajamas and a pink rubber nose, topped with a police officer's cap. He leaned in for another ear swab and I ducked into the kitchen.

I caught Matt's eye, the one not hidden by the patch. He winked. I motioned toward his bedroom. He nodded back. We danced down the hall and closed the door.

Whether it was the alcohol or the drugs or the ambience—didn't know and didn't care—I felt bold and emboldened, acutely aware of my body's desire for mouth on skin, skin in mouth. I tossed my hat into the corner. I flipped one boot off and pushed him onto the bed. He surrendered. His pirate costume had elastic pants. I stretched the waistband, pulled it down around his thighs. Stripping off my jeans, I straddled him and pushed him inside me. He smelled of sweat, a human musk I liked.

I moved on instinct, without feeling awkward or unskilled. I felt powerful. A power different from the one I felt at the parade and the women's march. All logic, all intention, all expectation—obliterated. This was rule *of*, *for*, and *by* the body.

I let Matt build, I let him writhe and moan. I got wetter and his hands got wilder, over and under me, what felt like through my body. I pulsed. We were now completely out of our clothes, skin to skin finally. No distance between our pores. His sheets were sandy, smelled of the ocean, and that sand rubbed my shins, and, when he flipped me over, my ass. I laughed. I said, "I feel like I'm riding a wave." Matt curled me into him. He *was* a wave and I was at the very center, the hollow between crest and trough. A calm, a pause, and a second crest, then a third. Waves collapsed and consumed me.

After Halloween, the push was on for the end of the trimester. When I wasn't in class, I spent all my time in bed with Matt. I had begun to see sex everywhere. Not sex really, but sensuality. Flowers smelled stronger. The sky was a piercing blue and, where it met a corner of a building, the brick—rich ochre—zinged into relief. Strong breezes made my skin ripple. Was this awareness, this brightness of colors and vividness of scents, love or lust?

I looked at other students in my classes and wondered, has he done it? Has she? Does her body writhe like mine? When people walked by me, holding hands, arms around each other, I wondered, how does he touch her? I thought I could tell if a couple was having sex by the ease they had with each other. He wouldn't touch her ass that way if they didn't know each other's bodies so well.

I wasn't the only girl in and out of The Terrace, in and out of beds. Stacy was one. For a time, she and Cal had a *thing*, very casual. Occasionally I saw Billie in Reid's room. Their affectionate was easy, friendly. They never kissed in front of us, but they'd hold hands on the couch. She'd put her head in his lap, he'd run his fingers through her hair.

The first morning I appeared from Matt's room and went into the kitchen for a glass of water, Reid was there. He raised his eyebrows.

"Don't look at me like that," I said. "I'm not doing anything you're not."

"True," he said.

"I was put on this earth to keep you honest," I said.

"Are you, you know, using protection?"

"Are you?"

He tousled my hair.

I was. I had taken Billie's advice and gone to the health clinic. The Pill regulated my period and I no longer had cramps. To me, that circular packet was on par with Mary's virgin conception, both miracles, both a taming of the body.

One thing I never let slip was my studies. If had a paper to write, I stayed at my desk in front of my typewriter. If I had chapters to finish, I read in the living room or I went to the library. The last thing I wanted was to fail. To stay here, I had to keep up my grades.

Billie didn't care much about her classes. She was coasting toward the end. Instead, she wanted to do what Betty Friedan had encouraged. She had started a women's consciousness-raising group. I often thought of her soliloquy at the Murphree statue. Even though I still had years before I graduated, I knew how she felt. This was the place of no *shoulds*, no *have-tos*. After only a few months, I had found my voice and a purpose that made school not just about grades and performing for professors.

My work with the Student Mobilization Committee and the Environmental Action Group—we picked up trash, we planted seedlings—was important. There was personal pride in simple activities. We pushed against authority. We didn't want money and status or comfort and security, the ideals of our parents' generation. Our brand of power was sovereignty over ourselves. We didn't want to be told by our government how to dress, talk, love, or fight. It felt good to speak up, to speak out. Betty Friedan was relying on me and that alone made me feel all-powerful.

The month slipped by and Thanksgiving was days away. Reid and I were headed home for the long weekend. Matt was staying put. He never went home. He and his family didn't see eye-to-eye about the war. Why spend all that money to go home and argue?

Cal and Paul were also staying in town. They and several VVAW and SMC members were fasting on Thanksgiving. This was part of a nationwide boycott to support the thousands of soldiers in Vietnam who had pledged to give up the few hot meals they received. I promised to fast with them, from afar. Reid wouldn't promise anything, he loved Thanksgiving, the one meal my mother went all out to prepare.

Billie was flying home for the long weekend. I had never been on an airplane and was impressed by the way she navigated the whole travel thing—driving to the airport to purchase the ticket and then dressing up to go on the plane the day she was leaving. Doreen left a day early. She *couldn't wait* to see Dwight. It had been nearly three whole months since she had held his *cutie putie li'l face*.

Matt kissed me goodbye and stood in the front yard waving as Reid and I pulled away. We blasted the radio. We smoked. Reid slid on his shades, rolled down the window, and hung his elbow out the window. I put my feet up on the dash—dirty and cracked from running around barefoot on campus.

The scenery slipped by, the horse farms of Ocala, the citrus groves of Orange County. When we reached the wetlands of the St. Johns River basin, which we crossed on a low-lying causeway, miles of sawgrass cradled the zigzagging river, the horizon broken only by clusters of palms. It was a landscape I had loved the minute we moved here. It reminded me of California. The flowers, the palms trees. The ocean breeze. Gardenias, bougainvillea.

I realized we had lived in Florida for five and half years, long past the time we usually moved to another state. I had time to both fall in love with the landscape and take it for granted. That had never happened before.

"You know what I just thought? We've been here longer than any other place."

Reid laughed and said, "Yeah, and I can't wait to get out."

"Only a few more months, my brother," I said. He would graduate in May. He never talked about what he would do next. I assumed, like Billie, he'd return home, get a job, eventually move out on his own.

I felt something I could only call *at home*. Never had I experienced this. The PCS had never appeared. I didn't know why. Maybe my father hadn't been offered a new assignment or maybe he hadn't put in for a transfer. Either way, I had stopped being a short-timer.

As we got closer to home, Reid said, "Don't mention anything about what we do. I don't. It's easier this way."

"Okay, got it."

"You know what Mom is going to say when she sees you? She's going to freak. She's going to think I corrupted you."

"What?" I feigned innocence, but I knew.

My hair, long and stringy, was only part of it. I hadn't shaved my legs or my underarms since I arrived at school. I wore a skirt made from a pair of cutoff corduroys and calico patches. My face was broken out. I used up all my mother's soap and never replaced it. I didn't care. Girls primping for boys, girls primping for other girls to compete for boys—I was done with all that. I cared about how we made a difference with our voices, not our looks. I cared about stopping the war and saving the planet.

My mother hugged me and took the ends of my hair in her hands.

"You—your hair—it's so… long."

My father eyed me guardedly. I looked nothing like the girl they dropped off at school and I didn't try to pretend otherwise.

I refused to eat on Thanksgiving. I sat at the table but only drank water. Reid—the one who promised nothing—wolfed down turkey and dressing. My parents exchanged a look when I explained my one-day fast. I expected the arguing to begin any minute. When it didn't, I baited my father with talk of the Homecoming Parade—the fake blood, the cherry bombs, the Guerilla Theater. I baited my mother with talk of Betty Friedan's speech. Neither said a word. Mom pursed her lips around her fork. Dad chewed. A lot.

I was now the one picking fights. Reid was silent. I nudged him under the table. *Help me out,* I said with my eyes. He acted like he had no idea what I meant.

The food smelled so good. I helped my mother put away the leftovers. I wanted to swipe a finger through the mashed potatoes and pop them in my mouth. I wanted a big bite of pumpkin pie.

I took a long, hot bath that night, something I missed. When I stood up, I was dizzy, but satisfied by my commitment.

I woke up early, starving, and broke my fast with leftovers. Gravy over dressing mashed together with potatoes and turkey and cranberry sauce. Yum! After I ate, I went to see Holly. I could tell that my appearance startled her as well. She was the same old Holly. Blonde and petite, in peddle-pushers, unlike me—I was plump, pimply, and shaggy.

"You look, well, I don't know, different," she said.

"It's just my hair. It's longer," I said, parroting my mother. "And your jeans."

I looked down at the holes in the knees, at the flowers Matt had drawn with pink and blue markers on the thighs.

"I can't wait for you to see what I'm planning," she said.

I knew from her letters that she was engaged to a business major. That hadn't taken long. They were getting married in June. They would live on campus in married housing—whatever that was. It sounded like she'd be married to an apartment complex. They had it all figured out, even what they would do after they graduated. He would be a business executive and she would be an elementary school teacher.

Whenever Matt and I talked about the future, our plans didn't include careers. He was a sociology major, but didn't want to be a teacher or a researcher. His fantasy was to buy a piece of land in the middle-of-nowhere New England and make furniture. Woodworking had been his hobby all through high school. He thought he was good enough to make money at it. In my imagined future, I too saw us in a house in the woods, although I wasn't so sure about the snow. The house would be on a plot of land where we could grow our own vegetables, raise chickens for eggs and goats for milk. We would be self-sufficient. The chapters on botany had always been my favorites in our science texts, and I thrived in my work with the Environmental Action Group. I never thought about marriage. Matt and I just *were*. It was fun to think of us, years from now, snug and happy in our own corner of the universe.

Holly had covered one wall of her bedroom with pictures of brides ripped from magazines; beautiful, smiling women in white and ivory and apricot. There was a time when I would have *oohed* and *aahed* over the pictures.

She filled me in on how she and Charles had met (at a sorority/fraternity mixer) and how he proposed (in the bleachers after the Homecoming game). I couldn't believe his name was Charles. She had found her Prince Charles. Was she sleeping with him? In the past this was something we would have talked about. I remembered our long-ago pact to tell each other when we lost our virginity. I certainly hadn't written to tell her about Matt. I wasn't going to put news like that on paper. I thought I might tell her now, but she wasn't confiding in me. All she talked about were flower arrangements and invitation designs. Then she showed me the three dresses she liked best and went over the pros and cons of each. This one had a lace bodice but no train. That one had a full skirt with a train but long sleeves—too hot for a June wedding.

I couldn't take it anymore. I said, "All this sounds very nice, Holly, but do you know what's going on out there?"

"I do, Celeste. I'm not stupid. But I'm getting married. You should be happy for me."

"This is kind of shallow. Guys are coming home in body bags. They're coming home maimed." I snatched a picture off the wall—a woman in an ivory beaded gown holding a bouquet of red roses—and waved it in her face. "Is this really all you can think about right now?"

She took the picture from me and taped it back up. "Wow, you've changed."

"And you haven't," I said. I heard meanness in my voice, but believed my tone was justified. Her concerns were small and petty; mine were universal, imperative.

When I got back home that afternoon, my bedroom, once a place of refuge, now felt small and confined. It didn't fit me at all. The house didn't even fit. It was too conventional, too middle-class. Just like my parents, with their uptight banter.

I took a stack of Dad's *Time* magazines to my room. Instead of wedding pictures, I ripped out pictures of the happenings around the world, good and bad, but mostly bad. I papered my walls with images of genocide in Bangladesh, the uprising at Attica, riots over inner city busing. The economy was tanking. Nixon was fighting with Congress over his Supreme Court nominees. *Jesus Christ Superstar* was on Broadway. Lieutenant Calley was on trial. Edmund Muskie was on the cover of the September 13 issue. He was being touted as the frontrunner for 1972. A surge of pride ran through me, remembering the day we stormed the Blue Key banquet. He had, as we wove our way through the gym, been speechless.

My mother came into my room with a sandwich. "What have you been doing all afternoon in here?"

"Just a little redecorating," I said.

"My God, Celeste. This is outrageous."

"It's my room," I said.

"Do you pay the mortgage? Do you pay the bills?" She put down the sandwich and looked around. "What's gotten into you?"

"It's the new me," I said.

I loved this feeling: bluster, bravado. Something Reid was so good at. I now knew why he had argued so often with our father about the war.

Along with tears, I saw disappointment in her eyes. Never again would I be her good-girl confidante. Never again would I be my father's rule-following, yes-sir, no-sir daughter. Both she and Holly were right, I had changed.

Matt welcomed me back with a big kiss, then he picked me up and carried me to his bedroom. Kissing Matt was urgent and harsh. Not like last summer with Adam. We had been slow-build, a low tide of ebb and flow. Matt and I were shore crash—all teeth-y and tongue-y. That afternoon, I held the tip of his penis inside me, teasing him. I let him slide in just a little, then out, in a bit more, then out. More, out. More and more, deeper, until he was all the way in and thrusting deep.

Even though Matt begged me to spend the night with him—*I haven't seen you in four days*—I didn't. I had homework to do before the start of Monday classes. Besides, I had vowed over the holiday to spend less time with him. I loved him, but I didn't want to be consumed by him. After all that talk of marriage from Holly, I felt I had to claim space for myself. I didn't want to fall into the trap of putting all my time and energy into a boy. If I wanted the kind of relationship Friedan spoke about, men and women as equals, both working, both taking care of a home—and I did want that—then I had to protect my independence.

Back at my dorm, which I now thought of as home, as my true residence, I opened the door to find Doreen unpacking. She told me how hard it was to return. In the parking lot, Dwight was balling his eyes out and her mother was begging her to get back in the car.

"I nearly had to pry myself loose from their clutches," she said.

While she had a flare for exaggeration, this scene was clear and poignant in my mind. I heard the wails of her mother and boyfriend whipping through the magnolia trees that surround our dorm. I saw Doreen backing away from them as they clawed the air. I took her for comfort food at the dining hall. We had meatloaf, macaroni and cheese, buttered rolls, and vanilla cake with pink frosting for dessert. It all tasted delicious.

We had three weeks left in the quarter. I had exams to study for, papers to finish. I mapped out a daily plan: Tuesday, write three pages of essay; Thursday, read pages 145-225 of history text. I only went to The Terrace if I had accomplished my goal. Once there, I found a mellow atmosphere. Everyone was enmeshed in schoolwork, faces in books, fingers flying across typewriters.

One afternoon after I finished twelve math problems and wanted to clear my head of numbers, I picked up *The Feminine Mystique*. As I read, I heard Friedan's voice. *What kind of woman do you want to be?* She had asked this question at the Mortar Board banquet. I had no idea. My examples were limited and limiting. I didn't know my grandmothers. In fact, I didn't know either set of grandparents. My parents had eloped. They were from small-town Ohio. His family was Catholic and hers Protestant. Neither family approved of the relationship. They returned home shortly after Reid was born, hoping a grandson would bring joy and acceptance. What they found was more religious conflict. Would Reid be raised Catholic? That was the question my father's parents asked. If not, they weren't welcome. My mother's parents wanted the opposite: a christening in their church by the same minister who had performed this rite for every member of her family. They left and never, not once in their cross-country travels, returned to Ohio.

My mother had, in marrying, given up her family. During her life, it seemed to me, she had been various women at various times, depending upon our location. When we lived in California, she dressed in waist-hugging dresses, sprayed her teased hair with a cloud of Final Net, and perfumed her wrists with White Shoulders. Other mothers on base came over for mornings of coffee and pastry. While they sat at the kitchen table, talking and smoking, we kids played outside, coming in only for food or a Band-Aid for a skinned knee. By afternoon, the mothers had replaced the coffee in their mugs with wine. When it was time to leave, they returned to their quarters to prepare dinner. For so long, when I was six, seven, eight, I thought I'd grow up to be exactly like those women. That, to me, *was* being a woman.

In Cheyenne, no mothers gathered to smoke and gossip. In fact, my mother made only casual friends with the women on base. She smoked by herself, often outside in the dark. Her coffee mug was filled with wine too early in the day. I could smell it, on the rim, on her lips when I kissed her: pungent, oaky. She no longer wore dresses or shellacked her hair. The Equality State, the first state to give women the right to vote, brought depression to my mother. She was afraid of rattlers and mountain lions. She hated the desert and the snow. She didn't want me to leave her at home alone. This example of a woman, unfulfilled and frightened, drinking too much, clinging to her daughter, was not the woman I wanted to be.

In Florida, she changed again. Free from the military base, she got a job. She developed friendships with women other than officers' wives. Had she read Friedan? The thought that my mother was one of the discontented suburban housewives had never crossed my mind. Maybe all along it had been disenchantment with her role.

Holly strove to be a traditional housewife, which made no sense to me. Billie, strong and independent, pushed against the life of her mother. From a large, close family, Billie was part of a very female-centered circle of relatives. Grandmothers, great aunts, aunts, sisters. She told me about the raucous conversations they had, mostly in the kitchen, their domain, and mostly about the men in the living room watching sports. She wanted to get away from this life, which was one of the reasons she came to a school so far away.

Billie was a leader and I admired that. She had no trouble speaking her mind. She wasn't shy about her assessments of others and of institutions. Our upbringings were so different. I was raised to be a prim and proper girl. She was a New Yorker, from a big Italian family who, according to her, fought about everything. She was worldly. She was smarter than I was. Nothing I had done impressed her. Nothing she talked about paralleled anything I had experienced. I hoped some of her outspokenness would rub off on me.

From his place on the wall, Jim Morrison stared down at me. He had all these songs about women. In "Twentieth Century Fox" the woman is so cool, collected, fashionable, cool to the point of being unemotional. A woman who glides into a room and all heads turn to watch her. I would never be that woman. The woman in "Woman is Devil" was not to be trusted. She'd take your money, take you on a ride. I would never be that woman, either, and that was fine by me.

Were we destined to recreate the life of our parents? Was I, as a woman, destined to be my mother? Could we just take pieces of those lives and make them our own? The only thing I knew right then was that I didn't want to become a profile in Friedan's book. I didn't want to be a woman bangle-braceleted to her stove and washing machine. A woman who focused all her attention on her children or let her husband dictate her decisions. I didn't want to become my mother.

All these personal choices we made—"we" meaning women—were, I saw now, political.

After I turned in my paper and took my final exam, I was ready for the final party before we all separated for winter break. My birthday—December 8th, the day I shared with Jim Morrison. He would have been turning twenty-eight. I was, finally, *of age*. I could drink and vote. When I arrived at The Terrace, Matt put a Burger King crown on my head and steered me into the kitchen. There, to hug me and wish me a happy birthday, was everyone—Reid, Billie, Cal, Paul, Stacy. There, lined up on the counter, were eighteen hashish bricks under jelly jars. One for every year I had been on this earth.

"Oh, birthday girl, you are loved. You are loved eighteen times over," Billie said, and flashed me a smile.

We lined up, me first. Cal lit a brick. Once the jar filled with smoke, I inched the lip off the edge of the counter, bent down and sucked it all into my lungs. We moved down the line, brick after brick.

Creedence Clearwater Revival was singing about a bad moon rising. But I was in too good a mood for a downbeat. I changed the lyrics in my mind. I saw good times on the horizon, days of sunshine and calm water. I heard voices of harmony, in harmony.

We danced. My skin throbbed. The snare drum was tiny buzzes of light in every follicle. Cymbals clashed and suddenly stars fell from the ceiling and pinpricked my scalp. The music changed and became a river and I swam in *Proud Mary*. It changed again. The Kinks sang about Lola and Janis sang about Bobby McGee. I felt in over my head in deep blue water that soon evaporated into air that was blue and blurry.

The furniture dissolved and the walls wavered. The walls, a vertical wave that roiled, built steam, ready to slam me to the floor. I froze. "Duck!" I shouted. "Swim!" If we hurried maybe we could get away.

Matt came over to me, "Hey, what's up? Where're you at, little girl?"

He put his arms around me and we swayed. Now we were on the ocean. In a raft, gently rocking. I felt safe. I remembered feeling like this the first time we slept together, as if we were on a body of water and yet we were bodies of water. All I had to do was let Matt hold me, rib to rib. I felt his hardness against my liquid thigh. Billie's fizzy hair bobbed around us. Cal and Stacy were there, barely moving, their foreheads together. On the couch, eyes closed, Reid was tripping in his own world.

I looked at the wall and it was no longer a tidal wave. We were on dry land. A hot island, steam coming off the walls. A spray of ocean, but warm. An ocean heated by electric eels and sting rays. I stripped off my sweater and in only a tank top I broke away from Matt and danced by myself. Flesh against air. Flesh dimpled by air, sizzling, making my pores once again come alive. I was a body that held both water and electricity. The music changed and Jim sang *touch me, touch me, promise me*.

I twirled around the room and the room twirled me. My arms, an undulating wave. Lovely, fleshy, muscular, tanned. In this hashy hazy watery world, I wasn't daughter or sister. I wasn't student or scholar. I wasn't friend, foe, good, bad. I wasn't woman, man, or child. The world at this moment could not be broken down into us or them. I was body; pulsing torso and gyrating ass. I was pleasure.

Centripetal Force

Reid stayed. Two weeks became three, three edged toward a month. His wood shavings carpeted the floor. Penny sniffed at them. Each time they tricked her, looking like fresh yummy morsels. Late into the night he remained at the table, sculpting, refining the menagerie. One of them looked like it would be a lion. But where was the tail? Another was definitely a cardinal, a serrated crest taking shape on its head.

Sometimes I sat with him and he told me funny stories about the Garden House residents. Mrs. Petrusky had tied a placemat on her head with the cord of her robe, like an Easter bonnet. While he was reading the poetry of Donald Hall, Mrs. Marsh thought they were playing bingo. She kept saying, "Was that N26 or O26?"

Evan immersed himself in Reid's books. They lay around on tables and the floor, turned upside down, tented. He picked them up at random, reading a poem from *Buried Portraits*, a poem from *Silver Alley*. When he discovered a phrase he liked, he read it out loud. *Scepter of shoulder. Knuckle-hole heart. Corrugated breath of moonshine.* I hadn't heard Reid's poetry since his last bookstore reading. I admit it was hypnotic, and my son speaking those words made it more special.

Since the party at Garden House, since I had come face-to-pixel with my childish scorn, I tried to temper my heart—melt the ice and cool the lava. I stopped pushing and picking at Reid. Just let it be. Let him be. We were all here together. For how long? Who knew? There was peace in surrender. I wasn't the only one to let down my guard. Penny was now a dog in love. Reid got down on the floor and wrestled with her until she was spent and then he gave her a long belly rub. He had found her weakness.

One evening, the weekend before the Fourth of July, Zink appeared the house. Sans Mustang. He zigzagged up the driveway on his skateboard. When he got to the end, where the flower beds began, the flowers that he recently crushed, he did a half turn, flipped up the board, and caught it behind his back. Impish, playful, he was Puck in the one and only Shakespeare production I had ever seen.

He saw me at the window. We had finished dinner. Reid served pork tenderloin marinated in olive oil, soy sauce, vinegar, mustard seed, and garlic. The sweet-and-sour tang still saturated the kitchen. I was washing dishes. Instead of shying away, the way most teenagers would, Zink came to the screen and said, "What's for dinner?"

"You're late. We've eaten. It was pork," I said.

"Thought I smelled roasting pig. May I come in?"

"Door's open."

Evan and Reid were in the living room, playing Scrabble. Not my game. Not Evan's either. The last time we played he was twelve and I blew him away with words he didn't even know. The box hadn't been opened since. This was Reid's idea, and if it was Reid's idea, Evan was in.

Zink had a clipboard in his hand. He set it on the counter and opened the fridge.

"We have leftovers. I can fix you a plate," I offered.

"I'll help myself, if you don't mind. That's how it is at my house. We fend for ourselves."

I handed him a clean plate.

"Lest you think I only came to siphon off the sweet meat of the porcine, I'm here on official business." He held up a clipboard. "Did Elba tell you about the skateboard park?"

"Who's Elba?"

"That's what we call Evan. You know, his initials, with an a at the end. To make it sound cool. You know, the island of Napoleon's exile. He lives so far out here, away from civilization. It's like he's stranded on an island."

"That's clever," I said.

I knew about the petition but hadn't read it. The boys planned to present it at the next city council meeting. It was official looking, neatly typed, beginning: "We, the undersigned, call on the city council to approve the construction of a well-designed and family-friendly skatepark facility to be utilized by all ages and all abilities."

Laughter came from living room. Zink cocked his head. "Who's here?"

"That's Evan and his uncle," I said.

"Uncle?"

"Yes, my brother. He's visiting."

"From where?"

"Colorado."

Then he said, "Oh, the prodigal brother."

Why was everyone getting biblical all the sudden?

"Let's join them," I said.

Penny rose to greet Zink. Her tail, a vigorous duster, wiped the board clean of tiles.

"Shit," Evan said. "Damn dog."

"Hey, watch your mouth," Reid said.

"Start over and I'll play," Zink said.

He stuck out his hand and introduced himself. They set up for a game. I sat on the floor with them, not playing but stroking Penny's belly, keeping her calm.

Zink started with the word *checkered* in the center. Reid followed with *concrete*. Evan put down *peak* quickly. On this turn, Zink took a long time—they had to use the egg timer—before putting down *examination*, the x getting a triple letter score. He was working the angles, trying to get the most out of every letter. No surprise, he was a shrewd player.

I decided this was a good time to find out more about Evan's new friend, pump him for information as he played the game. Reid beat me to it.

"Tell us about yourself, Mr. Zink." He was channeling our father, the way he used to question the boys who sat at our table, not just my boyfriends, but even friends Reid brought home, especially if they were civilian.

"What's to tell? Born and raised right here in Jim Morrison's old stomping ground."

Ah, a boy after my own musical tastes.

Reid gave me a meaningful look: who is this kid and how does he know about Jim Morrison?

"You must be a senior," I said.

"Labels, not for me."

"Is school for you?"

"I show up." He shuffled his tiles around in his holder. We were making him nervous.

"Zink's really smart," Evan said. "Last year he aced the SAT, highest score in the school. He's kind of a legend. Not the kind with plaques and trophies in the sports case, but the kind that—" He was at a loss on how to frame this, how to let me know that Zink was famous for his unorthodox behavior without revealing too much, lest I ban him from the house.

Zink took new tiles and shook them in his fist. The letters Z I N K were tattooed on his knuckles. Why hadn't I noticed this before? It looked like a homemade tattoo, ink and a straight pin. Infection city.

"Where did you get that nickname?"

"It's not some drug code, if that's what you think."

He was on top of his game tonight. Although, every time I had seen him, this being only the third, he was smooth, effortless with banter and comebacks.

"It's stupid. It's from when I was a kid and my mother rubbed that creamy white gunk on my nose."

"You mean zinc oxide?"

"Yeah. My brothers started call me zinc and it stuck. I changed the c to a k because it looks cooler."

Nothing renegade about that. Evan looked disappointed—crumpled brow and stunned frown. He couldn't believe that Zink wasn't as cool as he thought. Or maybe he couldn't believe Zink would talk so openly with us about his life. That he would talk, of all people, to me.

I looked at the clock. It was nearly midnight, which I translated, out of habit, to 23:45. Too late for Zink to skateboard home, even though I didn't know where he lived. I suggested he bunk here for the night.

"I'd hate to be an inconvenience," said the boy who had just shown up, helped himself to dinner, and beat Evan and Reid at Scrabble.

I threw a pillow at him and said, "Just stay. I'm sure your parents will understand. They seem so reasonable."

I took Penny out one final time before bed. Reid joined me.

"I don't trust him," he said.

"What's not to trust? Everything he says has a vague and slightly mysterious quality to it. He doesn't go to school. He seems to have no home."

The moon was high and bright.

"Perfect friend for your kid."

"Generationally speaking, he's really not much different from our friends."

"Haven't you heard, different times, different set of problems. It's a whole new world out there. The dangers are greater. Marijuana is laced with ecstasy. Coke is cut with levamisole."

I had no idea what levamisole was.

"Sounds like you speak from experience."

"I'm saying he's hanging out here because he wants something."

"There isn't anything he can get from me that he can't get at home." I told him about the Mustang.

"Rich boy goes slumming," he said. Slumming—I had thought the same thing, but coming from Reid, I took offense.

"Are you saying I live in a dump?"

He creased his brow. "You know what I mean."

"I don't think he's that bad," I said. Suddenly, because Reid was making a case against Zink, I was defending him. Offense, defense—I was playing all sides. Maybe all Zink wanted was a place where he was accepted, like Yost and now our house. It seemed to me Reid was here for the same reason.

"Either way," Reid said. "I'm keeping my eye on him."

The next morning, Sunday, a day I liked to sleep late, I woke to the sound of my name. I followed it to the kitchen. There, Reid stood on a chair giving a blow-by-blow of one of our protests. Evan and Zink sat at the table, having peanut butter and jam toast.

"And then your mother got up on the podium and whipped the crowd into a frenzy." He formed his hands into a bullhorn. "She said, *If you want to stop the war, you have to use your voice, you have to let O'Connell know you want all government investments off this campus.*"

I froze. Here we go again. To mount a defense or not? Part of me wanted to retreat, to go back to bed and ignore this display of bravado. Instead, I stepped into the room. Engage, I thought. See what happens.

"I never said that."

Even though he didn't drink it, Reid had brewed the coffee. Zink poured me a large cup and refreshed his own, which he drank black. I loaded mine with cream and sugar.

"Who's O'Connell?" Evan asked.

"The university president," Reid said, irritated. That fact was beside the point. "I'm telling you, she was a natural. I was so proud of my baby sister that day."

Baby sister? Those words made the warm fuzzies rise up through my center. Again.

"Mom, you were a radical?" Evan raised his eyebrows, intrigued.

"Your uncle's exaggerating."

Reid jumped off the chair. His landing jiggled the floor. In the lemony morning light and with me this sleepy, I was amused rather than mad. Maybe Zink's presence leant an unreal quality to the scene, our triad broken by a fourth. Or maybe it was Reid's showman quality. This wasn't about me at all. This was performance art.

Besides, I had to pick my battles, like every parent who had to deal with a toddler or a teen. You couldn't nag all the time. Your voice began to sound like all the adults in the Peanuts TV specials. *Wah wah wah wah wah.*

Reid shoved Zink's clipboard across the table. "Petitions are for chumps," he said. "It won't accomplish a damn thing."

Zink fidgeted with his left eyebrow ring, twisting it, tugging. So far, he had said nothing.

"What do you suggest?" Evan asked.

"When you go to the meeting, you need to make some noise. Show them you're serious."

Evan leaned close. *Go on, I'm listening.*

"If you want, I can go with you."

Maybe this was a job interview—Reid wanted to be their guru, their commander-in-chief.

I looked at Zink, wondering what he thought of this proposal. He wasn't paying attention to Reid. He threw a piece of crust to Penny and she crunched it down.

"We don't feed her people food," I said.

"Sorry, not yet up on all the house rules."

I tightened the tie of my robe. "Why don't you just blow city hall to the ground. That'll show 'em."

"Cool," Evan said.

"I was kidding," I said.

Zink laughed. "Good one, Ms. L."

Hyperbole, a tact I hadn't yet tried. It deflated Reid—he was quiet, sitting on the floor petting Penny—and enlivened Zink.

This was one thing I could give Zink. A place where people talked, engaged with each other. A place of easy teasing mixed with a modicum of rules. Evan, because he had such a home, didn't fully understand its value, at least not yet. Zink, the neglected rich kid, craved it. Reid, I gleaned from his continued presence, wanted it as well. That was what he said in his postcard. *I'm coming home.*

Zink became an intermittent presence. I never knew when he would appear in the driveway in his Mustang or at the backdoor with his skateboard. I never knew when he would walk out of Evan's bedroom in a T-shirt and underwear, embarrassingly scratching his crotch. Embarrassing to me but not to him evidently.

He'd open the fridge. "Any OJ?"

"Any parents?" I'd asked.

"Oh, I have parents. But I'm number four, so they're pretty sick of the whole kid scene."

He had no shame. I liked that about him, and, against my better judgment, I liked having him around. He laughed at my one-liners. He actually cleaned up after himself and offered to do chores. It turned out we shared a taste in music. He told me he had a thing for members of the 27 Club. Hendrix, Joplin, Brian Jones, Jim Morrison, Kurt Cobain—all dead at the age of twenty-seven. He had checked out all of Morrison's writings from the library. Long ago I had done the same. They were fairly puerile, but I could see the appeal for someone like Zink.

Soon there were others, boys named Chex and Louse. They all wore the skateboarder's uniform: baggy shorts, slogan T's, and tennis shoes with no socks. Evan pulled out the mini-skateboard park, the ramps and rails he and Keith had built. They spent hours in the driveway doing nose bones and kiwi flips. How many more were there? Needy boys, who on the outside appeared to be tough, but on the inside wanted to be mothered and fed. Bring your rude skateboarders, your unwashed, your deodorant-free, your foul-mouthed. They were particularly attracted to my son.

I asked Evan about Chex. Every time I saw him, he had on the same clothes and they got dirtier and more torn. He never tied his laces and I worried they would get caught in the wheels. His skateboard was stenciled with miniature black skulls. Evan didn't know much about him. He said he had been going to Yost for only a few weeks.

"Why do you call him Chex? Is it like the cereal?"

"No, Checks. Like he stole welfare checks and tried to cash them and that's why he was in juvie."

Great. Better to keep the enemy close, I thought.

"So, Louse, does his name have anything to do with picking up a bad case of head lice?"

"God, Mom," was all he said.

On one particular Thursday evening they were out there showing off for Reid. I watched from the kitchen window. The asphalt took on a mirage quality, a shadowy blue-black that at times made it looked like the boys were skating on water.

Evan did an Ollie. Before you can do anything on a skateboard, you have to master an Ollie. I had seen Evan do this trick many times. He started at the top of the driveway, by the garage, and skated down toward a pair of cement blocks, one stacked on top of the other. Crouching as he approached the blocks, he jumped and, at the same time, popped the back end of the board against the asphalt. By shifting his weight from back foot to front, the board appeared to hug his feet as he soared over the blocks, landing perfectly. All this happened so fast the viewer didn't even notice the mechanics of the move.

I knew this was simply gravity. Skateboarding, at heart, was physics. The formula, when I looked it up on Altavista, was: $Fc = mv^2$ over r, where:

m = mass of moving body,

V = velocity with which it's moving,

r = radius of circular path.

This was gobbledygook to me, but I understood the basics, was able with my unscientific mind to apply it most readily to the gravitational pull of the planets. We—the earth—were drawn to the sun. It was a path from which we never strayed, like the moon in orbit around the earth.

The confidence on Evan's face when he landed made me smile. He was good at this. It was his talent, like poetry for Reid. And Reid appreciated it as well. A look of pure admiration replaced the mock smile I had seen so often since he'd been back.

Checks made a run toward a stacked rail. Attempting a spin, he landed on his ass. The boys heckled him and then, abandoning their skateboards, sat down on the grass.

Their rest didn't last long. Reid roused them and gave a tutorial on passive resistance. He had passed the job interview. He was now the grand poohbah of Operation Black Skull, his name for their mission to convince the city to fund the skatepark. I surmised the name had to do with the decoration on Checks's skateboard.

Reid boasted about his experiences protesting nuclear proliferation and overseas sweatshops. He gave lessons in going limp when a cop tried to arrest you, in locking your arms and legs if they tried to pick you up. Deadweight, he said. That was the goal.

He loved to be the center of attention. At Garden House he had all the women hanging on his every poetic word. This was the only way he knew how to connect with others, through organizing and leadership. Through taking control.

I had once been a part of his group. I found it hard to resist his good humor, his ability to make even the most mundane statement sound enlightened. I knew how his voice could sound conspiratorial, as if it was just us, as if I was in on something special.

Reid was a force, *the* force, that we revolved around. My mother and I had been doing it all our lives. Even in his absence—the long absences between visits—he was the nucleus. We vied for his attention, his love.

The following weekend Evan went to his father's. Typically, he spent most of July and August with Keith. Reid's appearance had thrown off that schedule. Evan begged to stay here and Keith gave in. Our custody was easy that way; not cemented in bad blood. Trading days, especially as Evan grew older, was common.

So, it would be Reid and me, bouncing around the house by ourselves. I was anxious. Did I have to entertain him? I could take him to the beach where I walked Penny. Or we could go to the White Bridge Café, one of my old favorites, for fried clams and beer. The deck was right on the water and at sunset you could watch the dolphins feed on mullet. A shift in scenery might be good for us. Somewhere neutral we could talk. If it was reconciliation he wanted—to be a part of the family—we'd have to start slow. I wanted to know him, *him*, my brother, not the famed poet.

When I got home on Friday night, he was in the middle of making us omelets. They were filled with grated onions, zucchini, and cheddar, topped with an X of bacon strips. He handed me a glass of tequila on the rocks. We sat on the patio.

"What's your favorite color?" I asked.

"Purple. Why?"

My mother was right. Should I have known this? All I could think of was the battleship gray walls of his bedroom.

"No reason," I said. "Tell me about where you live. From the postcard, it looks really beautiful."

"Why do you ask?"

I swallowed a mouthful of omelet. It was delicious, but I felt like I was swallowing my pride.

"I want to know about your life. Is there something wrong with that? You're staying at my house. You're practically living my life. Tell me something about yours."

"Okay. I rent a small house that butts up against the mountains. I like the town. Good people. Creative types. I never thought I'd stay in one place this long."

This was going well. I continued. "Why can't you write?"

"It's complicated. I know you think I'm here for some nefarious reason, but really, I'm not." He set aside his plate.

I spoke too soon. His veneer was harder to crack than expected.

He took out his knife and a piece of basswood. It looked like an owl, the body taking on a conical shape. He wiped the edge of the knife on his pants. Bent forward, forearms on his knees, he shaved off thin slivers that fell to the ground like ash. As he worked, he seemed to be still and in motion at the same time.

I went deeper. "I don't know how to think of you. How to see you in the right perspective. You've always overshadowed me." Overshadowed, I thought, like a plant in the shade.

"And you've always been a better person than me."

"Oh, please," I said. "That's what people say to excuse their own bad behavior."

"Guilty." Whittling, like writing, was solitary. It was also a way, when done like this, while we talked, to avoid looking at me directly.

"I love you and I hate you," I said, my attempt to be honest, to let him know how I felt.

"Same here," he said.

"You hate me? I don't think so." I wanted to jump up, get into his face the way I did when I was young. "After everything I did for you?"

"Everything you did? Wait. What are you talking about?"

A sour burning rose in my gullet. Tequila? Onions? No—anger. So buried an emotion, I almost didn't recognize it.

"You're the one who keeps bringing up the past. You're so eager to tell Evan what we did at school." I slid away my own plate. The silverware clattered on the table.

"What's the harm of him knowing? We were fighting for something important."

"Fuck this," I said. "You know what, if you want to tell him, just tell him. I'm not playing this game anymore."

Penny barked. I doubted she had ever heard me raise my voice.

"These kids, they're soft. They have nothing to push against." He drained his drink. "Besides, you didn't do anything wrong." He still held the wood and the knife, but his focus wasn't on them. He looked at me, and that look—fierce, direct, commanding—made me squirm. It sent me right back to the streets of Gainesville.

"Yes, I did, Reid, and so did you." I lowered my voice. This next question—I didn't want to ask it in anger. "Here's what's been on my mind. Why did you just assume I'd take the fall?"

"I didn't assume anything."

"Don't you remember the day you and Dad picked me up from the police station? We went to the hotel. He told us if we didn't—well, he wanted to know what happened. And that whole time you said nothing. I was left to explain everything and I had no idea what to say."

"Memory's a faulty instrument."

"That's convenient." If he thought a cute aphorism would shut me up, he was wrong.

"You didn't say a word, but you didn't have to. Remember? You looked right at me, the way you're looking now, and shook your head, which meant—this is how I interrupted it—to *not* say anything." I had replayed this scene so many times over the years. "Then, later, at The Terrace, you all just. All of you just assumed."

He bowed his head, went back to whittling. Was he mulling this over or just ignoring it? Was he trying to take away the sting of his gaze? His hand was tightly wrapped around the wood, strangling the innocent creature.

Finally, he said, in a voice far lower than mine, "Let me ask you something. Why didn't you ever go back to school? You're drowning in domesticity."

That hurt. He had turned on me.

"I have a son, I have responsibilities," I said. "Something you know nothing about."

"Don't blame that on me."

This was the nitty-gritty of my resentment—a nit, a piece of grit that had calcified into an ugly, ugly gem: I wanted Reid to be grateful. I wanted him down on his knees, a supplicant, groveling, kissing my toes, vowing eternal devotion.

A chunk of wood fell. He had cut off the owl's head. *We inflict damage on those we love.*

"I dropped out of life, too, you know," he said. "I felt guilty and I dropped out."

"I don't see it that way at all. You're famous. You're Reid Layman."

"Famous? That's debatable." He fingered the jagged edge of the wood.

"You've been interviewed by Bill Moyers. How much more famous could you be?"

He got a kick out of that. I was the court jester at Garden House *and* at home.

"Bill and I aren't best friends or anything," he said.

Moyers was the only journalist Reid respected. He said his Vietnam War coverage was unimpeachable. The interview had taken place after Reid won the National Book Award. During the hour—no commercials on Public Broadcasting—Moyers tried to pin my brother down about his early life. Reid shied away from talking about himself. He spoke about language and how we use it to structure our world. If we can't speak it, we can't imagine it.

The knife slipped out of his hands.

"I'm scared shitless being here. I'm scared every minute of every day," he said. "I can't write. Ever since I won that, that, that—" He couldn't even name the award.

I didn't buy it. The pose of the tormented artist was stale. I let my gaze drop.

Moyers had asked Reid what he, as a poet, wanted people to know about him. Reid thought for a moment, then finally said he believed he was a conduit. He was put on this earth not to tell his own story, but the stories of others. "I'm a listener, Bill," he said. "That's all."

I wondered if he had heard, really heard, what I said. Had we talked around each other, our words bobbing and weaving, not making impact?

I was spent. He was ashen, all the Rocky Mountain high-altitude color drained from his cheeks.

"Let's call it a night," I said, standing. Penny came to my side, wagged her tail.

Reid picked up the knife and began to pack his supplies.

"Thanks for dinner," I said, squeezing his shoulder as I passed.

In the days that followed, Reid and I were polite, cautious in our interactions. Our conversation stayed in my thoughts, but neither of us brought it up. On Saturday night I met Holly for dinner. We went to White Bridge Café. The sunset was lovely, but no dolphins came. She wanted to know all about Reid and his visit. How things were going. I didn't have the heart to get into the details. Fine, fine, everything was fine. On Sunday Evan returned. The week started up.

Free from Garden house, I had time on my hands. I worked, but after work—what to do? Reid had taken over. He visited Mom, entertained Evan, walked the dog, cooked. Without the busyness, I felt useless.

Not seeing my mother brought a trinity of guilt, relief, and *so there*. *If you can't remember my name, so there*, I won't visit. It was perverse and left me feeling giddy and nauseous most days.

I scheduled a dental appointment for Evan, a vet appointment for Penny. I ran errands, replacing toilet paper and toothpaste. I stripped and remade beds, washed all the laundry, only on odd days because of water rationing. I scooped dog poop up in plastic bags and tossed them away. Chore after chore. Check, check, check.

All this was not much different from how I had lived for years. That reality was highlighted by Reid's presence. He was right, I was drowning in domesticity. I rushed to get Evan to school, to get to my job. I rushed back to school to take Evan wherever he needed to be: soccer and baseball practices, piano lessons, appointments, his father's. I squeezed in a visit to my mother. I rushed home to make dinner and help with homework.

I came up with a formula to describe my current situation:

m = me, my mass. I was a forty-four-year-old divorced woman; a little heavy in the thighs; the skin around my eyes and mouth wrinkly. I had a practical haircut—a shoulder-length bob with bangs—that fit my wash-and-go lifestyle. My clothes were just as practical. Denim skirts and cotton shirts; jeans and tank tops on the weekends. I didn't have a degree. All my mom jobs didn't add up to a career. I was smart, but hadn't used my brain in any serious way for years.

V = the speed with which I travelled to accomplish all my daily responsibilities.

r = the path I continued to tread, a rutted and monotonous circle.

This was the woman I had become. I had no center-seeking force. Reid had poetry, Parker had classic cars. Holly had real estate. My mother, after my father died, had the job at the gift store. Later, she had a group of friends she played cards with and met for Sunday morning brunch. My son, all of fourteen, had skateboarding.

I had never asked myself the question Reid posed: Why didn't I go back to school? If I thought my life was small, why didn't I make it larger? If I stopped looking outward, what would I find inside? *If we can't speak it, we can't imagine it.*

And what about the other part of our conversation? Reid might not recall his silence after my arrest, the way he shook his head—*Don't tell*—while we stood in the hotel room, our father demanding the truth. But I wasn't wrong. My memory on that point was clear. This led to another question I hadn't asked myself: why had I assumed responsibility for my brother's actions?

For a long time—and maybe I still did—I viewed my life as *before* and *after*, the split being the nights I spent in the Alachua County jail. It had nothing to do with the jail itself, but the fact that Reid left me there. They all did. Matt and Billie and Cal. I had eighteen years of *before*. At the time it was forever. I had no reason to believe there would be an *after*.

In May of 1972, I understood—instinctually, in my bones—I should tell no one why I was in that cell, especially my parents. My father was convinced it was Reid's fault. He was supposed to be watching out for me. His Pumpkin wouldn't do such a thing unless she was led astray. I didn't try to convince him otherwise.

To my mother, I had broken the code—so many codes, what was expected of me as a military daughter, a daughter of the 1950's, as her daughter. It didn't matter, going forward, how silent I was or how conscientiously I followed the rules, mistrust was a shim between us. Once I accepted this, there were many *afters*: after I fulfilled the terms of my probation, after I got my job at Paperbark. I lived for *afters*. I let them take over. The more *afters* I experienced, the further I was from 1972. Meeting and marrying Keith, having Evan, the house in town, the house by the river—these were all *afters*.

Reid and I were now in kind of *after*. This one didn't adhere to any rules I could follow.

When I was young and really wanted to irritate him, I took down one of the model airplanes he had hung from his ceiling and twirled it above my head. All those kits he bought at the post exchange—C46 commando transports, P51 mustangs, B36 Peacemakers—all those hours spent putting them together. Touching them was bad enough, but untacking them, that got a rise out of him. He threatened me. *Celeste, if you don't stop…* The feeling of the taut string in my hand, the outward tension of the plastic, not heavy but solid enough, made me smug. I was the source of both motion and my brother's anger. As long as I kept my hand moving, the plane stayed in the air. Perpetual motion. Perpetual ire. Until my arm grew tired or Reid snatched it away.

If my life was one of those spinning plastic planes, I should take a pair of scissors to the string.

If my life was a sun-loving honeysuckle struggling for light under a canopy of pines, I should dig it up and replant it out in the open.

I took Penny to Plum Beach, a secluded beach about thirty miles from home where dogs ran off leash. They gamboled in the surf, chased Frisbees and each other. We, the owners, talked. About dogs and the weather. I didn't know any of their names, but I knew the dogs. Rosie, a drool-y and barky Rottweiler. Jack, a terrier whose way of saying *Chase me* was to nip ankles. A reserved mutt, Zig, who for some reason liked Penny and played exclusively with her.

The whole experience was uncomplicated and uncomplicated was exactly what I needed. Just watching the dogs dip and yip and sniff—it was bliss.

I like the ocean—churning surf, salt spray, cockle shells—but it was the exact opposite of my beloved river, always in a hurry, always pulled and pushed by the fickle moon, always clawing and raking the shoreline. These days I only went there for Penny to play.

On the way home, I took a detour. Veering off U.S. 1 and driving under the I-95 overpass, I went straight to Fellsmere. Left on Vernon Street. Right on Old Bear Creek Road. Right on Tall Pines. I remembered the way to Paperbark. Was it even there anymore?

The town had seen little construction or growth. Trailer parks were still the primary housing of choice, as it had been in the mid-1970s. Convenience stores, package stores, and a dollar store were the primary commerce. No, the nursery was no longer in business, but I found the site, overgrown with dodder and kudzu. I pulled over. A corner of one of the greenhouses peeked out of the mesh of vines. Far in the back of the property, not visible from the road, was the house where I had lived. Where Keith and I lived.

When I met him, my body was starved for touch, for skin-on-skin. I had dirt-on-skin. I had dirt-on-dirt, in crevasses that chafed. I didn't wear a bra because it was too restrictive and sweat ran down my chest. By the end of the day, my areolas were black with dirt.

Keith was so shy I had to make the first move. I invited him over for dinner, which was just avocado sandwiches, and after we ate, I led him up to the sleeping loft. His hands were as dry and dirt-veined as mine, but their touch was supple and smooth. He quickly found the places I liked: inner thigh, lower back, my erect nipples. And I found those same places on his body—my fingernails digging into his ass; my tongue caressing his lower belly, the zipper of hair that went from bellybutton to pubic bone.

When Evan was born, he fit seamlessly into our life at Paperbark. As a toddler, he wobbled around the land, no shoes, no clothes except a diaper. He tasted dirt and decided it wasn't as good as the food we grew in it. He let fuzzy caterpillars crawl up his chubby legs. He learned respect for things that stung, bit, hissed, or buzzed. I marveled at his intense exploration of the world. He squatted and watched a line of ants for half an hour. When that was no longer amusing enough, he poked holes in a banana frond and studied the web of fiber threads.

I wanted to live there forever. We had an organic garden of lettuce, broccoli, arugula, and watercress. The place smelled at all times like compost and fermenting apples. Keith, however, decided he was sick of grime and back-breaking work. Without telling me, he got a job at a department store in the mall. The mall? The one that had taken over the orange grove. Retail? Selling things—decorative pitchers and valences in just the right shade of ecru? Up to that point, we both shunned this kind of consumerism. I didn't understand and I didn't speak to him for a week. My mother was overjoyed. She thought of it as a step up the economic ladder.

I admit that in the end, my anger was assuaged by the first paycheck.

I couldn't remember any of the names of the people I worked with at Paperbark. I mostly took direction. When it was time to transfer seedlings from greenhouse to soil, I picked up my trowel and hauled my wheelbarrow into the field. I listened to talk of variegation and soil acidity. I listened to debates about the best habitats for orchids. The leaves of orchids grown in humid climates were thinner and more elongated than orchids grown in drier areas.

Oh, yes, now I remembered. The owner's name was Marcus. He taught me that ponytail palms were neither palm nor tree, but succulents. He taught me that the color of flowers was determined in large part to how they were pollinated: insect or wind. I know the best time to prune frangipani is in winter. I know bromeliads live only on air and water. Marcus urged me to look closely at tree bark. Black cherry had scaly bark. Birch had slender outer layers that peeled away in curly strips. When a maple was attacked by a fungal infection, the bark cracked in concentric circles.

I was about to let Penny out—we could wander around the property together—when I heard the rumble of an approaching vehicle. I got back in my car, feeling silly. What was I doing? Here was another area of my life Reid brought into relief: the fact that I didn't have a passion. I ricocheted between responsibilities. I never touched the ground. Was I a gardener at heart? Was this the profession I now thought I should pursue? Or was I meant to keep doing what I was doing, writing copy for Sun Power? Maybe my destiny wasn't any of these. Maybe I hadn't yet found it.

Did I need one all-consuming passion? I was a dabbler. Wasn't that okay? But as a dabbler, I didn't take any one thing seriously enough. Nothing was expected of me and so I did nothing. That seemed the worst possible betrayal of self.

There were no Fourth of July celebrations. Governor Chiles banned the possession and use of fireworks, even sparklers. The stock car race at the Daytona International Speedway was postponed. Russell decided to close Sun Power for the whole week. He was taking a vacation. We weren't making any money anyway. He put a sign on the door. "Gone fishing. Be back on July 9." This date was significant because it was the two-year anniversary of the opening of the business. Before he left, he took down the fire maps. When he returned, he hoped there would be no need for them.

Garden House had an indoor picnic. The dining room was decorated in red, white, and blue. Flags and bunting were taped on desks and walls, the adhesive coming loose in places, a display of patriotism that was flap-eared, comical. Balloons, tied to the backs of chairs, bobbed in the Gulf Stream of the air-conditioning, on full-blast. Wheelchairs and walkers were draped with construction paper chains. Had this been a craft project? I tried to imagine arthritic fingers cutting paper, folding and gluing the strips. Maybe Sophie had made them all.

It was billed as a cookout, but the food was the standard dining room fare: no open flame or barbeque. Hamburgers and potato salad cooked in the kitchen. Many of the women needed their meat cut and served with no bun. In general, it wasn't bad. I had eaten there several times in the last year. Evan said the bread pudding was to die for.

Families were also dressed in appropriate patriotic attire. Watching all this, I knew I had made the right decision to move my mother here. It was filled with involved families and caring staff.

My mother looped her arm through Reid's and let him escort her around. This was the kind of thing Evan used to do. I didn't know if he felt replaced, but he stuck close to Reid, or as I thought of it, as far away from me as possible. Reid was king. Everyone knew him. Everyone stopped and talked to him, laughed with him. He glad-handed, like a politician. He was charming and articulate.

With reverence, my mother said, "He's a poet." The world's poet, with a capital P. It was as if she said Doctor or Attorney. Professions her generation esteemed.

I, the wicked daughter who put her here in the first place, volunteered to staff the refreshment table. Refreshments in this case included the bar. Wine, tea, soda, and water. I was told to ration the goodies. I poured wine into tiny plastic cups, not much bigger than pill dispensing cups. I drank five in a row, like shots. Gut rot that brought instant light-headedness. I was to keep count of how many glasses each resident drank and only allow those with a blue wristband to partake. I didn't need instructions. I had worked many a party. I knew Mrs. Bliss was a diabetic and couldn't have any Pepperidge Farm Milano cookies. I knew Miss Chase's digestive system wasn't compatible with dairy of any kind. No Cheese Whiz for her.

When I poured my mother a glass of wine, she said, "Thank you, aren't you a kind girl." Today I was neither sister nor daughter.

Mrs. Kline came over for her third glass of wine. Ah, a drinking buddy. I poured one for her and one for me. Her hand quivered as she raised it to her lips, but not enough to spill. She wasn't about to lose even one drop of this potent elixir.

"Hit me again," she said.

I didn't see why she couldn't have another. The glasses were so small and so what? Everyone here was on their last years. Why not go out with a bang?

"Who's that man?" she asked, pointing to Reid.

I explained that he was my brother and he lived in Colorado, didn't visit often. I said he was a poet, trying to capture for myself the glow that emanated from my mother every time she mentioned his profession.

"A what, dear? A plumber?"

"No, Mrs. Kline. A poet."

"A potter?"

"He writes poetry," I said.

"Well, that's not a profession," she said.

Yes, some people saw it that way. Sometimes I saw it that way.

"One more for the road," she said, plunking down her tiny cup.

I took the opportunity to fill one of the larger punch glasses for myself.

Reid came over, wanting another glass of wine for Mom.

"Hello, Mrs. Kline," he said. He flashed a smile and put a hand on her arm.

Before she tootled off, she said, "I'm on to you."

I didn't tell Reid this was her standard line. It meant nothing. Let him believe someone was watching him, not buying his act.

"What was that about?"

"I guess she doesn't trust you."

"What's not to trust?" Again, the smile, somewhat smarmy and self-effacing.

"She's been around a long time. She's seen 'em come and go."

"You're not making any sense."

"None of this makes any sense," I slurred. The alcohol was bringing out my old friend, my gem. Hard-earned resentment.

"I see the fox is guarding the hen house," Reid said, nodding at my cup.

"A cliché. That's not like you. Besides, I don't think *hen* is a word you want to use here," I said. "In a place like this, that's two strikes against you. Misogyny and ageism."

I gulped the last of my wine.

He returned to our mother and Evan returned to his side. Helen put on music. Not *God Bless America* or the *Star-Spangled Banner*, but Tommy Dorsey and Glenn Miller. The ladies danced. Swing, shuffle, step-ball-change. Reid took my mother and waltzed her around the room. The look on my mother's face—she beamed, once again. She didn't care that everyone was looking at her. She was in the arms of her son. The families and staff moved back, creating a makeshift circle that was now a dance floor. He led her across the floor with expertise, as if he had been doing this all his life. Just like in a movie, they were star and co-star.

My heart—such a fickle muscle—opened, just a little. Enough to let my brother in. *See, look how happy he makes her.* I had to face it, Reid was our sun.

I began to make plans. I could help him find a place to live. I'd give him some of our parents' furniture. I had a garage full of it and he was entitled to half of it anyway. He'd start to write. He'd keep teaching poetry at Garden House. We could work through our differences, air them out and settle them. We would be together in caring for our mother. This was how I had once imagined our adult relationship: supportive, allied.

For a few days, we got a reprieve from the fires. Scattered showers arrived, dampening flare-ups. The mandatory evacuation order was lifted in Flagler County. No more homes had burned. Volusia County residents were allowed to return to their homes, although they were cautioned about food and water contamination that might have occurred as a result of extended electrical-power outages. President Clinton arrived to thank the firefighters for their dedication. With our sighs of relief, we breathed in clean air.

I came home one night, a Tuesday, to find that dinner wasn't made and the dog was whining and scratching at the door. No sign of Reid or Evan. The air conditioner wasn't on. It was crushingly hot. I let Penny out and she went off on her own.

Reid was at the patio table, curled over a pad of paper, a pen moving quickly across the page. He was intent. In the zone. He was writing again. How long had he been like this? Should I disturb him? Pull him out of his reverie? It wasn't reverie, it was his work—the job he was paid to do.

I approached. He showed no indication he was aware of my presence. Was he writing about me? Was he sitting there critiquing my life in the form of a sonnet?

Not everything is about you, Celeste. This I heard in my mother's voice.

Penny raced by me and right to Reid. He looked up, looked my way, but didn't seem to really see me. His eyes were unfocused. He was still in the dream space.

I stepped closer. The distance between us felt like miles. There were too many steps. I had a shimmer of memory: Reid and I at the last protest, the asphalt and smoke, a flicker of fire that I saw out of the corner of my eye. I was pinned down and Reid was free. He was stepping back, away. He was turning.

I touched his shoulder. "Hey," I said. "You're writing."

"I am," he said. "But don't tell anybody. You'll break the spell."

"There's a spell?" I laughed.

"Oh, yeah, there's a spell. It's a spell so long and convoluted and secret that sometimes I forget it."

"What brought it back?"

I sat. He clicked the pen double-time.

"Something happened at Mom's. Two things, actually."

At Mom's? I didn't think of Garden House as Mom's home. It was where she resided, not where she *lived*. She probably felt that way, too. We needed more time for it to become hers.

"Mrs. Pruitt wrote a beautiful poem. And I don't mean an old lady sweet poem. I mean a genius poem. I was jealous. I thought, why hadn't I written that?"

"Wow, what was it about?"

"It wasn't about anything. I mean, there was something about a lake and the decaying of the body. When she read it, I cried, in front of everyone, there in the rec room."

"Is that the first thing that happened?"

"What?"

"You said two things happened."

"Oh, right." He let Penny lick his face. He still looked dazed, here and not here. He was back at Garden House. What else could have happened? Sophie had declared her love? Or her mother had? Maybe a resident peed on the floor. I had witnessed that.

"She forgot who I was," he said.

"Mom?" I hadn't thought that was even possible.

"She called me George and made some comment about the cows and how they were food, not friends."

"George, her brother. Oh, she talks about him all the time. That's nothing new, Reid."

"It's new for me," he said.

My heart opened even wider. Up until now, his time with my mother had been parties, poetry, and tea time. It was fawning nurses. Finally, he was coming to see reality. I knew that reality and it was painful.

The next night Reid didn't come home. I discovered this fact in the morning when I saw Evan and Penny on the pier, alone. I had noted that he hadn't been home at dinner—well, I noted that he hadn't provided the dinner—but that had happened once or twice before, if he stayed at Garden House or went out with a friend. I went to bed not worrying about him.

Evan came through the door, looking as if he had lost a prized possession. His skateboard, for instance.

"Where's Uncle Reid?" he asked.

"I was going to ask you the same thing."

"Did you kick him out?"

Penny wound around my legs. Her morning without Reid didn't seen to bother her.

"No," I said. "Why would you say that?"

"You don't want him here. It's obvious." He slid into a chair at the table.

I didn't want to fight. I hadn't yet had coffee.

"Maybe he left early to go see grandma," I said. That seemed plausible, though not likely. It was 07:00. How much earlier could he have left?

I called Helen. She was about to call me, she said. Reid hadn't shown up for the poetry group on Wednesday. The ladies—yes, that was how she referred to the residents of Garden House—were concerned.

"I hope everything's okay," she said.

"I'm sure it is," I said. I covered with a white lie. "He probably went to visit a friend. He might have mentioned it and I forgot."

Maybe he had done just that. He had many friends in town. He even had friends in other parts of the state. Cal still lived in Gainesville. Why worry? He could take care of himself.

We didn't see him the next day either. Evan spent two nights at Keith's. By the time he returned, Reid hadn't come back. Evan spoke to me in grunts and mumbles.

I went to see my mother. She was in the midst of doing what she called calisthenics, which was touching her toes and reaching for the stars.

"We have to stay in shape, you and me," she said.

Her face was red with exertion. She was absorbed and seemingly pleased with her activity. In all the time she had been at Garden House, I hadn't seen her this active. Something was working. Reid's presence or my absence.

On the bureau were two of Reid's birds, the cardinal, still in process, and an owl, a different one, just taking shape. The eyes were over-large and off-center. Caricature-ish. I thought of the head of the other owl, landing in the grass.

"Aren't those the cutest?" my mother asked.

"They are," I said.

"He's so talented." She wagged her fingers over her head.

As always, Reid was here but not here. Here, not. It didn't matter that neither of us had seen him in the last four days. His physical presence had never been the issue. Not here, here. *That* was a talent.

I called Holly later that night. Did I really think Reid might be there? As we talked, I could tell she was puttering around her kitchen, taking dishes from her stainless-steel Bosch dishwasher and stacking them into her solid oak, glass-front cupboards.

"I haven't seen him," she said. "Why? What's wrong?"

"He hasn't been home since Tuesday."

"Well, that's Reid," she said.

She wasn't at all worried. Maybe I didn't need to be either.

The first time I went to her new house I stood in front of the huge windows looking out at the Atlantic. I ached with the feeling that I had done nothing with my life. This was what a life on the straight and narrow provided. Holly, of course, had not married Prince Charles from Florida State University. She never lived in married housing. She had come to her senses, finished her degree, and returned to marry a hometown boy. She had a beautiful home, a beautiful family. She was right to not be ashamed. She and Grant did work hard. They had earned what they had.

Was that what I thought success was—the ability to drink your morning coffee standing in a 3,000 square-foot house staring at the beach? No, I wasn't surprised Reid had not gone to visit her. That was the last place he would want to be.

On Monday, I drove to Parker's business. He was in the office on the phone. I looked around. This was the cleanest service station I had ever been in. He was a collector of 1930s paraphernalia: Coca-Cola machines; Nylint toy trucks; signs advertising Kola-Pepsin gum, Nosegay tobacco, and Gulflube motor oil. There was an assortment of tire repair tins on a shelf: Redi-Spare, Match-Patch. The lettering was faded and the tops were rusty.

Parker had never married, although over the years he'd had a few long-term girlfriends. Stephanie, the beautician. Kathy, the pediatric nurse. When things didn't work out, he'd say "she was bossy" or "she wanted me to get a real job." A real job was any job that required him to wear something other than coveralls. I thought of him, at this point, as a man set in his ways; no woman was going to tell him what to do. His house was about a mile away, tucked away in a neighborhood that bordered a reserve. He had a life that suited him.

"Have you seen Reid?" I asked when he got off the phone.

"Not recently. We had lunch at Crawford's about two weeks ago. I haven't heard from him since."

"You were downtown and you didn't stop in to see me?"

"He didn't want to. He wanted to get back to your mother's place."

"He hasn't been home for a few days. Did he tell you anything about his plans?"

"Your brother's not a planner. Surely you know that by now."

A neon sign for Electric Auto-Lite Service flashed on and off above his head.

All through high school, Parker had a part-time job at a gas station. He was always working on cars in his driveway, his legs sticking out from under the front fender. He had found his niche early in life. But I did wonder if he was satisfied with the way his life had turned out. If his tour in Vietnam had derailed him in some way.

"Parker, are you happy?"

"What's this all about, Celeste? Is this about those goddess heads you put up? Is this about Reid? I mean, don't worry about him."

"His visit does put some things in focus," I said.

"What, like, about your life? You've got it all. Your son, your house, that cool new job."

"I know."

Someone pulled into the station. He waved to Parker.

"I gotta get this," he said, waving back. "By the way, how's your car running? You're gonna need an oil change soon."

"Fine. Good. I'll make an appointment."

"No need. Just come in next week. And to answer your question. Yes, I'm happy. Would I have made some decisions differently? Sure. Who can say they wouldn't? Maybe I should have married Kathy."

"Yes, she was pretty great. Thanks, Parker."

I sat in the car for a long time, watching Parker talk to his customer, watching the neon light flick off, flick on, flick off.

I had let Reid into my life. Let him see the good—my son, my land, my river—and the bad—my son, my nonexistent profession, the gaping hole of my self-doubt. And then, just as I accepted the good and the bad he had to offer, he was gone. Again.

PART TWO

The Past

The Blind World

Christmas of 1971 was a dreary, tense affair. My mother had removed the magazine pictures I taped up over Thanksgiving weekend. The walls were repainted a soft rose. She called it the guest room. My belongings were in boxes in the garage, she said. If I wanted any of it—knickknacks, clothes, books, yearbooks—I was welcome to take them back with me to school. It was tough love. She didn't approve of the new me.

I said nothing. I didn't whine or challenge. I simply tossed my suitcase on the new white bedspread and said to her, "What time's dinner?" I knew it was a dismissive question, implying all she was good for was preparing meals, and half the time she didn't even do that. As soon as I said it, my face flashed hot with regret. If I had learned anything from Billie and Betty Friedan it was not to put down other women. For the rest of the trip she treated me with cautious dismay.

My father treated me the same as always. He asked about my classes, he asked about my friends. I think he imagined me sitting around with my dormmates braiding each other's hair and talking about boys. Or whatever innocent young co-eds did in their all-female dorm. He certainly didn't think I was hanging out with derelicts anymore. He never asked me about Reid, how he was doing, what he was doing. He thought we were running in two separate worlds. He did ask if I was staying safe. Of course, I was, I said.

Ever practical, he decided it was time for me to learn how to change a tire. We spent a few hours in the driveway talking jacks, lug nuts, and tire pressure. I appreciated the attention and the advice. You never knew when this skill would come in handy.

On Christmas morning I opened my presents, seeing judgment in each one: a purple sweater, a beige pleated shirt, a necklace with a gold and enamel butterfly pendant, and bath beads. The clothes were square. The necklace, while beautiful, wasn't me at all. It was something I would have worn at twelve. I thanked my mother and wondered if in her eyes I was like a butterfly, coming out of my chrysalis. Right now, I was in an awkward stage, not yet as beautiful as this one made of gold, but hopefully in the future I might grow colorful wings.

Bath beads? Did she not remember that I had no bath tub in the dorm? Did she think I stank because I had stopped using deodorant? Maybe I did. But to me I smelled just like everyone at The Terrace. Earthy. Natural. Matt never complained. I took none of this back to school. I stashed it in one of the boxes in the garage before I left.

Reid and I spent New Year's Eve at the beach with a group of kids from high school, including Holly and Adam. Adam brought sparkers and firecrackers to light at midnight. We built a bonfire and drank cheap wine and beer. The sound of the waves and the smell of the fire—so soothing.

Holly said she had seen Parker recently and had invited him to join us. Since his return from Vietnam, he was living at home and working at a gas station.

"Not that you care, but the war has really messed him up," she said. "Not physically. I mean, emotionally."

"Of course I care," I retorted.

"Holly, you don't know what you're talking about," Reid said.

"Guys, guys, it's almost 1972, let's be friends," Adam said. He had changed from surfer to frat boy, cutting his long hair and wearing preppy shirts. "Let's hug and kiss and talk about anything but the war."

"Whatever you say, Adam," Reid said.

At midnight, according to Adam's new digital watch, we set off firecrackers and lit sparklers. Reid and I smiled at each over the coils of light. We didn't care that we were here with all these unenlightened former friends. Soon we would go back to our real lives at school, back to the real business of stopping the war. For now, we were together and a little drunk.

Parker arrived after midnight. He looked ragged, his hair dirty and matted. He had on a pair of fatigues. I noticed a POW/MIA bracelet on his left wrist, tucked under his CPO jacket. He pulled up his sleeve and showed it to us: Major Thomas Keene, 11-6-68.

"Poor sucker," he said. "But then again, we were all suckers."

Adam gave him a beer.

"Elixir of the gods," he said, chugging it.

Reid, Holly, and Adam went down to the surf, kicking at the waves, splashing each other. Others continued to set off firecrackers. I asked Parker if he wanted to take a walk and we headed south, toward the boardwalk.

He had been stationed in Da Nang. When he enlisted, he believed he could just go and get it over with. But when he got there, he knew he had made the wrong decision. His unit spent their days going into villages in search of Viet Cong or Viet Cong sympathizers. When they found none—and, really, how would they know, they couldn't speak the language?—it didn't make a difference anyway, innocent or not, the soldiers had to burn the houses of every village.

"So, tell me what happened," I said.

"I don't like to talk about it."

"I'm a good listener."

"Celeste, you're good at everything you do."

Is that how he thought of me, as good? The good student, good sister, good friend? I wanted him to know what we were doing at school. I described the Homecoming parade, remembering the search and destroy mission we had reenacted. He cut me off.

"Listen, I get what you're doing and okay, I'm all for it, but really, you have no idea."

We stopped and sat on the steps of the boardwalk.

"There was this time, when we were—it doesn't matter where we were—it was hell. My CO told us to fire into the jungle. He heard a noise, he said. Later, after we lay there for hours and nothing had happened, no return fire, we went in. We found dead men and women. No children, thank God. But one of the women was pregnant and you could see her belly moving, like the baby moving inside, under the skin. We just left her there. We just walked away."

He dropped his head to my chest and cried. I had no idea what to say, how to handle this horror. I had acted like I could. *Tell me, tell me* I had begged. He had and I was useless.

My chest was wet with his sweat and tears. I wished I hadn't pushed him. It made me angry that the men in Washington, that Nixon, McNamara, and Laird could send a boy to do that.

A firecracker went off in the distance and he flinched.

"I think I'll head home, he said." "This is why I didn't come earlier. I know they're just firecrackers, but the sound, it gets to me."

After he left, I went back down to the beach and found the others lighting more sparklers. I lit two, one for each hand.

The joy had gone out of the night. The sparks stung my hands, electrical zaps that hurt—hurt so good.

    Reid and I returned to Gainesville on New Year's Day. For the next few days I had the dorm room to myself. Classes began on January 4 and I knew Doreen wouldn't return until the bitter end of vacation. She wanted to spend every moment she could with Dwight. I snuck Matt in the side door and up the stairs. We stayed there for the next two days. Activities of the dorm, much quieter than usual—many students hadn't yet returned—continued around us. We heard girls opening and closing doors, asking each other to borrow shampoo or a skirt. We heard the telephone ring and snippets of one-sided conversations. But I felt like we were alone in a way we couldn't be at The Terrace. No high school boys would knock on the door wanting draft advice. We wouldn't be drawn into a debate over Nixon. We didn't have to listen to Cal's high-pitched complaints about how nobody in VVAW but him was pulling his weight. When Matt needed to go to the bathroom, he put on my robe and, after I had made sure the coast was clear, dashed down the hall and back. When we needed food, I went to the dining hall and doubled up on chicken, mashed potatoes, salad, and the vanilla cake I loved so much. We ate on the floor on a blanket, then got back into bed.

    I was learning new things about Matt's body. His penis—such a strange addition to my repertoire of knowledge. Once it had been as foreign as a place I had never traveled to, Antarctica say. Suddenly, I knew it intimately. I had some control over it and it also had a life of its own: one minute soft and floppy, the next large and hard. Matt talked about how, when he was going through puberty, he couldn't control it and felt so self-conscious when he got a hard-on unexpectedly.

My body and its capacity for intense pleasure surprised me in this same way. It could be unruly. Sometimes my T-shirt rubbed against my nipples in a way that aroused me. Sometimes in the shower I touched myself the way Matt did. I came with streams of water sliding down my belly. During sex, I went so deep into sensation that I had no awareness of sound or surroundings. Anyone could have walked in the room and I would not have heard them.

Each part of my body revealed a new sensitivity. My feet had always been ticklish, but I never knew that if someone traced a figure eight over my arch, a tingle would run up my thigh. And my thighs, the insides burned every time Matt licked them. My neck, my earlobe. The very tops of my shoulders, the tendon-y flesh where shoulder met neck, a nibble right there made me swoon.

That word, swoon—so common in romance novels—I had once scoffed at it. Now I knew what it meant: your knees *do* weaken; you melt into the body next to you, your love. It meant, *I have to have you inside me, right now*. I had read Jacqueline Susann's *Valley of the Dolls*. I had read *The Carpetbaggers* by Harold Robbins and *The Best of Everything* by Rona Jaffe. But what I learned in those books was too vague. Too black-and-white, like print on page, not the color of ruddy, lustrous flesh.

Doreen returned, brought back her Southern charm, filling the room with hours of talk about the holidays at her house, traditions like stringing popcorn and opening all their presents on Christmas Eve. She showed me the pearl necklace Dwight gave her and the fuzzy slippers her mother thought she would need this winter. She seemed happier, cheerier than I had ever seen her. I thought maybe when she went home this time, she might decide not to return or, if she did, it would be days of tears and intense telephone calls.

"You know what," she said. "I'm glad to be back. My mother was driving me crazy."

"Mine, too," I said. This was the first common ground we had ever met on.

"Her apron strings are awfully tight." She pronounced tight as two words: *ti-eit*.

She told me a story about how she went to her father's grave and let it all out, how much she missed her mother and Dwight and wanted to come home. She begged him to let her out of her promise.

"I said, *I know I made a promise, Daddy, but I don't think I can fulfill it. You have to tell me what to do.* All the rest of the weekend I waited for a sign and this morning before I left, I got my sign. There was this little bird singing. It was the kind of bird Daddy liked, the ones with purple feathers on top. It was singing and it said *Go back, go back. There's time.* Just like that. So clear."

"Like a purple martin or something?"

"Celeste, it doesn't matter. I'm here and I'm staying. I'm done fighting. Dwight can wait. This is my time."

With that, Doreen put an end to Billie's prediction that she wouldn't make it through the year.

A cold front settled over central Florida. The heater in our dorm didn't work. In the late afternoon, when the sun went down, a gloom settled over me. I wrapped myself in a blanket and tried to study. I finished a lab on mitosis. I could still smell the fermented onion root I had sliced and examined under the microscope that morning. I had French to study. Why had I decided this was the term I'd learn French? *Je vais, tu vas, il va, nous allons, vous allez, ils vont.* And that was just the present tense. I still had to learn the future tense, the imperfect.

Each morning ice laced the edges of my window. Luckily, this term my first class didn't begin until ten so I had time to warm up in the shower before I went out. Sometimes I went to the library to get warm and study. I found a cushioned chair on the third floor, in front of a window, with a heating vent at my feet.

Along with French and Biology II, I was taking the second section of history and English. I no longer went to my study group, though. At Billie's urging, I joined her consciousness-raising group. Every Tuesday night, we met in the basement of the Union. The room was suffused with perspiration and honey. Someone always brought carob brownies or applesauce cake. We took off our shoes and sat in a circle, knees touching. The one thing I found immediately interesting was the fact that in this room Billie wasn't the leader. She didn't even pretend to be. She voiced her same old complaints—guys on campus never listened to us and girls on campus were too docile—but this room was strictly an egalitarian space, and Billie took that seriously.

The topics were not clothes, makeup, and guys. This was about us and what we, as women, wanted. It was about patriarchy as a political institution. How it kept women down, kept us silent, held us back, on our backs or in the kitchen or barefoot and pregnant. We talked about popular culture—how movies, television shows, and advertising perpetuated the image of women as objects. Were women only concerned about laundry stains and spotty dishes? Why, in so many situation comedies, like *My Three Sons* and *Family Affair*, was the mother dead, leaving a father or uncle to parent rambunctious kids? Only men could be main characters?

Willow, a girl who wore a purple poncho all the time, showed us an ad for Tipalet cigarettes. A man blew smoke in a woman's face, with the slogan, *Blow in her face and she'll follow you anywhere.* What woman wants smoke blown in her face? Willow pointed out that the image implied women were foolish enough to follow a man just because he had a nice, cherry-smelling cigarette. The other Tipalet ad was a woman with a cigarette in her mouth and the man standing behind her. The slogan was: *Give her your Tipalet and watch her smoke.*

"Sexual innuendo," Willow said. "It's all about making a woman into a sex object."

Billie said, "I understand, sister. There's so much work to do, on ourselves, as young women in America."

I remembered seeing that ad in a *Time* magazine.

Willow held up ad after ad, denouncing each as sexist.

Love's Baby Soft. Woman in a white dress, with a lollipop up to her lips. *Because innocence is sexier than you think.* Women should remain little girls.

National Airlines. A picture of a smiling stewardess. *I'm Jo. Fly Me.* Fly me implies fuck me.

Delmonte Ketchup. *You mean a woman can open it?* Women aren't strong.

Women portrayed in kitchens, on the hoods of cars, in bathing suits next to a man fully clothed, with an iron in her hand, with a baby in her arms—the messages subtle but effective.

The Virginia Slims slogan—*You've come a long way, baby*—I had thought of it as catchy. But now I knew that calling women *baby* was just another way to sexualize us, to keep us young and infantile.

I was reminded of Friedan's words, the ones she expressed so passionately, the ones I myself was too tentative to verbalize. With this group, I felt a connection. I was finally defining the woman I wanted to be.

In mid-January, Nixon announced the withdrawal of 70,000 troops from Vietnam. The vibe on campus was hopeful. Two weeks later, though, in a Tuesday night address, Nixon revealed that the U.S. had been conducting secret talks with North Vietnam, via Henry Kissinger. Cal became enraged. He stormed around the house, spewing about Nixon. "He's a liar, bargaining with the lives of young men!"

We were having one of our family dinners, a once-a-week gathering Billie had spearheaded. She made everyone commit to showing up and helping to cook. Spaghetti and meatballs was the main course that night. Billie chopped onions, I chopped tomatoes, Matt made the meatballs, and Reid peeled garlic for the bread.

The meal was *so* delicious—we were used to cafeteria food or pizza from Leonardo's. Cal was bouncing off the walls. He'd jump up, walk around the table, sit back down. He shoveled forkfuls into his mouth and got up again.

"Nixon doesn't care about peace. He just doesn't want to look like a weakling," Cal said.

"You're saying this whole war is about saving face?" Billie asked.

"I'm saying our protests aren't working."

He continued pacing. He mumbled and raked his fingers through his beard.

"We need something else to get O'Connell's attention," Reid said.

"If you're serious, I have some ideas," Matt said.

"What do you mean?" I said, popping a meatball in my mouth.

"At Case Western, we did other things. We didn't just burn draft cards. We burned flags and set fire to stuffed hawks—you know, like the war hawks in Washington."

"Groovy," Billie said.

"We set trash fires to hold off the pigs. Made Molotov cocktails. They may not have heard our words, but they sure heard our bombs."

"You know how to make a Molotov cocktail?" I asked. I had never heard any of these stories about Matt's years in Cleveland.

"It's not that hard, man."

"The FBI is on my ass. We can't get involved with any violence," Cal said.

He was convinced that because of his VVAW activities the FBI was monitoring his comings and goings. Black Suits, he called them, and he saw them everywhere. His room was bugged, he said, and the telephone tapped. He had told us that if anyone approached us with questions about him, we were not to answer.

"But I thought you just said what we were doing isn't working," Matt questioned.

"Fighting violence with violence? Not cool," Reid replied.

"I don't know. I just don't know." Cal shook his head.

"You don't always have to use them," Matt said. "They show you mean business."

Cal's intensity picked up speed. He paced faster. "The government is holding our troops hostage. Keeping our men over there with no plan is as bad as them being in POW camps." Then he swept his plate off the table, leaving a bloody tomato mess on the floor.

"And women," Billie chimed up. "There are women there. Maybe not on the frontlines, but at military hospitals. Nurses, for instance. Now I know nurses aren't considered *people* by *you* people, but they are over there."

She got a roll of paper towels and wiped the food off the floor.

Cal looked at her, down there on her knees cleaning up, and said, "Point taken."

There was no more discussion of trash fires or Molotov cocktails. There was only Cal, storming around the house, toppling everything within arm's length: a floor lamp, stacks of books, and full ashtrays.

Matt picked up the lamp. He clicked it on, but the filament was broken. We were all tired. Cal had worn us out. Reid lit a joint and passed it to him. He brushed it off, grabbed his army jacket, and left.

"Should someone go after him?" I asked.

"Nah, let him blow off some steam. He'll be back." Matt too a long drag.

Later, as Billie and I washed the dishes—somehow we were the only ones cleaning up— she asked, "Did you hear what Cal said? *Point taken.* It's like he just slapped me in the face."

"But he acknowledged you."

"Sure, he's learned to say as little as possible to me to shut me up. It's like he thinks that by just saying a few words he can placate me."

"What more do you want?"

"A voice. Equal representation in the movement."

"No, you want the podium," I said.

"You're right. The podium, that's what I want. I want to be off the pedestal and behind the podium."

Were we just groupies to their protest movement? I hoped not. I wanted to be on the podium, too. Why did I remain silent? Why did I stand around thinking the guys would invite us up or hand us the microphone? No, we had to take it. Billie was right to want her voice heard. No, she had *a right* to have her voice heard. We both did.

I spent that night at The Terrace. When Matt and I were alone in his bedroom, I lit candles and the room grew serene, glow-y. We were snuggled under a blanket.

"Do you think Cal's being watched by the FBI?" I whispered.

"Just because we're not Berkley or NYU, our passions are real," he said. "We're part of the movement and we're a threat."

"I'm not questioning anybody's passion. I'm with you. It's just sometimes, he seems, I don't know, over the top."

"That's just Cal. He's intense."

To me, Cal was more than intense. I had never seen any black cars parked out in front of The Terrace. I had never seen any men in suits wondering around, asking questions. His obsession, I worried, bordered on paranoia.

The next morning, Matt left earlier for his work-study job. I made myself a cup of tea and got back into bed. I thought I'd study, but conjugating French verbs just made me sleepy. There was a tattered paperback copy of *The Lottery and the Draft: Where Do I Stand?* on Matt's floor. It was a book that floated around the house, from coffee table to kitchen counter to the tank of the toilet in the bathroom. Cal thumbed through it often. For him, it was a bible. He could recite whole paragraphs. He used it as a reference when kids from Gainesville came over for advice.

I leaned over and picked it up. I read about the Selective Service classifications. In the past, I had paid little attention to Cal talking about two-S, five-F and one-A-O. They sounded like algebra equations and math wasn't my strong suit. I never cared about solving for X. But now it was important. I needed to know how to solve this equation of who went to war and who didn't. It might not affect me, but it affected almost every guy in this house, in this institution. Reid, Matt, and Paul were on student deferments. II-S status, as written in the book. The military loved Roman numerals.

I read about the year of vulnerability. Vulnerability—I had also heard that word when Cal and Reid counseled kids. I hadn't thought of it as having anything, technically, to do with the draft. I thought it was just a feeling, an emotion all those boys felt as their eighteenth birthdays loomed. A fear, really. Once you signed the Selective Service papers, your life was out of your hands.

Who was vulnerable? Everybody, it turned out, was vulnerable for a year after he registered, unless he had some of kind deferment. Of course, student deferments were temporary. After they ended, the year of vulnerability picked up again. The book gave the examples of two guys, Louis Luckless and Willy Winner. They both had student deferments, but Louis, poor Louis—his draft number was two. He was doomed. When his deferment ended, his year of vulnerability began. His number was low, so he was more likely to be drafted.

Willy Winner had a high lottery number, 355. He was lucky. After he graduated from college, his chances of being called up were slim.

Reid's number was 207. The randomness of the lottery system created fear and uncertainty. What were the odds Reid would be drafted after he graduated? More math I didn't want to think about. There were so many variables. In fact, there was a section in the book on variables and a section on predictions, the gist of which was, there is no predicting. It was pure luck.

The real question was, who wasn't vulnerable? The answer: vulnerability ended only after you turned twenty-six. What would happen to Reid and Matt in May? I was having so much fun, the months had slipped away.

I threw down the book and went to find Reid. Stacy and Billie were in the living room, playing gin rummy. Billie had a cigarette hanging between her lips, smoke curling through her halo of hair.

"Where's Reid?"

She nodded toward the kitchen, and he came out carrying a bowl of potato chips. He had three beer cans tucked between his forearm and belly.

"Hey, sis," he said.

"Are you eligible to be drafted after you graduate?"

"Yes," he said.

"Why didn't you tell me?"

"Tell you? Come on, Celeste, what do you think this is all about? All of us are eligible when we graduate. Matt, Paul. And it's not just about us. It's about all those guys who come here and sit around that table. They don't have deferments. They're poor, they aren't in school."

"What can we do about this?" I asked.

"Exactly what we're doing, trying to stop the war," Reid said.

I knew all this intellectually—the way I knew time marched on, the days added up, and June would, eventually, arrive—but I hadn't absorbed it emotionally; in my gut, in my heart. What was going to keep Reid and Matt from being drafted?

"He can get me pregnant," Billie said, snuggling against Reid.

"You can do that?" I asked.

"Well, I know the mechanics." He pulled the tab off the beer and fizzy foam bubbled up.

Of course, I had seen that in the book. Fatherhood deferment: III-A.

"He can pretend to be crazy or gay," Stacy said.

Not qualified because of physical, mental, or moral standards: IV-F.

"He can shoot off a toe or cut off a pinky."

"That sounds good," I said, calculating which appendage to spare. "Baby toes are worthless."

They burst out laughing.

"Oh, my dear Cherry," Billie said. "You crack me up. So sweet. So naïve."

I had willed myself into a state of suspended belief. We would live here forever, lolling around on these couches, opening the treasure box, ingesting whatever mind-blowing substance was inside, and talking about how we were going to change the world. We would party, we would dance, we would move from bedroom to kitchen to living room. We would step over whoever had crashed on the floor and we would make coffee for him—or her, though it was usually a guy—and listen to the crazy night he had. Sure, I believed that the war needed to end and that our actions—joining our voices with those across the country—could be influential. I had been thinking about Cal and Parker and what they had been through, but I hadn't seen what was right in front of me: my brother and my boyfriend were approaching their year of vulnerability.

After that, every time I went to The Terrace, I looked around to see if a strange car was parked on the street or if I could spot men in black suits hiding in bushes. The only thing I noticed was an increase in the number of boys and young men coming to the house to talk with Cal and Reid. Instead of one or two, they came in groups.

They brought paperwork from the Selective Service and unopened envelopes from local draft boards. By not opening this correspondence, they pretended, for just a little longer, that the military wasn't coming for them. They weren't much older than I was, but they looked young and nervous, with faces that didn't even need shaving and chests that barely filled out their T-shirts. Cal and Reid sat with them at the dining room table, reading through the notices, making calls, agreeing to meet with their parents or a lawyer. Sometimes they had to deliver the bad news: this time there was no getting out of; you show up at the induction center on Monday morning or you'll be arrested.

They asked questions. Was it true that if they cut off a finger, they wouldn't have to serve? How hard was it to get across the Canadian border? How could they find a sympathetic doctor to give them a medical deferment? Could they go queer? How does one go queer?

Vets in Army fatigues also came. They sat around talking about their year in Vietnam. The jungles, the rain, the mosquitoes, the asshole CO's. They talked about the things they had done and the things they wished they had done, like disobeying orders. It reminded me of our women's group. They never shied away from opening up, no matter who was at the house.

Reid read to them from Walt Whitman, Rupert Brooke, Randall Jarrell, and Robert Lowell. The poetry of war. I liked listening to my brother. He went into a kind of trance. His voice sonorous, his cadence sharp. I pretended, if I were, say, on the couches studying, that we were alone and he was reading only to me. These days, we never got any time alone, just us. But my illusion didn't last long. Often, when Reid was done, the men cried, openly. Messy male snotty tears. Then I wouldn't be able to listen anymore and had to leave the house.

In March, the new issue of the *Florida Quarterly* came out. There on the first page was Reid's poem, published under the name Reid Layman.

The Blind World

Soil pit eyes
tear gas eyes
tear stained lies.
Rice fields blood stained
fields of death
fields of crosses
boots on hallowed ground.

Razor wire cut, napalm smut
smug mug hawks.
Burn the flesh, burn the flag.
Stars and stripes
stars over rice paddies
over stars under soil
silver star pinned under
soil silver with blood
blinding us all.

I walked over to The Terrace to see if he was home. I wanted to congratulate him. I also wanted to talk to him again about what he was going to do in the coming months. The house was quiet. The only person in the living room was a guy I didn't know asleep on the La-Z-Boy.

Reid was in his room at his desk. There were books all over the floor at his feet and he was frantically typing.

"So, Reid Layman, how does it feel to be a published poet?" I stuck my fist under his chin as if it were an interviewer's microphone.

"Ah, I see you've read the poem." He leaned back and stretched.

"I have. I can't say I understand it, but, hey, good job."

"What do you think of the pen name?"

"Now that I get. You're trying to be a regular guy. An *Everyman*." I picked up a book. "What are you working on?"

"An essay on Whitman." He grabbed the book away and read these lines out loud:

Henceforth I ask not good-fortune, I myself am good-fortune,
Henceforth I whimper no more, postpone no more, need nothing,
Done with indoor complaints, libraries, querulous criticisms,
Strong and content I travel the open road.

"Wow, that's beautiful," I said. "What's it from?"

"A poem called 'Song of the Open Road'." I don't know if you can hear it, but when I read it, I hear music, I hear a kind of melody that just—sorry, it sounds crazy, I know. It's just that I love his words."

He didn't sound crazy. He sounded like someone passionate about what he was studying. I admired that, but I wasn't about to tell him. It would go to his head and he was already too full of himself. Still, wasn't that why we were all here, to find the thing we would spend the rest of our lives doing?

"I can see why," I said.

I liked having my brother all to myself, even for a moment, and this moment reminded me of winter storms in Cheyenne, on the days school was canceled. We were allowed to watch television all day and the black-and-white of the screen matched the black-and-white out the window, everything drained of color by wind and snow. The whole universe was muffled and colorless. We were safe and warm.

"Listen," Reid said, "I can't talk now. I've got to finish this. It's due in the morning." He turned back to the typewriter.

I stepped out of the room, turned, and ran into Cal. Literally, I turned so quickly our foreheads slammed together. I bounced back against wall. Tears sprang into my eyes.

"Celeste, I'm sorry," Cal said. "Are you all right?"

I felt a knot beginning to form above my eyebrow. "I'm fine. Are you?"

"Sure. Come and sit down."

He led me into his room and I sat on his unmade bed. He went to get an ice pack. The room was a disaster. Clothes were everywhere, mounds on the floor and on his desk, as if for a whole year he had taken off whatever he had worn that day and left it where it landed. It smelled funky.

His desk was made out of a door—the door to his room, hinges still intact and facing out—stacked on cinder blocks. And there on the corner was a pile of dried and shriveled— what? They were oval, oval-ish, and had a beige-y, pink-y tint. I remembered the rumors about Vets bringing home human trophies, the ears of Viet Cong worn on a string around a neck.

Cal returned with a few cubes of ice in a smelly dishtowel. I put it to my forehead. He saw me looking at what I now thought could be human ears.

"Oh, yeah, well, we cut off ears and fingers all the time. We were crazy over there." He pounded his head like he was trying to pound out memories. He paced the room. "We killed babies, Celeste. We torched the place. We cut them open and pulled out their hearts and ate them."

I got his point—he was exaggerating, acting macho and psycho, like the war had really fucked with him.

"Cal," I said. "I'm sorry."

"They're apricots, you silly." He laughed. "Billie's always trying to get me to eat these things, says they're good for you. We had a food fight the other day. Guess I didn't clean up."

I laughed too, self-conscious relief. I had believed the stereotype and was ashamed. Didn't I know Cal well enough to know he wouldn't do something like that? I wasn't sure. We spent time together in the group—we weren't close personally. I had never asked him about his time in Vietnam. I was afraid to, because of my encounter with Parker. What could I possibly understand about his experience? Still, listening was something I could do.

"I know this is a little too late, but if you want to talk about it, I'm here."

He was direct. "We patrolled. We got into firefights. We survived. The truth is I killed some people. Nobody wants to hear that."

I apologized again. His mistrust was valid, based on experience. It must be alienating to be on this campus. There were a lot of veterans, but he lived in a house of mostly privileged kids who were on student deferment.

Over the next few weeks I wrote my papers, read my books. I ran between my room and Matt's bedroom. Sometimes I went to dinner with Kim. She was interested in getting involved with our demonstrations, but she was on probation—the Student Housing Board had taken notice of all those parties and she couldn't afford to lose her resident assistantship. It was how her parents afforded tuition.

Matt got a job at Leonardo's Pizza. He was behind on both tuition and rent. That put an end of our family dinners. Sometimes, I would go to The Terrace, crawl into his bed, and wait for him to return from work. He smelled of pepperoni and tomato sauce when he finally slid between the sheets. I pushed my ass against him and he hardened. He pushed into me. We rocked. We fell asleep with him still inside of me.

I continued to go to the Tuesday night women's meeting. Doreen was suspicious of the whole thing. One night when I was getting ready to go to the Union, she asked, "What do you do at these meetings anyway? Whose *conscious* are you trying to raise?"

She was sitting on her bed, drawing. She had joined the art club. Her medium was pastels and her once-pristine eyelet bedspread was covered in smears of pale green, blue, and orange.

"Why don't you come and see for yourself?" I teased.

"Here's the thing I don't get. If it's the guys with the problem—that's what you think, that they don't respect us—then why don't you bring in a bunch of guys and read them the riot act?"

"We're trying to get women to think about their lives without men. In spite of men. Get your own job. Have your own life. You don't have to depend upon a guy to be happy."

This was the first time we'd had a conversation about feminism. Since the purple martin told her to come back to school and embrace her time here—that bird she believed was her father—I wondered if she ever questioned what had all along seemed inevitable: her marriage to Dwight.

"Well, we need men. Unless you expect to do everything yourself. Mow the lawn *and* satisfy yourself. Sorry, but self-gratification is not for me. You certainly need them for children, and that's what life is all about."

"It doesn't have to be. Don't you want more than being a wife and mother?"

"I have Dwight and that's all I need," she said. "Anyway, you're all so hairy. Why don't you shave? Plus, I hear you sit around staring at your private parts in the mirror and tasting your own menstrual blood. Gross, gross, gross, and gross."

"That's ridiculous. First, we keep our clothes on, and second, some of us shave our legs." I wasn't one of them, but some did. "And third, we don't taste our blood. Gross."

Was that how other women on campus saw us, as hairy, masturbating, vagina-obsessed, blood-tasters? That made us sound like witches.

At the meeting, I listened more carefully to the discussion. I wanted to make sure we weren't really pagan worshippers. That night we talked about the movie *Carnal Knowledge*. A bunch of us had gone to see it over the weekend. The question on the table was: are you Candace Bergen or Ann-Margaret?

Bergen plays a strait-laced girl seduced by Jack Nicholson's character, a womanizer with no interest in marriage. He introduces her to his best friend, Art Garfunkel. He's sweet, passive. Just the kind of boy a proper woman in the 50s was expected to marry. Bergen does marry him and there's no passion in their relationship. Ann-Margaret is a good-time girl. She gets involved with Nicholson, and when he refuses to marry her, commits suicide. Both women ended up miserable and the audience ended up depressed. At least I did.

"Me, I'm the anti-Bergen," Rain said. She wore glasses that fell down on her nose and she constantly pushed them back up. Her legs were so hairy—dark black hair—that sometimes I couldn't take my eyes off them. Women's liberation aside, I wouldn't want to walk around with a blanket of fur on my legs. I definitely would have shaved. Okay, one of us was very hairy.

"Well, I'm a pro at getting as good as I give, but that was too much. That was giving away your soul," Billie said.

"Garfunkel's not my style," I said.

"Oh, he's mine," Willow said. "He's my dream husband."

I saw us veering toward a typical female rap session about men.

"If I had to decide between a mouse or a rat, I'd stay single," I said.

"That's what this is all about. Imagining a different kind of future than we've been told we have to have. We have choices."

"That's the whole problem with that and many movies. They give such narrow paths for us."

I learned, for the first time, about the virgin/whore split. I had, up until then, never known about this idea that men view women as one of these archetypes, and that they sleep with the whore but marry the virgin. I wondered if Matt thought of me this way. Was I Ann-Margaret, good enough to sleep with but not to marry?

"What do you expect," Rain said. "The movie was written by a guy."

At the end of the meeting, we stood in a circle and put our arms around each other in a big earth-mother group hug. No, we were definitely nothing like Doreen had described us.

Winter term ended. To celebrate, we went mushrooming. It was an annual event, Reid said. Not to be missed. Matt said it would blow my mind, but that was all he would say. He wanted me to have my own trip and if he told me too much, my expectations would get in the way.

When I showed up wearing tennis shoes they looked at me and said, "Are you sure you want to wear those?"

Cal had on galoshes, Matt and Reid had on hiking boots. Billie wore those horrible chunky shoes I teased her about.

"Why not? They're just shoes. Do I need to be wearing something special?"

"You'll see."

We thumbed out of Gainesville on Route 441. The first car to stop was a guy with a pick up. We jumped in the bed and enjoyed the ride. Matt and I sat with our backs against the cab, thigh to thigh, holding hands. The wind blew my hair around my face. After an hour on the road, Reid rapped on the back window of the truck and the driver stopped. We were in the middle of nowhere, between Gainesville and Micanopy. All around us nothing but cow pastures. And cows in those pastures.

"Which way?" I asked.

"There is no way. This is the place." Reid shimmied between two strands of barbed wire.

Everyone followed.

"Wait, where are you going?"

"Just come on," Matt said.

I climbed through the fence and was met with my first cow pattie. Luckily, it was hard and dry. This was why they had on boots. We tromped through the field. I took care to step over and around all the lovely surprises the cows left for us.

The cows watched us with bored interest. They chewed their cud. We didn't change their monotonous life in any way.

"What is a cud?" I asked.

"It's regurgitated food. From the cow's first stomach."

I had thought a cud was some kind of gum or something they had in their mouths. Like they chewed the sides of their cheeks all the time.

"Wait, cows have more than one stomach?"

"It's a good thing you're not a biology major, Cherry," Billie said.

Cal spotted the first clump of mushrooms. He bent to pick them, right from a fresh, fertile cow dropping.

"Yuck," I said.

"That's because you've never experienced the wonders of these little beauties."

"They're slimy and ugly and covered in shit," I said.

"It's just fertilizer," Reid said.

"Just wait, darling girl. You'll see."

I did see. Indeed, I did.

We found a cove of pines, far away from cows and cow patties, and settled in. Reid's backpack supplied a blanket, water thermos, crackers, and a box of figs. It was a picnic with the most boring food.

Cal made a fig sandwich, slipping a mushroom between two pieces of dried fruit. As unappetizing as it appeared, I fixed one for myself. The mushroom was a sour, soggy filling. Around it was a sweet, but grainy coating. I only had to eat one.

I saw globes of light. I saw, like a drunken Dumbo, pink elephants dancing on the back of a cow. No, they weren't elephants, they were feathers. Pirouetting, arabesque-ing, glissading feathers. No, they were butterflies, in pinks and purples and yellows, neon floating through the air, alighting on Cal and Matt's foreheads. One landed on my nose. I reached up to take it onto my finger, but instead I crushed it, the yellow smearing on my palm. I started to cry and then I laughed because suddenly my hands were yellow paintbrushes. Every time I moved them, they drew beautiful pictures in the air. Pictures of elephants and feathers and butterflies. My hands had been dipped into the phosphorescence of a lightning bug. I spun around, my hands making pictures. My hands were sparklers, drawing in the air, lighting the world on fire. My whole body turned yellow. I hugged everyone: Billie, dear friend Billie; my brother Reid, Reid, I love you so much; Cal, combustible but kind Cal; Matt, my one true light. I left my yellow body-print on each of these people. I hugged the trees. I plastered my yellow body against a pine and I was one with the pine. My feet planted firmly on the ground, my arms wide and tall and willowy. I was sap and bark, needle and cone.

The next thing I remembered: I puked up all the yellow in my body and I passed out. I woke up with dung and pine needles in my hair and didn't even care.

Spring on campus was beautiful. The trees leafed, turning a pale green. Azaleas and magnolias blossomed, pinks and whites and yellows. The air was warm but not humid. Everything looked brand new. There were so many activities and I wanted to do them all. I had made good grades, so it was time to slack off. Have some fun.

The Residence Halls Committee hosted the Spring Frolic, a Saturday of games like wheelbarrow and potato sack races. Matt and I partnered for the three-legged race and won first prize. We celebrated Earth Day by piling a bunch of seedlings into a grocery cart—Cal brought home the cart and we had no idea where he got it—and walking around campus, stopping to plant golden rain trees or red buds. We carried signs with antipollution slogans: L.A., DO YOU REMEMBER WHEN YOUR AIR WAS INVISIBLE? and IN THE AIR, IT'S A BIRD, IT'S A PLANE, IT'S SUPERSMOG!

John Ciardi read poetry at the Rathskeller. Senator McGovern spoke to a packed University Auditorium. The Carpenters played at the gym. We all went even though it wasn't our kind of music. We thought Karen and her brother were hokey but it was something to do. When we got there, we discovered we all knew every word to every song. Matt held me and we swayed to "Close to You." We went to see Mudcrutch at the auditorium, a band more our style. Billie and I instantly developed crushes on Mike Campbell and Tom Petty.

For a few weeks I was just a fun-loving student. Then it was May. Celebration ended and the reality of war was once again in the increasingly muggy air.

Ocean of Storms

The first week of May Neil Young was everywhere on campus. I couldn't walk down the dorm hallway without hearing his voice coming from behind a closed door. I couldn't walk to class without hearing his voice from a passing car. I couldn't pass the Plaza without someone strumming a guitar, trying to match his tenor. *Four dead in O-hi-o*. It was our anthem. The second anniversary of the Kent State and Jackson State shootings was days away. We got ready for the commemoration rally.

At The Terrace, we spent the Saturday before the rally cutting wood and nailing together planks to make dozens of crosses. They represented those from Gainesville who had died in Vietnam. Billie and I painted them white.

Paul was in charge of getting the list of events written up and into the newspaper: noon rally followed by a march to Van Fleet Hall, the ROTC building. We'd plant our crosses as part of a die-in. Later, at dusk, we'd hold a candlelight vigil at the Selective Service Office in downtown Gainesville.

Reid and Matt drafted the list of demands: get ROTC off campus once and for all; stop supporting the government by taking millions of dollars in defense contracts; open up the university's Foundation funds for public inspection.

On the morning of May 4, I ditched my classes. I slipped on my armband—the same kind Matt had been wearing that first day at The Terrace, with a white peace sign—headed to the Plaza.

A cloudy mist hovered over the proceedings. Any minute the sky might open up. There were hundreds on the Plaza. They filled the green and overflowed into the courtyard between Peabody Hall and Library East. They hung all over the Murphree statue, clambering for the top spot. My chest expanded with the sight of it all. This was the first rally to bring out so many. The biggest crowds I'd seen all year were for student president election speeches and the Earth Day plant-a-thon. I pushed closer to the platform stage, which was set up at the south end. Reid was up there, mic in hand.

"We're cowards," he said. "All of us. Yes, I mean you and me. I'm up here protesting the war, but still I ask myself, have I done enough? I'm one man. What can I do? I can raise my voice. I can urge all of you to raise your voices. Join us in the call to end the war. Show O'Connell we mean what we say. The worst cowards are in Washington and in the White House. Nixon and Kissinger and Abrams."

His strength as a speaker came from his direct appeal, his ability to display emotion. He used "I" instead of "us" and "them." He made you feel that if he could do it, so could you. If before today you hadn't done a thing to try to stop the war, it was okay. Now was the time.

Reid introduced Cal, but he needed no introduction. I doubted there was a student in the audience who didn't know Cal. He had spearheaded the draft card burning at Tigert Hall two years earlier. He had introduced Jane Fonda. He had been to the convention in Chicago. He had been arrested countless times. He had been highlighted in the article Paul wrote about the Vets fasting for Thanksgiving.

Cal's voice was thunder. It was a sound I was familiar with—so many nights listening to him rail against the government—and here, on this afternoon of high tension, in this public space, it took me by the shoulders and shook me. He was in your face—in my face.

"My fellow students, we live in an imperialist country, and this institution is part of that. This university is part of the problem. The military industrial complex is alive and well right here. President O'Connell takes millions from the government."

The crowd booed and Cal continued.

"That money goes to secret testing. For all we know, they're developing the next chemical weapon right over in our science labs. They think we don't know. But we know, we know. Your school takes the money and propagates the death of innocent women and children."

Boos mixed with jeers mixed with calls of "Make 'em pay, make 'em pay."

Cal turned over the bullhorn to Billie and the roar grew even louder. Billie—everyone knew her too. She strutted around, continuing to shout *Make 'em pay* until it was deafening. Then she finished up with a rousing call and response.

"Is this an unjust war?" she asked.

"YES-IT-IS!" we shouted back.

"Is this an immoral war?"

"YES-IT-IS!"

"Is this institution profiting from war?"

"YES-IT-IS!"

"Do you want to stop the war?"

"YES-WE-DO!"

"Do you want to stop imperialist practices?"

"YES-WE-DO!"

"Then follow me! We're going to Van Fleet. We're going to get warmongers off this campus. We're going to lay down our bodies!"

We carried our crosses high above our heads. We walked through campus and chanted. *Out now! Peace now!* At Van Fleet, we planted our crosses. Reid read *The Blind World* and two other poems I had never heard, and as he read, we each silently sank to the ground, falling in slow-motion, as if shot. Matt writhed on the ground. He moaned. I mimed a bullet to the leg, to the chest. I screamed until my lungs were hollow. Moans and screams came from all around me. Then, as planned, everyone went quiet. For the next half an hour, we lay motionless—dead. Around us, students milled, spread out, dispersed, nudged us to try to get us to move. We didn't. Police were several hundred yards away, ready to intercede if necessary.

The clouds opened and sun heated the grass, my shoulders. As I lay there, I thought of Parker, his fear of fireworks, the story he had told me about the pregnant woman. I thought of Cal and the apricots I mistook for trophy ears. He knew I believed the worst about him, believed he was someone who could do that. He played along. He wanted to scare me, to make me think he was crazy.

I could never know what it was like to be in war, in this particular war—that was what both Parker and Cal had told me. *You have no idea.* I didn't, but what I couldn't do, didn't want to do, was be passive. I had to further embrace my activism, and to do so I had to acknowledge the advantages we had within the secure walls of the university, a comfortable cocoon. We were middle class, as white as our crosses. The men had student deferments. The women—we had gender on our side.

The following Monday night we were all together at The Terrace. The Rolling Stones were on the turntable and Nixon was on television. We were splayed on the couches, a pitcher of cranberry rum punch on the coffee table. My belly was warm with the glass I had already downed. A joint was making its way around the room. When it came to me, I took a drag and held the smoke as long as my lungs could take. I passed it to Cal. Reid was next to Billie, his arm around her.

We had begun the evening expectant. Nixon was giving yet another national address and maybe, just maybe, he had seen the error of his wicked tricky ways and he would finally say, *No more talks between the United States and North Vietnam. No more seven-point peace plan that isn't working. We're leaving Vietnam.*

After nearly five minutes of the same old *blah blah blah*, we had tuned out and turned down the sound. Mick Jagger's voice permeated the room. The camera tightened on Nixon's face—large, bumpy. He had a patch of sweat at this left temple. Matt threw pretzels at the screen, bopping him on the nose.

"Look at his hands," Billie said. "Those are the hands of a murderer."

Just then Paul came in. He had been at the newspaper office and UPI was reporting that Nixon had announced he was mining all major ports to North Vietnam in an effort to stop the supply of arms. We would also continue air and naval strikes.

"Turn it up, you goons," he said. "You're missing it."

We heard only the final snippets of his speech. *You want peace, I want peace … at this moment we must stand in purpose and resolve … an enemy that has shown utter contempt for every overture of peace we have made.* Reid was shouting, "No, no, man, you're the one showing contempt," and Cal was shouting, "We haven't offered peace. We've offered dead babies and burning villages," and Mick was singing, "Gimme, gimme me shelter."

I threw my plastic cup at the television screen. Punch splattered on Nixon's forehead and oozed down his cheeks: sweat made real; tears he never wept.

"What does this mean?" Billie asked.

Cal picked up a handful of markers from the floor, markers we used to make posters. He drew a map of Vietnam on the living room wall, beginning with the physical outline in black. The country was shaped like a large comma, inserted between Laos and Cambodia (he filled those in with brown) and the South China Sea (he slashed that with blue scribbles). He called it a comma monster. At the center of its head was the eye—Hanoi. He colored it purple.

He kept drawing, filling the whole south wall with the rivers, the mountains, the forests of Southeast Asia. I was surprised he could do this freehand and by heart. He knew the country well enough, had studied it not just from the inside—while he was there—but from the outside—in books, on maps. He wanted us to understand just as deeply as he did. I had never seen Cal quite like this. His body moved lithely and confidently.

"Mining means bombing, you know that, right?" Cal said. "This is a policy of death. He's just killed 10,000 more American lives."

In Nixon's final comment, he asked for the support of the nation, his "countrymen," and said, "Our purpose is not to expand the war, not to escalate the war, but to end the war."

I looked at the television. Walter Cronkite, a talking head, was parsing Nixon's speech. His face was splotchy with dried punch. While his lips were moving, he wasn't saying a damn thing.

That night all my dreams were full of images of Nixon, his smarmy face with sweat cascading off his chin. The next morning over coffee and toast—Billie was the cook—Cal said we needed to march over to Tigert Hall and demand that O'Connell publicly condemn the mining of Haiphong Harbor.

As we walked, chanting *No more war, No more bombs*, we picked up others. By the time we stationed ourselves in the hallway outside President O'Connell's office, there were at least a hundred of us, with more students spilling down the stairs and out the door. Crammed in, shoulder to elbow, thigh to knee. For five hours. My butt hurt. My toes were cramping. I had a headache and I wanted to eat. I was dreaming about a cheeseburger.

Four campus cops blocked O'Connell's office door. When they first arrived, their puffed-up chests and crossed arms were menacing. Now, like me, they were slouchy, two of them leaning back against the wall, trying to take a load off their tired feet and aching backs. They weren't frightening at all. We could push right past them if we wanted.

A half dozen other police paced the perimeter of the hall. They too waited for O'Connell, but they were waiting to see when or if they could arrest us. Reid was standing by the office door, talking with Cal and Paul.

When O'Connell finally opened his office door, he looked haggard. He was tall and thin, with a beak nose and a long face, deeply wrinkled. He said he would talk with a representative. Reid and Cal went into his office. Billie and I pressed against the door to see if we could hear anything.

After only ten minutes, they returned to the hall. O'Connell said they had a fine talk and he asked us to file out quietly. He didn't want anyone to get hurt.

"What did he say?" Matt asked.

"Same old thing," Cal said. "He's just trying to get rid of us. Saying what we want to hear so we'll go home."

More police arrived and told us to clear the hallway. We were a fire hazard.

"Let's go, folks," one of the cops said. "You want peace, let's have a peaceful exit."

They hustled us down the stairs. Outside, there were more cops, cops in the same beige uniforms, but with billy clubs and in helmets, with mirrored sunglasses so we couldn't see their eyes. I had never noticed how not seeing a person's eyes made them ominous, unreadable. One of them pushed Cal and he fell on the final set of steps.

"Filthy pig," Cal said, jumping up, shoving into the cop's face.

"Filthy punk," the cop said. He had a dark and overgrown moustache that hid his lips.

"I'm gonna sue this university. I know my civil rights."

"I think you're mistaken, young man. You tripped."

They were nose to nose, spit flying between them.

Matt pulled Cal away, but Cal broke free and scrambled onto the parapet above the stairs.

"Hey, did you see that? These pigs just pushed me down."

It was hard to hear him with so many students shouting at the cops. Matt handed up the bullhorn and Cal continued, his voice loud, clear. He urged us to surround Tigert Hall, to link arms and create a human chain that no pigs could break. I slipped my arms through Billie's and Stacy's and soon everyone was connecting, forming a circle around the building.

I remembered Abbie Hoffman and his call for protesters to levitate the Pentagon. At the time I thought it was silly, but here, now, it seemed that if hundreds of interlocking arms could enclose the building, we might contain the malevolence. Quarantine it inside. Only voices for change would be let out into the world.

My hands shook—I hadn't realized I was scared until I saw them—and I locked my fingers, not only to keep them still but also to keep the cops from breaking them apart. We sang, "One, two, three, four, we don't want your fucking war!" Two cops were pinned inside the circle, up against the brick corner of the building. Stacy and Billie taunted them.

"Sooey, little piggie. Are you in your filthy sty? You dirty pigs."

The cop with the bushy moustache, took out his billy club and slapped it against his palm, a threat, as if to say, *One blow and you'll be down.*

Cal urged us, walking around with bullhorn to lips. "We've almost made it, people. Almost there. Don't give in, don't give up."

The other cop came right up to Billie and slapped her. She was stunned and then spit in his face. He grabbed for her, but she twisted away and ran. Our link in the circle broke apart. I heard sirens and a line of Gainesville police cars pulled up and parked on the grass. Up until now, we had been dealing only with campus police.

"It's time to take over these streets and show this town that we mean business!" This was Reid. He now had the bullhorn. "Not business as usual, but the business of war at home!"

Cal crossed the green and ran onto 13th Street. We followed, dashing around and between cars. Now that we were all jammed into one block in front of Tigert Hall, I saw that our numbers had doubled, tripled even. Hundreds of students were bringing the traffic to a standstill.

Thirteenth Street bordered the eastside of campus. It was a main thoroughfare, lined with campus buildings and apartment complexes. Horns blared. Exhaust spewed. Students hung out of windows, sent calls of encouragement. The atmosphere, at the beginning, was festive. Someone in one of the apartments put a speaker against the screen and blasted the Stones. People danced. Some kids walked around with guitars, singing Bob Dylan.

The jubilance was brief. More cops arrived, in full riot gear, helmets replaced by gas masks, making them more menacing. They walked in a line down the street, trying to force us off so traffic could pass. We had nothing to defend ourselves with, except what was within reach—rocks, sticks, clumps of cracked asphalt. Someone threw full cans of soda that splashed and fizzed against shields. Other spontaneous weapons: bottles, books, a slingshot. Cal picked up a trash can and hurled it.

I had a rock in each hand when the first tear gas canister lobbed over our heads. It landed on the west side of 13th Street. I didn't close my eyes or hold my breath fast enough. The gas entered my throat and I couldn't breathe. The second canister was sent in the other direction. It forced us to turn around. The strategy, I saw too late, was to corral us in one place.

Coughing, sneezing, with burning eyes, I stumbled and everyone kept going, right over me. I crawled toward the only landmark I could think of, the Krystal's restaurant on 1st Avenue. I managed to just get myself deeper into the crowd. I was kicked in the ribs, and when I tried to get to my feet, I was kneed in the chin. I bit my tongue and blood filled my mouth. The butt of a billy club landed in my gut. I was down again. Everything went silent. I knew, intellectually, that the air was churning with noise. Rocks against shields, shrieks, heckling, boots on asphalt. I heard nothing.

I looked for Reid, for Matt, for Billie. I didn't see them or anyone I knew. The protest had taken a life of its own, apart from us, the initial organizers. It wasn't what we had planned, but there was power in numbers. I called out. My voice echoed through the crowd, a whisper, a squeak.

Even though I could barely see, I ran. It was a half-mile back to the house. Once I crossed over to the north side of University Avenue, the crowds thinned out. I dashed behind the gas station and came out in a part of the neighborhood I recognized. I turned left, right. I spit out blood. I ran my tongue around my mouth to make sure I had all my teeth. I touched the spike of a chipped upper molar.

At The Terrace, the living room was full of students, battered, bleeding, bruised, crying tear gas tears. They gulped water and complained about the pigs. Paul was on the couch. He cradled his wrist, bone pushing against skin. It was swelling and turning purple. His glasses were broken and falling off his nose. He didn't seem to notice.

"You need to get to the hospital," I said.

"I feel like I'm going to pass out. I can't get off the couch." He slumped left and closed his eyes. That was where I wanted to be, in deep sleep so that nothing hurt anymore.

I found Stacy in the kitchen, bandaging some guy's forehead. She had a regular Florence Nightingale station set up at the table. Students leaned against the counter, waiting their turn.

"How did you get back so soon?"

She shrugged. She dabbed hydrogen peroxide on my lips and on the scrapes on my face and upper arms. She filled a glass with half water, half hydrogen peroxide.

"Rinse your mouth."

"Yuck," I said.

"Do it," she said.

I did. The stuff fizzed in my mouth, burned at the site of the cut. I spit out blood-tinged hydrogen peroxide.

In Matt's bedroom, I stripped to my bra and underwear and crawled into bed. I was crying and my stomach hurt. I would wait here for the others. When I heard them, I would get up, learn what happened to them. Where were they? Had they been arrested? Images carouseled in my mind. I tried to pinpoint where it had gone wrong. The moment it turned from peace to pandemonium. I remembered the rock in my hand—I didn't remember reaching for it. I saw a cop coming at me with a billy club. I saw my palm full of dirt and rocks. That gesture, my arm raised, releasing the rocks, kept flashing in my mind. I wrapped myself in the sheets and I fell asleep.

I woke up blind. I tried to open my eyes, but they were stuck together. Crusty sleep, tear gas residue, and dust had created a glue. I rubbed them. My vision fuzzed into clarity. Matt was next to me in bed, his arm across his face. I leaned down and kissed him, but he didn't wake. There was a purple bruise on his elbow. Two guys I didn't know were on the floor. I nearly stepped on them when I got up. My legs felt weak. I made my way—slow, sloggy—to the living room.

Reid, Billie, and Cal were crashed on the couches. They too had bruises marking their flesh. Billie looked like she might be getting a black eye. I had no idea what they had been through or what time they returned. Paul was nowhere to be found. I hoped he had gone to the infirmary. Stacy came out of the kitchen with a pot of tea.

"Want some?" she asked.

The hot water stung my tongue and the gums around the broken molar.

She handed me two newspapers, *The Florida Alligator* and *Gainesville Sun*.

"You've already been out?"

"What can I say, I'm an early riser." She laughed. "You realize it's almost eleven."

The article in the *Alligator* was written by Paul. His headline, *Antiwar Demonstration Rips UF*, was accompanied by two photographs, one showing a guy lying on the ground, his face covered in blood, and one of a woman being carried by cops by her arms and legs. Both were unidentified and I didn't recognize either.

The *Gainesville Sun* headline read: *200 Arrested in AntiWar Protest*. Students had been charged with disorderly conduct and unlawful assembly, both misdemeanors. One student had been arrested for trying to run an officer over with a car. He was charged with a felony, intent to commit murder. We had been up against eighty state troopers, fifty city police, and fifty sheriff's deputies. How had they arrived so quickly?

Anticipating another night of "unrest," the mayor was calling for help from around the state, another hundred police officers were expected to arrive today. *Unrest*, such a prim word for what had happened. I felt rage—clinched teeth, heat simmering at the back of my throat. I began to sweat, my hands sticking to the newsprint.

And we weren't alone in our unrest or our rage. All over the country students were responding to Nixon's announcement. Thousands at Michigan State took over the busiest intersection in East Lansing. At the University of Minnesota, protesters were sprayed with pepper gas from a helicopter. Amherst College, University of California, University of South Florida, Yale, Princeton: they all had held protests.

I noticed, below this article, at the bottom of the page, a piece of news six lines long, as if it were a passing fact: The Selective Service was calling up another 9,000 men. Men with draft numbers 1 through 35.

Another rally was slated for early afternoon. We only had two hours to get ready. I woke everyone up. Matt made coffee while Billie and I cooked breakfast. After, we gathered our supplies to make signs: poster board, paint, stakes. We were tired and subdued, but then Reid put on Deep Purple and we grooved through our work.

Billie told me what had happened to her and the others. They had gone to one of the apartment buildings to get more trash cans and had been cornered by two cops. Cal created a diversion, going crazy, charging and kicking at the cops, so everyone else could get away. Cal himself had finally crawled through the underbrush and escaped.

"What happened to you?" she asked.

"Some pig got me good. Then I ran home. I tried to wait up for you guys." I had fallen asleep crying. Not from the pain, but from anger, how we were treated by the cops. Now I resolved to get revenge.

My first sign said GET YOUR DICK OFF MY PEACE, a reference to Tricky Dick Nixon.

"Whoa, Cheery," Billie said.

"What, don't you get it?"

"Oh I get it, but it's a little over the top."

"What you mean is I'm not your little cheerleader cheery fuck face cherry bomb?"

I had no idea what I was saying. I was tired and my whole body throbbed.

"You've changed, girl," Billie said. Her sign read WOMEN UNITE AGAINST THE WAR.

I tore up mine, grabbed another placard, and wrote BANISH PHALLIC IMPERIALISTS.

"Is that okay with you?"

"Settle down," she said.

"No, Billie, we can't settle down. We're under attack," I said. "Now, let's go."

She followed without another word.

By the time we got to the Plaza, there were more students, and cops, than the day before. They were fanned out around the green, in full riot gear. Evidence of last night's protest was everywhere. Toppled trashcans spilling litter. Street signs were bent. Shrubs were pulled up by their roots around the library.

Stuart Burgess, Blue Key president, had commandeered the microphone. His pitch: as long as the rally remained peaceful, the police wouldn't interfere. That was bullshit and we knew it. I looked at the nearest cop. He rocked on his heels, one hand on the nightstick holstered at his hip. He scanned the crowd. Sun glared off his helmet shield. His twitchy stance coupled with Burgess's arrogant grin made bile rise in my throat. I remembered the feeling I had the night before, running home, thinking how it felt when that cop knocked me to the ground. His face was pure evil. He wanted me gone. Not dead, but taken care of. Away. Burgess had been like that at the banquet we crashed in October with Betty Friedan. He wanted women, especially, to know their place and stay in it.

"The police will keep their promise. You should too," Burgess repeated.

"Why should we?" shouted Matt. "No leader in this country keeps his promise."

The crowd reacted in unison. "Yeah, why should we?"

"Calm down," Burgess said.

"We will not calm down," Matt said. "Silence is consent. O'Connell has to speak out. He has to go on record that the university is against the war."

The crowd rang out: *No more silence. No more silence.*

"You, Burgess, you get down. Get off the stage."

Get down. Get down. Get down.

Cal jumped to the platform and took the mic away from Burgess. "We're here to show the people of Gainesville that this minor inconvenience is nothing compared to what the people of Indochina are experiencing," he said.

I dropped my sign and stepped up next to Cal. He gave me the microphone. I didn't have time to hesitate or think about what I was going to say. I wanted another confrontation. It was exhilarating to be out here again, to use voice and body for our cause.

"This war is evil. Each day hundreds of boys are losing their lives. We're bombing innocent civilians. If we stay silent, we're no better than Nixon and Abrams. We're no better than O'Connell. We need to let this city hear our voices. We need to take over the streets again."

With our fists in the air, Cal and I chanted *Take the streets.* Soon everyone was with us. *Take the streets. Take the streets.*

Burgess called for restraint, but no one heard him. Without the mic, his voice was drowned out.

"When Nixon shows restraint, so will I," Cal said. He picked up a rock and threw it into the line of police officers. It ricocheted off a shield and hit another officer. Cal laughed and threw another one.

We moved, as if on cue, as in sync as if we were one unit, toward the administration building. I reclaimed my sign and we marched over to Tigert. We still wanted to hear from O'Connell. He had made no statement other than the one asking us to remain calm, which was in fact just another ploy to silence us.

Matt was behind me and he put his arms around me. "Stay safe," he said. "This is going to get messy."

Take the streets. Take the streets.

"Don't worry about me," I said. "I can take care of myself."

What do we want? Peace! When do we want it? Now!

It was at first organized chaos—students once again spreading out over the lawn in front of Tigert, spilling into the street, stopping traffic, banging on the hoods of cars, kicking tires—then it was just chaos. A wall of police officers awaited us. Again, rocks and sticks were our ammunition. Theirs, it turned out was, instead of tear gas, water. Two fire engines screamed up the street. We backed away, but too late. The force of jet spray stung my skin. We huddled in a group, our backs facing out, keeping the spray on less vulnerable parts. It felt like being pelted by buckets of gravel.

We ran out of the stream, ran north, toward the intersection of 13th and University Avenue. This was the same place we had performed our Guerilla Theater during the Homecoming parade. Here the traffic was heavier, but we ran between cars, pounding trunks, shouting, *No more war* and *Take the streets*. Horns blared.

Police on horseback wove through the cars as well, chasing us away. We gathered on the south end, by the gas station. Certainly they wouldn't ignite tear gas so close to fuel. We barricaded the street with anything we found. Benches, boxes, branches, trashcans, a folding chair from one of the houses close by.

We held the corner, keeping the police at bay with rocks, for maybe an hour. I was still in pain from the day before and each time I threw a rock those tender spots on my shoulder and hips flared. I had a kind of a tracking vision—any movement caught my eye and I was on it, able to tell if the target was friend or foe. If friend, I held back. If foe, I hit my mark every time. Shield, helmet. Bam, bam. Adrenaline inflamed my veins. I felt a zap of pain that gave my arm Superwoman and Wonder Woman strength—double the super-power strength.

At sunset, they came at us full force. Clubs swinging. Horses with flared nostrils, stomping hooves. Tear gas bombs. I pulled the bandanna over my mouth and nose. Reid got a club on the side of his head. Cal was kicked in the face by a horse. Matt helped him up. He grabbed me and all three of us ran.

Clothes still wet, we arrived home bruised and bloody. I had a cut over my right eye, a growing knot on the back of my head and skinned knees and palms. I didn't care. We had escaped again. I was energized.

It was two in the morning. Paul was at the dining room table typing up an article—one-handed, since he still had a splint on his left wrist.

He had heard that the police were handcuffing anyone they caught, putting them on buses, and taking them to jail. Now the jails—both city and county—were overcrowded. There was no place to house everyone arrested. The buses just drove around the city for hours. He had also heard stories of abuse by cops: beating innocent bystanders and reporters.

Everyone collapsed on the floor or the couches. I couldn't sit still.

"That's what we should do," Billie said. "Tomorrow night—I mean tonight—we get arrested. We'll cram their jails so full they have to give in."

"But it's not the pigs we want to give in. It's the university," I said. There was a tear in my jeans, at the thigh, and as I walked around the room, I pulled at it, making it larger.

"But the pigs will put pressure on O'Connell," Billie said.

"We're thinking too small," Matt said. "We need to fight fire with fire."

I stared at Cal's Vietnam map. Over the past few weeks, he had been expanding it. Now the whole wall was a portrait of Southeast Asia. He had added other materials to create a relief. Paper sacks had been ripped, molded, and spray painted into mountains. Blue pipe cleaners were twisted into rivers. Cities were labeled with words and letters snipped from the newspaper. Cambodia was red and the corner crease ran right up the middle of the country that Nixon vowed we had not invaded. Cal had created a work of art.

"He's right. We need to make a statement," I said. "They'll just keep on with the pepper spray and the hoses."

"Tonight and the next night and the next, we can spend all day and all night on the streets of this town and O'Connell isn't going to budge. He needs proof that we're serious," Matt said. "Did you see those students dancing? They think this is a party."

"Maybe the first night they did, but not now," Billie said. "All those students in jail, you think they're not serious?"

"I'm ready. We need to make the Molotov cocktails," I said.

"It's too dangerous. The FBI will be all over us," Cal said.

"What do you think, Reid?" I asked.

Reid was the only one who could, if he wanted, change Cal's mind.

"What if every cop out there, every administrator on campus, including O'Connell, stopped defending the hawks? What if they joined us? We could all walk down University Avenue together. Peacefully. That's my vision."

I didn't want to listen any longer. I wanted action.

In Matt's room, I sat on the bed. With both hands, I ripped the leg right off my jeans. I tried to visualize O'Connell coming out of his office, picking up one of our abandoned signs—one that said STOP THE FUCKING WAR!—and leading the rally right down the middle of 13th Street. That would be progress. If I took this ideal further, I imagined Abrams standing at a podium saying, "We will bring every one of our troops home. Today!" Nixon would make an announcement, finally admitting he had been wrong. No more war. No more draft.

As it was—in reality, in the world where men with draft numbers 1-35 had to report to their local board by June—the government was both withdrawing troops and calling up more men. How could this be? Cal believed Nixon was saying all the right things, the soundbites that America wanted, but was secretly planning more attacks. I realized I had never asked Matt about his draft number. Like those boys who came to The Terrace afraid to open envelopes from Selective Service, I was afraid to know.

When he came into the room and sat beside me, I asked. His response was defeatist. *What does it matter?*

"Of course, it all matters. Why else are we doing this? In the big picture, it matters. Don't you see?"

"I see pretty clearly, Celeste. My number is forty-seven." His birthday was July twenty-sixth.

"That means—"

He cut me off. "Don't say it. Like I said, I know what it means. It means none of us really have a choice. The government has us by the nuts. They own us. In a month, we'll be spit out of this institution and into another. The United States Armed Services."

"I think we should do it," I said, standing up.

"What?"

"The Molotov cocktails. We should make them for tonight."

This was a cause worth making a statement, even if that statement included violence. I was ready to put my life on the line to stop the killing, stop the war. I went to Matt's chest of drawers, gathered a bunch of T-shirts and ripped them into rags. He lined up all the bottles in the house on the edge of the bathtub. We dipped the rags in a mixture of motor oil and turpentine, stuffing them into the bottles.

Billie came in to use the bathroom. "What in the hell are you doing?"

What had she accomplished simply by being a loud-mouth? I admired that she stood up for herself with these guys and she made herself into a one-woman wrecking ball, but it was time for more than words. Sure, she wanted to be up on the podium. But did she want to get down in the mud and muck of the fight? The real fight. We had to show them the truth. *Them* was O'Connell and his side-kick, Provost Hale. *Them* was the police and guardsmen. *Them* was Nixon and the others in Washington. There was something larger at stake: The 50,000 dead Americans in Vietnam and 70,000 men still there, used by Nixon as a bargaining chip.

"Either help or get out," I said.

"Well, you're no longer cheery or a cherry," she said.

I no longer wanted to be like the boy at the Pentagon placing carnations in the rifles of Guardsmen. I wanted bottles filled with fire.

Billie pulled Reid into the bathroom.

"This is what you wanted," I said to him. "A true revolution. You can't do that playing nice, which is what we've been doing."

Reid looked at Matt.

"Hey, talk to your sister, man," Matt said. "All her idea."

"We have to fight back. I'm not going to lie down and be tear gassed again."

"We have to show strength," Matt said. "It's the only way."

"It's your way," Reid said. "Not mine. If you're planning to bring these tonight, don't come. I mean it."

They left and Matt kissed me. We smelled like turpentine. The skin on my fingers tingled. We washed our hands in the sink, sharing a bar of soap. It slipped from my hand to his. Suds bubbled on my forearm. I lathered his hands and our fingers linked and unlinked. His thumb dipped and dove and I chased it with mine until we were playing the thumb game and laughing. He took an old nail toothbrush and cleaned under my nails.

Our hands twined and twirled, and for a moment, looking at our coil of arms and fingers I couldn't tell where mine ended and his began. Without toweling dry, without turning off the water, Matt pushed me into the bedroom, onto his bed. With his wet fingers, he opened my body. I heard the water still running and I felt submerged. I let Matt cover me, rock me like a wave, roll me. With each motion a part of me stung—tender bruises, sore bones—but I also hummed, my thighs, my nipples. Matt came and I came and I didn't think or feel anything other than a contented ache.

We slept in. When I finally woke, my legs were weak and my arms achy. The bottles were in a milk crate in the corner of the room. I needed a shower and clean clothes. I told Matt I would meet him at the protest later. He'd have to bring the bombs.

I walked across campus, passed the libraries and Century Tower. The Plaza was scattered with debris of yesterday's speeches. Flyers blowing across the grass. Placards with broken sticks leaning against tree trunks. I stopped in front of the auditorium. I had stood here back in September, the *F Book* in my hands, taking in the history and tradition of the university, innocent, the whole school year in front of me. Now, classes were going on as usual, students hurrying from one building to another. I had been one of those students, always making sure I went to class and always on time. I no longer felt innocence or reverence, not since I'd had the shit kicked out of me by the pigs.

The dorm was business as usual. Girls heading to and from the bathroom, to and from each other's rooms. Some of them looked at me askance. I was disheveled, my clothes torn and smeared with dried blood. When I opened the door, Doreen jumped up and grabbed me.

"Where have you been? Well, I know where you've been, but your parents have been calling and calling."

I knew this would happen, our parents finding out about the protests on the news.

"Don't worry about it." My tone was dismissive.

"I am worried. You're crazy. You're all crazy. And you look like hell. It's all gone too far."

"My brother might be going to war soon, Doreen. What's too far to stop that?"

I didn't call home. I didn't want to talk to my parents. At this point, I didn't even want to talk to Reid. I wasn't sure how he would react when Matt showed up with the milk crate. For all his past crusading, he was, at this point, thinking too idealistically. Did he believe O'Connell would just up and join us in a peace rally?

I showered, the water stinging my skin, reminding me of when the cops turned the hoses on us. Afterward, wiping away steam from the mirror, I took a good look at myself. My shoulders and back were splotched with bruises. My eyelids were turning blue and yellow. The abrasions were beginning to scab, but the cut over my right eye was an open, raw gash. Still, my wounds made me smile, and even that felt satisfying. I had fought hard and I'd be back tonight.

I dressed for battle: jeans, jean jacket, headband, bandanna. I made my way to the corner to meet the others. It was a clear night. A full moon sat low on the horizon, right above the trees. I felt, looking at the moon, how strange it was that this same moon—the one lighting my way— was the same moon everyone, all over the world, saw. The same moon that shone over Vietnam.

Thirteenth Street was overrun with students, more than the night before. A thousand students or more, I guessed. Drivers of the stalled cars honked and shouted out open windows. "Get the hell out of the way." They were fed up with us.

Tear gas was rife in the air. I blocked it with my bandanna. A group of students came by and said the protesters were moving north to University Avenue. I let myself be carried away with the natural flow of the crowd.

In front of an apartment complex on 13th Street, students dragged out two love seats, as if they were creating a grandstand. I thought they were silly. Not just silly, but part of the problem. They wanted to observe the action, not be a part of it. This was the kind of apathy we were up against.

At the intersection, students were rebuilding the makeshift barrier from the night before. Most of it had been cleared to the side of the road, making way for the day's traffic. Reid and Matt were carrying over a bike rack. Cal and Billie had boxes and folding chairs. Another student rolled over two trashcans. I joined them, dragging a piece of plywood and propping it against the trash cans.

Matt saw me and pulled me to him, kissed me. Behind our barrier we again had our ammunition: rocks, slingshots, sticks. At his feet was the milk crate, the Molotov cocktails packed tightly inside. The trashcans were overstuffed with debris. Matt lit them. Waves of heat flickered, catching the attention of the cops.

"Are you ready?" he said.

I nodded.

A double wall of police came toward us, more city and state police, more National Guard. Police on horseback. Police in riot gear. They advanced in formation down 13th Street.

We hunkered down, intent on holding this corner—not letting any traffic pass and not letting any cops close enough to arrest us. A riot wagon trolled University Avenue, heading right toward us. Tear gas spewed from a nozzle on the top.

Matt lit and threw the first bottle, sending it right in front of the wagon. Over the sound of the engine and the students shouting, I heard the *shatter, pop*—a flame burned but sputtered out quickly.

He threw another one, into a bush at the side of the street. It flared, then caught fire, stopping the cops from reaching us. For a few minutes, at least. They re-grouped and advanced again from the other side.

Cal grabbed the next bottle. Matt lit and pitched it. It landed twenty feet from one of the horses. The horse reared and the officer fell off. He rolled over, got up, and grasped a rein.

My attention was drawn to the students on the love seats. Cops were yanking them up—by their hair, by their ankles, dragging them way. More students jumped in their places. They resisted, curling into fetal position or clutching armrests. Passive bystanders forced to become active mutineers. One guy blindly sent out karate-kicks, connecting with the cops' faceplates and shoulders.

"Look at those pigs," I said.

"Fascists," Reid said.

He grabbed a bottle by the neck. Matt lit the rag.

Billie yelled, "No, don't."

I turned to Reid, then back to the love seats—he was aiming right for them.

I reached out but was too late. Reid let loose and the bottle landed on the sidewalk, shattering, sparking the cushions. One student dodged away in time, another tumbled backward. Fire engulfed the sofa. A cop, still trying to wrangle the students, stepped away, but the leg of his uniform flashed to life. Another cop tackled him and snuffed out the flame.

The cops were all over us, charging from behind. I hit the ground, on all fours, my knees and palms eating asphalt. One cop seized me around the waist and knocked the wind out of me.

"This is her," he said. "She's the one who threw it."

"Let her go. Stop it!" Reid screamed.

He, Matt, and Billie lunged toward me, but the cops shoved them back with their shields. I wrestled myself free long enough to roll over, and I started kicking, wildly. I made contact, hoping it was in the guy's balls.

In the struggle, I saw a club strike Reid. A bloody gash opened on his forehead. He crumpled. Two cops lodged a shield against his ribs, forcing him into a submissive position. Billie put up a fist-swinging fight and wrenched herself away. She ran. Matt was dragged away between two officers, face down. He was shouting my name.

I was pinned again, this time on my back with a billy club at my throat. I couldn't run, I could barely breathe. Then, the cop flipped me and stuck his boot deep into the middle of my back. My cheek ground into the pavement.

Around me, I heard a shuffling of boots. A boot toe caught my temple. Pain knifed through my skull; light zapped behind my eyes. I screamed.

My hands were cuffed. "Get the fuck off me."

"Shut the fuck up," the cop yelled back. He yanked me up by the chain of the cuffs, wrenching the socket of my left shoulder. With the spasm of muscle, my knees buckled. I screamed again.

"Shut the fuck up, you raging bitch," he said.

Blood seeped into my eye, dripped down my cheek and into my mouth. I spit in his face, a mix blood and saliva.

My eyes were swelling fast. Soon I wouldn't be able to open them. I went limp when two cops tried to put me on the bus. No matter, one of them slung me over his shoulder and dropped me on a seat at the back.

Confusion and noise and murky gloom. Through slits, I saw the moon glinting off the window of another bus. There was a place on the moon called the Ocean of Storms. After we moved to Florida, NASA launched several lunar probes that landed on this spot. One of those probes transmitted the first pictures the public ever saw of the moon. The surface was rocky, pock-y, crater-y. The moon, made of basalt and magma, had no atmosphere. No storms, no oceans. I had no idea how this area got its name. I did know that what we saw in those pictures was the near side of the moon. It was the face of the moon we saw every night, the face I had seen earlier that night, just before the explosion.

Year of Vulnerability

The transport bus circled the city for an hour. My bones hurt and my eyes were quickly swelling shut. We cheered every time we neared the jail; booed when we drove right past. I remembered Paul telling us that so many students had been arrested, they didn't have room for us all. We grew nauseous. We complained—*When are you going to let us out of this goddamn paddy wagon?*—and drummed the backs of the seats. A boy with a blood-soaked T-shirt tied around his head threw up.

When we finally stopped, there was a crowd of students in front of the jail, cheering and jeering, demanding to know information about their friends. We were ordered off the bus, and while I wanted off, instead of standing up, as commanded, I went limp again. I refused to take orders, to aid in my own incarceration.

Two cops stood in front of me: tall, wide-girthed, with large, helmeted heads.

"So, this is the way it's gonna be?" one said. I could tell, by his gruff voice, he was the cop who carried me on board.

My show of resistance was no match for him. He clasped my wrists and the other gripped my ankles. They dragged me down the aisle, my hair slopping through the puddle of vomit, my back scraping the sidewalk. I was dropped on the floor, just inside the lobby, my head hitting concrete. Nothing solid came into focus. I heard footsteps, indistinct conversation. I smelled coffee overheating on a burner.

I was fingerprinted right there on the floor, the inky mess leaving marks on the tile. At that point I found my situation humiliating and got up. With no mention of my right to remain silent or my right to counsel, I was escorted down a hallway between a bank of cells.

There was a sign taped to one of the cell doors. I leaned in close to read it. "Please don't tease the animals. By request of the Gainesville City Zoo." Hand-written on the back of one of the Student Mobilization Committee flyers, it was somebody's idea of a joke. *Somebody* being one of us, a protester arrested and held here. It made me laugh. The cop took this as a comment on the conditions of the cell.

"That's right, believe it. This is where you're spending the night," he said. Up close and without the riot gear, he wasn't intimidating at all, just a regular man, with sandy hair and chubby cheeks.

Two dozen women were in a cell built for two, with a metal bunk bed, a sink, and a toilet. Was the dominant stench sweat or urine? I couldn't tell—both mingled equally in the fusty air. Someone came to me, stroked my hair.

"Look what they did to you, sweetie."

It was Willow from my women's group. Her shirt was ripped and her arms were streaked with blood. Not her own, she said. It belonged to a guy she tried to help. The cops were beating him over the head, even though he was flat on his belly. They wouldn't stop, until Willow threw herself between the body and the batons.

"I thought they were going to kill him. He didn't deserve that."

"None of us deserve to be here."

"Right on, sister."

With so many in the cell, there was nowhere to sit but on the floor. Willow and I squeezed into a corner and sank down. I put my head on her shoulder and closed my eyes. I saw Reid lifting the bottle and Matt lighting the rag. I heard the click of the lighter, even though at the time it was too chaotic and noisy to hear such a sound. But now the memory was crisp. I saw, even, the blue at the center of the flame.

Why, after his objection to us even making the bombs, had he thrown one? When he comes to get me, I thought, when he and Matt and Billie come, all this will be settled.

"My parents are going to kill me," Willow said.

I opened my eyes. Hours earlier Doreen had mentioned my parents and I hadn't thought about them since. Dad's face emerged: stern, disappointed, his eyes hardening, the way they did when he and Reid fought. They were the cold sheen of steel. That would finish me off. My mother wouldn't be surprised in the least. She had seen the changes in me, been the target of my cutting comments. She knew what I was capable of. Had Reid called them? Were they on their way? What would I say to them?

Picking at the peach polish on her nails, Willow told me that bail had been set at $100 for disorderly conduct and $500 for unlawful assembly, both misdemeanors. The student credit union was giving loans for bail. She was waiting for a friend of a friend to bring her money.

None of that applied to me. I was pretty sure what I had done—what Reid had done, but already I was absorbing his actions into a narrative that put me, like the cops believed, here—starting a fire and injuring a cop—was not a misdemeanor. My bail might be $1,000 or $10,000. How would Reid come up with that kind of money? Or our parents?

"I can get you a loan," she offered.

"That's okay, I'm sure my brother's going to come soon."

I wasn't sure at all.

I slept lightly, with a vague sense of what was happening around me. Women talking, women crying. And the men, across the hall but out of sight—they moaned, fought, shouted. "Hey Mr. Piggy, I'm dying. You want my death on your hands." Occasionally, a cop called out the names of those being released.

In the morning, there were only five of us. I moved to sit on the bottom bunk. The mattress was so thin the springs dug into my legs. Every time someone was set free, we heard cheers from the crowd outside. The cops grudgingly delivered care packages. *Guess you kids have rights.* They were sullen and their uniforms disheveled. They'd been on duty for days, just like us. The care packages were bags full of potato chips, Little Debbie snacks, and soda. Some had notes inside, words of encouragement and updates on bail. A pizza was delivered. The smell of pepperoni made my mouth water. It was gone before I got a piece. I ate an Oatmeal Crème Pie in two bites.

Willow finally left around noon. She gave me a handful of Tootsie Rolls.

"See ya on the outside," she said.

I sucked on the candy. Melty, chocolately, the sweetest thing I had ever tasted.

When Reid gets here, when Reid gets here, when Reid gets here. What? I'll be free? The truth will come out? Yes, both these things will happen when he comes to bail me out.

I lost track of time. I had no watch. There were no windows. The lights were always on. Soon I was the only one left in the women's jail. I was given a sandwich, bologna between slices of Wonder Bread. I fought sleep. I needed to stay awake to hear my name.

Twice I was taken to the main room with two police officers. I kept my head down, not making eye contact. They asked me who my friends were, who I had been with at the protest.

"Give us names and we'll let you go."

I glanced up and recognized one from the first day of the protest at Tigert Hall. He was the one with the mirrored sunglasses who spit on Billie. With his glasses off, he looked harmless. He smiled, trying to convince me he was a good guy.

"I want to help you," he said.

I put my head back down. I sent my thoughts back in time, back to home and Reid's room, where I had listened to Jim Morrison. I heard Morrison's words. *You know that it would be untrue. You know that I would be a liar.* I saw the stop sign on Reid's wall, the wall he had painted gray. *Don't say anything*, I thought. I had no idea what they would do to Reid or Matt or Cal if they caught them.

Where was Reid? Matt? Had they left me here to die? No one came. No one sent a care package or bail. The sign about the zoo wasn't so funny now. The cell was polluted, a nuclear waste site. There was no toilet paper. I dripped dry. I held my bowel movements. At last I asked if I could use the station bathroom. The sandy-haired cop looked at me and said, "Sure, kid, just hold your horses," and he didn't return for hours.

When he did, he brought me a can of cola. I asked how many of us were left.

He pointed toward to the men's cell. "It's down to you and two guys over there, and missy, I don't think they're getting out anytime soon."

The coke was too acidy. One sip and it burned my gums. I handed it back to him.

"Why don't you tell me what happened," he said.

I said nothing.

"We have witnesses."

I didn't believe him. He was trying to scare me into talking.

"There had to be others. You didn't do this alone, missy. Tell us, we'll tell the judge, and chances are things'll go easier for you."

The dismissive *missy*—I hated that.

"Between me and you, what did you do?"

"Nothing," I said.

"That's what you all say. Let me tell you, I know what you did and the nothing you did is a felony. Harold's a friend of mine. He's still in the hospital."

My bowels dropped. Now there was no mistaking the rampant smell. He kindly took me to the female officer's bathroom. I cleaned up and was given a pair of underwear—new, still in the wrapper—and sweatpants. Both were too big.

Later that afternoon, the officer woke me.

"Leahy, you're up," he said.

No cheers greeted me outside the jail. No Reid or Matt or Billie or Cal. Only my father.

"Good God," he said.

I knew what I looked like from my trip to the bathroom. My hair was matted. Both eyes were black and blue. The scraps on my right cheek were inflamed. My lips were split and still occasionally broke open and bled, especially when I toothed the loose seam.

When I reached the car, I saw Reid in the front seat. So he had come for me. Been forced to come. I got in back. The seat felt so comfortable I wanted to curl up and sleep.

"What do you have to say for yourself?" my father asked, looking at in the rearview mirror.

"Nothing," I said.

"That's not an answer. You know this is serious. Aggravated assault and arson are felonies."

Again, that word. *Felony.*

On the streets of downtown, the people of Gainesville were going about their business, walking into a store, out of a restaurant. I heard church bells.

"What day is it?" I asked.

"Sunday. Mother's Day, by the way," my father said. "Do you know what this is doing to your mother?"

"I'm sure she's upset," I said.

"She's devastated. We both are."

My father drove us to the Holiday Inn. Taking the elevator up, I stood next to Reid. I nudged him, shoulder to shoulder, my way of asking: *What's going on? What did you tell Dad?* He didn't flinch or push back or even look at me. What did that mean?

The hotel was right on the corner of University and 13th. From the window of our fourth-floor room, I saw the debris from the riots, pieces of the barricade pushed to the side of the road. Stacks of chairs, a bench, plywood, trash cans, the bike rack, the burned love seat—all waiting to be hauled away on the next garbage collection day. Black streaks from the fire marred the sidewalk. Traffic moved smoothly through the intersection. The American Oil station was open for business. On the first night of protests I had snuck behind the building, between the fence and the dumpster, to get away.

To the north, I could almost see the roof of The Terrace. So close, so far.

"Tell me what happened," Dad said.

The same appeal had come from the cop in jail. From him, it was a trap. From my father, it felt like a chance to tell the truth. It seemed Reid hadn't yet said anything.

"It's not what you think," I said.

"Wait," Reid said. He had his hands up, as if trying to stop me from talking.

"I knew it," my father said, turning to Reid. "This is all about you."

Why did he always think the worst of Reid? Did he really believe I was so good I'd never be involved in a demonstration unless coerced by my brother?

Here we were again, the all too familiar dynamic. Dad and Reid facing off, me trying to prevent a blow up. My mother was nowhere in sight, but she was very much present. *Your mother is devastated.* Why was it my responsibility to keep the peace?

I sat down. Pain seared my tailbone, reminding me of my battered body, and I stood back up.

"The way I see it, this can go one of two ways," my father said. "You can tell me what happened and I can work with the authorities to figure something out. Or I can just get in the car and go home. Let justice take its course."

He was bluffing. He wouldn't let either of us go to jail. Reid and I stared at each other. Was he going to speak up? Should I?

For the first time, I thought about—no, I scrutinized— my dilemma. No one knew Reid had thrown the Molotov cocktail. Not the police, not the university, not my father. Yes, he had been at the sit-in and had been a large part of the protests, but he hadn't been arrested. If I told the truth, what would happen? Would Reid be expelled and lose his student deferment? If so, his year of vulnerability would kick in. If Nixon called up more troops, he could be among them. That had happened to Louis Luckless.

And what if Reid was arrested? Could a criminal record disqualify him from service? Maybe he should confess to the crime. Maybe that was his way out of Vietnam.

Then what? It would cement Reid's place in the family as a hothead, a loser. Would my father let him return home? The fact that he was blaming Reid when he—my father—knew nothing about what really happened, made me hold on tighter to my secret.

I needed to talk with Reid, alone, just the two of us. I had to find out what he was thinking, planning. Maybe he would want me to tell the truth. For now, I had to keep my mouth shut and wait.

"Well?" my father said.

Reid looked down and then up again. He shook his head. A gesture I interpreted as *Don't say anything*. My impulse all along.

"I got caught up in something I shouldn't have," I said, the most benign thing I could think of. It wasn't accusation or admission.

My father sighed and put an arm around me. "Okay, okay," he said. With this new information, he was reassessing the situation. It seemed to him, his daughter, his *Pumpkin*, had committed a crime.

The room was stuffy. I walked over and turned on the air conditioner. The drone relieved the tension.

"You," Dad said, pointing to Reid. "Go back to your place, get some sleep. We'll finish this in the morning." He handed me a bag of clothes. "Here. Your mother packed these. Why don't you take a shower? I think you'll feel better."

I looked at Reid one more time. He stood there, hands at his side, shoulders slumped—none of the defiance he had on stage the day of the rally. I cleared my throat, but he wouldn't look at me.

I showered. The hot water pounded against my back and neck. There was a large bruise on my belly, darkening. I didn't want to think about any of that right now. I just wanted to feel heat and smell soap. I wanted to scrub my skin clean. I changed into the clothes my mother had sent. My girlhood clothes. At least they were clean and fit. My own underwear—what a luxury!

Reid was gone and my father had gotten McDonald's hamburgers for our dinner. We ate at the little round table in the corner of the room. He told me the plan. He was a planner and he liked everyone to know the plan. That way, the schedule advanced like clockwork. No glitches. No one was late. Breakfast was at 0700 hours; dinner at 1800 hours. Every vacation we were given an agenda and if you weren't in the car at the designated time, my father threatened to leave without you.

Tomorrow he would find a lawyer. After that, we'd go to my dorm room and pack up. Reid would help us. I was going home.

"What?" I asked. "A lawyer? Home?"

"You think you can just go back to class as if nothing has happened?" my father questioned.

Maybe. I didn't know.

"But I have exams," I said. "I have friends. I have a life here. I have—"

"And who do you think is footing the bill for this life?"

"I can get a job." I thought about Matt. He had two jobs, one on campus and one at Leonardo's.

"Celeste, you've been expelled," my father said.

The food sat in my belly like a meat-dough rock.

"Can't you fix that?" I asked. "Talk to school officials?"

"No, I don't think I can."

Now I was the one reassessing. I wouldn't be going back to school. I might even be going back to jail. I had to put my fate in my father's capable, military-trained hands. He would pull strings. He would demand things. What things, I didn't know.

He got in one bed, I got in the other.

When I was certain my father was asleep—lightly snoring in the next bed—I took the key and left. The air was saturated with humidity. The electric sign in front of the hotel buzzed. Except for that sign, the streets were eerily quiet and dark. It felt like the whole town was asleep. The whole world, even. I saw no one as I walked to The Terrace, and when I got there, no lights were on.

I felt like I should knock. I had been away only a few days, but it was long enough for me to feel like an outsider. I didn't belong.

Had it really been eight months since I stood in front of this door for the first time? Back then I didn't know Matt or Billie or Cal. All was ahead of me. If I had never opened it at all, none of this would have happened. If I had been the daughter my parents expected of me, I would be in my dorm room now, braiding Doreen's hair.

I heard movement inside—a loud laugh—and opened the door. The smell of the house brought tears to my eyes: full ashtrays, vanilla candles, congealed bacon fat in an unwashed frying pan, damps towels, sandalwood incense, and underneath all that stale marijuana.

Matt and Cal sat at the table in silence. Light came from a lamp in the center of the table. Maps of upstate New York, New England, Ontario, and Quebec were spread out in front of them.

"Who's going to Canada?" I asked.

Matt got up and embraced me. "Oh God. Oh God, Celeste. I was so worried about you. We all were."

"Why didn't you come get me?"

Cal appeared beside me, put his hand on the back of my head. "We couldn't," he said. "Too dangerous. The pigs are turning over names to the FBI. If you get arrested or try to help anyone in jail, your name goes on the list."

"Come off it, Cal," I said.

"I'm serious. They're all around us now. Just waiting."

"We tried," Matt said. "But they wouldn't let us see you and then Reid said your father was coming."

"Where is he?"

I didn't wait for an answer. I walked to his bedroom. All his clothes were piled in the middle of the bed. Billie was taking each shirt, each pair of jeans, and folding them. There was a duffel bag open and waiting to be filled.

"What's going on?" I asked.

They lunged, enveloped me in a double-hold bear hug. Billie started to cry—I had never seen her cry. She volleyed questions at me. Was I okay? What was it like in jail? Did the cops suspect Reid? What about my dad, was he really getting me a lawyer? Too fast, too loud—I couldn't take it in. I froze, said nothing.

Reid guided me to the bed. "Sit down," he said.

I sat. A stack of shirts tumbled against me. By now, Matt and Cal had entered the room. Matt sat cross-legged at my feet and took my hands.

"What exactly is the danger?" I asked. "You haven't been caught doing anything."

"Destruction of property, Celeste," Cal said.

"That cop was burned," Reid said.

"And I lit the rag," Matt said.

"But no one knows that," I said.

He didn't answer.

"I can't stay here," Reid said.

Their rationale was confusing. The agreed upon narrative seemed to be that the correct person—me—had been arrested. However, they were protecting Reid, not me. I was disposable. But I was also a threat. I couldn't be trusted not to tell the truth. Consequently, Reid and Matt had to leave. On the other hand, every time I said I hadn't told, they looked at me as if I had nothing to tell.

"Do you have a plan at least?" I asked, taking a lesson from my father. If I knew the plan, I could settle it in my mind.

"Billie's cousin in taking us to New York. From there we're going to Maine. There's a place where we can cross to Canada."

But if he didn't do anything—and that was the revised history—why did he have to leave?

"It's naïve to think any of us are going to get away with this," Billie said.

"You're Reid's sister," Cal said. "There could be witnesses, cops who know what happened." This was the first hint that someone understood the truth and it was coming from the most unhinged out of all of us.

Billie put her hands on either side of my face. "You have to let him go. You can do this Cheery, I know you can."

I removed her hands and asked everyone to leave the room.

Reid and I were finally alone. He took over folding his clothes and gathering items from his drawers. If he remained in motion, he wouldn't have to look at me. Really look at me. I had just spent three days in jail for him. Or was it four days? I wasn't sure anymore.

"Stop packing," I said.

"I have to go. You see that, don't you?" he said.

"Not really. I haven't said anything more to Dad. I won't tell."

"Tell what?" Again, a disregard for the facts.

"Reid, you threw the bomb," I said, so softly I wasn't sure he heard.

He said nothing.

"Did you hear me?" I spoke louder.

When he didn't answer, I said, "Going to Canada, that's one plan."

If he went, it was possible he would never be allowed to return to the United States.

"You have another?" He stuffed a few shirts into the duffel bag.

"Dad can help. He can, I don't know, pull some strings," I said. "He's getting a lawyer. Or maybe if you join the Air Force he can get you a desk job, stateside."

"I don't want his help."

"But you want mine."

Once again, he didn't answer me directly.

"You can go back to classes, still graduate," I said.

"Who gives a fuck about classes? I can't go home. I'll die there. This is my only chance."

"Your only chance to what? You don't have anything to run from."

Matt and Billie came back into the room. Billie handed Reid his wallet. He put it, along with the rest of the clothes, into the bag. He sat down. Shoulders slumped, head in hands, he said, "Let's sleep on it. We're tired. We'll see how things look in the morning."

How could any of this look different? Morning, noon, night. It is what it is, I thought.

"Stay here tonight," Matt said. "Just one night."

I didn't want to walk back to the hotel. I didn't want to see my father. The exhaustion, the need to be held, to feel Matt's arms around me, was overwhelming. I stayed. In Matt's bedroom, what had been our sacred space, he kissed all the cut and bruised places, lightly, a barely perceptible touch of lips to wound, enough so that I felt a healing begin. The knot of flesh in my shoulder unclenched. Torn skin on my knee formed the first delicate rind of scab. He ran his tongue down my neck and my belly. He entered me and all the hurt evaporated.

I slept, once again in this familiar bed. I slept and forgot everything. It was just another night at The Terrace.

In the morning, Reid and Billie were gone. I knocked on the bedroom door and when neither answered, I pushed it open. Empty. The duffel bag was gone. They had tricked me, and also Matt. They had left without him.

No, Reid hadn't tricked me. I knew, when I went to Matt's room, that he would leave before dawn. I knew, with my silence, what I had agreed to—I'd take the blame. This was how I would keep the peace. How I would keep Reid safe. For me, a girl, the consequences were not life or death. I couldn't be drafted. For me, a girl, education wasn't a must. I didn't need a degree to be a secretary. Or to marry and have children, like my mother and *her* mother and *her* mother. No one—my father, my mother, the *authorities*—expected anything more from a girl.

I stood in the living room alone. The room had lost its sheen. Not that it ever really had one. It was always a dump. It only felt special because of the people. It glistened, to me at least, with warmth, love, smoke, anger, and purpose. It burned with hot-house voices arguing over ideals and strategy.

The coffee table was heaped with dirty dishes. On top was Reid's moleskin notebook. Next to it was Matt's guitar. Billie's fringed suede jacket was on the floor, along with a pair of Cal's jeans, VVAW patches on both knees. His map of Vietnam looked like the drawing of a fourth-grader. The couches were dirty and ripped. These couches—where we had crashed, feet to head, feet on belly, head in lap, like crayons tossed into an old cigar box.

I was nowhere in this house. No piece of me anywhere. Not a pinch of skin, a hair fiber, or a crumb that may have fallen from my lips.

I walked back to the hotel. There, at the intersection, I had an urge to cross the street and stand in front of the remains of our protest—trash cans, wood, love seat—but I didn't. It wasn't an altar. At this point, it was more like a grave. The sun beat down on the pavement. It would be another hot day. I smelled the burnt cushions. I smelled my own shame.

At the hotel, my father was waiting for me outside, by the pool. He had our bags packed.

"Where the hell have you been?" He was so mad the vein at his temple pulsated.

"Reid's not coming, Dad," I said.

"What do you mean he's not coming?" This was one of my parents' most annoying habits, the what-do-you-mean question.

"Don't you get it? He's not coming to help us. He's not even going to finish school." I had never spoken to my father this way, with the full force of my anger. "He left. He's on his way to Canada."

"What do you mean, Canada?"

Canada, to my father, was where the weak and the weasel-y went. It was where a man went to get out of his obligation. He sat down in one of the lounge chairs. Had he really thought Reid would fall in line? Did he think this was a phase and Reid would snap out of because of my arrest? I couldn't tell if he was mad at Reid, at me, at himself. All three, probably. That was how I felt too. I was mad at everyone.

"I failed you kids. I moved you around too much. I wasn't home enough. I couldn't keep you safe. This war, this damn war."

I wanted put my arms around him and tell him he was wrong. But he wasn't and I had no compassion to give.

At Mallory Hall, my dad stayed in the lobby while I went upstairs to pack. He wasn't letting me out of his sight. Doreen sat in front of her make-up mirror, hot rollers in her hair, preparing for an end-of-the-year sorority gala. Her dress—yellow chiffon with a high ruffled collar—hung on the back of the closet door.

"Oh, Lordy, girl, look at you." She touched my cheek. "Does it hurt?"

"Only when touched."

"Sorry."

"I'm kidding."

"And she jokes her way right through the pain." She smiled.

Doreen buzzed with information. She told me that community sentiment had shifted in the last three days. Claims of abuse of power by police had come to light and the student protesters were no longer thought of just as long-haired rabble-rousers. Several reporters had published accounts of how they were beaten. Their cameras were taken away or detroyed. Damning photographs in the *Gainesville Sun* confirmed it all. Student government had set up a legal aid center for collecting even more evidence. The mayor announced that all misdemeanor charges would be dropped after six months if the individual wasn't involved in any other "unlawful acts." A blue-ribbon commission was being formed to study how the demonstrations turned violent so quickly. I didn't care what color the ribbon was. It didn't matter to me. I was going home.

There was a yearbook sitting on the bed.

"Oh, yeah, I got that for you," she said. "I didn't know if you wanted it or not, but I thought—I don't know what I thought."

I flipped through it, the pages filled with images of ordinary college life. Crowds at football games, students studying on the green, a tug-of-war on collegiate day, bicyclists riding across campus. Clubs. Greek organizations. Smiling administrators in ties and jackets. Candid shots of speakers (McGovern, John Kerry, Betty Friedan) and musicians (Karen Carpenter, Mudcrutch, The Guess Who). There was a photo of homecoming queen Cassandra Martin waving from a parade float.

I had spent all this time in a totally different place from Doreen or Cassandra Martin. I had lived in the world of anger and escalation, of defiance, of raised fists and tear gas. Cassandra had lived in a world of compliance. It was her world just as much as it was mine. What would she tell her children about her days at UF? Dances and parties and football games and sorority sisters. What would I tell my children? Oh, yeah, I wasn't having any children. But if I did, the answer was nothing. I'd say nothing about this dark period.

"I'm so sorry, Celeste," Doreen said. "I knew all that stuff you were involved in was trouble."

That was the closest anyone had come to saying *I told you so*. Leave it to Doreen, but I couldn't leave it. She wasn't innocent. Anyone who didn't speak out was complicit. I still believed that.

"Let me ask you a question, Doreen. Why isn't Dwight in Vietnam?" I asked.

"What do you mean?" Her eyes were big with a frank sincerity I no longer believed.

I didn't have much venom left. But I had this: "You know what I mean. Don't act all innocent and naïve, like *little ol'*

Dwight, he's just a *good ol' boy* who knows nothing about the *bad ol' war*."

She turned away, back to her make-up mirror, and began to unroll her curlers. Tonight, at the dance, she would be charming, wholesome, pretty. There was no denying it, Doreen Carlisle was fulfilling her father's wish in the best way she knew how.

I packed up my stuff: books, record albums, clothes, bedspread. I had so much less than when I arrived. No commissary soap left. I pulled Jim Morrison off the wall, crumpled him and tossed him away.

Doreen stopped me on my way out the door.

"He has flat feet," she said.

Back home, in my parents' guest room, and like a guest, I was polite. I helped with meals, dishes, and chores, then retreated to my room. I didn't want to know how my mother felt. I couldn't take one teaspoon of her pain onto the gallons of pain I carried. I could only make her days easier by helping around the house. I shaved my legs and armpits. I put on deodorant each morning.

I feared she might breakdown, that during dinner one night she might cry or scream or blame. She remained impassive, though, putting to use her years of training as a military wife. I didn't know how she made sense of this turn of events. This loss of her son. Did she connect it to the loss of her parents—the choice she made to marry my father against their wishes? One gain, one loss. For my part, I embraced my new old role. It appeared the only road to salvation for us all.

The house held a different kind of silence now. Beyond the chatter of daily living—*Good morning. How are you? What do you have planned for the day?*—my parents barely spoke to each other or me. It was real silence. I couldn't fill it with cheer.

Both of them worked all day, my mother now fulltime at the gift shop. Still, I didn't spend much time out of my room, a nesting of walls decorated with botanical prints my mother had chosen. I was absent, without life. Every time I closed my eyes, I saw the fire. I saw the moon through the small window of the bus. I saw Reid packing his duffel.

I knew I was scheduled to appear in court in Gainesville at the end of May. Dad didn't share the plans for the arraignment, and I didn't ask. I stayed blissfully ignorant in my room for the next three weeks.

On Sunday, May 28, we drove to Gainesville and checked into the Holiday Inn. This time our room was on the north side of the building, with no view of where we protested. We met with the lawyer on Monday morning. The arraignment was a formality, he explained. A plea had been negotiated. The police officer suffered second-degree burns and was recovering. He was due to return to work in June. My charges were reduced to disorderly conduct, unlawful assembly, and destruction of property. I was given two years of probation and released into the care of my parents. A judge pounded a gavel and that was that. O'Connell and a panel of administrators had already decided I wouldn't be returning to the University. A group of men were in charge of my fate. I hated that just as much as being called *missy*.

Standing outside the courthouse, I noticed the *Gainesville Sun* in the vending box. There was a picture of the Duke of Windsor on the front. He had died. I thought of Doreen, across campus crying her eyes out, thinking of poor Wallis Simpson. It was the end of a great love story.

Just a summer earlier I had been on the beach, making out with Adam, learning to surf, dreaming of the year ahead, of college, of hanging out with my brother. Now, I avoided sun, sand, and surf. The air outside was stifling and I didn't want to see any of my friends. Holly called the house, but I didn't take her calls. Eventually, she gave up.

I read just enough to keep up with the war. Nixon was still bombing North Vietnam. What began with the May 8 announcement continued for the next six months. Cal had been right. Nixon had no plans to pull back. He was prolonging the slaughter in yet another way. Jane Fonda went to Hanoi and denounced the bombing as war crimes. A picture of her sitting on an anti-aircraft gun appeared in the newspaper. She became the most hated woman in America.

Another shocking picture appeared in the paper: crying children running down a village road with the dust of a napalm blast behind them. The girl in the middle was naked, the skin on her arms burned.

That image turned many Americans, my father among them, against the war. I found him alone in the living room one night, long after my mother had gone to bed. He was drinking scotch and listening to Marty Robbins.

"I'm sorry, Dad," I said. I was sorry for everything, even for Jane Fonda and the little girl in the village.

"Aw, Pumpkin. I know, I know." He had called me Pumpkin. I dropped to my knees, took his hand, and kissed it.

"I don't worry about you," he said. "You're resourceful. You know how to sit back and observe a situation. Make an assessment. I'll bet you don't think so, but you have an analytical mind. You don't think so, what with all the trouble, with the situation, but you are. You think things through. Not like your brother."

He was a bit drunk, slurring and repeating words.

The record player arm clicked off. The refrigerator compressor clicked on. I didn't move. I wished I could pour myself a scotch and drink with him.

"Maybe I'll go back to school, somewhere else," I said.

He sighed, took another sip. "Yeah, maybe you will."

The resignation in his voice said it all—I wouldn't be going anywhere. He wasn't paying the tuition. Find a husband, he said without saying a word. Let him take you off my hands.

Not long after that night, on a Saturday in August, just after midnight, the phone rang. My parents were in bed and I was on the couch, watching *Please Don't Eat the Daisies*. I ran to answer but before I could, my father's voice, a strident bark, came from down the hall: "You have the gall to call this house."

I picked up the kitchen extension.

"Reid, Reid, don't hang up," I said.

"Hey, sis. How are you?"

I'm a mess, I'm wrecked! I wanted to say.

"Where are you?" I asked, instead.

"Can't talk right now, just wanted to call and tell you goodbye."

"Celeste, hang up the phone," my father yelled. His voice came to me from the receiver and as a delayed echo from down the hall.

"No, Dad, I want to talk to Reid."

"Don't ever call here again," my father said, a forceful and final command.

I heard my mother say, "Give me the phone, William. Let me talk to him."

Their end of the line became muffled, as if they were tussling over the phone, and then the handset clattered to the floor.

I took the opportunity to say, "If you're really leaving, leave. But once you cross the border, there's no coming back."

I didn't want to be stuck here, waiting for his return. We each made a choice: mine was to lie; his was to leave. Reid never cared if he graduated. He never planned to come home or to get a day-in, day-out job, like teaching.

My mother recovered the phone and spoke. "Reid, he doesn't mean any of those things."

There was no answer.

"Reid," she said.

"Mom, I think he hung up."

She called his name again. I hung up. On the television screen Doris Day romped on a playground with a bunch of kids, singing and strumming a ukulele.

Six weeks later, my father had a heart attack. We, my mother and I, took shifts at the hospital. I stayed with him at night. In his room, in semi-darkness, just me, my sleeping father, and the life-buoying machines—the buzz of ECG, the whoosh of oxygen—I closed my eyes and implored: *Dear God, please let him be okay.* Night after night it was the same. I bowed my head. I begged, but I didn't bargain or promise anything in return. I couldn't, because even if my prayer was answered, I knew I wouldn't suddenly become a nicer person, a better person, a more faithful person.

One afternoon when I was home by myself, I dialed the phone number at The Terrace. I had no idea who might answer. Could Matt or Cal still be there? Matt, I figured, had graduated and moved on. Maybe he had gone back to Cleveland or moved to New England to the farm he had dreamed about. It was possible Cal was sitting at the dining room table right now, counseling a group of boys scared shitless to go to Vietnam.

Someone answered with a slurred hello. I asked for Cal.

"Just a minute." He put down the phone. A minute passed, two. Five. This was going to cost a fortune. My father, when he got out of the hospital, would see the bill and blow up.

Finally, he came back on the line.

"There's no Cal here."

"What about Matt? Is there anyone named Matt there?"
"Who is this?" he asked.
"Who's this?" I asked.
"Nathaniel."

I imagined he was a freshman, newly arrived at the house. He could have taken over my brother's room. Or Matt's.

"Do you know Reid Leahy?"

"Sure, I know Reid. Knew. But I can't tell you where he is."

"I'm his sister and it's my dad. Our dad. He's had a heart attack. He's in the hospital.

"Is it serious?"

"He's in the hospital. Did you hear me? It's serious."

"I've been sworn to secrecy," he said. "If I tell anyone, Reid's ghost will come in the middle of the night and stab my eyes out."

"Are you drunk?"

"Drunker than you. You're missing a great party."

Yes, there were loud voices in the background, faint strains of music.

"I need Reid's number," I said.

"Look, I'll call him and leave a message. Those are my instructions. I call him and he calls back. If he wants to that is."

Reid never called.

My father died on the last day of September.

My mother and I moved through the following weeks with resignation. I helped her settle the estate: will, life insurance, survivor benefit from the military. I taught her how to pay the bills (my call to Gainesville had cost $4.80) and how to do simple things around the house, like fill the water softener tank with salt.

She could have buried my father at Arlington National Cemetery or any of the national cemeteries in Florida, but she wanted him close. That's what she said—*I want him close*—so the service was local. At the funeral, she kept looking over her shoulder, toward the door. Maybe she was just scanning the guests—friends, acquaintances, military colleagues, Colonel Perkins and his wife. But I suspected she was looking for Reid, certain he would come to his own father's funeral. I, too, hoped he would come. I didn't want to bury my father without him.

Afterward, in the car back home, she said, "Will her ever come back."

Richard Nixon was reelected on November 7. But no one in our house cared. For Halloween we had turned off the lights and sat in the dark listening to the trick-or-treaters on the street squealing with delight. For Thanksgiving, I heated two cans of chicken noodle soup. By way of a blessing, my mother said, halfway through the meal, "You're a comfort to me."

Christmas was as pitiful as the year before. No, more so. I gave her a framed photograph of my father and she gave me a blank stare.

After the holidays, she went back to work. We had a routine that went something like this: we woke at eight. I made eggs, she made coffee and toast. We read the newspaper at the kitchen table. We didn't speak. Dinners were the same. We were on autopilot. I did the dishes and went to my room and slept.

In February, a postcard arrived from Reid. It was postmarked Cutler, Maine. When had he written it? Maybe he hadn't gone to Canada. Yet. Or someone else had mailed it, like Billie.

The postcard said, in his unmistakable tiny and neat writing, "I love you both." Did that mean he knew our father was dead or that he just didn't love him?

I was so excited by this measly gesture, I got dressed and drove downtown to show my mother. Through the shop window, I watched her at the service counter. She smiled, chatting away with customers as she rang up their purchases. Purchases with the heft of air, like greeting cards. She wrapped and boxed porcelain figurines as if they were sacred. She was different here, with these people who knew her only in this role as a competent merchant. She looked happy, an emotion I hadn't seen in her for years.

It made me mad. She had moved on, forgotten all about her husband, my father. All these years, since the night he broke Reid's peace sign necklace, she—I believed—had been angry with him. His death had released her. She no longer had to play the role of supportive wife.

When she got home from work that night, I accused her of being glad he was dead.

"It's as if you don't love him," I said. "You've just gone on with your life."

"Don't be a baby, Celeste," she snapped. "I loved that man with all my being. But I have to work. Who's going to pay the mortgage? The lights? Not you. You haven't left the house in months."

She was right. I stayed in my bathrobe all day. I smoked at the kitchen table the way she used to. But she no longer smoked, and had gained weight, while I was quickly losing body mass. My father's death had released me, too, from having to do anything constructive. Betty Friedan had been counting on me to change the world. My parents had been counting on me to stay safe. I could do neither. There was no way to walk that line, be a little bit rebellious, a little innocent. The world narrowed, pin-holed. All I could see in front of me were days of nothing.

This realization did not thrust me into action. I tied the belt of my robe tighter and hunkered down on the couch.

During the day, I watched television, game shows and a new soap opera called *The Young and the Restless*. I was back to eating frozen dinners and watching the news, this time by myself. My old friend Walter Cronkite—my father's friend, really, and listening to him was comforting—he kept me up-to-date: the World Trade Center opened; John Mitchell was fingered as the architect of the Watergate break-in; Bobby Riggs beat Margaret Court; Skylab was launched; the American Indian Movement activists surrendered at Wounded Knee. Always, always, as soon as my mother returned from work, I turned off the television and went to my room.

Finally, on a Tuesday morning in May, she forced me out of bed and into clothes. I tried to push her away, but she ran a brush through my hair and handed me the car keys.

"Do not return to this house until you have a job," she said, shutting the door behind me.

I drove around. No destination. I found solace in the tires mowing down the asphalt. I turned right. I turned left. I took this freeway and that byway. With the radio turned up, way up, I let music consume my thoughts. I could always rely on WRBZ to play The Doors and, sure enough, Jim sang to me that afternoon. He sang of fire and mire and a funeral pyre.

I thought about what I would do now. I had vowed not to wait around in this town for Reid to return, but I was stuck doing just that. If there was any money from my father's life insurance, I could go back to school. Or I could go away, like Reid. Just leave, go back to Gainesville, to The Terrace. I knew a boy named Nathaniel who lived there. Or I could go to New England. To Maine. That was as close to Reid as I could get. I wanted to be near him even as I rejected him. Push, pull. How could it be both? Just the way Nixon was conducting the war.

On a dirt road in a small town thirty miles from home—Fellsmere, a town I had never been to—there was a sign in front of a nursery called Paperbark. *Help Wanted*.

I parked and got out. The land was lush with plumbago, allamanda, crotons, and juniper. Two workers about my age, maybe a year older, were shoveling soil into a wheelbarrow.

They called out, "You want a job?"

I bent and grabbed a handful of dirt—dark, perlite-speckled, almost smooth it was so rich and loamy. For the first time in a year, I felt alive.

PART THREE

The Present

Fireproof

Reid had been gone six days. I seethed. I had whiplash. It was 1972 all over again. Somehow, I was in the *before*. My brother had left me to pick up the mess. Evan was convinced it was my fault. I had said something to piss Reid off or my general bitchy nature drove him away.

"You told him to go, didn't you?" he asked.

"Of course not," I said. "This is what he does. He comes and goes. You know that."

You know that? No, he didn't. But I knew.

Each morning, Evan went out on the pier, meditating by himself. No, Penny was with him. From the back, they looked forlorn. His shoulders slumped. Penny looked left, then right. Left again. Searching.

It was disorienting. For weeks we'd had a clockwork routine. Evan and I returned from our days—his at Yost and mine at Sun Power—to a home aromatic with saffron rice, roasting chicken, and Moroccan couscous stew. The good-humored chef had already straightened the house and walked the dog. At dinner he regaled us with tales from Garden House. We, in turn, let him in on the secrets of the lives of delinquent boys and the solar power industry. We gave of ourselves as if *we* were gifts, objects he might cherish. Now we felt neglected. He had unwrapped and inspected us. He found us undeserving. We didn't fit into his duffel bag, and, anyway, we were too heavy to carry on his travels.

On the sixth night, Zink showed up. By now, we had eaten all the leftovers. Each bite was delicious—spicy paprika, savory rosemary—and bitter—an unground peppercorn caught between my molars and made me tear up. I ordered a pizza.

Evan was a grouch and Zink was a motor-mouth. He couldn't stop talking about plans for the skateboard park and how he thought this was his calling—organizing, sticking it to *the man*. He thought he could be like Reid—like those of us who had organized during Vietnam. The city council meeting was the next night, but without Reid, Operation Black Skull was defunct. That was also one of the reasons Evan was so sulky.

"What about you, Ms. L?" Zink asked. "What did you want to be, you know, when you were our age?"

I had no words. No one had asked me that in years. I hadn't asked myself. My mind flashed on a box of memorabilia in the hall closet, my youth stuffed inside. I unearthed it, a box labeled *College* under a stack of other boxes. I brought it back to the living room and dumped the contents on the floor. We were surrounded by photo albums; yearbooks; my student ID card and my SDS card; concert ticket stubs, play programs, protest handbills and articles from the newspaper; a baggie full of slogan buttons; my signed copy of Betty Friedan's *The Feminist Mystique*; the *Florida Quarterly*, with Reid's first published poem.

Evan and Zink laughed at the photos of boys in striped bell-bottoms and girls in mini-skirts and white knee boots. They asked if we really wore love beads, if we put flowers in our hair. Yes. Yes, sometimes, we wore flowers in our hair, behind our ears, or around our necks.

Did we turn on, tune in, and drop out?

Yes, yes, well, I was kicked out.

Did we burn our bras?

No, I never burned a bra. They cost too much.

Did we really believe we could change the world?

That was the crucial question, and for me, the answer was, yes, I had believed.

Evan spread out the slogan buttons. *Draft Beer Not Students. War is not healthy for children and other living things. Stop bombing. Out Now.* Several of them were just black with white peace signs. He pinned them all to his shirt.

Here I was, letting Evan into my past and Reid was nowhere to be found. I opened one of the college yearbooks to the picture of Jane Fonda giving her speech. She stood at a podium on a wooden platform over the water of Graham Pond. A pair of ducks floated in the foreground. Students sat on the banks of the pond, crowded together, some on each other's laps. In the background, students hung out of the open windows of a dorm.

"That old actress came to your campus?" Zink asked.

"She's not that old," I said, though that was beside the point.

"What was she doing, giving a performance?"

"No, she was talking about the Vietnam War."

"She was a communist, right?" Zink asked.

Hanoi Jane. Would she ever shake that image? Maybe not, even with all the public apologies.

"Did you people ever wear shoes?" Evan asked. In many of the pictures, students are barefoot, a foreign concept to him. These days, shoes, or more importantly the right sneakers, were a status symbol.

He held up a picture of Reid and me. We were outside in front of The Terrace, our arms around each other. I couldn't pinpoint exactly when it had been taken. It must have been early in my arrival at school. There was a scattering of leaves on the grass and I was still wearing shoes.

"You look—" Evan said and stopped, unable or unwilling to complete the sentence.

I had long hair and wore a midriff top and hip-huggers with a macramé belt. Looking at the picture, I could almost smell the crisp autumn leaves in the air, feel the reassuring weight of Reid's arm around my shoulder. I had felt loved, a part of something, something bigger than myself. Looking closer, I saw Cal in the background. He was turned away from the camera, but I recognized his bushy hair. He had on his camo vest, as he so often did.

"What? I look what?" I asked.

"You were kinda pretty," he said.

That must have been difficult for him to admit. He could have changed his mind during that too-long pause and said anything, said that I looked young or weird or stoned, which I probably was.

"Did you guys with your crazy hair and your bare feet really think you could change the world?" This was Zink, asking again. He found it hard to believe this motley crew could do anything but fire up the bong.

"I'm telling you, we wore shoes. Look, I have on shoes," I said.

"You dropped out?" Zink asked.

I should have known he would dig deeper than Evan.

"Kind of. Not really."

"What about football games?" Evan asked.

At his high school, everyone went to football games. Not necessarily to watch the game, but to meet up, hang out, smoke, and make out under the bleachers. At least that was what I imagined these herds of late-twentieth-century teenagers did for fun.

"I never went to one football game," I admitted.

"Seriously," Zink asked again. "What about you, Ms. L? What did you want to be when you grew up?"

That question cut too deep; to the core. Here it was again, my lack of accomplishments. I quickly scooped everything up and put it in the box.

"I'm pretty much grown up now," I said, putting an end to the conversation.

With Evan and Zink in bed for the night, I couldn't resist: I opened the box again. There were a handful of other pictures from The Terrace: Matt and Cal from the Halloween party; Billie holding up a sign that read "Make Love Not War"; Cal, Paul, and Matt sitting in the living room drinking from cans of beer. Cal's beard hid the hint of a smile.

In all these years, I had never seen or spoken to anyone from The Terrace. My separation had been swift and final. What I knew about their lives I knew from Reid or searches on Ask Jeeves, or what I read in the newspaper.

Paul Fielder became a respected newspaper reporter. He worked for the *Miami Herald*. I saw his byline often, especially now, in his coverage of the fires. Stacy was a theater professor at the University of South Florida in Tampa. She was married, had two sons. Cal still lived in Gainesville and was involved with local politics. Keeping the county commissioners honest, I imagined.

It was Matt I had missed the most at the beginning. Even more than Reid. I had loved him, once. My brother had loved him. They were like brothers. We didn't have an Austen ending, a misunderstanding or a letter never received. We didn't find our way back to each other at all. After he graduated, he moved around for years, even joining Reid on several of his cross-country adventures. Finally, he settled in Western Massachusetts and was a woodworker, making one-of-a-kind tables, chairs, and bookcases. He was married and had a daughter. She was probably in her early twenties now. I had every reason to believe he was a good and loving father.

Billie. Besides Reid, I felt the most betrayed by her. In the end, sisterhood wasn't powerful enough for her to stick by me. She and Reid had what I would call a Brontë-ian ending. She followed him all the way to Maine, but at the border of Canada, she chickened out. She returned to Florida and received her diploma with her whole family in the stands. She went back with them to New York and worked as a writer, not at the *Times* but at alternative newspapers like *The City Sun*, the *New York Observer,* and *The Village Voice*. She took to the streets to fight for women's issues every chance she got. She marched with Betty Friedan and Gloria Steinem in Washington in July of 1978 in support of the Equal Rights Amendment. I had once thought I might see her again, or at least talk with her. If I called, out of the blue, I was certain she wouldn't miss a beat. "Hello, Cheery," she'd say, and begin to tell me about her latest triumph. "You should have been there…" Her voice, so distinct, so out-of-breath and in-a-rush—it would have been wonderful to hear again. In 1995, Reid told me she died of ovarian cancer. She never married or had children. The heartache of this news was nearly as overpowering as when my father died. I had taken for granted that she would be there, always, and especially when—if—I finally decided I was ready to get in touch.

I didn't need to look up Doreen Carlisle. Every year, I received a Christmas card from her. That was Doreen, a zealot of proper Southern etiquette. She was still Doreen Carlisle, because, all along, she and Dwight had the same last name. She never had to confront the issue of the day: would she take her husband's name or not? She had four children, two girls and two boys. They were grown now. She sold Tupperware and must have been pretty successful because in her note last year, she wrote that she was named Georgia saleswoman of the year. *Saleswoman!*

As she promised her father, she graduated, summa cum laude, with a degree in sociology. Cal, Matt, Billie, Paul, and Stacy had walked in the University of Florida graduation ceremony three years before her. It was the Leahy siblings who never received their diplomas.

For most of the mid-70s I didn't own a television and I didn't read the paper. Changes taking place in the country went largely unnoticed by me. Roe vs. Wade legalized abortion in January of 1973. University of Florida President Stephen O'Connell resigned in June of 1973. That same year, the gas crisis hit. I had a car, but didn't drive much—I lived where I worked and grew most of my food—so I didn't sit in long lines at filling stations. Nixon resigned on August 9, 1974 and eight months later Saigon fell.

I had to go to my mother's house to watch recaps of the days leading up to the evacuation of the American Embassy: the line of people snaking up the stairs to the roof to climb into the belly of a helicopter; South Vietnamese trying to push through the gates, blocked by Marines. Just like old times, I thought, sitting there with her, with the smell of dinner in the air. It wasn't the way I had imagined the war would end: all this chaos, this failure. Long ago I wanted a world-wide celebration. I wanted the people to take over the streets with dancing and public inebriation. I even believed I'd feel gratified at being a part of the voices that helped stop the fighting. Instead, I felt over-heating sorrow. I had to go and stand at the sink, open the window and breathe fresh air.

After that, it was chin up. I got involved again. When protesters tried to block women from abortion clinics—even those getting basic healthcare, like pap smears—I was an escort, running the gauntlet from car to door. When I was pregnant, I canvased for Anderson. In 1982, during the Florida vote to ratify the ERA, I linked arms with other women in the rotunda of the state capitol building and sang *We Shall Overcome*. With four-year-old Evan, I went door-to-door for Mondale. When he was seven, we went to the protest at Cape Canaveral Air Force Station for the testing of the Trident II missile. Right in our backyard, nuclear warheads were being launched from the Atlantic.

He was too big for a stroller, but I made him sit in one for the long walk from the rally grounds to the air base. There were hundreds of us, the most famous being the pediatrician Benjamin Spock. He was the first to climb the fence, the first arrested. Police began handcuffing and dragging people way. Evan cried. *What are they doing, Mommy? Make them stop.*

My last protest ended with Evan clinging to me, his face in my belly, afraid of the police. I mourned that part of myself. I missed her. But back then I mourned so many things. The loss of living at Paperbark in our cabin. The loss of the ideals I thought Keith and I shared. Not too long after that we divorced. Evan was eleven.

At the time, Holly had said. "Why now? You've almost made it. Just coast for a while because it's going to get hard again. Adolescence will hit you like a bus. You won't want to be on your own for that."

I have since learned that people often make a change during the calm. In a storm, we may fight, but we're in it together—animosity and all. In the quiet moments, we create chaos.

The first night I spent by myself in my new home—Evan at Keith's for the weekend—I sat on the couch in front of the sliding glass doors looking out at the backyard, so long and green and pristine, ready to be made into anything I wanted. I looked at the glimmer of the river. It was mine. Not really mine, no one owned the river, but at any time I could walk down to the pier, take in the briny smell, the jumping mullet, the cheery swamp sunflower. I could find peace there. I had extricated myself from a marriage that had turned sour. I hadn't waited for someone to step in and take charge, to rescue me.

There were nights I was so lonely when Evan was with Keith. I learned to channel that emotion into getting chores done so that when he was here, our schedule ran more smoothly. If all the laundry was done, the beds remade, and floors clean, then I could just be with him. So, I cooked and froze meals. I even sent meals to Keith's. Evan liked only my lasagna, so why shouldn't he have it there, too? I busied myself. I was good at that.

I wasn't good at pleasure. I had thrown my whole self into Keith and when it ended, I waited a year before I dated again. I had two semi-serious relationships.

One was a man named Rich. Appropriately named, he was wealthy. He had been an investment banker who spent time in the Philippines before retiring and moving to Florida to play golf. He spoke of small-cap funds and Lipper ratings, of tee times and putters. I didn't understand any of it. He was great in bed, though, so I stuck it out longer than I should have.

After that was Jeff. He wasn't great in bed and I tried to coax him, to teach him, but, alas, he wasn't trainable. Even when I prompted, *Ah, right there. Slow, oh, slow down.* He was rushed and too heavy-handed. I faked it more than I should have.

I hadn't dated since.

My life quickly became all about the practical. This was just an *after*. Another *after*.

I drove Evan to the city council meeting. First thing, he re-tuned the radio and turned it up. We listened to Puff Daddy until a stabbing pain developed behind my left eye.

City council meetings were held once a month. I had never attended a single one. I considered the whole affair a snooze-fest. Bring a pillow—it will be a long and boring evening. When Evan was four, a group of parents trying to get the school board to institute all-day kindergarten, urged me—shamed might be a better word—to join a series of meetings to plead our case. I begged off. Since then I rarely gave much thought to small town politics.

When I got to the parking lot, I was curious. Not about the meeting itself, but about how the boys would present themselves. Would Zink take a combative tone? What exactly was Evan's role? I couldn't imagine Checks speaking at all. He spoke so infrequently.

"Mind if I come in?" I asked.

"Why?" There was panic in his eyes. How might I embarrass him?

"Do you mean why would I come in or why would you care?"

This was one of those questions that boggled my son's mind. I knew it. I used it to my advantage and didn't even feel bad about it. He had his own cache of weapons—sarcasm being one of them.

He said nothing. He might have been thinking about Reid. Missing Reid.

"I won't say anything. I'll be like a family representative, if for any reason they need me to, I don't know, vouch for you."

"Okay," he said.

Zink and his friends were by the door, cupping cigarettes.

"Good to see you, Ms. Leahy," Zink said.

"Just happy to be a part of the team."

"The team?" Louse asked.

"Just supporting the cause," I said.

"Oh, right. Sure." He stuck his hands deep into the pockets of his cargo shorts.

"You got the petition, Checks?" Evan—known in this group as Elba—asked.

Checks nodded. He had a large mole on his chin.

"Do they have an agenda?" I asked.

"That guy there." Zink pointed to a man in a powder blue suit jacket. "He's handing them out."

"Okay. Good luck. Break a leg."

"What do you mean?" Louse asked. He was clueless. It was a good thing Zink was running the show.

I picked up an agenda and took a seat in the back. The boys were up last. First, we had to bow our heads for the invocation from a minister of the Church of Christ. That rankled me. Where was the separation between Church and State? Then we had to stand for the Pledge of Alliance, words I hadn't said since high school. There was roll call, approval of minutes, approval of the budget, a fire status report, a discussion of the proposed installation of downtown parking meters, a discussion of zoning concerns for a proposed addition to a homeless shelter. How could we compete against the homeless?

By the time Zink's name was called—Stephen Byers—my back ached from the hard chair and I wished I had a pillow, not for napping but for lumbar support.

Zink had created a poster-sized sketch of his design, well-drawn, detailed. The park would be 100 feet by 150 feet, made of contoured earth and rebar covered with concrete, a kind of undulating moonscape. He had used color pencils to define the features: skate bowls, ledges, half-pipes, slant rails, banked wedges, stairs, flows.

The gist of his speech was: Skateboarders need a safe place to skate.

Mayor Kemp said, "As opposed to Monroe Park?"

"If you'll allow me to continue," Zink said.

All he got was blank stares. Jaws dropped, hung open. Flows and wedges, slants and cradles—that all sounded vaguely sexual. They had no idea what a funbox was, but they sure as hell knew they didn't want the teenagers of their town to install one. Half-pipe, for all they knew, could be drug-related. Councilwoman Charon couldn't believe her ears. She actually ran her index finger around the rim of her ear, as if to dislodge wax.

Zink had lost them. I couldn't sit still as promised. The situation called for an adult voice. I joined him at the microphone, stated my name and my relationship to the boys, my son being the one in the backwards hat and Nike T-shirt. My role, I thought, could be one of character witness. These were, for the most part, good kids. They had done their research and worked hard to gather signatures on the petition. Also, I wasn't totally uneducated about the topic. I had done my own bit of online research. The city of Palm Beach had built a skateboard park three years earlier, to great success. It kept skateboarders out of public parks and gave young people a place to hang out. It closed at dusk, to forestall late-night mischief.

"But do we want them hanging out?" Councilwoman Charon probed.

"They do now," I said.

I liked it, being in the spotlight, being an advocate, going up against the stodgy old traditionalists. It was true, the city had important issues to deal with: the homeless, the wildfires, how to spread around a fixed amount of money. Still, the skateboard park had value, relevance.

"But do we want them to?" Her hearing was clogged, not with wax but ignorance.

I looked over at Evan. He kept his eyes down, his chin tucked.

"I understand the issues of liability," I said. "But do we really like to walk downtown and have to skirt the skateboarders who have no place to go?"

"Food for thought, Mrs. Leahy," Mayor Kemp said.

With that, the gavel went down. Meeting adjourned.

Behind me, a chair scraped against the floor, a noise that made me turn to see Evan standing up.

"No way, man," he shouted. "You can't dismiss us like this."

His voice impressed me, strong and deep, emphatic.

"Young man, the meeting is over," Councilwoman Charon said.

"We're not leaving until we get an answer." He slapped the back of the empty chair in front of him.

Checks and Louse stood up. Was this planned or was it a spontaneous outburst? Reid, I thought. This was all his fault.

Mayor Kemp looked at me. The parent, the responsible one. My chest heated with embarrassment. At the same time, I was proud. At least Evan was speaking up. An officer stepped into the room. I had seen her when we first arrived, pacing the lobby. All I had thought at the time was *Boring assignment. Hope you have your pillow.* Now she stood behind Evan, arms crossed. Tall and solid, she was imposing. The gear on her belt—radio, baton, handcuffs, pepper spray—added to her authority. No holster, I noticed. No gun. But the butt of a knife hugged her side.

Checks, the silent one, said, "We have just as much right as anyone here." His tone went up at the end, revealing his uncertainty.

"I got this, Ms. Leahy," Zink said. He was all confidence.

"No, I got it," I said, walking over to Evan.

The cop smirked, implying I had lost control over my son.

The morning I found Zink at our house, I had tried, with my stance, my height, to let Evan know I was still the parent. I still had influence. But he wasn't two, or five, or even ten. I could no longer control him. Guide him, yes. In this instance, guidance meant, to me at least, letting him have his say. If the council couldn't take the time to open their minds and their ears to these kids—screw them.

Evan ignored me and said to the cop, "You can't make us leave."

"Oh, you don't think so." She took a step closer, her chin to his forehead.

"Hey, back away from my son," I said.

"Excuse me, ma'am," she said. Her two-way radio crackled.

Evan kicked the chair. It skidded and fell over. The officer tensed, put a hand to her belt. I spotted an exchange, a mutual nod, between her and the mayor: *Not worth it.*

What were my options? I could pinch Evan's his ear and drag him out. I could coax or cajole him. I could try to reason with him. More than likely he'd rebuff me and the scene would escalate. He wanted to be Reid's nephew. He wanted a story to tell.

"Let's go," I said.

I started for the exit, not looking back, willing him to follow me. It was the best way I could think to get him out and let him save face.

The warm night cloaked me in sweat. Evan had followed me. My relief palpable in every pore on my skin, every bone in my body. I took a deep breath.

"I don't know what that was in there, but if it was some attempt to channel your uncle—"

He cut me off. "You did it, and worse from what I hear."

I was tempted to use the if-I-jumped-off-a-cliff cliché, but the truth was Evan's actions were child's play. I didn't fear that because he stood up to the city council he would turn into a *juvenile*.

The others appeared, Zink, Louse, and Checks.

"Dude, you're my hero," Checks said.

"Whatever," Evan said. Now he seemed to be embarrassed.

On the way home, he called all six members of the council douchebags. I hated that word. Every time he used it, I told him to come up with an insult that was less offensive to me. So he used the abbreviations DB. Mayor Kemp was the biggest DB of them.

He said nothing about my broken promise to keep quiet or how I came to his rescue. For all I knew, in his eyes I was an even bigger DB than the mayor. I shouldn't have forced my way into the meeting. I should have just stayed in my seat. Maybe Evan's eruption had nothing to do with Reid, but was about me—about showing me he wasn't a kid anymore. I needed to find a different way to communicate, to respect the ways in which he was growing, changing.

"You're right, I said. "Kemp is a serious DB."

We seemed to be in collusion, at least over this one topic.

I decided we needed a distraction. I popped popcorn and put the video I had rented a few days earlier, *Bettlejuice*, into the VCR. We laughed every time Michael Keaton burped, farted, or hocked a loogie. It was the first night we had been together without the shadow of Reid between us. I wanted to lean over and hug him. I wanted to tell him that even though the meeting had been a bust, I was proud of him. But I was afraid anything I said would ruin the moment.

I fell asleep on the couch and woke with the glare of sun in my eyes. The television was off. I tried to remember the end of the movie. Had the Deetzes and the Maitlands decided to live happily ever after in the haunted house? I had no idea. It was 06:30. Evan and Penny weren't in lotus position on the dock. He must have slept in. This was my chance to revive my routine. I put on coffee and as it brewed, I called to Penny to join me. She trotted out of my bedroom.

The grass had a slight dewy shine. In the distance, the river looked like crests of light, flashing. Penny was way ahead of me, sniffing around something in the yard, halfway between the house and the river. One of the lawn chairs tipped over? A tarp blown in from a neighbor's yard?

I caught a patch of blue—Evan's jeans. I saw a shoe, his tennis shoe, in the grass by the oak tree. Penny licked his cheek and he didn't move. He was passed out, with Reid's precious bottle of tequila, empty, next to him. I tried to remember how much had been in the bottle. It hadn't been touched since Reid left.

How much had he drank? A quarter of the bottle? Less? The smell coming off his clothes was pungent. My guess was that he had spilled more than he ingested. I toed him in the thigh. Gently, at first. When he didn't stir, I dug the tip of my tennis shoe in harder.

He pulled his knees to his chest and rolled into fetal position.

"Get up," I said.

He opened his eyes. The sun made him squint.

"Oh, God," he moaned and wrapped his arms around his head. *Don't see me.* That was the kind of thing he did as a toddler. When he did something he knew he shouldn't, like pull all the toilet paper off the roll—when caught, he'd put his hands over his face, believing if he couldn't see me, I couldn't see him, and if I couldn't see him, I couldn't scold him.

His brain, now steeped in alcohol, had shrunk, rendered him infantile.

"Get up and get in the shower. You'll be late for the center."

He pushed onto his hands and knees and gagged.

"I can't go to the center like this." His head must be on fire.

"That's exactly where you're going. For the next six hours you're going to feel like shit. That's exactly how you should feel. Your gut will ache. Your head will ache. That's punishment for the stunt you just pulled."

He wobbled into the house. I continued my walk down to the pier. Smoking and making a public scene were now the least of my worries. This was the way he would go off the rails.

The goddesses simpered at me, bad mother, the mother who hours earlier thought she had done a pretty good job. Was this the first time he had ever had a drink? And if so, why had he drunk that bottle? Was he trying to be Reid? Was he trying to have some kind of spiritual cosmic mind-meld with the Aztecs? Or was he just trying to piss me off?

Inside, Evan sat at the dining table, head in hands, the smell of alcohol replaced by soap. I poured coffee. I toasted and buttered two slices of bread.

"Are you doing to tell Dad?" he asked.

'No, because you're going to tell him. I don't care how or when, but by the time you return home today, you will have told him." I handed him the toast. "You probably don't feel like eating this, but you should have something in your stomach."

We heard Keith's horn.

"Ow," Evan said.

"Drink lots of water today," I said. He gathered up his backpack, but left his skateboard on the floor by the door. Rumbling around on asphalt wasn't going to feel any good today.

"Good luck," I called after him, even though I knew he couldn't hear me.

True to my word, I called Keith that night. I let him do the talking. Before I said anything, I wanted his take on Evan's behavior. Did he find it alarming or normal adolescent behavior? Wasn't this the kind of thing he dealt with all the time with the boys at the center? Alcohol, drugs? It was part of his job to offer guidance.

Even though our different parenting styles were one of the reasons we divorced, I had never questioned Keith's parenting decisions. When I was pregnant, he read every book on the subject. He read about how to handle a teenager when Evan was one. I read nothing, not even the classic *What to Expect When You're Expecting*. I didn't care what everyone else had to say. This was my experience and I would have it the way I wanted. I often felt like I was parenting not with my husband, but with a coterie of experts. Often those experts contradicted each other.

The other cause of our divorce was Keith's job. As he rose up the retail ladder, he wanted the new, the shiny. Our A-frame wasn't enough. Our sheets were threadbare (which I liked because they were soft) and our couch was saggy (which I liked because it felt like an embrace at the end of a long day). He wanted to live closer to work. He wanted a real house in a real neighborhood where Evan could go outside and play with other kids. He took me to see the house he wanted us to buy, a house Holly had found for him. It was a bungalow in the heart of downtown. Evan was starting kindergarten and I could walk him a few blocks to the school. There was a small backyard. I could plant a garden. I gave in. Okay, maybe I wanted to live there, too. It was cute and clean. A tidy house for a tidy family.

I consented, too, to the store-bought couch, the Cuisinart pots and pans, the fresh-off-the-lot Mazda, and each time I did—although I didn't understand this until years later, when I decided to leave—I lost my connection—to both nature and Keith.

After we divorced, he suddenly left retail and began teaching, an honorable profession. It was as if my harping had driven him to hold on tighter to something he didn't even believe in. A cause-and-effect I had no idea I was triggering.

Before long he was hired as the director at Yost. It was a job that suited him. He could converse with all sorts of people, teenage boys, their parents, and, when he had to raise money, the big shots in town, business owners and bank managers. He still lived in the house we had purchased in town.

"I kicked his butt today," he said now. "I didn't let him sit down once. When he wasn't running to the bathroom, he was running with those kids."

"Did he have lunch?"

"Yes, he ate. And drank lots of water."

So, we were good in a crisis. We were as one, a united front.

"All the alcohol is out of the house," I said.

I had poured out all the beer and the wine.

"Does this have anything to do with Reid?" he asked.

"Does this have anything to do with Zink?" I asked reflexively, pissed he was accusing my brother even as I did the same thing. Maligning Reid was my job.

I adjusted my tone—Keith wasn't the bad guy here—and asked what he knew about Zink, about his family, and why he came to Yost. It turned out my initial assessment was largely correct. He was from a wealthy family. The parents often went on trips and left him—the youngest—at home. His rap sheet was petty crimes. Child's play, a way to get attention. A candy bar from the drugstore; truancy; possession, less than an ounce. (Ironically, that's what my friends and I used to do, drive around with one fat joint, smoking it with the windows open, tempting the cops—pigs—to come and bust us.)

"You know, he's going to UC Berkeley in the fall. He's a smart kid."

"I had no idea," I said. Or maybe I did. There was a reason I liked having him around. He got my historical references and he had his own set of inane trivia: Alaska is the only state name you can type out on a single row of keys. The Ms in M&M's stand for the last names of founders Forrest Mars and Bruce Murrie.

It turned out he had graduated in 1997 and had taken the year off before plunging back into a rigorous academic program. He was bumming and slumming. He was playing us.

Why, then, I thought, had he been so intent on the creation of the skatepark? He wasn't even going to be around to finish the job or to use it.

"Evan's a good influence," he said.

"I'm not that crazy about Evan being this kid's good example."

"I don't mean with Zink. With all the kids here. You'd be surprised how mature he is. How empathetic. He has a real skill with people. Plus, he's a hard worker."

All this made my heart swell.

"You'll keep an eye on him? Zink, I mean. Evan, I mean. Both of them." When we were married, I didn't have this much restraint. I only learned the "co" in co-parenting after we were divorced.

He said he would, then he added, "Why doesn't he stay with me for now? I'll take him over to visit my parents."

My sense of relief surprised me. Yes, take him off my hands. Take both boys. There was no reason for Zink to be here without Evan.

Keith's parents, Doug and Martha, lived in Tampa. Every summer they entertained their only grandson. They spoiled him, took him to Busch Gardens, Adventure Land Waterpark, and the Lowry Park Zoo. He could be a kid there and I was grateful for the break.

Over the next few days I slipped back into my pre-Reid routine. Penny and I walked down to the pier every morning. She plunged in. I counted the smokestacks. I said a silent and stupid prayer to the goddesses. Were they powerful enough to bring an end to both the fires and my anger at Reid? At least I had them back, all to myself.

The water was static with algae and reeds. Bass skimmed the surface, snapping at gnats and dragonflies. Kingfishers dove for brim. A pair of osprey had built a nest in a bare willow limb. With binoculars, I could see the heads of their three chicks.

I worked. My new project was making cold calls to schedule appointments. I averaged one hit per twenty-five dials. Russell went on site visits. His ratio was far less than mine, maybe one sale a week.

He asked me about Reid, said he had some poetry of his own he'd like to show him. This didn't surprise me. Many of Reid's fans wrote poetry. At his readings, they handed him sheaves, hoping he could help them publish.

"My brother's gone," I told him.

"Already? He didn't even say goodbye."

"Easy come, easy go." I gave a brisk wave. *No big deal.* Push that emotion down.

In the evening, in the quiet house, I sat on the couch and read the newspaper I filched from the office. Russell picked up a copy every day and read it front to back. Sometimes he clipped out articles, so I'd turn the page and come upon a hole. That was fine when it was the story of yet another Catholic Church sex abuse scandal or the sex scandal of our president. More often, the missing articles were about the fires. That didn't mean I had no news of the fires. We never really got away from them. A brush fire in New Smyrna Beach had flickered to life and an old growth hammock outside Daytona was raging.

My meals were strips of chicken wrapped in romaine lettuce, fried egg sandwiches, Grape-Nuts with a handful of almonds. I didn't call Holly. I didn't go by and see Parker again. I pulled into myself. I wanted to be alone.

The yearbook still sat on top of the box in the living room. I lifted it, put it back down. There were no pictures of the protests inside. No evidence of what I or Reid or Matt or Billie had done. Or not done.

During our conversation on the patio, I asked Reid why he assumed I would take responsibility—why, in essence, he let me—but the real question, the one I had avoided all these years, kept coming back: why was it *I* assumed I should take the fall?

The answer was like the layers of paint on the walls of my dining room. Anytime I accidently nicked a spot with the corner of a chair, I saw chips of mauve, cobalt, and orange underneath the Venetian Gold I had applied. The paint of *before* and *after*. Or more precisely, *at-the-time* and *now*.

At the time, I did it to save Reid from going to war. Information about the draft was rumor and rumor was information.

No one knew when or if they were going to be called to service. The system seemed random, as if boys were at the mercy of Nixon's whims. My sacrifice seemed less than him going to war.

At the time, for all my burgeoning feminist ideals, I had fallen for the script: girls—women—were expendable. My father never encouraged me to go back to school—he certainly wasn't going to pay for it—and I got the message. You don't need an education. You'll marry and be taken care of. You'll be a wife and mother. It was okay for me to not have a career, to give up parts of myself for a man. My mother had done it.

But there was something else, and this I hadn't yet admitted to myself: I wasn't innocent. I made the bombs, Matt and I. I had convinced him to make them. I wanted something of my own that had nothing to do with Reid, I wanted to show Reid—show them all—I was a part of the group, not a groupie. Without that crate of bombs at the protest, no one would have been injured. No crime, no jail. Legally, I could have been charged as an accessory, although I didn't think of this *at the time*. Morally, I was culpable.

The Thanksgiving Evan was two—we were at my mother's, all us in the kitchen, Mom and I peeling apples, Keith peeling potatoes, and Evan serenading us with a wooden spoon on a Tupperware drum. I opened the oven to baste the bird, and just like that, less than a blink of an eye, Evan put his hand on the hot door.

The burn sent us to the emergency room. Evan screamed as the doctor pronounced a second-degree burn. A nurse made him a gauze mitten and sent us home with ointment and instructions on care. But each time I changed the bandage—those blisters accusing me—I thought of the police officer burned by the bomb Reid had thrown. I had never forgotten his name. Harold. I didn't know if that was his first or last name. Over time, Evan's wound healed, but if you look at his left hand, you can see a coin of wrinkled skin on his palm. That wound was my fault.

I thought of that police officer more often, probably, than Reid did. He was a part of my *now*.

Yet another day went by without Reid. And another. I visited my mother. Everyone at Garden House asked about him. Had I heard from him? When did I think he'd return? They missed the poetry workshops. I shrugged, feeling like Evan. Now I understood why he did it so much. Sometimes there were no answers. Sometimes there just wasn't anything more to say.

My mother alternated between gleeful and anxious, similar to the way she behaved before Reid arrived. She didn't ask about him. She didn't use any names: not mine, not my alias. Not Reid's. She talked about *the boy*.

At the end of the week, I brought her a new pair of pajamas. She rubbed the fabric against her cheek.

"Silk. It's so soft," she cooed.

"It is."

"Do you know where I put my winter boots? I'm worried about my boots."

"You don't have to worry, Mom. Winter's a long way off."

"It smells like snow." That must be dinner prep, what smelled like Brussel sprouts frying in bacon fat.

"It doesn't snow here. We're in Florida. Remember?" It was the stupidest thing to say. Remember? Asking an Alzheimer's patient if she remembers was like talking to the deaf in a louder voice.

I sat and held her hand, changed the subject. Evan was a safe topic. She liked to hear about what he was up to. The previous night he had called to tell me his grandparents had taken him to a restaurant in Ybor City, the oldest Spanish restaurant in Florida, The Columbia. They served, according to him, the best yellow rice he had ever tasted. He couldn't stop talking about the Flamenco dancers. I described them to my mother, the twirl of their red dresses, the chatter of their castanets, just as he had to me. She appeared to be listening, her smile over-wide. The smile she gave when I talked about Evan, as if everything he said and did was a first. But when I finished, she said, "I'm telling you, it's going to snow."

Agitation showed in her fingers. They twirled and tightened the elastic in the pajama bottoms. I folded the pajamas and put them in the drawer. I turned on music. That calmed her. An aid came in, not Sophie but another young girl whose name tag said Patrice. She would help my mother get ready for bed.

When I stepped outside, I saw my mother was right: the wind had changed again, bringing from the north a blizzard of ashes. It stank. A cinder halo had developed around the sun. I shivered, a chill that sputtered up my spine and then broke out in sweat between my shoulder blades.

On the radio, I heard a Readiness Level 4 had been issued, the second most serious level.

For the first time, a fire had breached the Brevard County line. In fact, fires from three counties—Volusia, Seminole, and Orange—had converged to create one large and fast-moving conflagration. Between 200 and 300 homes were threatened.

Pyra was falling down on the job. Myra and Tyra weren't much help either. Still, the active blaze was sixty miles away. Five hundred more firefighters were being requested and helicopters were being dispatched to drop suppressant.

At home, my neighbor Derek was standing in the middle of our street. He flagged me down. He didn't have his dog. He wasn't taking a walk. He was assessing the situation.

"What do you think we should do, Celeste?" he asked.

"I'm not sure," I said. "I think I might stay the night and see how things are in the morning."

"That sounds fair," he said.

Fair had nothing to do with it. He probably meant *reasonable*. But reason had nothing to do with it either. My hands trembled on the steering wheel, my foot was shaky on the brake. I had no idea what to do. What if I left and my house burned to the ground? What if I stayed? It was the dilemma everyone in the path of the fire had faced all summer.

I stuck my hand out, caught some flakes of ash, and rubbed them into a smeary mess. The goddesses didn't stand a chance against what was coming our way. They were old and dried out. They would be the first to go. If I stayed, I'd go with them.

I turned on the television. From above, the land was a patchwork of scrub flat and pine hollows. At the edge of the quilt, an S-shaped line of fire obscured the fine stitching of trees. A scene of ravished houses, of smoke that was the white of smolder and the black of active burn. The skeletons of palmettos were charred and eerily black and white, looking like the writhing limbs of a mythological creature, struck down. The only color was a stand of green oaks far in the distance. Containment efforts had failed.

The newscaster suggested everyone in Brevard County prepare for evacuation. Gather your vital records and valuables, your sentimentals.

If the fire chief knocked on your door and said you had an hour to pack up and leave, what would you take? Setting the timer on the stove, I gave myself an hour to gather a bag. Where to start? For a moment, my mind went blank. Vital records? Values?

I kept all my documents in a filing cabinet in the closet of the guest room. I rifled through and pulled out my birth certificate and Evan's. I also found Keith's. We must not have gone through all these folders before the divorce. I found our marriage license and divorce decree. I also took my will and the power of attorney for my mother. Surely Garden House had a copy on file. Yes, of course, they did. I gave them a copy. Still I needed my mother's will. I needed my father's death certificate and his military papers. And her life insurance policy. All this paperwork, a facsimile of life. And death.

The box of college stuff was still on the living room floor, but I didn't bother with it. Too big and bulky, loaded with livewire emotional baggage that might ignite on its own. In the hall closet were other keepsake boxes: Evan's baby photo albums; his old toys, stuffed animals, and baby clothes. I opened one and saw his baby book. I took it but nothing else. I couldn't pack my car with only memorabilia.

I packed a suitcase. Underwear. Tons of underwear so I didn't get caught wearing only the ratty and ripped comfy pairs. Such an inane thing to think about right now. Time was running out. I had fifteen minutes.

I went back to my room to find one more thing: the valuables. Jewelry. I had my engagement ring and wedding band, buried deep in a drawer in a drawstring pouch. There were also several heirloom pieces my mother had given me: a set of jade earrings and necklace, a diamond bracelet my father had given to her. I had forgotten all about the cameo broach until I saw it in the pouch as well. It belonged to Keith's mother. She gave it to me the night of our rehearsal dinner. I wore it once and never again. It wasn't my style. So that was two things I had of Keith's I needed to return.

In the bottom drawer was a cookie tin, one of those large tins that people send you at Christmas time. Royal Dansk, with a sled whooshing over snow trails. The sight of it brought me to a halt. I felt queasy, remembering what was inside. That was where, when I moved here, I had stowed all the postcards Reid sent over the years. I took it out and placed it on top of my luggage.

Right then, the timer buzzed. My hour was up. I had a sad pile of miscellany. The phone rang and I jumped. The two sounds, buzzer and phone, one right after the other, jangled against my nerves. It was Helen. In a voice both calm and wise—she was wise to appear this calm—she told me they had decided to leave now. They were putting the residents in the traveling van and heading to a companion facility in Stuart. It was the protocol used during hurricane season. The ladies would have to double up in the rooms, but it was a safe palace. Did she say *palace* or *place*? I misheard *palace*. I asked if I should come and help out. No, she said, they didn't want to create alarm. She gave me the telephone number of the facility.

I sat down at the dining room table. So tired. What about this table? What about all the furniture? The sideboard? The antique mahogany desk my mother had given me, with the scrolled legs and leather top? Of course, it was all just *stuff*. They are replaceable. That was what everyone said in a situation like this. People, loved ones, are not.

I rubbed my hand on the surface of the table. It was where I had sat the night I told Keith how unhappy I was in our marriage. I told him, finally, how all the times I had given in to his desire for more stuff I felt my soul die just a little. As I talked,

I ran my thumbnail along the crack where you pulled it apart to add the leaf. It was a nervous habit. As I tried to make Keith understand abstractions like *stuff* and *soul*, I laid out the specifics. He was never home. Retail demanded nights and holidays. He was too consumed by consumerism. It wasn't what we valued. It wasn't *us*. With Evan, he had become punishing, not nurturing. Somewhere along the line, he had decided that his way was *the way*.

Back and forth went my fingernail, collecting bits of varnish. I thought of the times we had opened the table to make it bigger for company. In that moment, I realized I wasn't sharing my feelings so we could begin to rebuild our relationship. I wanted a divorce. And even though it hurt and even though I felt like I was pulling apart our family, I knew I was doing the right thing.

This was my epiphany table, where the space that opened for the leaf wasn't a void, but an addition. It expanded to make room for more. This was the table where we dumped all our stuff at the end of the day. Purse, keys, the mail. Evan's school books, permission slips needing a signature, sometimes his soccer ball. This was the table where we sat the night Reid arrived. It was where he served us dinner and whittled his small animals. And now, the fire might eat it up.

It was dark. I hadn't even noticed the sun going down. Penny had. She wanted to go out one last time before settling down for the night. We stood in the yard, taking in the atmosphere. It felt lighter than when I had returned home. She sniffed. Even she smelled the difference. A decrease in the barometric pressure. Maybe the wind had shifted once again. I was hopeful. Maybe by morning, the fire would be under control. I prayed to the goddesses. I couldn't see them, but they were out there, on sentry duty. I pleaded with God, just like always. I begged, but offered nothing in return. *Please don't let our houses burn down. Please don't let people die.*

I needed sleep. Replacing the television for the radio, keeping it low, I laid down on the couch. Penny curled on the ground. I reached down and scratched her back.

I dozed lightly. At dawn I turned the television back on. I sat, mesmerized by the images. Nothing good had happened in the night.

Until now, the authorities believed the fires would be stopped by the Buck Lake Conservation Reserve, 9,000 thousand acres of wetlands along the St. Johns River. Surely the fire couldn't jump over that much boggy marsh. But it did. It had torn through cabbage palm hammocks and pine flatwoods, banked east towards Mims and Titusville, densely populated towns.

The county commissioner broke down and started crying on national television. Homes had been reduced to ash. Shelters were full, overfull. People camped out on the floors of churches and schools, their belongings in sacks and suitcases that created cubicles of artificial privacy. One young boy cried into his Pokémon pillow case. My sense of time warped. I wasn't sure how long I sat there before I heard—really heard—the newscaster say Brevard County was, in fact, under a mandatory evacuation order.

The phone pulled me off the couch. This time it was Holly. She and Grant were going to Coconut Grove to stay with a friend. We could join them. I might, I said. Or I might go to Tampa. Doug and Martha would take me in. I couldn't make a decision. I just needed to get in the car and drive.

I carried everything I had packed to my Honda. The air was the air of hell: blistering, throat-choking, and ash-obscured. Derek pulled out of his driveway, Buddy sitting beside him, suitcases tied to the roof. He rolled down the window.

"I see you're heading out, too," he said.

"I don't think we have a choice," I said.

I had a feeling he wanted to say something else, something more than good luck. The next time we saw each other we might be standing in a pile of rubble. I had seen that carnage on TV, beams smoking, furniture charred nearly beyond recognition.

"Stay safe, Derek," I said.

In a surge of adrenaline, I thought I should gather up all my hoses and hook them together. I should douse my house. That might help. Shouldn't I *try* to save everything I had worked for?

Penny barked. Oh, Penny. I hadn't packed any dog food. I went inside, and when I returned with the bag, she was galloping toward Reid—walking up my driveway.

Pleasure and Pain

Reid once told me—years ago, when we were in college, driving back to school after Thanksgiving—that the five states he had lived in were like the five senses.

Central Illinois was taste. He had only been a baby there and babies put everything in their mouths. He remembered dipping a dump truck into the dirt and tilting the bed to his lips. He remembered our mother putting her finger in his mouth and scooping it out.

He associated South Carolina with sight. This was where he learned, through observation, military protocol. He watched our father dress for work every morning. He watched the way men on base stood so erect, the way they saluted with precision. He learned the meaning of insignias and rank. All this cemented in his mind who we were as family, as Americans.

Texas, touch. Humidity on skin, dust on skin. Sun on scalp.

California was all about smell. Because there was eucalyptus in the air, because there was gardenia and jasmine; lemon and olive trees. There was the funk of fertilized fields.

Cheyenne was sound. The wind whipping across the land. Airplanes taking off and landing at the base. Coyotes. Cattle. Snow plows. The rodeo.

I counted out the states. He was one ahead of me. Florida was my fifth state, his sixth. I asked him, then, what sense that made the Sunshine State.

"Consciousness," he said.

"Heavy, man," I said, dismissing his metaphor as baloney, as him trying too hard to sound like a poet.

Now I wondered if maybe he was right. This was the place where we had come of age, where I became aware of myself as a young woman. It was also the place, after years of moving, I felt at home. On that same drive, the one going home for Thanksgiving, as we crossed the St. Johns River on State Road 520, I looked out at the bald cypress and palm trees, at the marsh grasses that lined the water's edge—tawny green tassels against the deep blue—and I knew I had landed in the right place.

The evacuation was bumper to bumper on I-95 South. I drove. We hadn't spoken a word for two hours. Exhaust seeped through the a/c vents, the air inside becoming foul. Reid had retrieved his belongs from the house. What were his valuables? His sentimentals? Penny was in the back seat, leaning against his duffel bag, panting with car sickness. When the traffic eased up and we were able to accelerate to twenty-five, I could stand it no longer.

"Where the hell have you been?" I asked.

After five agonizing minutes, he said, "I had to get away for a bit."

"Too much family for you?" I asked, a snarl of spite in my voice.

I turned on the radio. I no longer wanted to hear what he had to say. Firefighters were releasing ping pong balls of suppressant from airplanes, hoping to stop the fire in its destructive tracks. I changed the station. We listened to Don McLean and Stevie Nicks. Like some cosmic joke, a Doors song came on. Not "Light My Fire," which would have been over-the-top, but "Love Me Two Times."

As Jim sang about one for tomorrow and one for today, my mind drifted to the movie Oliver Stone made about The Doors. I had been excited to see it in 1991, twenty years after Morrison's death. Val Kilmer as Jim. Who couldn't get into that? I dragged Holly with me, wanting to us to relive the summer twenty years earlier, when we hung out at the beach, reading, listening to the transistor, getting high. The summer I learned to surf. But the movie was nothing more than the egotistical imagination of Stone. The final scene, with Jim in the bathtub, his arms spread out on either side, Christ-like—I whispered to Holly, "Give me a break," and she shushed me.

Reid turned up the radio and said, "Oliver Stone."

I felt my reaction in my body, an instant recognition, a warming in my chest, like love—he remembered—and then a rock in my throat, like distaste—he remembered. Our shared history.

"Yeah, that movie sucked," I said.

Frustrated with the traffic, I turned off the highway, taking isolated back roads. I had no idea where they would lead, but it was better than where we were. Reid took the wheel. We drove for two more hours, west with a turn north on County Road 700, and finally I gave up.

"Let's find a hotel. A motel. Whatever," I said.

The first two motels didn't allow dogs. The woman behind the desk at the third took a look at Penny and said, "She seems sweet enough." Bless The Cadillac Motel of Sebring, Florida. Were there two rooms? I asked. Yes, there were. Boy was I greedy. I didn't want to spend the night in a tiny box with my brother.

I stashed my stuff in the room and took Penny for a walk. She deserved it. The smells, every shrub, post, and hydrant, were from another planet. I stopped at a convenience store, heated two burritos, and bought a six-pack. I knocked on Reid's door, left him a burrito and two beers.

"You wanna come in?" he asked.

"No thanks. I'm going to get some rest."

The rooms were 50s kitsch, red vinyl chairs, green bedspreads, and burlap lamp shades. Maybe it wasn't meant to be retro. Maybe it was just that old.

Penny jumped from one bed to the other, like a kid in a place where rules don't apply. She tried to dig a hole to the core of the earth. Finally, she plopped down. I opened a beer and picked up the phone. Time for yet another round of calls, a repeat of ones made earlier. For the first time, I wished I owned a cell phone. My mother was safe in Stuart. Helen had been smart to leave early, so they had been there for a day and were managing well enough. Holly and Grant were safe in Coconut Grove. Their drive had been as slow and tortuous as ours. I told her where I was and that I had decided to hunker down here until we received the all-clear. Keith and Evan, in Tampa, were glad to hear Penny and I were safe. Keith offered me a bed at his parents' condo, but I said we were fine in the middle of nowhere. I didn't mention Reid in any of these conversations.

I opened my bag and took out the last thing I had packed. The tin of postcards. I wanted to read them, to see if I could gain any insight into my brother from this one-way conversation. In the weeks he had been here, he seemed to be playing a part, the part of big brother, devoted son, famous poet. Did he think those were the only roles expected of him? He seemed phony to me, his voice too much like the one he feigned in his books. The jaded, sharp-tongued critic of all that was wrong with America. Had he been that way in college? Or had his voice matured over time? So far, we had had two real moments. Both of them had been centered around his writing.

Spread out on the bed, the postcards were a puzzle of neat-edged rectangles that fit together only in one way, chronologically. I began to put them in order.

March 17, 1978, New Orleans, LA.

November 30, 1983, Tucson, AZ.

May 5, 1987, Yakima, WA.

January 11, 1991, St. Louis, MO.

Some of the postmarks were blurry, so I had to guess when they might have been written.

The first one came from Buffalo, NY. All it said was *Au revoir my lake of Eeriness, goodbye lady of the falls.*

Much of what he wrote was like that, random thoughts, cryptic phrases, and scraps of poetry. Some of it made little sense to me, as if I were stepping into a dialogue already in progress.

Missouri River: *Thinking of Mark Twain and his Huck. Of racism and small town small-mindedness.*

Woodstock, NY: *I missed the music fest by years, but there are many here who are trying to recapture the joy and communal spirit.*

Black Hills National Forest, South Dakota: *I can't stop thinking about the drive we took through the park. I knew then I would one day come back and stand among the buffalo.* This brought bile to my throat. The tugging of heartstrings.

I remembered that trip. We lived in Wyoming then, and my father thought it was essential to see Mount Rushmore. When we traveled, he liked to rack up the miles and hours as efficiently as possible. The first time you said you had to go to the bathroom, he said, "Tough. Hold it." The second time, "Hold it just a little longer. Ten more miles." Twenty more miles and you asked a third time. He began looking for a rest area or an exit with a service station. By then it was too late. He had to pull over and one of us would run into the bushes and drop our shorts.

Once we got to Mouth Rushmore, Reid and I looked at the famous heads and said, "Oh, yeah, there is it. Wow." We ran off to play in the nearby woods. It seemed like a letdown after all those hours in the car and after seeing it a million times in books. We stayed for lunch then hit the road. Driving through Custer State Park, our car was stopped by the crossing of a free-range herd of buffalo. My father wasn't pleased, but my mother rolled down the window and stuck out her hand. The buffalo weren't close enough to touch, but their smell permeated the car, sweet-ish and manure-y.

My mother said, "Aren't they beautiful? Such beautiful, beautiful beasts."

She started to laugh. Her laugh giggly and incongruous with our surroundings—vast prairie on one side, towering Black Hills on the other—and my father started to laugh. He threw back his head, something I rarely saw him do. In profile, his features were slack and unguarded. He wasn't worried about time or rules or the miles we yet had to go. Reid and I joined in. We couldn't help it. The laughing was contagious. We laughed so long and so hard tears came to our eyes.

Asheville, NC: *There are vets living on the street. I'm ashamed of how our country treats those who gave their bodies and their psyches for the war.*

In North Dakota, Reid mined uranium; in Kansas he picked corn. From Bakersfield, he railed against the way migrant workers were treated.

On one card, he wrote: *I think you know why I can't return.* I did know. My brother and I were immersed in a kind of blame-off. Both of us felt guilty about what happened. He blamed himself. I blamed myself. But the police also blamed me.

With all the postcards laid end-to-end, there in front of me was my brother's life, a straight-line narrative told through the zigzag of travel, travel punctuated by erratic phone calls and visits. And my life? Well, I had always been right here.

I finished my second beer and took Penny for another walk, shorter this time. Then I went to see Reid. The television was on, showing the long lines of traffic still on I-95. I handed him the last beer. We sat on opposite beds, Penny next to me.

"Let me ask you something, why did you come back? Why are you so suddenly interested in my life?"

"It's not sudden. I've always taken an interest in your life."

That sounded so clinical, as if he had been studying me.

"Stop talking to me as if I'm your audience. I'm not Bill Moyers. It's just you and me."

"How long are you going to blame me for the decision you made?" He had been studying me. He knew I was unhappy.

"The situation you forced me into," I said.

"So, make a change," he said. "Do something."

"You make a change," I countered.

"I did, I came here."

"Oh no you don't. You can't make your change on my turf."

"Your turf? The truth comes out."

He was digging in. No elevated language, no metaphor or verbal trickery. I was amused and curious. I kept at him.

"How long are you going to blame me for believing you couldn't come back?"

"I didn't want to come back," he said, a croak in his voice.

"Yes, you did. Every postcard was a plea," I said. I had realized this while reading them all. It wasn't in anything he wrote, but in the fact that he wrote and sent them. He had longed for connection to us. "In your poems, you're Mr. Unfettered. But all those postcards you sent—you were homesick."

"What do you want from me?" He stood and paced.

The question hurt my heart, hurt so much I was afraid of it. I wanted to joke. I wanted a light-hearted quip to steer away the attention. It was the easy way out. Easier, I had always thought, than facing the truth. But I didn't tell a joke. I didn't defend. Instead, I asked for what I wanted.

"Admit that when I came to see you after I got out of jail, you had already decided to leave. You didn't care what happened to me. You used me as an excuse. Say you're sorry. Say thank you."

I didn't expect either, but I waited. How would he respond? Was he capable of telling the truth?

"I'd change things. If I could," he said.

I had received my answer. He wasn't able to tell the truth. He looked at Penny. She whined, wanting him to pet her. He leaned forward and stroked her chest. She settled right down.

Had we come to the end? Was that all there was to say? My throat ached. My eyes were dry. I was ready to let it all go. To go back to my room and let it all sink in. We were at an impasse.

Then he said, "I did it on purpose."

"Did what? Left me there?"

"Yes, no. I mean, I threw the bomb on purpose. I didn't want anyone to get hurt, but I wanted a reason to—" he paused, trying to come up with the right word. He stuttered, then said, "Flee."

I hated that he used the word *flee*—so poetic. He didn't even know how to be real.

"I couldn't see a way out. I was graduating, with an English degree for God's sake. What was I going to do, teach high school brats the joys of Whitman and Yeats? Was I going to return home and live with Dad? I couldn't stay at The Terrace. Billie wanted to get married."

I didn't know that. She had joked about it, but I thought that was it—a joke.

"And then there was my student deferment. I had no idea what was going on with the draft. I actually thought of enlisting, but that would have betrayed Cal and it would have made Dad happy. No way was I going to make him happy. I mean, that was my thinking at the time. What I'm trying to tell you is that I was fucked up, I admit. I wanted to burn up my life. I had this notion, and it was pie in the sky, that if I got away, I could write. I could have a career as a poet. I couldn't do that at home or teaching or even staying in Gainesville. I had to have a clean break. A break that would leave me with no attachments."

"No responsibilities?" I asked.

"It was more than that," he said. "And I'm being honest here. I wanted no family, no past, no present and no future. No obligations of any kind."

I had felt that way at Paperbark Nursery. On my knees in the dirt, planting or weeding or harvesting—that was all that mattered.

The air in the room was yeasty from the open beer cans on the bureau. We sat facing each other, spent.

"So, now, you're lonely and you want family. You want friends. You want community. That's why you came back?"

"Yes," he said.

"You sacrificed my life for yours?" I asked.

"Yes," he said.

That word, yes. Two yeses in a row. In effect, an apology and a thank you.

When I got back to my room, I stood over the bed and looked at the picture postcard puzzle. Reid finally told the truth. I had finally accepted my part in the truth: Reid's decision to leave may have been at my expense, but I used him to keep myself stuck, safe. The fact that I had been spinning around my brother like a yo-yo was a choice, not a result.

Penny jumped onto the bed and the postcards scattered, lost their order. I picked up Lake Erie. Then, because I could and because these dispatches were no longer important, I ripped a half-circle around the lake, separating land from water. It now looked like any body of water. Nothing special. All that was left on the back was a bit of our home address: 54 Circle Drive. I picked up Mount Rushmore. It was much harder to tear around the outline of Washington, Jefferson, Roosevelt, and Lincoln. My fingernail slipped and I cut right into Roosevelt's nose. Once I desecrated this monument, I felt free. I didn't need scissors. I could do this with my bare hands. I picked up another and ripped it in half. I quartered those halves. I quartered again and tossed. Penny got into the act. Even though her puppy chewing days were long over, she put a postcard between her paws—the way I used to find her with one of my sandals—and shredded. I had done this same thing to the maps on our long, long-ago drive down to Florida. I had wanted then to sever my link to the West, to the Midwest, to all the states I never wanted to live in again.

There were enough postcards to blanket the floor between the beds, snow-covered shag carpet. I wanted to leave them and just walk away. But then the housekeeper would have to clean up and housekeepers were usually women. I didn't want to add to her burden. I needed to clean up my own mess.

I slept well that night. A deep sleep I hadn't experienced since Reid arrived. The next morning, officials reported on the heroics of the firefighters. Fires, not just in Brevard County but in two other counties as well, had responded to the suppressant chemicals and firebreaks. Homes and businesses were spared. Later in the afternoon, roads would be opened, letting evacuated residents return. The state was once again on Level 2 readiness—a return to normal operations, alert and monitoring.

When Penny and I went outside, Reid was leaning on the car. He had coffee from the convenience store. He handed me a cup.

"It's a good morning to return home," he said.

I could tell my brother goodbye in any number of languages. He had taught me that. I had some slang of my own. I could tell him to scram in French: *fichez le camp!* I learned this from a class I took at the Community Learning Annex when Keith and I were planning a trip to Paris to revive our relationship. (The money we had saved went for divorce lawyers instead.) In Spanish—something I got from Evan when he took it in eighth grade—I could say *!vete al carajo!* Go to hell. I could say *umalis ka*, or something like that, which meant buzz off. That I got from Rich, the banker I dated who had worked in the Philippines. In truth, I didn't want to say any of these things. I didn't want him to misunderstand my meaning in any way.

"Reid, I think it's time for you to go home," I said. "Your home, wherever that is."

"You're going to leave me here?"

"You know how to get around," I said.

"Are you okay?" he said.

"I'm fine and I want to be very clear," I said. "I've said it before, I love you and I hate you. And, yes, that's part of my contrary nature. But I don't want you in my life right now. Or in Evan's life."

He was flummoxed, mouth agape. There was a word—*agape*—a world-famous poet might use. I left him standing in front of The Cadillac Motel, in his lace-up sandals, holding his duffel bag. Whether he knew it or not, he was right where he wanted to be, ready to stick out his thumb and hit the road.

I stayed on the back roads: miles of cattle pastures, palmetto scrub, golden rod, and tall stalks of purple blazing star. It was stark and beautiful. A flock of sandhill cranes lurked in a drainage ditch. I pulled off the road and rolled down my window. Their red foreheads were bright against the dull and patchy weeds. They eyed me, displeased by my ogling. All at once, they opened their javelin beaks and emitted a bugle of trills. Tuneless, maddening. I laughed and Penny barked. The cranes barked back. The more I laughed, the more Penny barked. The cranes took flight.

I never understood why my mother had started to laugh that day in South Dakota. Maybe the absurdity of such huge beasts with their wise yet woeful eyes. Maybe she was just happy, pure and simple. What made my father laugh? For him, the buffalo were a delay. Did it finally dawn on him just how rigid it was to travel this way? The journey wasn't about getting someplace, it was about how we got there. Why did I laugh? Because I had the laughing bug. And Reid, had he just caught the laughing bug too?

I understood here, in the middle of this old Florida road, after leaving my brother behind, that we all laughed for our own reasons, and that was okay. It was a rare day. We were all happy at the same time.

There was more to my life than the in-betweens of Reid's visit, more than the *before* and *afters*. I just hadn't seen it that way until now: This was the *now*. I had a home, a son, friends, family. And what I didn't have—a degree, a profession—I could get. Why did I have to pick one thing and do it for the rest of my life? Why was that the gold standard, the sign of a successful life? I could make my own backyard into an Eden all its own. Growing not only flowers, but vegetables. I could go back to school. I could quit my job with Russell and find another. Or throw myself into solar power, the energy of the future.

Maybe I would go back to South Dakota and stand in the middle of the buffalo in Custer State Park. I'll smell the patties and feel the wind on my face. I'll laugh. Like my mother did, like we all did. Maybe I would go to Paris. I've never been on a plane. At the very end of Stone's movie—after the ridiculous Christ-in-the-bathtub scene—the camera pans through the cemetery where Morrison is buried. Père Lachaise. His grave is covered in flowers, burning candles and empty liquor bottles. The gravestones around his are tagged with graffiti. *Je t'aime Jim. Morrison Hotel. Break On Through.* One day I'll stand on that spot.

I couldn't sum up my life in a neat package. *Neat?* That was never me. I was all the messy parts. I wanted to own my heady days at the University of Florida—my strong voice and physical pleasure. I wanted dirt from Paperbark. I wanted a dash of Keith. I wanted to be a dutiful daughter and a kind friend. I wanted—and this was the most defining role of all—to be a mother, even if I was less than perfect in that role. All those things I pushed against and thought dragged me down—they were life.

I wasn't really sure where Reid would go. Maybe he wouldn't go anywhere. Maybe he'd return and continue to visit our mother. If so, that was fine by me. I didn't expect to never see him again. In fact, I knew I would see him. But for now, I had a feeling he was on his way back to Colorado. He had never meant to stay here at all.

I arrived home in the late afternoon, the sky heavy with low gray clouds. A skunk-y odor hit me when I got out of the car. Keith and Evan stood in the driveway. They had been worried about me, about the house, and had returned. Zink, for some reason, was with them. I didn't ask. I just accepted. Penny stuck her nose in their crotches.

My house, my tumble-down house, stuffed with possessions, some mine, some Keith's, some my mother's, stuffed with love—my house was intact. We walked all around it, just to make sure, then down to the pier. Penny galloped off ahead of us, eager for a swim. Evan and Zink raced down the slope of the yard, just like two kids having a good time.

Standing on the pier, I took in the mimosas, lacy-leafed and parched, and the knotty trunks of red cedar. Sun-scorched barnacles created an almost perfectly horizontal line on the breakwall, long abandoned by receding water. Penny dove in, parting the pepper grass and milfoil. The family of osprey circled over the water, the chicks learning to fly.

"Are you really okay? That was quite a scare," Keith said.

My head vibrated with fatigue. "I'm fine. We're all fine."

There were the goddesses, smiling unnervingly at us.

"I guess they did their job," I said.

"Are you a believer now?" he asked.

"Let's put it this way. I'm not not a believer."

Lightning bugs came out and Evan chased them. Both he and Zink caught several and smeared them on their upper arms, making skeleton streaks.

When it was time for them to leave, Zink kissed each of the goddesses on their full and silly mouths. We walked up to the driveway. There was the Mustang. I hadn't seen it earlier. It was packed full of boxes and suitcases.

"I'm heading to Cali," he said.

"Why?" Evan asked, thrown off by this news.

"Florida's over, man," he said. He had a new piercing, a loop in his bottom lip.

"Over for you," Evan said. He didn't understand what was happening, but he took it for what it was: Zink going his own way, just like he always had.

From the back seat of his car, Zink pulled the poster of the skateboard park and a stack of notebooks. He handed it all to Evan.

"To you Elba, I bequeath all my worldly skateboard park research," he said. "Go back to those city council douchebags and make it happen."

I hugged Zink, whispered, "Berkeley's perfect for you."

"Don't blow my cover, Ms. L. I got a reputation to uphold."

The Mustang shot out of sight.

Keith and Evan were leaving, too. Going back to town, to the other house. Evan would stay at Keith's for the rest of the month. I hugged my ex. I hugged my son. He seemed taller and heftier. His hair had grown out. I felt only the tasseled remnants of the peace sign. For the next four years, I would have to stay close to him. Not too close, but enough.

It was just Penny and me. She shook out her wet coat and we went inside.

The next morning, when I arrived at Garden House, it was in shambles—understandable, given that they had just returned from their evacuation to Stuart. Unpacked suitcases sat in the hallway. Two overturned walkers blocked the public bathroom. Mrs. Kline was trolling the floor. She didn't shake her finger at me. She didn't say *I'm on to you*, even though today I was up to no good. Today I was the bearer of bad news.

"Hello, dreary," she said.

Did she say dearie or *dreary*?

"Hello, Mrs. Kline."

"You're a sight," she said.

I probably was, all shamble-y and shaken myself. The last few days—few months, really—had taken a toll on us all.

"Good to see you, too," I said.

My mother was standing in front of the bureau, staring at something on top. It wasn't her brush and comb set or her makeup or perfume bottles. I stepped close and saw it was Reid's cardinal. He had finished it. It was painted a dusty red with a yellow beak. No sign of the half-finished owl.

This time I was direct. Harsh, you might say.

"Mom, I'm sorry to tell you this. I don't think Reid's coming back. He's gone. Maybe back home, to Colorado."

She said, "Well, that's terrible dear. Was he a friend of yours?"

"He was. He was my brother."

She stared at me. I saw the return of the twisted lips and searching eyes. Was she trying to pull up a recollection, fish out the name, a thing long buried and replaced by another? Or was she, in a calculated way, putting it all to rest? Maybe she decided that things were better the way they had been all these years: our lives without Reid.

"I'm so sorry for you," she said. "There was that boy you liked in college. He left, too. Ran away, I think. There are so many runaways. Living on the street. It's sad."

"I think you're right." She was talking about a boy from her neighborhood, a boy she had a crush on. I knew this story. I had even seen a picture of him. His name was Robert Silver. He went off to World War II and never came back.

"Do you think the tea will come soon?" she asked.

"It will, I'm sure."

We had tea, my mother and I. My mother and Estelle. Special morning tea brought to us by Sophie. We picked up where we left off, talking of nothing or not talking.

I looked at the picture of my father in uniform. It was several years after he had died that she told me why we never moved again. She had refused, giving my father an ultimatum: retire in Florida or go to the next city without her. I liked that about my mother, her quiet strength.

Before I left, I went out to the back garden and sat on the bench by the koi pond. The koi, seeing my shadow, came up, their mouths saying *feed me, feed me*. Around the pond, hosta flourished, as did dozens of orchids, hibiscuses, and bromeliads. I liked bromeliads just as much as orchids. They were a perfect combination of stern and supple, with their stiff and spiky leaves protecting blossoms so soft, yielding. Blossoms that were cherry-red, sometimes orange, sometimes purple. That was how I felt now, my heart so hardened to Reid all these years and now so soft that it broke. I broke. I cried, right there in front of the goldfish.

The palms and bamboo were thick enough and tall enough to create a secluded shade: it actually felt a few degrees cooler inside this canopy. And I felt alone. I missed my brother. I missed my father, as well. I missed them all. My mother who was here and not here.

My gut hurt—all that blubbering. I twirled my fingertips in the water. Tepid, algae-green. The koi scattered then returned, curious, nibbling.

Before I left, I picked a red hibiscus. It was a bomb, detonating yellow pollen all over my hand.

I ran into Sophie on the way to my car. She was leaving, getting into her VW bug.

"When do you think we'll see Reid again?" she asked.

"I'm not sure," I said. "You just never know with him."

"Everyone loves him," she said. "Especially my mom."

"I know," I said. I loved him. I just didn't want to love him so close.

On the drive, I listened to Joan Baez warble. I had never been a Baez fan. I switched the station. Janet Jackson, Savage Garden, Boys II Men. No, no, and no. I settled on Paula Cole. At least she was of this decade. By the time I got home, the flower had begun to wilt. I placed it in a glass of water and, before long, it perked up, a splash of red that made me happy.

That night it rained. Abrupt, violent, like the thunderstorms we had every year in summer. Thunder woke me and the irate downpour, heavy and threatening on my patchy roof, kept me awake. With this much rain, the fires would be smothered for sure.

I went out to the living room and stood at the sliding doors. A funnel of water poured off the eaves. The low grunt of a fog horn echoed off the house. The dampness made my bones ache. Or maybe it was just the distorted events of the long, long day.

When I was young, I was fascinated by thunderstorms. Once my mother found me, at age five, when we were living in Texas, standing outside in the rain, holding my arms up toward the sky. I told her I wanted the lightning to touch my skin. Horrified, she sat me down and explained that lightning could kill. I was never to go out during a storm. Reid had teased me about this for years: me and my lightning bolt skin. I didn't remember why I had done this, but I could see how a child, awed by the beauty and force of a storm, might want some of that power for herself.

The rain turned to a sprinkle and the moon made an appearance. A filmy, almost-full moon, casting an eerie shimmer on the grass. The lawn looked like an alien landscape. I opened the door and went out. The air was heavy with the intense smell of sun-dried fish. The grass, when I stepped off the patio, felt chilly. Shrubs had been pummeled, their branches drooping.

The hem of my robe was soaked and clung to my ankles as I walked around the yard.

More clouds passed and the moon brightened. I stood under an oak and pulled the lowest branch, sending fat drops down onto my shoulders and neck and face, a moon shower. In the distance, flash-bulbs of lightning, the lament of thunder.

I opened my mouth to feel the drops on my tongue. I took off my robe and lay down in the grass. Wetness seeped through my nightshirt. It felt good, cool, water pinging my skin. I hadn't felt this physical pleasure in years. Scissoring my arms and legs, I made a rain angel. There, on the bare parts of my skin—the backs of my thighs, my upper arms—the grass was supple now, tingly.

Reid might say, if he were here, *It's a sign. I think we're healed, Celeste.* It didn't matter what Reid said or what Reid wrote, or even where he went next.

It began to sprinkle harder, but I didn't move. With my voice clear and strong, I greeted the shower—"Hello, rain,"—and saluted the goddesses—"Thank you, gals." I let my now drenched body sink deeper into the earth.

About the Author

Photo credit Stacey Doyle

Tina Egnoski is the author of three books: *This Invisible Beauty*, *In the Time of the Feast of Flowers*, and *Perishables*. Her work, both fiction and poetry, has been published in a number of literary journals, including *The Carolina Quarterly*, *Cimarron Review*, *Hawaii Pacific Review* and *The Masters Review*, as well as in the anthologies *Forgotten Women* and *Shoreline*. She studied English at the University of Florida and later earned an MFA from Emerson College. She has received literature fellowships from the Rhode Island State Council on the Arts and the Colorado Council on the Arts and Humanities. From 2016 to 2019, she was the director of the Ocean State Writing Conference. She currently works in the Liberal Arts Division at the Rhode Island School of Design.

Acknowledgements

Two librarians at the George A. Smathers Library patiently provided documents that enhanced my understanding of the academic and social milieu of the early 1970's at the University of Florida: Archivist Peggy McBride and Curator of Manuscripts and Archives Carl Van Ness.

Stevan Nikolic gave my manuscript a home at Adelaide Books and took special care with the editing and publishing process.

Mia Garcia provided savvy expertise in the areas of editing and public relations.

Jody Lisberger read many drafts. Her friendship, wisdom, and sound writing advice are everywhere in these pages.

Karen Lee Boren read the final draft and her suggestions were instrumental in deepening the narrative voice.

Editor Tanya Gold and novelist Marcy Dermansky provided invaluable guidance.

Members of the Historical Fiction Collaborative offered encouragement on very early drafts.

My husband Dan is a wise reader and grammarian. I benefitted from his nuanced understanding of the comma.

My son Patrick—my singular joy—is at the heart of everything I write.

Made in the USA
Middletown, DE
09 March 2020